For Keith
with deepest thanks, love
and many blessings,
Hiro

Shahnaz

A Novel

Hiro McIlwraith

OOLICHAN BOOKS
LANTZVILLE, BRITISH COLUMBIA, CANADA
2000

Canadian Cataloguing in Publication Data

McIlwraith, Hiro, 1949-

    Shahnaz

ISBN 0-88982-188-7

    I. Title.

PS8575.I524S52 2000   C.813'.6   C00-911143-3

PR9199.3.M318S52 2000

We gratefully acknowledge the support of the Canada Council for the Arts for our publishing program.

The Canada Council | Le Conseil des Arts
for the Arts | du Canada

Grateful acknowledgement is also made to the BC Ministry of Tourism, Small Business and Culture for their financial support.

BRITISH
COLUMBIA
ARTS COUNCIL

We acknowledge the financial support of the Government of Canada through the Book Publishing Industry Development Program for our publishing activities.

Canadä

Published by
Oolichan Books
P.O. Box 10, Lantzville
British Columbia, Canada
V0R 2H0

Printed in Canada

For Gordon, Jesse and James McIlwraith

and for

Ron F. Smith
and
Keith Harrison

Chapter 1

I don't want to worry about her any more.

It's five o'clock in the morning. I lie in bed next to my husband, Shahrukh, listening to him snore as the big clock in my parents' sitting room strikes its deep gong six times. Ever since the last rainy season its mechanism has gone awry. It announces the time, then adds an hour to it. My grandfather bought this clock in England when he was a young man studying law at Cambridge. Since he trusts no one in Bombay to fix it, it continues to chime in its own eccentric fashion, and everyone in the house just mentally deducts an hour from the sum of its resolute bong-bonging.

The dawn light filtering in through the window illuminates all the familiar objects I will soon be leaving behind. Here is the desk at which I sat and did my homework for so many years. Its scratched surface is cluttered with an assortment of unmatched frames containing photographs taken at various family celebrations. That dreamy-eyed girl in a sailor dress lying on the floor with her chin cupped between her hands is me, on my fifth birthday. My father took that photo while we were on holiday in Mussoorie, in the foothills of the Himalayas. My mother wasn't with us. Next to it is a picture of Perin aunty, my mother's younger sister, taken that same day in Mussoorie. She is wearing a striped sari with a heavy cardigan, and is carrying my sister, Roshan, in her arms. I am standing next to both of them, holding onto Perin aunty's sari with my left hand, my right hand shading my eyes against the sun.

The steel almirah, which still stands in a corner of this room, used to hold my clothes. Now it's stuffed with old saris, torn strips of muslin and other assorted bits of cloth that my mother saves for who-knows-what purpose. She keeps the almirah locked, as though it contained priceless jewels. The keys to it, and to every other lock in this house, hang from a giant keyring hooked onto the waistband of my mother's sari petticoat. This causes her to jingle as she walks, giving me time to slip away when I hear her coming. But now I can almost see her sitting in that Burma teak armchair in the corner of the bedroom, scowling at me.

The calendar on the wall has today's date circled in red ink: September 11th, 1972. This is the day of our departure. I want to cheer and clap my hands and jump up and down. Goodbye, house of misery!

Goodbye to hands that hurt and words that bite.

Goodbye mum! She is angry that my husband and I are leaving India.

I'd rather face a rogue elephant than confront my mother when she's angry.

Against the wall directly across from my bed, I can see my reflection in the triple mirror of the rosewood dressing table. My hair sticks up at the back of my head; the triangle of my face is split by a big smile. I look like Silloo aunty, my father's youngest sister, who gave me this dressing table as a gift for my eleventh birthday. I have her wide, full mouth, her almond-shaped eyes, her crooked front tooth and high cheekbones. When I was twelve, Silloo aunty ran away with an Goan doctor from Marmagao, and was disowned by my grandfather for three whole years. I would sit beside her on the dressing table's padded, embroidered stool, watching her put Yardley's "English Rose" lipstick on her lips. It was a ritual that held an unending fascination for me. Gripping the golden cylinder with the tips of her slender, tobacco-stained fingers, her lips taut against her teeth in a wide O, she would smooth on the colour with long, firm strokes. Her mouth looked wet and luscious, like the inside of a pomegranate. I wanted to be just like her when I grew up. I vowed I'd wear "English Rose" lipstick, and drink gin fizzes in tall, frosted glasses. I would smoke gold-tipped cigarettes and wave my hands in the air when I talked. I, too, would wear silk dresses with "sweetheart" necklines, and Ma Griffe perfume in the cleft between my breasts.

Now Silloo aunty lives with her husband and two children in Fort Lauderdale. And Shahrukh and I are on our way to the other side of America, to Eugene, Oregon. We'll go to graduate school there; I'll be able to visit Silloo aunty once we're settled.

My husband, Shahrukh, who is twenty-two — a year older than me — is lying next to me, fast asleep, looking cherubic and pleased with himself. I stroke his curly hair, hoping he'll wake up, but he turns his back on me and mumbles something incomprehensible. "Shahrukh," I whisper loudly. He snores. "Shahrukh, wake up!" I blow gently in his ear, smiling as I see the tiny hairs on his temple wave in my breeze. Nothing. I weigh the merits of leaving him to sleep against the sudden urgency of my need to talk. How can he sleep on a day like this? It would be better if he woke up now. "Shahrukh!" He pulls his pillow over his head. I sigh, and roll over to my side of the bed.

I look around the room, wishing it were time to get up. Outside, I can hear the clink of milk-bottles at the small Aarey Dairy booth where a long queue of people must be waiting patiently in the semi-dark, ration cards in hand, to collect their daily supply of pasteurised buffalo's milk. Sunder ayah used to get the milk for us each morning. She'd let me peel the blue foil off the top of the bottle, and scoop out the cream with a

9

teaspoon. I'd eat in the kitchen while she made breakfast, the cream smooth against the roof of my mouth, sweet on my tongue. I'd sit on a low wooden stool and watch her chop onions for omelettes, happy to be near her. She worked squatting on the kitchen floor with the wooden base of the sickle-shaped knife gripped between her feet, which were splayed and cracked around the edges from years of walking barefoot in all kinds of weather. She would hold the onion in both hands and slice it swiftly against the blade, her small body rocking back and forth with each slice, her round face intent. I'd beg for a story, and she'd begin in her soft, musical voice. Her stories were filled with goddesses and demons, heartaches and wonder. Often, they were about young girls who grew up to be heroic women. Listening to her, my back and shoulders straightened and my spirit expanded until I felt powerful enough to perform miracles as effortlessly as she sliced onions. Ah, Sunder! What will I do without you?

Three families live in makeshift shelters on the road outside our compound wall. Through the open windows of the bedroom, I can hear them hawking and spitting as they brush their teeth with twigs from the neem tree. They quarrel about access to the one municipal water tap which serves them all for drinking, bathing, laundry-washing, and cooking. The women are the loudest and most aggressive of the lot. Their strident voices shout obscenities in Marathi. Always this anger, these arguments. I pull my pillow over my head to shut out their noise, but it's no use. One of them begins haranguing her children: "Get under the tap, you lazy good-for-nothings! Only ten more minutes and the water will be turned off!"

Their lives sadden me. And yet, by tomorrow I'll be at the other end of the world. I can choose my life in ways that they cannot. I feel deeply guilty about this, but I can't wait to get on that plane.

I hear the rasp of a match stick strike against the side of a wooden match box, then the whoosh of flame as their primus

10

stove catches, sputters, settles down to a steady hum. Sunder ayah used to pump up our primus stove every morning while Roshan and I squatted on our heels beside her. Her glass bangles would clink and jingle as she lit the stove, rolled out chapattis, and cooked them on the hot griddle. She would sprinkle the hot chapattis with sugar, tear off pieces with her fingers and feed us, one bite for Roshan, one for me. Her hands smelled of ghee and flour and the Lifebuoy soap she used. Her fingers were work-worn and rough-skinned, but her touch was tender as she caressed my cheek, then put the rolled-up chapatti in my mouth.

Yet Sunder ayah, whose love has sheltered me since the day I was born, is no longer allowed in our house. My mother has decreed it. She has banished both Sunder ayah and Perin aunty, forbidding them entry to our home, and throwing terrible scenes when she encounters them in public. So these two women, whom I love more than anyone in the world except for my father, no longer come to family gatherings, or attend any events where my mother might be present. I said goodbye to them yesterday. We hugged each other, and cried, and I clung to each of them in turn, knowing I might never see them again.

The harsh cawing of crows brings me back to the present. I can see them through the bedroom window, perched in a row on the electrical cables high above the street outside our compound. Then I hear the first handcarts roll by, their wooden wheels rumbling noisily along the pavement. I'll miss these sounds.

Most of my family refuses to talk about the fact that Shahrukh and I may be leaving India for good. My father and grandmother act as though our trip is nothing more than an extended vacation. This is typical of them; when something upsets them, they pretend it doesn't exist. My mother is furious, but so far she's remained uncharacteristically silent. When our visas arrived from the U.S. Embassy in Delhi, her lips tightened and her nostrils turned white, but she said nothing. This scares me; I keep waiting for the explosion. Perin aunty is the only one willing to talk with me about it. She tells me she'll miss me, but she's glad I'm going. Sunder ayah just hugs me and cries.

I smell the familiar fragrance of burning sandalwood. Khorshed aunty — my father's oldest sister, who has been living with my parents for the past year and helping to take care of my mother — is up, saying her morning prayers. The first thing she did when she moved in was to set up a shrine in her room, with a round silver tray which bears the implements of Zoroastrian piety. On the front of the tray sits a fat silver brazier lined with white sand. It's piled high with miniature sandalwood logs which crackle and burn and fill the air with fragrant smoke.

The scent of sandalwood has accompanied all the celebrations and disasters of my life. It evokes in me a yearning for my abruptly terminated childhood, a longing to be free of memory and responsibility. I feel the prickle of tears in my eyes, and snuggle closer to Shahrukh for comfort.

Khorshed aunty's voice rises and falls in the cadences of the Zend Avesta. In addition to the sandalwood brazier, her tray holds an oval silver frame intricately carved with roses. Inside is a portrait of Zoroaster, his head wrapped in a white turban and surrounded by a misty halo, his eyes raised heavenward, communing with an invisible deity. Behind the frame is a tall silver flagon filled with rosewater, with tiny holes in the stopper. My aunt will use it to sprinkle the fragrant water all around the house once she's reached the appropriate place in her prayers. Each part of this ritual is carefully prescribed. Its unvarying nature comforts me, even though the God my aunt worships bears no resemblance to the playful, creative spirit I know, in my heart, as God. My God is more friend and lover than patriarch. Yet I recognize, in Khorshed aunty's devotion, the same wholeness that sometimes fills my body with such joy and wraps me in a love so profound, that I need nothing else.

My favourite bit of this trayful of treasures is a tall silver receptacle shaped like an inverted cone. It is filled with rock sugar and if I time my entrance correctly, Khorshed aunty will fill my mouth with lumps of crunchy sugar to sweeten my day. The tray bears, in addition to all this, a whole coconut, a small heap of uncooked basmati rice, a garland of fresh flowers. Each item is symbolic of something: prosperity or fertility, blessing, sweetness, devotion.

A tiny silver bowl with a fluted edge contains the red kumkum with which Khorshed aunty will mark her forehead when she has finished chanting and praying. I breathe in the mingled fragrances of sandalwood and jasmine, roses and lilies and marigolds. Every doorway in my parents' house is festooned with garlands of flowers, as is the daily custom. And today, there will be elaborate designs drawn in powdered lime of many colours laid out on the threshold to provide us with a festive and auspicious farewell.

As the cries of the fish-hawkers sound outside my window, I wake Shahrukh by nibbling on his ear, stroking the soft skin at his throat until he purrs like a cat. We consider getting out of bed, but are cool and comfortable beneath the silk monsoon quilt in our bedroom. We start to make love, but give up quickly, inhibited by the proximity of my parents and the squeaking of the old teakwood bed. We sit up instead and talk about our impending trip.

"I thought I'd be glad to leave, but now I can't believe we're actually going. You think we're crazy?" asks Shahrukh.

"We're doing the right thing," I reply, with a certainty I don't feel. "We can't stay here, Shahrukh. We've been through this a million times already."

"I know, I know. But . . . We have everything we need, here. A house, good jobs, money, servants. There, we'll have nothing. We'll be bloody paupers."

"Shahrukh! You wanted to go too; this isn't all my doing."

13

"I want to go. I do. Once we're there it'll be a blast; I just . . . . Part of me is scared. Aren't you? A little bit?"

I take a deep breath. Emigration has been my idea. I've wanted to leave India ever since my high school principal, Miss Lambert, first proposed it, back when I was fifteen. But at the time, my father thought I was too young to go by myself. Shahrukh and I have been talking about emigrating almost since the first time we met. Neither of us wants to live our parents' lives. But left to his own devices, Shahrukh would probably stay in Bombay, work in his father's business, live the life he was born to live as the only son of wealthy Parsi parents.

There is a seductive ease to the luxury and idleness of our days here. I look at other Indian women I know, and I dread falling into that silken rut. Their days are filled with visits to the beauty salon for facials, manicures, pedicures; shopping; drinks and dinner parties every evening. These things, which seem to satisfy my friends, bore me. I want adventure, freedom to learn and grow and find out what I'm capable of accomplishing. So, over the past six months, I've written to various American universties for application forms for both of us. I've done all the leg-work, choosing the University of Oregon, handling the details of visas and foreign exchange. I haven't allowed myself to question the wisdom of this course of action.

I look at Shahrukh. He's a handsome man, with clear brown eyes, a wry smile, eyelashes longer than mine. He makes me laugh; his sense of humour is sardonic, and cuts like a knife to the heart of things. I cherish this in him. Having him with me makes it easier to leave.

I want to create a life of my own, some place where no one knows me. I feel disloyal and guilty even thinking this, so I've pushed away all doubts, remained intent on my goal. My mother's life has disintegrated like an imploding star, and even though I haven't lived at home since I was fifteen, the dense pull of her gravity threatens to engulf me. I don't want to worry about her any more.

Leave. Just leave and never come back. I take a deep breath, to assure myself that I can still breathe. Then I get my dressing-gown and head for the bathroom.

After a long, two-bucket-bath I emerge feeling light-headed and relaxed to find that everyone else is up as well. The house is full of relatives chattering like a flock of sparrows: my grandmother, Shahrukh's parents, his sister Zenobia, my sister Roshan. Then there are various aunts and uncles, cousins, nieces, nephews and second cousins from both sides of my family. Also, assorted children, and relatives who only show up on special occasions — marriages, navjote ceremonies, funerals and the like. They are all here to see us off at the airport this evening.

My aunts have spent the past several days in an uproar of cooking, determined to make us eat all our favourite dishes in the short time we have left with them. They have filled the house with the familiar fragrances of pomfret-in-green-chutney-cooked-in-banana-leaves, and goat-pulao-with-saffron-and-spices, and thousand-almond-chicken-cooked-in-double-cream. My new blue jeans, acquired at great expense from our friendly local smuggler of foreign goods, strain at the seams and pinch uncomfortably at my waist.

I wander out into the dining room, attracted by the voices raised in mock argument. My uncles and cousins and those aunts who aren't busy making dhansak for this afternoon's farewell meal sit around our dining table, which can seat twenty-four adults. They play canasta and tease my cousin Navaz about her habit of staring blankly at her hand of cards when it's her turn to play.

Feroze uncle calls out from across the table: "Arre, Navaz, you'll never catch a bridegroom if you play your hand at love the way you do at canasta." This remark is greeted with snorts of laughter from the younger uncles, giggles from the other cousins, and sly looks from her sister who knows that Navaz has a boyfriend at college. This boyfriend is a non-Parsi. His

15

existence remains a secret from the assembled relatives and, most particularly, from her parents, my Dilna aunty and Eruch uncle. They pride themselves on being broad-minded, but would revert very quickly to the lock-her-up-and-throw-away-the-key school of parenting if they discovered that their darling Navaz were straying from the Parsi fold. Since Navaz's sister, Sarosh, has confided her secret to me, and since I have difficulty keeping any secret for long, I duck out of the dining room before any of them notices me.

On the verandah, a slight breeze wafts in off the sea, carrying with it a whiff of briny air and the pungent smells of drying fish from Juhu Beach. Here I find the abundant remains of breakfast laid out on the dining-table: spicy omelettes, and platters of freshly baked bread from the Irani bakery down the road; butter and karvanda jelly and homemade mango preserves; freshly squeezed sweet-lime juice in tall glass jugs, and slices of ruby papaya; mango fool and fried-red-bananas; golden vermicelli sauteed in butter with raisins and almonds; freshly made chapattis, and guavas picked from the trees in our own garden.

I sit down to eat, relishing this moment of quiet and solitude. I feel overwhelmed by all the people in the house, all the attention focused on me on this day of my departure. So I take my time, buttering the warm bread, savouring each mouthful.

Just as I'm finishing my breakfast, the children wander in, sleepy and rumpled in their sweaty pyjamas. They ask me questions for which I have no answers.

"Shahnaz aunty, how big is Eugene? Is it like Bombay?" asks my cousin's daughter, Farad.

"Stupid, it's much bigger than Bombay. Don't they teach you anything at that school you go to?" says her brother Cyrus, with the lordly scorn of a twelve-year-old.

"Actually, it's a lot smaller than Bombay," I say.

"Do they have big-big cars there, with shiny chrome, like in the movies? And too-tall buildings high as the clouds?" This from ten-year-old Jamshed, who breathes heavily through his mouth because he has a deviated septum.

"I don't know, Jamshed. I've never been to Oregon."

The children look disappointed, and one youngster pipes up: "Behram uncle would know, he's been everywhere."

"Why don't you go and ask him?" I say. Then, feeling ashamed of my ill humour, I offer the boy a slice of guava.

"Will you meet Elvis Presley there?" squeaks Parviz, who is thirteen and has posters of Elvis pinned up all over her room.

"I don't think so. He lives a long way from Oregon," I reply. And then, seeing her face drop, I add, "I'll send you one of his albums when I get to Eugene, okay?"

She brightens, and slips her hand into mine.

"What about the food?" asks my chubby nephew Xerxes, raising a laugh from his young cousins. "Can you get pomfret there? Or mangoes?"

"Who will cook for Shahrukh uncle and you?" my niece Homai asks with a worried frown. "Are you taking Sunder ayah along to take care of you?"

"No, sweetie, Sunder ayah has to stay and look after Perin aunty." As a soon-to-be-foreign aunty, I am expected to know more about the mysteries of faraway places than the other adults around here. But I have few definite answers to most of their questions, and eventually the children, bored by my vague replies, drift away.

I stay in my seat a while longer, listening to my family chatter and laugh inside the house. The murmur of the surf, the cawing of crows, the mellifluous song of a bulbul soothe me. Through the open door, I see Shahrukh walk into the living room and look around for something. He searches under the sofa cushions, picks a stack of magazines off the coffee table and puts them down again, wrinkles his forehead. Then he stands in the middle of the room rumpling his hair with one hand, looking dejected. I half rise from my seat to ask him if he needs help, but he walks away, into the dining room.

17

As I get up from my seat, I hear Behram uncle striding up and down the garden, declaiming loudly to the crows who sit on the wall and who punctuate his discourse with cacophonies of cawing.

Behram uncle was once a distinguished barrister who practised law with my father in the family firm. He was the bachelor uncle, who went on holidays to France and Italy and indulged his passion for exotic cuisines and even more exotic erotica. Some of the cattier aunts whispered about other tastes which were also indulged on these solitary expeditions, but as soon as they realised we kids were in the room, they'd immediately change the subject and start talking about something boring, like finding a good match for the latest cousin of marriageable age.

All of the kids loved Behram uncle. For one thing, he talked to us as though we were his own age. He never condescended or kept secrets. He also had a marvellous fund of mildly risque jokes, which he would tell us with great gusto. He usually returned from his travels with gifts which delighted and surprised us and, on occasion, shocked our parents. On my tenth birthday he gave me an abbreviated edition of Sir Richard Burton's Thousand and One Nights, complete with pictures of nubile young maidens swooning bare-breasted into the arms of virile, scantily clad young men, and harem wives in seductive poses being hauled by their long, long hair into the presence of their masters. The book looked old, and must have been quite valuable, although I didn't think of that at the time. Its value to me lay in the cachet it gave me with my older cousins, who had to beg me for a look at "The Book," as it came to be called, and promise me various favours in return. I am still grateful and amazed that my parents allowed me to keep this somewhat unorthodox gift. Khorshed aunty was appalled, and wanted to lock the book away in her vault, but my father insisted that it was mine and I had the right to keep it.

In the past few years Behram uncle has succumbed to the

madness that seems to be such an inevitable part of Parsi families, with their generations of inbreeding and inter-marriages. He no longer pleads cases at the Bombay High Court and, although he still goes to his office every day, dressed in immaculate linen suits and monogrammed silk cravats, he no longer sees clients.

His secretary, Miss Cawasjee, is a spinster of indeterminate age and absolute devotion. We've often suspected that she harbours a secret passion for our dapper uncle. She takes dictation from him every morning for two hours, and transcribes her notes into perfectly typed letters on heavy bond paper which my uncle signs with a flourish. She then files them away with all the other unsent letters he has dictated since his slide into premature senility.

Barred from oratory in the court-room, our uncle now practises his art on any available audience, be it human, bestial or, as today, ornithological. The crows listen to him for a while, then, discovering the greater delights of our breakfast table, swoop down on those dishes that have been left uncovered. They carry off in their thieving beaks bits of omelette, guava, fried banana, chapatti. Hopping a short distance away, they regard me comically, with their heads cocked to one side. In a burst of generosity, I uncover all the dishes left on the table and go back into the house, hearing their jeers — caw-caw-cawww. As I head up the steps, I wonder, do they have crows in Oregon? And who, indeed, is going to cook for Shahrukh and me, since neither of us knows how to boil an egg?

At the top of the stairs I hesitate for a moment. I don't want to talk to anyone right now. Veering right to avoid the living room, I head into the familiar quiet of my father's library. The wooden shutters are closed. The sun quivers in narrow golden bars across the granite floor. The room is dim and cool, with high ceilings and leather armchairs which look like browsing animals in the half-light. Bookshelves line all four walls. There is a familiar smell of dust and mildew and silverfish, and the glue that binds the books. Underlying this complex architecture of smells is the rich brown fragrance of my father's pipe tobacco. I walk over to a chair by the window, and curl up in its tan leather arms. Tucking my legs under me, I rest my cheek against its cool brown back and close my eyes. In the dim silence, I smell something that causes the hairs on the back of my neck to prickle. The smell of a dead mouse, which is the smell of my mother when she's manic.

My mother is somewhere in this room. I know by her smell that she's here. My face flushes, my heart pounds, the palms of my hands are damp with sweat. I sit up, suddenly alert, and pull open the shutter closest to me. Sunlight floods into the room in a wide gold shaft. I look around, but see no signs of her. I hold my breath, so I can hear better. The walls in this room are thick. No outside noises penetrate. I hear a faint jingle and a soft thud, which seem to come from high in a corner of the room. I turn around and kneel on the chair. Resting my chin on its high back, I scan the ceiling to see if my mother is hanging batlike from the rafters. This expectation that she might be up there in defiance of gravity doesn't strike me as strange. My mother is capable of anything.

I hear a thudding behind me, and swivel around to meet it. My mother is perched on top of one of the bookshelves, which stretches three-quarters of the way to the ceiling. She is swinging her legs, banging her heels against the books on the topmost shelf. The shelf is bolted firmly to the wall, so it won't topple, but it's not very wide, and I'm afraid she'll fall. I take a deep breath and strive for casual unconcern.

"Oh, there you are! I was looking for you. What're you doing?"

She doesn't answer, except by swinging her legs harder, thudding louder against the wall of books. Her face is in shadow, but I can see the white gleam of her teeth in a feral smile. "Mum, come down from there. You'll fall." Despite myself, my voice is edgy, strained. Damn.

"Oh no." Her voice in reply is girlish, teasing, with giggles frilling the edges of it. "I'm very very well. I was born here. I'll come down tomorrow."

Lord, I think to myself. Here she goes again. I'm fiercely glad I'm leaving. Someone else will have to take care of her.

But who? My father is a dear and loving man, but he sees only what he wants to see. When my mother is prancing around in Never-Never Land, or is up in the corner near the ceiling, my father leaves. Urgent business in Delhi or Calcutta or Bangalore rescues him from the knowledge that his wife, my mother, is not all there, has fled, in fact, into the swamps and swirls of manic-depression. Nervous Breakdown, they call it, my aunts and uncles and grandparents, who talk about her in whispers. I think of her nerves twanging and breaking like wires that are pulled so tight they snap and stick out of her brain in lethal metal curls.

She giggles, and rocks back and forth setting the bunch of keys at her waist jingling. She looks like a sly and very intelligent monkey, perched up there near the ceiling, banging and jingling, peering and giggling. I get up and walk to the foot of the library ladder she has used to climb onto her perch.

"Come on down, Mum. I'm going away soon. Come and talk to me."

"Sssssss."

She bends over and hisses at me, sending a spray of saliva flying at my upturned face, which I wipe with the sleeve of my t-shirt. Feeling angry and helpless, I want to walk away, but am afraid to leave her there alone. I put my foot on the bottom rung of the ladder. One last time, I tell myself. Soon, I'll be on the other side of the world. I climb up the worn rungs of the teakwood ladder until I am looking directly at her knees, covered demurely in a sky-blue cotton sari. She is still rocking; her movements make the ladder wobble. I wrap my right arm around her legs. My left hand holds firmly onto the rung of the ladder above me. The smell of dead mouse is in my nostrils and I swallow hard as a wave of love and nausea sweeps through my body. I set my jaw and take a deep breath.

"Mum, come down, please? I'm leaving this afternoon. Come and help me get ready?"

She looks down at me through the mass of frizzy black hair which hangs over her forehead like a leafy bush.

"You don't want my help. You're going away so you won't have to see me any more."

Her voice is flat, matter-of-fact, without complaint. Sometimes, in the middle of her manic storms, she has these moments of heartbreaking lucidity. My chest aches with sadness. I let go of her legs and reach up with my right hand to stroke her cheek. To my surprise, it is wet with tears. I look up at her, and am about to say something tender and consoling, and untrue. She jerks both knees up hard against her chest and gives me a tremendous push with her feet and legs, launching me and the ladder into empty space. I feel my body arc through the dusty air, feel the acid bite of panic seize my throat and flutter through my flailing limbs. My last conscious thought, before the ladder and I both hit the floor, is that she has got me again.

Chapter 2

It's three o'clock in the afternoon. We are at the Air India counter at Bombay's Santa Cruz airport, checking in our luggage and watching the bored attendant staple the stubs of our luggage tags onto our tickets. LAX means Los Angeles, she tells us. We'll have to clear U.S. customs there before catching a connecting flight to Eugene. I feel a shiver of excitement race up my spine. My face has congealed into a pointless smile, which, try as I may, I cannot erase. I look at our baggage tags. The names are magic; I conjure them in my head. LAX, Los Angeles, California, USA. They have a rhythm all their own. I watch Shahrukh's hands as he puts our tickets back into their folder. Little-boy hands, with dimpled knuckles. I'm putting my future into these hands. I bite the tip of my tongue and look away.

Turning around I recall, with relief, the presence of our relatives, all fifty or so of them, milling about and gesticulating wildly, arms filled with garlands of flowers. They jabber excitedly amongst themselves, wave at us from the outer concourse, which is separated from the departure area by walls of glass. The male members of the family pat their sweat-beaded foreheads with crumpled white handkerchiefs while the women weep and blow their noses with great vigour into inadequate squares of embroidered cambric.

The children run around playing hide and seek among the pillars of the open hallway. I'm only twenty-one, I think to myself. I want to run out and play too! I turn back to the Air India counter with something like despair in my heart. I force myself to stand still, to keep from grabbing our bags and running back through the glass into the world I know.

The check-in formalities completed, we now have a three hour wait before we board our plane. Air India operates on what is jokingly referred to as "Indian time." This means that our aircraft, which is scheduled to take off at five p.m., is almost certain to remain earthbound until six or seven or eight o'clock in the evening. The actual time of departure will depend on the vagaries of the weather, the mood of the pilot, the digestive health or otherwise of the air traffic controller, the results of the latest round of negotiations between the ground crew's union and the Air India brass, and a host of other factors both numerous and unpredictable. The only thing we know with any certainty is that we won't be leaving anytime soon.

Shouldering our cabin bags, Shahrukh and I make our way back through the crush of passengers and uniformed skycaps wheeling loaded trolleys. We emerge into the main concourse where our families have assembled.

My mother is hanging onto my father's arm; she looks pale and timid. He shouldn't have brought her here. Crowds leave her frightened, bewildered, once her manic mood has passed. I stroke her arm. She looks at me blankly, then buries her nose in my father's shoulder. I walk around my father, cocking my head to one side and peering at her upside down, trying to coax a smile from those pale lips. She will not meet my gaze. She glances sideways at me, her eyes raised no higher than my waist. I can feel the back of my head throbbing where it hit the stone floor this morning. It seems a long time ago. I search for words to reach her, some way for our hearts to touch across the gulf that separates us. My throat closes; the words won't come. Instead, I feel tears prickle at my nose. I kiss her wildly curly hair, and she pulls away, startled. I feel a sadness so deep, I want to lie down on the floor and go to sleep.

We are separated as my aunts, my sister, Sharukh's mother, and children of various heights and ages swirl around me. They drape me with garlands of flowers, tug at my skirt, clasp my hands between their own damp palms, hug me again and again. My grandmother circles my head with trembling, blue-veined hands, the knuckles swollen with arthritis, and sprinkles grains of rice over my hair and shoulders, pressing some of the grains onto my forehead in an ancient gesture of benediction. The men take Shahrukh aside for some last-minute advice, delivered with great gusts of laughter and general hilarity. I glare at them, resentful of the air of jollity. All the advice given to me these last few days has been about duty and responsibility and working hard to make my family proud; why is it that whatever these men are saying to Shahrukh is so lighthearted and carefree?

My father makes his way through the crowd. He puts his arm around me and draws me behind the privacy of a concrete pillar. He looks at me with such tenderness that my knees give way. Glancing quickly around, he pulls an envelope out of his pocket. It smells of his pipe tobacco, and I lift it to my nose to breathe in this familiar aroma. Hurriedly, furtively he pulls my hand down and urges me, in a low voice, to put the envelope out of sight in my handbag. I do this with as casual an air as I can muster, aware of the watchful eyes around me, and the necessity for discretion in the face of stringent regulations governing the export of foreign currency and gold from India. I don't want to undergo a tiresome and potentially dangerous interrogation by airport police or the C.I.D., whose spies, so the rumours go, are everywhere. My father must have made a last-minute acquisition; otherwise, he would never have given me whatever the envelope contained in so dangerously public a place.

The P.A. system screeches into action to announce that the Air India flight to London and Los Angeles is now ready for boarding. My aunts and sister and cousins move in to say their last goodbyes, wailing and hugging and sobbing and hugging and crying and pressing damp kisses onto my damp cheeks. They urge me, variously, to call every week, to write every day, to take care of myself, to take care of Shahrukh, to call the instant we arrive in Eugene, to eat properly, to hold my purse firmly with both hands, to hide my money in my brassiere, to watch out for rapacious cab-drivers and suspiciously friendly foreigners, and on and on and on until I am completely overwhelmed and gasping for air.

I crane my neck to see if I can spot my mother, but she is nowhere in sight. Shahrukh rescues me from these doleful farewells by grabbing my hand and dragging me off towards the departure area. I wave and blow kisses, looking backward as I walk away from the home of my birth and enter the tunnel of the departure gate. I feel as though I'm making my way through a long, serpentine birth-canal. It ends abruptly at the open door of the plane which will carry me away to foreign shores and grown-up adventures.

Chapter 3

It is eight o'clock in the evening, Indian Standard Time, and we have been flying over the Arabian Sea for the past half hour. The lights of Bombay's elegant crescent-shaped harbour, known colloquially as the Queen's Necklace, long ago gave way to an inky sea and deepening sky. Shahrukh and I have had our seats upgraded to First Class, thanks to my uncle, who is chairman of the board for Air India. We lounge in decadent comfort, eating Beluga caviar and toasting each other with vintage Veuve Cliquot champagne generously provided by the chief steward, an old school chum of my cousin, Dinshaw. Then we chat for a while, too keyed up to sleep, but tired and subdued after the heavy meal and the emotional send-off at Santa Cruz airport.

Sharukh pulls out the inflight magazine from the seat-pocket in front of him, and begins to read. It dawns on me, with a sudden frisson of anxiety which causes my scalp to prickle that we really are leaving. Shahrukh and I were married two years ago, shortly after my nineteenth birthday. Although he's a year and a half older, he's never travelled outside the borders of India until today. I've been abroad with my family, to England and Europe, to Southeast Asia and Japan, but they've been short trips, filled mainly with shopping and sightseeing.

For most of our lives, Shahrukh and I have been sur-rounded by a warm, enveloping cocoon of family and friends, traditions and customs which we have imbibed with our mothers' milk.

We've grumbled often enough about the lack of privacy, the way everyone seems to know our business and to assume the right to lecture us on everything from what kind of bed we should buy, to how we ought to raise our kids, and when we should have them. But this . . . nothing in my past has prepared me for this formidable isolation. We haven't even left the East-ern hemisphere, and already I am appalled at the irrevocable nature of this act of emigration. What have we done? I look up, involuntarily, for the emergency-cord which, on Indian trains, one can pull to bring the train's momentum to an abrupt halt. This plane, of course, offers no such amenity. Shahrukh, reading my upward glance instantly, grins at me and covers my cold hand with his own warm one.

I rest my head on his shoulder and close my eyes, while my mind scampers over unfamiliar terrain: did I choose the right man? Will he be able to keep me safe, so far away from the shelter of family and home? Or will he look to me for safety? And if he does, how will I manage? What if one of us falls ill? My mind natters its way through scenes of mayhem and disas-ter until I terrify myself into absolute exhaustion. Gradually, the throb of the big engines lulls me into a stupor, and I drift off into an uneasy sleep.

When I wake up, the sky is tinged with rose and the sun streams in through the small window beside my head. Below us is a patchwork of fields and plains with a silver river wind-ing through them, flowing into a silver sea at the edge of the horizon. The cabin crew are quietly and efficiently taking or-ders for breakfast. One of them comes by with a tray of orange juice which I accept gratefully. I am thirsty, and I remember, with a smile, my grandmother's injunction to drink lots of flu-ids, to keep from getting dehydrated. Shahrukh is not in his seat, and I feel a momentary panic, which I hurriedly quell by telling myself he has almost certainly gone to the loo.

I find my toilet case in my blue carry-on bag, and walk over to an unoccupied bathroom at the back of the cabin. As I sit down on the toilet seat, my stomach lurches and I feel faint. Bending over with my head between my knees, I find myself suddenly engulfed in tears, a wild desolation seizing my heart. The bruise at the back of my head throbs and burns. I wrap my arms around my body and rock back and forth to comfort and console myself.

After a long while my heart feels calmer. I raise my head, which is now engorged with blood from hanging upside down for so long. To my surprise, I am hungry. A good sign, I suppose. I brush my teeth and make silly faces at my reflection in the mirror, then unlock the bathroom door.

As I walk down the aisle I see the back of Shahrukh's head in the seat next to mine. With his new, short haircut, the nape of his neck looks tender, exposed. In a rush of relief and love, I bend down to kiss him before sliding into my seat. He smiles up at me, the gap between his front teeth making him look twelve years old. As I settle into my seat, the stewardess comes by with perfectly cooked Eggs Benedict which Shahrukh has ordered for me, knowing them to be my favourite western-style breakfast. He takes the tray from her, and places it on the fold-out table in front of me. I smile gratefully at him, all the fears of the previous night dispelled in this golden light high above the world. I lift the first forkful into my mouth, savouring with pleasure the burst of golden egg-yolk, the tang of Hollandaise sauce, the salty bite of ham, the chewiness of English muffin. The sun, through the window, lays a warm wedge of light on my arm.

Chapter 4

The early morning sun streaming in through the open window of my bedroom warmed my cheek and brushed the surfaces of the room with gold. I was home with my parents for a week-long visit — the first one since my wedding. Shahrukh and I had been married for three months by then. We lived in a large, airy flat in Old Alipore, in Calcutta. Shahrukh was away on a business trip, and I had taken a few days off from my job at the British Council to spend the week in Bombay.

"Shahnaz! Aerogramme for you, from Florida!" my sister Roshan called from downstairs. She had just finished high school, and would be starting college soon.

"Hang on, I'm drying my hair." I heard Roshan run up the stairs, taking them two at a time. Her face appeared in the mirror behind me, looking flushed and round-cheeked. She thrust the letter impatiently at me.

"Open it, it's from Silloo aunty, I want to know what she says."

I laughed, finished drying my hair and switched off the hair dryer. I took the letter from her, slit open the blue envelope and pulled out the pages, which crackled as I unfolded them. And there in front of me was Silloo aunty's flamboyant scrawl, in purple ink, on mauve paper.

To me, everything about Silloo aunty had always seemed larger than life. Especially when I was younger. She was sophisticated and sharp, slender and quick. She had a narrow, triangular face, a nose like a scimitar, high cheekbones, amber coloured eyes which slanted up at the corners. Her voice was deep, a sexy, throaty, gravelly growl which she owed, in part, to the ferociously pungent Balkan Sobranie cigarettes she smoked all day. She slept on the spare bed in my room when she came to visit, and would read my palm instead of a bedtime story.

Grasping my right hand in her left, she would trace, with her manicured index finger, my life-line, head-line, heart-line. Pointing to each one as she told me its story, her polished fingernail lingered on crossroads and climaxes along this mysterious map of my life. "So much sorrow, Shahnaz," she would say, shaking her head sadly, letting the cigarette smoke drift out through her nostrils towards the ceiling. "You have a hard life ahead of you, my darling. See this square here, on your heart line? And that cross there?"

Eagerly, I would examine my palm. If I squinted a bit, I could sort of see the square she traced on my hand. Although its corners didn't look much like corners, and if I'd drawn those lines in my geometry book, Miss Shelton, my geometry teacher, would have made me stay after class and draw them over again with a ruler. But, eager to please my glamorous aunt and wanting to hear more about the "sorrow," which made me feel all solemn and important and grown-up inside, I nodded my head sagely as she mused over the portents etched on my hand.

"You will travel far, sweetheart," she drawled in her deep, dreamy voice. "All the way across the world." Then she'd sigh and shake her head and look pityingly into my eyes.

I'd hold my breath, dying to know what she saw in my future but knowing better than to ask. At the first hint of open curiosity, of eagerness, from me, she would thrust my hand back into my lap, her nostrils flared with distaste, her voice turned brisk, impatient, falsely gay. "It's all nonsense anyway. Off to bed, little monkey. Sleep tight!" And turning off the light in my room, she would swish out to the verandah in her ivory silk dressing gown, her bare feet padding softly on the tiled floor. I would hear her swinging back and forth on the verandah's large swing-bed, creakcreeeak, creakcreeeak, until I drifted off into foreign lands and nameless sorrows.

When I was twelve, Silloo aunty met a man, uncle Claude, who was Goan and Roman Catholic. I remember the day she arrived at our house with her new husband, looking defiant, sly and scared as she got out of the car in our gravelled driveway.

It was a Sunday morning in early March, the air muggy but relatively cool. I was swinging on the swing-bed on our front verandah, talking to my father, who was bent over the verandah railing pruning the jasmine bushes that lined the front of our house. When the familiar black Humber drove up, he looked up with a smile to greet his youngest, his favourite sister.

His smile of welcome faded into a puzzled half-frown as she emerged out of the passenger side door of the car. She wore a sleeveless white blouse, and a red raw-silk skirt which swirled around her calves as she walked. Her red high-heeled shoes clicked on the stone steps as she climbed up them to kiss my father's cheek. Then the driver's side door opened with its usual reluctant creak; I watched in amazement as an elegant man dressed in white trousers and a khaki bush-shirt emerged and stood smiling at my father and me. He was tall, the tallest man I'd ever seen, with a small, straight nose, which made me realize he probably wasn't a Parsi. Our community is noted for its imperious noses. He had a black moustache which bristled over a generous mouth, and he wore black horn-rimmed glasses.

There was something odd about his presence in our driveway, a kind of disturbance that fluttered in the air around him, like the unease that precedes a late summer thunderstorm. He stood there, still smiling, looking from Silloo aunty to my father to me. When it became obvious that Silloo aunty wasn't going to introduce him to us, he strode over to my father and stretched out his hand, which was large, with broad, clean nails and white half-moons at the base of the cuticles.

His voice was a surprise, a light, clear tenor at odds with the height and heft of his muscular body. "Hello. You must be Sorab. I'm Claude. Silloo's husband."

My father, usually the soul of courtesy, gaped at him, his mouth opening and then closing again so comically that I almost laughed. It took me a moment to realize what the man had said. Husband? I looked questioningly at Silloo aunty, who was, by then, walking into the house. She turned and looked over her shoulder at her husband as though she didn't know why he was there, as though he'd followed her home and she was wondering if she'd have to keep him.

Clearly, this was a man who wasn't easily flustered. He remained calm, with that half-smile still flickering on his face. While my father struggled to respond to his greeting, Claude turned to me with a nod and said, "And you're Shahnaz. I recognize you from your pictures. It's a great pleasure to meet you at last. Silloo has told me so much about you."

Eventually my father found his voice and his manners. He shook hands with Claude, hugged and congratulated my aunt and ushered them both into the house, calling for my mother as he went. I followed, excited and fearful, wondering what my grandfather would say to this sudden marriage.

My aunts and uncles and cousins were gathered at our house for Sunday family dinner. They exclaimed in surprise, and laughed and cried and hugged my aunt and her new husband. Khorshed aunty demanded to know how they'd met, and when and where they had got married. She insisted she was going to give them a proper wedding reception as soon as possible. When were they free, she asked? Meanwhile, my grandmother slipped quietly out through the back door. I supposed that she had gone to break the news to my grandfather, who was stretched out in a long chair in the back garden, reading the weekend edition of the Times of India and drinking his afternoon tea. Keeping a watchful eye on the back door, I added my hugs and congratulations to those of my other relatives.

Silloo aunty bent her head towards mine and said quietly, "He's a wonderful man, Shahnu. He makes me happy." I kissed her, troubled by the air of impending disaster that hung like a monsoon cloud about her happiness.

We heard a muffled shout from the garden. A few minutes later, my grandmother came in the back door and hurried through the living room, into the kitchen. We heard her talking to the bearer, asking him to take a jug of water out to Soli Pappa. Then she came back into the living room, where the rest of the family stood, hushed and expectant, waiting for her to answer the unspoken questions that hung quivering in the air. Only Silloo aunty looked away, her face pale, her amber eyes glittering with tears.

Uncle Claude disentangled himself from the mob and, putting a protective arm around my aunt, led her to a couch by the window. They talked in low voices. Meanwhile my grandmother said, in her quavering voice: "He turned all red in the face, so I said to him, Soli, she is our daughter. After all, whatever we may feel, we must make him welcome. He is our family now. But what to do? The man won't listen, he starts shouting only, and his veins are swelling in his head and I'm saying to him, Soli, you are going to have a stroke, so calm down."

Just then, we heard the crash and tinkle of shattering glass, followed by my grandfather's roar. Looking frightened, Ramesh, the bearer, ran up the stairs from the back garden. He ducked his head into his shoulders and hurried off into the kitchen without meeting anybody's gaze. Two of my aunts, and my cousin Naushir, followed him out to the kitchen.

My grandmother called across the room to Silloo aunty: "Don't worry, darling. He is hot-headed only. You know how he is. He will shout and scream, but in the end, you are his favourite daughter. I will go and talk to him. Sorab, you come with me and help me knock some sense into his head."

Squaring her diminutive shoulders, my grandmother walked briskly out the door to the back garden. My father followed, dragging his feet. Claude looked confused. Silloo aunty cried. The others hovered around, patting and reassuring both of them. I hung back, angry at this upstart who had shown up from God-knows-where, laying claim to my beautiful aunt and wrenching her away from me.

The day ended badly. My grandfather ordered my aunt to get out of his house, and to take her so-called husband with her. He shouted at my grandmother that she had nurtured a cobra in her bosom to poison his last days on earth. It would have been better, he proclaimed, if the child had died of typhoid fever at the age of eight — at least then he would have been spared the sight of her turning her back on her family and forsaking her religion. Since she had married a non-Parsi, she would not be allowed at his funeral; it was the Parsi law. He was alternately furious and tearful about this. He raged and shouted at her, his voice cracking: his own daughter would not be able to pay her respects to him when he was dead.

The rest of the family clustered around him cooing and clucking like a flock of pigeons. He told them they were never to mention Silloo aunty's name again: she was no longer his daughter.

After that, I saw Silloo aunty only a few more times. She and Claude moved to Chichester, where he got a job as resident psychiatrist at the County hospital. She took a course in tapestry weaving at West Dean College, and sent us photographs of her work from time to time.

Her tapestries were beautiful and troubling. In a corner of each one she wove the figure of a medieval monk, emaciated, tonsured and robed, his back to the viewer. Sometimes his robes were brown, sometimes purple or black or midnight blue, intricately woven, sombre in colour. But he remained faceless, his upright stance proclaiming rectitude, judgement, retribution. Always, on his left, there was the reclining figure of a woman. Soft, Rubenesque, voluptuous, her hair and clothing in disarray. Her face was turned away, or shadowed, almost but never quite visible. These elements, though not central to her work, disturbed me with their quality of mystery, their sorrow.

My aunt's tapestries became well-known. She exhibited her work in London, Paris, Milan, New York. She and Claude moved to Florida. She wrote to me at least once a month, sent us cards every Christmas. I missed her.

∾

The dressing table I sat at that day was the one Silloo aunty had given me for my eleventh birthday. Her last postcard, with a photo of the Grand Canyon, was tucked into the frame of the mirror.

"Read the letter!" urged Roshan. I scanned it quickly.

"Listen to this," I said. "She wants me to come to America. She says there are many good universities there; she wants me to apply for graduate school. She and Claude will sponsor Shahrukh and me for visas, if we get admitted to an American university."

"I don't want you to go so far away. I'll never see you!" Roshan looked at me in dismay.

"It's not so far. You could come too, once you finish school."

Roshan shook her head, her eyes filling with tears. "You'll go away like Silloo aunty and you'll never come back, I know it."

"Don't worry, sweetie," I began. But Roshan interrupted me.

"Mummy went away to America for two years and look what happened to her. Don't go!"

Her words caught me by surprise, and I felt a sharp unease underneath my breastbone. My mother. America.

I shook my head and pushed the thought aside. There was much to do. My aunt had enclosed a list of American universities, both on the East coast, where she lived, and in California and the Pacific Northwest. She had sent me addresses to write to for application forms. I hugged myself with joy. This time, I knew I was going to leave India. I would not let anyone stop me.

Chapter 5

My dream of leaving India began with the letters my mother mailed to us from various cities in the United States during the two years that she lived there. The notepaper was crisp and smelled deliciously foreign. The photographs she enclosed were of thrusting skyscrapers, of snow-quilted prairie glittering under an immense cobalt sky. In those photos, geysers spurted hundreds of feet into the air, faces of US presidents were carved into mountainsides, their nostrils huge as houses. There were pictures of my mother looking diminutive and radiant amongst her friends — men and women with pink American faces and broad American smiles, their bulky American bodies clustered around her so that she was cocooned in magnitude. America seemed to me, then, a place of fabulous size. A place with so much room that people and landscapes and even buildings could grow there to an unimaginable stature.

I was twelve the summer I first realized that living in India meant I would be pruned into a miniature — the size and shape considered perfect for an Indian woman. I wasn't a woman yet, but I was old enough to see my future and know that the price I'd have pay to remain in the country of my birth would be to stay small.

That summer we went, as always, to Udvada, a tiny fishing

village several hours north of Bombay, where my family had a bungalow on the beach.

Just before it was time to go I tiptoed to my parents' room, hoping to say goodbye to my mother. Neither of my parents ever came with us on these annual trips to Udvada. My father claimed he couldn't get away from his law practice. My mother made no excuses, she simply didn't come. Each year, we'd wheedle and cajole and try to get my father to change his mind. But neither my sister nor I made any attempt to persuade my mother to come with us. For all her head-in-the-clouds vagueness, there was something flinty, utterly unyielding inside her. We recognized that we had a better chance of pushing the Western Ghats into the Arabian Sea than we had of moving her by anything we could say or do.

I can't remember when I first realized she didn't like children — didn't like my sister and me. She would stiffen, flinch if one of us inadvertently touched her. We learned to hold ourselves at a distance, to knock before entering any room she was in. Even then, we could not avoid seeing her distaste, the tightening of her mouth, the lines that turned white on either side of her nose when we entered, as though our very presence repelled her. I learned to become invisible, to take shallow breaths and use up as little air as possible when she was in the house.

Before she became ill my mother was a mathematician and theoretical physicist. I saw her at work once, when I went with my father to pick her up from her office at the Atomic Energy Comission. Standing in the doorway of her office, I realized I was looking at a woman I had never seen before. She looked so happy, her face soft and glowing, her eyes intently focused on the papers in front of her. Then she glanced up and saw us in the doorway. Her face congealed into the familiar rigid mask; her eyes turned vague, opaque.

So we travelled to Udvada with our aunts: my father's oldest unmarried sister, Khorshed aunty, who lived near us in our grandfather's compound at Juhu Beach, and my mother's younger sister, Perin aunty.

Khorshed aunty was large and stern, with a bosom like a bolster and white hair pulled tightly back into a bun. She carried herself rigidly upright — head high, chin raised, nose in the air like a camel. Her voice was deep, her diction perfect; every consonant was precisely articulated; every sentence proclaimed her utter superiority to us lesser mortals. She was always chastising us about our lack of proper form, and what she called our "hooliganism."

Perin aunty, who was my favourite person in the world next to my dad, was tiny and beautiful. She had large, dark eyes that brimmed with laughter, curly, shoulder-length black hair, and a smile so radiant that even small children who came into her clinic for immunizations were enchanted and forgot to cry when she gave them their shots. It was Perin aunty, not my mother, who made sure we got new clothes when we needed them, who helped us with our homework, who told us stories and taught us new songs, and played Scrabble with us on dank monsoon weekends. Perin aunty organized our trips to Udvada each summer, and made sure we had our hair cut before we left so we wouldn't have to fuss with it on our holiday. I could hear her talking to Sunder ayah on the verandah, giving her last-minute instructions about shopping and meals.

Before we left, I went and stood in the doorway of my mother's room, wondering if it was safe to go in. The air in her room was heavy and stale: a faint smell of urine, dead flowers and rotting oranges: the odours of putrefaction. As my eyes adjusted to the gloom I could see my mother lying on the big four-poster bed with her back to me. I had a feeling she was awake, but there was no invitation in that silent back. I didn't dare disturb her.

I could feel the unspoken misery that had spread throughout our household that year pressing against my body as I waited in that doorway. It had something to do with my mother's return from the United States, and the illness she suffered from being home. The weight of her unhappiness settled on my chest, stifling me. I tiptoed out of her room as quietly as I could and ran down the front steps to the car.

My sister Roshan had already claimed the window seat in front, next to my father. I climbed into the back, where Khorshed aunty was seated, and tried not to touch her doughy body, which radiated heat and irritability. Perin aunty hurried down the steps and got in on the other side of me. I leaned my head against her shoulder, and she rubbed the top of my head with her cheek.

My father drove us through a maze of downtown streets that I hardly recognized even though I'd travelled through them thousands of times. I had never seen them as silent and as empty as they were at this early hour. We travelled through the heart of Bombay's business district to Victoria Terminal, whose cavernous interior echoed eerily with the clank and rumble of trains being shunted in from the railway yard. There were several huddled families asleep on the wide platforms amid their boxes and bedding, and a few idle porters in faded red uniforms taking their morning tea at the only tea-stall that was open.

Our train, bright lights blazing on its great black engine, chugged in from the railway yards a few kilometres away. Its windows and doors were closed and gleaming with dew as it hissed up to the platform. When it had come to a stop, my father and I walked alongside it, searching the yellow reservations lists posted on the outside of each bogie for our names. I had to skip-run to keep up with my father's long stride, and I felt happiness fill my whole body like a smile. I tucked my hand into my father's large, warm palm, rubbed my cheek against the sleeve of his bush-shirt. He smelled deliciously, as always, of Dunhills pipe tobacco and shaving soap. He smiled down at me, saying, "So, beta, you will write to me, no?"

"Of course I will! I always write to you, but you never write back," I said. My father smiled his fond, absent smile, that made me want to grab him and shout: Look at me! I'm here, right in front of you, look! But I didn't. We found the first-class compartment that he had reserved for us. I let go of his hand and stepped back a pace as he signalled to the porters, who were waiting patiently on the platform with our bags and boxes.

The coolies loaded our baggage into the compartment. My aunts bustled up to the train with my sister and settled in with much fuss and fretting. The station-master waved his green flag. As the train whistle sounded, we hugged our father goodbye and ran over to kneel on our seats and wave to him through the bars on the windows.

Our train had an old-fashioned coal-fired steam engine, which belched out black, gritty smoke as it slowly steamed out of the station. Despite the heat, Khorshed aunty insisted on closing the windows so we would not get coal dust all over ourselves and our belongings. We waved to my father, mouthing goodbyes through the dust-streaked window-panes until we could no longer see him.

"It's too bad your daddy couldn't come with us. He needs to get away from all this heat and whatnot," said Perin aunty. I nodded, but was too excited about the holiday ahead to worry about him for long.

As the train picked up speed, the darkness outside slowly bleached into daylight. We jogged past railway colonies whose tall tenement buildings were festooned with laundry — wrinkled sheets and shirts, pants, blouses and saris — hung out to dry on small crumbling balconies. Past sprawling slums which stank, even through the closed windows, of open sewers: miles of grey, makeshift shelters pieced together out of cardboard boxes, rags, flattened tin cans, leaning against each other for support.

Roshan stared sombrely out the window, then pointed through the glass and cried: "Look at that boy — he's eating rubbish!"

He was small, no more than two or three years old, with a

bulging belly and rust-coloured hair. A black string tied around his waist protected him from the evil eye. He toddled barefoot and naked over a mountain of steaming garbage. In one tiny hand he clutched a crumbling chapatti; with the other, he stuffed something runny and yellow into his mouth.

I wanted to cry. I felt his hunger in my belly. Why was this little boy eating garbage when we had more food than we could possibly eat? It was no use asking my aunts — they never had answers for me. It's very sad, they would say, but what can we do? Then they would go back to their meal, undisturbed. In the corner of our compartment stood our stainless steel tiffin carrier stuffed with food. The sight of it, along with the heat, the lurching train, the stench of open sewers, the child outside the window, blended into a bitterness I could not swallow. I ran to the small sink and vomited.

Both my aunts fluttered around me, cooing with distress. They couldn't persuade me to lie down, but had to content themselves with placing a wet handkerchief on my forehead. Perin aunty kept stroking my head, checking my temperature with the back of her hand. My mouth tasted sour. I looked resolutely out the window, at the grim industrial outskirts of Bombay, where factory chimneys chugged and steamed, turning the air sulphurous with smoke. I wanted to bang my head against the dust-streaked window; I wanted to hit something. But my aunts were watching, so I raised my chin and breathed shallowly until I was floating in a jellied sea just above the twist in my belly.

And then finally, we were out of the city. We rolled past a yellow and brown patchwork of fields and small farms. Dusty villages of mud huts, their walls and roofs smeared with fresh cow-dung, baked in the sun. Bare-chested boys rode the backs of sleek black water-buffaloes, children and animals splashed and played, cooling themselves in shallow irrigation ditches and muddy ponds. They looked so happy, those laughing boys.

I'd almost forgotten what it was like to play, to splash and fool around with my friends and have fun. All that had disappeared from my life once my mother came home. She began to fall apart and my world dissolved around hers. I craned my head to look at those laughing boys as they receded into the distance. The train joggled on past women carrying water in brass jugs on their hips, balancing baskets filled with dried cowdung patties on their heads, graceful as ibises. They walked single-file through the fields, looking like a straggling line of gladioli in their brightly coloured saris.

Everyone tiptoed around the subject of Mum's illness, pretending there was nothing wrong. The adults avoided talking about her when I was in the room, would not answer my questions about what was the matter. I persisted. I pestered them to know why she was always in bed during the day, why she prowled the house at night. She'd come into my room, switch on the lamp beside my bed and glare at me with such a look of hate in her eyes that I lay shivering in the heat, unable sleep after she'd left. When I demanded to know what all this meant, the grownups pinched their lips together; their faces congealed into that long-suffering, righteous look that meant they were about to lie to me. They acted as though the screams I heard from her room at night, the early morning visits from the doctor, who came and gave her injections that left her as pale and quiet as a corpse, were figments of my imagination. I couldn't trust my own senses, which told me there was something very wrong with her, while all around me the adults insisted she was fine, fine.

I brooded on all this as I watched my family chew their omelette rolls. Then, thinking I might get a real answer if I caught my aunts off-guard, I began chattering about my cousin Sarosh's upcoming wedding. "Khorshed aunty," I began, "Do you think I could wear a sari to Sarosh's wedding?"

My aunt shot me a startled look. "You want to wear a sari? Really?" Then: "Hmmm. I don't know what Sorab will say to that. You're still a bit young."

"I'm not! I'm twelve. Almost twelve. Nergish wears saris sometimes and she's twelve." Nergish is my cousin.

"Nergish is big for her age. Poor child, she developed very early. Got her monthlies when she was only ten years old, that's why her mother lets her dress up like a grown woman," Khorshed aunty grumbled, her voice a mixture of disapproval and pride.

"You'll trip on the pleats the first time you try to walk and the whole thing will fall down around your ankles, Shahnu!" Perin aunty looked up from her breakfast and laughed — the first laugh I'd heard from her in days.

"I won't! I'll practise. You can help me. I want to wear your peacock blue tanchhoii! Please? Daddy'll say yes if you say I can! And then," I carried on, bouncing on my seat with excitement at the possibilities unfolding in my imagination, "I could wear Mummy's sapphire necklace and earrings. And her ring too. Although the ring might be too big, what do you think? And I could get Binky to set my hair in a French roll and. . . ."

"Not a chance," teased Perin aunty. "You think I'm crazy enough to let you wear my best sari? You'll go galumphing around in it like a tomboy and rip the border, or spill Goldspot on it at dinner. Oh no. You can wear it at your own wedding if you like."

"I'm never going to get married! I'm going to be just like you when I grow up," I blurted out, then blushed. Perin aunty froze for a moment, her face blank and empty. Then she raised her eyebrows and rolled her eyes in mock hilarity.

"If Shahnaz gets to wear a sari, I want to wear one too!" Roshan piped in.

"I'll ask Mummy; she'll lend me one of her saris," I boasted, knowing, even as I said it, that I wouldn't do anything of the sort. I was too smart to court rejection.

Roshan looked slyly at me. "Mummy won't lend you her sari. She never lends anyone anything. She slapped you the other day when she caught you trying on her perfume."

"She did not!" I was furious. I didn't think anyone had seen. I'd never had a hand raised in anger against me before. "She did not slap me. She just told me not to touch it."

"She did! I saw her. She really let you have it — one solid phataak, on your cheek. You cried in the bathroom and then you had five red finger-marks on your face."

My aunts exchanged looks over Roshan's head. Then Perin aunty turned to me and said, gently, "I was just teasing, Shahnu. You may wear my sari if your daddy says yes. I'll help you do up your hair. And you can wear my emeralds too, if you promise to take good care of them and not go running around like a jungli at the reception."

I mumbled my thanks, and glared at Roshan as she whined, "But what about me? I want to wear a sari too, if Shahnaz gets to wear one."

I'd almost forgotten why I'd launched this sari conversation in the first place. "Perin aunty, when do you think mummy will get better?"

Perin aunty shot me a wary look above the tops of her half-moon glasses. Then she looked at Khorshed aunty and shrugged. Just as she opened her mouth to reply, Khorshed aunty cut in: "There's nothing really wrong with your mummy, darling. She just needs rest."

"But why does she need rest? She doesn't do anything. She never goes out any more, not even to her office. She just sleeps all day. Then at night she wanders around the house screaming. She comes into my room and says terrible things to me."

"That's enough, Shahnaz. There are some things you are much too young to understand." Khorshed aunty's voice turned steely. "Your mummy is just needing some rest. Now come and help me tidy up the breakfast things, then you and Roshan can play Scrabble."

I turned my face to the window to hide the tears of frustration that sprang into my eyes. Perin aunty put her hand on my shoulder. "Come walk with me to the dining car, Shahnu. I could use a nice cup of tea. You can have a cold lemon-barley if you like. It'll help settle your stomach."

Lurching against the jolting of the train, I followed her down the narrow corridor. Several times we had to turn sideways to squeeze past other passengers before we finally reached the dining-car, which was almost empty. A waiter in a stained white uniform showed us to a table by a window. We sat down facing each other. My aunt ordered tea for herself and a cold glass of lemon-barley water for me. When the waiter left, she turned and put her hand on my arm, which was resting on the table top.

"Shahnu, darling," she began, looking embarrassed, pleading. I kept my eyes stubbornly fixed on hers. Perin aunty sighed. "It is very difficult, sweetheart." Her voice dropped to a dramatic whisper and she looked around quickly before adding, "She had a nervous breakdown, your poor mummy. Due to some female problems . . . You know that operation she had last year? Well . . . She had trouble with her insides after that."

My Perin aunty is a doctor. Trouble with her insides?

"What trouble? What exactly is her problem?"

"Well, darling, she had heavy bleeding, and so they had to remove her internal organs, you see, and she . . . "

"What internal organs? You mean her intestines? But then how does she eat? She must . . . Could you please just tell me what's wrong with her?"

Perin aunty darted a worried look over her shoulder and opened her mouth to speak, but I couldn't stop myself, I had to know: "What does nervous breakdown mean? Is she crazy? I don't understand!" I said. My aunt glanced quickly around again and shook her head to silence me.

"Keep your voice down, Shahnaz. We don't want the whole world to know our family's business." Then, leaning across the table until her mouth was just inches from my ear, she murmured: "Your mummy had a hysterectomy. Do you understand what that is? It means she had her female organs removed surgically."

I was grateful for the confidence, but still confused about the link between the "female" operation and my mother's increasingly bizarre behaviour.

"Hysterectomy." I tried out the word. "Is that like hysterical?"

Just then the waiter returned with a dented silver tray laden with thick white railway-issue china. He placed a small round teapot and a tea-cup on the table in front of my aunt. He then put a sweating glass of lemon-barley water on a small doily next to my elbow. We remained silent while he clinked down teaspoons, tea strainer, and bowls of sugar and cream on the table between us. When he left, I launched into my protest once again.

"I don't understand why you won't tell me, straight out, what's wrong with her. All this talk of taking out her insides and nervous breakdown. I don't know what it means."

Perin aunty looked at me with an infuriating mixture of exasperation and pity. "You'll understand when you're older. Just now, your daddy needs you to be his strong girl and not to worry him with a lot of questions, darling. He has a lot to handle, poor man."

"I wish you'd all stop treating me as though I were a baby." Then, as Perin aunty opened her mouth to protest, I cut in: "Fine, I won't ask any more questions. But I want you to stop pretending she's all right! There's something wrong with her. You have to do something. She scares me. You don't know what it's like!"

I was close to tears. Why wouldn't anyone listen to me? At that moment I wanted to do something desperate, so my family would have to pay attention. Something dramatic and final, like yanking open the door and jumping out of the hurtling train. I had a momentary vision of my body slamming down on the tracks, being sliced through beneath the heavy iron wheels, lying splattered and broken on the gleaming rails.

I shuddered, and drank down my lemon-barley, leaving a half-inch of liquid at the bottom of the glass, as I'd been taught was the polite thing to do. But for whom was I being polite, I

48

asked myself, despairingly. Who benefited when I deprived myself of this last half-inch of my drink? The half-inch which had all the best parts — the crunchy, semi-liquefied sugar and tangy lemon-pulp that settled on the bottom of the glass? It made no sense to me, but I obeyed like an idiot.

Perin aunty said her tea was cold and she no longer felt like drinking it anyway. We made our way back to our compartment, where we found Khorshed aunty reading a book, with Roshan fast asleep on the berth beside her. I got my own book out of my sling bag — I had just begun reading Middlemarch — and wedged myself into the corner of my berth with my head against the window. The khattata-khattata-khat of the train made a soothing counterpoint to the story and soon I was absorbed in the world of the Brookes. It helped me push all the turmoil surrounding my mother to the very back of my head.

The rest of our journey passed quickly and uneventfully, though the little compartment we were in got hotter as the morning wore on. Khorshed aunty resorted to splashing Eau De Cologne liberally on her bosom, her neck, underneath her hair, to cool herself off, so that the whole compartment reeked of her cologne. It was almost noon by the the time the train steamed into Udvada station.

The station was really nothing more than a double platform with a bench at one end and the station-master's tiny office, which doubled as a ticket booth, on the other end. The lone porter was a small, wizened old man with bow-legs and a face like a walnut. He was a fixture in the village, having worked there for as long as I could remember. He hauled himself up into our railway carriage and, in the five minutes allotted to the train for disgorging passengers and taking on the mail, managed to unload all of our baggage onto the platform while we disembarked. Then the station master clanged his brass bell and waved his green flag. The train pulled away with a great hissing and clacking and whistling.

The porter loaded all our baggage onto his person with an

alacrity that belied his years. He had the boxes balanced on a small wad of cloth on top of his head, suitcases under each arm and more bags dangling from both hands. Feeling ashamed at having such an old man carry my bags, I followed behind him as he trotted off at a brisk pace towards the village's only taxi, which was waiting just outside the station. My aunts trailed behind me, half-carrying half-dragging Roshan, who coughed and complained about the heat and the dust.

The taxi was an ancient black Buick with cracked imitation-leather upholstery. The driver was an even more ancient Parsi gentleman named Mr. Naushirvaan. As we walked up to the car, he doddered out of his seat, his large head quivering like a jelly on his scrawny neck. He patted my sister on the shoulder, exclaimed over how much I'd grown, and shook hands formally with both my aunts. He showed the waiting coolie where he wanted our baggage stored. The suitcases were tucked into the boot of the car, the boxes hoisted onto the roof and tied down with lengths of hemp rope. The four of us squeezed ourselves into the Buick with the rest of our bags. Perin aunty paid the coolie, who salaamed and went off smiling his betel-stained smile and wagging his head with delight at the unexpected generosity of the tip she had handed him.

Mr. Naushirvaan tried several times to start the car, but after it had wheezed unh-unh-unh a few times, the engine failed to turn over and simply died. He climbed out of the car again, moving at the pace of a waterlogged snail. Roshan began to whine: "I'm hungry! Why is he taking so long? I want to go!" Khorshed aunty shushed her sternly, while Perin aunty fanned herself with her book. I was hungry too, but there was no point in complaining, so I smiled apologetically at Mr. Naushirvaan and settled back in my seat, prepared to wait.

Tottering over to the front end of the car, Mr. Naushirvan inserted a long metal crank under the grille and heaved mightily, cranking one, two, three times. Finally, with a choked gurgle, the engine sputtered into action. Then, moving faster than

I'd ever seen him move, Mr. Naushirvan doddered back into his seat and drove down the bumpy dirt road with his nose inches from the windshield. He drove in second gear the entire way, the wind blowing red dust in through the open windows. Perin aunty smiled stoically through the flying grit and kept up a running conversation with Mr. Naushirvan about who had got married since she last saw him, who had died, which couples had been blessed with new babies. Khorshed aunty kept her white cambric handkerchief clamped firmly against her nose and mouth and looked as though she had swallowed a piece of rotten fish. Me, I was happy. I could smell the sea, even though I couldn't yet see it, and the summer stretched out in front of me, enticing as a new book, full of possibility.

We drove down the road a few miles, Roshan and I exclaiming excitedly over familiar landmarks. Khorshed aunty radiated silent disapproval as we clambered over her to point out our favourite places along the way. Finally, we spotted the grey stone wall that marked the boundaries of our compound. The wooden gates were open, the mali and his wife, who lived on the property and took care of it year-round, were waiting for us in the driveway. My aunts had sent them a postcard letting them know we were coming so that they could get the house aired and ready for our arrival.

The mali, whose name was Mohan, was a balding, harassed-looking man about fifty years of age who had a gift for making almost anything grow. Our bungalow was surrounded by gardens that rose in lush, stone-lined tiered beds from the circular driveway all the way to the high stone walls girding the compound. Some of the trees and shrubs in these gardens were several hundred years old. Besides the many varieties of roses, there were two different kinds of jasmine, honeysuckle, lantana, queen-of-the-night, and champa trees, spicy carnations, tall pink phlox and rows of bright red canna lilies. Tamarind trees, with their feathery leaves and finger-like fruit, swished against the verandah roof in the small breeze that blew in off the sea.

As we coasted down the driveway, the mingled perfume of wet earth and roses, chameli blossoms and frangipani, crowded in, clamouring to be recognized. When I was younger, I had named every bush and shrub and tree in this garden, spent long hours in or on or under them. Now I waved to my garden friends.

The taxi jolted to an abrupt halt at the foot of the wide stone stairs leading up to the verandah which ran along the length of the bungalow. Mohan greeted us with folded palms and deep namastes. As always, he was knee-deep in children. A couple of toddlers with runny noses and bare bellies clung to his legs. Then there were three or four older boys who stood at various heights around their father, and a little girl who hung back, scratching her calf with the toes of one small, bare foot. Mohan's wife, Mangala, a tall, stately woman who never seemed to grow any older despite her constant child-bearing, held a brand new baby against her breast, and another, about a year older, slung on her hip. At a sharp command from Mohan the children clustered around the taxi, many brown hands lifting bags and boxes out of its rusty old boot and carrying them into the house.

Mangala told us we had just missed a major storm. Some of the tiles had blown off the roof and crashed onto the well-head at the side of the house. "Hai Ram, thank God the children were all safely inside when it happened," she said, wagging her head in a gesture that signified amazement, gratitude, relief. "Vishnu was taking care of us. Such a storm, tobaa! That tall coconut palm that used to grow right by the well blew over and cracked the well-cover." She murmured on, her mellifluous voice lending the litany of disaster the grace of a prayer. The roof had been mended, she said, but new tiles would have to be brought in from Bombay. Meanwhile, her husband had improvised and patched it as best he could with old ghee cans beaten flat and nailed down. The water-level in the well was low, so they had not been able to water the rose-beds twice a day, but the canna lilies were doing fine and the love-apple and jackfruit trees were heavy with fruit.

My aunts settled down in the teak long-chairs on the verandah to catch up with news of the house and the village. My sister and I, restless after the long train ride, raced around the side of the house and onto the beach. There, the sand stretched endlessly in either direction; the sea crashed and glittered in the noonday sun. The yellow sand was littered with debris flung there by the storm — coconut shells, cracked open and washed up by the tide, dead crabs, great fronds of seaweed.

We ran along the beach, prodded at stranded giant jellyfish with driftwood sticks, scooped up the first shells and coloured pebbles of the summer, gathering up our skirts to make a cradle that would hold our treasures. The sand burned our feet through our thin-soled sandals. The wind tangled in our hair and blew right through my head, leaving it gloriously empty. My mother's craziness, my father's peculiar unconcern, school and classes and the stench of Bombay were scoured out of my skull by the wind and the sun. Splashing each other, laughing and gasping in the heat, Roshan and I ran in and out of the water.

Eventually, when it got too hot to stay outside, we went indoors for lunch, unloading our treasures on the verandah steps. We ate at a long table on the front verandah, overlooking the sea. Khorshed aunty was having a nap and didn't want to be disturbed, so lunch was a giggly, silly-headed affair. Perin aunty, being my mother's younger sister, was more like a cousin than an aunt. We joked and teased and played and mock-wrestled with her as we'd never dream of doing with Khorshed aunty, who was much older than my father and stern, unrelenting when it came to matters of Good Form and Doing The Right Thing. After lunch, we laid down on the swing-bed and fell asleep to the roaring of the sea and the dry rustling of the palm-trees.

We played on the beach for the rest of the day. As night fell, we sat out on the verandah and told stories, each of us making up a story that started with the last sentence of the one that had gone before it. The tales grew taller as the night grew darker. Mohun lit the kerosene lamps, each lamp casting a small circle of radiance, making wild shadows dance along the walls and up the ceiling. The house was so old, it had no electricity or running water. There was also no indoor toilet. As bedtime drew near, we begged for one more round of stories, just one more, please! Anything to avoid having to go to the outhouse.

The outhouse was in a corner of the garden, a long, dark, scary walk from the main bungalow. There were snakes in this part of the country. Poisonous ones — cobras and vipers. And scorpions. One of the mali's sons had died of a scorpion bite a few years earlier. We had been vacationing in Udvada when it happened. His skinny brown left leg looked incongruously normal next to his grotesquely swollen right leg, which was the colour and texture of a ripe eggplant. The skin looked as though it would burst.

The boy was stretched out twitching and trembling on a palette his mother had improvised for him on the floor of the back verandah. I could still smell the stench of burning flesh, as the village medicine man applied hot coals with a pair of tongs to the boy's calf to cauterize the puncture wound. I could still hear the screams of the boy as he lay in delirious agony in his mother's arms. All the while the pundit had chanted mantras and laid powders and potions and amulets on various parts of the child's body. None of it worked. The boy was dead before the village taxi returned from the nearest town with a real doctor. If Perin aunty had been with us on that trip, she could have saved him. Thoughts of him were vivid in my mind that night as my sister and I got our nightgowns on. Carrying a battery-operated electric torch apiece, we stepped carefully along the garden path lined with fragrant queen-of-the-night bushes towards the looming mass of the outhouse.

The outhouse was built on a high brick platform, with many shallow steps leading up to its door. The sickly stench of phenol mingled with the odours of urine and feces grew stronger as we got closer to it. I took a deep breath before I entered, and, holding my hand over my nose and mouth, tried to do my business as quickly as possible so I wouldn't have to breathe in any of the stinking air.

Later, ears alert for any sound, particularly the rustling that might announce a snake, I waited outside for my sister to finish. Then we ran as fast as we could back to the safety of the house. We shook out our sandals, tucked them in under the mosquito-net, and climbed into bed, breathless with fear and excitement.

By the time Perin aunty came in to kiss us goodnight we were weak-kneed and giggling with relief. Her kerosene lamp cast wavering shadows on the whitewashed walls. Setting the lamp carefully on the small teak table beside our bed, she raised the side of the mosquito-net and slipped into the giant four-poster bed. We squabbled over who got to lie next to her, a familiar ritual which ended with Roshan crawling over Perin aunty's body to the outside of the bed so our favourite aunt was ensconced between us.

With one arm around each of our shoulders, Perin aunty told us a story. She was a natural storyteller, her imagination as vivid and unfettered as our own. She acted out the parts of each of her characters, her voice dropping to a tense whisper or rising in a swooping shriek that had us shrieking too, with fear and delight.

That night she told us of the spirit woman who dwelt at the bottom of our well, waiting there until the end of eternity to be reunited with her dead husband. "Her name is Laila," said Perin aunty, solemnly. "Each night she emerges streaming from the dark, cold waters of the well to sit by the phosphorescent surf and comb her long green hair. Her moaning is the sound of the wind; her singing is the music of the stars. Her voice is as rich and bright as diamonds, and she weaves a tapestry of dreams into the tresses of her hair as she plaits it by the light of the crescent moon. If she remains faithful to her dead love, all her suffering will be redeemed. The dreams she weaves will, at the end of Time, spring to life and take form," said Perin aunty, her eyes shining in the lamplight.

"But that's too long!" I protested, appalled at this vision of suffering womanhood. "She's still alive, even if her husband is dead. She can't just sit there wailing and singing and waiting for him forever!"

Perin aunty ignored my outburst and continued her story: "Each night, Laila waited for her husband, Jagannath, to come to her from the sea. He had been a great fisherman, who lured such quantities of silver fish into his nets that the Lord of the Sea became jealous of his prowess. One day, just as dawn was breaking and he was turning his boat homewards, the Sea Lord whipped the winds into a frenzy until they blew up a great storm. He churned the waves with his mighty forearms so that they towered and crashed over Jagannath's boat. The boat, its crew and its cargo perished in the storm, swallowed by the Lord of the Sea.

"But Laila would not let her husband go. She wept by the sea-shore until blood flowed from her eyes and shone on her breast like rubies. She demanded justice from the gods. The Lord of the Sea had no reason to quarrel with her husband, she said. He had always made his offerings at the shrine of the fishermen before he embarked on any voyage. The gods, in turn, argued with the Sea Lord but they could not bend his steely will. In despair, Laila flung herself into the well in our courtyard and drowned in its dark waters. But her spirit still sought her Jagannath.

"So every night, as the moon rose in the sky, the incomparable Laila swam up from her watery dwelling-place and sang so piercingly that the Sea Lord's stony heart was moved to pity. For those brief moments between the time when the first rays of the sun become visible over the edge of the horizon and before the moon disappears into her daytime slumber, he gives Jagannath permission to leave the depths of the sea and embrace his Laila. The fronds of seaweed you find on the beach," said Perin aunty, "are the strands of hair she leaves behind. If you take a strand and place it under your pillow, you will dream of the man you will one day marry."

Roshan giggled at that and nudged me but I felt something harden stubbornly inside me. I turned to Perin aunty: "But why does she have to live at the bottom of a well for eternity just because her wretched husband drowned? If I were her, I'd be sad for a while, of course, but I wouldn't kill myself."

Perin aunty hugged me to her. "Oh, you'll see, Shahnu," she laughed. "One day you'll fall in love with the right man and then you'll do anything to be with him always."

"No I won't. I'd never sit around in the bottom of a well waiting for my husband to turn up alive when I know he's dead. Maybe I'd pack my bags and take my beautiful voice to La Scala or Covent Gardens. Or I'd make my own records and become as famous as Galli-Curci or Callas — I'd be a star!"

But Perin aunty just opened her eyes wide in mock terror and said: "Listen. Sssshhh! Hear that wailing? That's her, Laila, singing for her Jagannath."

I fell asleep that night to the hiss and roar of the surf outside our window. I dreamed I was that woman fated to spend eternity lurking in the bottom of a deep dark well waiting for a dead man to return. My lonely song echoed off the stars.

The next morning we were up early, eager to swim, to explore. But our aunts had other plans for us. Udvada is a holy place for Parsis. Although the village is tiny, consisting of no more than a few dozen families who live there year-round, it is home to the most sacred Parsi fire-temple in India. Here, legend has it, burns the eternal flame that was carried across the sea from Persia when the Zoroastrians, (called Parsis because they came from Persia), fleeing Muslim persecution, crossed in tiny boats and landed on the west coast of India in the eighth century A.D. To house the sacred fire, they built this temple in Udvada. Tended by the temple priests, that flame has been kept burning ever since. I loved the idea that the fire I saw there each year had been burning for over twelve hundred years, symbol of the undying flame of truth.

That morning, Khorshed aunty told us, we were to bathe, put on our sudra and kustee, the muslin undershirt and sacred thread that are the emblems of our faith, and go to the fire-temple. My aunts were having a special ceremony conducted by the priests in comemmoration of Khorshed aunty's grand-father's birthday. Her grandfather, my great-grandfather, died when I was six. I didn't remember much of him. He was a quiet, short, man with a pink, bald head like a baby's. He collected coins, and rare stamps. He had once spent an afternoon with me, showing me his Penny Blacks and the rest of his prized collection.

The ceremony we were to attend that morning would go on for several hours. The dasturjis — Zoroastrian high-priests — would sit cross-legged around the holy fire, dressed in pristine white muslin trousers and starched white duglis. Their beards would curl around their chins and they would rock back and forth as they chanted prayers in the ancient language of the Zend Avesta. In front of them, the fire in its great silver urn would crackle and fizz as they leaned over from time to time to feed its flames with fragrant sandalwood logs.

As the morning progressed the priests' assistants would glide barefoot across the marble floors, bearing silver platters piled high with fruit — pomegranates and oranges, custard-apples, papayas, pineapples, mangoes — and special ritual sweetmeats and foods. The priests would bless the food, passing their hands over it and intoning prayers, sprinkling it with rose-water from silver shakers. When the ceremony was over, we would take those foods home, each piece of fruit, each sweetmeat, redo-lent of sandalwood. Later that afternoon my aunts would carry the blessed food to friends and neighbours — other Parsi families who lived in the village — and I would get to see my friend Arni.

My sister and I grumbled as we put on our good clothes. If our father had been there he would not have made us go — he claimed to be agnostic, although he said his prayers every morning like all the other adults in our household. On the other hand, I loved the cool marble floors and cavernous quiet of the fire-temple, the frankincense which filled my nostrils with a fragrance that reminded me of something I once knew but could no longer quite grasp. I loved the slant of golden sunlight that flowed like liquid fire through the slits in the shuttered windows, the feeling of endless space, limitless time, that descended on me when I became quiet and still inside. In any case, our aunts would brook no arguments; we must go with them. And of course, afterwards, we'd get to eat all the yummy sweetmeats that were only made on such occasions.

So we dressed. We went out to the driveway where the ancient taxi awaited us. We drove to the fire-temple, where my aunts were greeted in hushed voices by other women dressed in white georgette saris with their sudras and kustees conspicuously displayed for the occasion. They patted Roshan and me on our heads, exclaimed over how tall we'd grown. They told me I looked just like my father when he was my age. They told my little sister she was beautiful, like our mother. Same big, brown eyes and fair skin, they said. Then their voices dropped to conspiratorial whispers as they turned away from us to huddle with my aunts.

"How is she?" they asked, directing furtive glances our way to see if we were listening. I feigned an elaborate lack of interest, by becoming intensely preoccupied with smelling the yellow roses that bloomed in a stone urn in a corner of the wide terrace.

"Any improvement yet?"

"Poor thing," said one old crone, her caramel eyes gleaming with feigned sympathy and barely hidden malice. "God has given her such a hard life."

"What about the children?" asked another woman. "And Sorab? How is he managing?" They all glanced at us again, pityingly.

I wanted to scream, to slap the sly looks off their wrinkly old faces. But it wouldn't do. Only crazy people behaved like that. I grabbed my sister's hand and dragged her out onto the broad stone steps that led down to the fire-temple's garden.

Roshan didn't want to go with me. She whimpered: "I want to stay with Perin aunty!" Furious, I dropped her hand and pushed her away. She fell on the top step and skinned her knee. As she tried to stand up she tripped on the hem of her dress, which ripped and unravelled. She began to bawl. I could hear my aunts exclaiming and calling our names. I ran down the stairs and out into the garden.

My belly hurt and I wanted to wail out loud like my little sister. I might look like my father — everyone always told me I took after him — but inside, I was angry and and filled with bad feelings, like my mother. What if I went crazy like her? I couldn't think clearly. My head swarmed with other people's thoughts and feelings so that I couldn't see myself from the inside any more.

I hid in the bushes until the ceremony was over. My aunts came down the stairs, followed by the priests' assistants, who carried the heavy trays of fruit and food out to the waiting taxi. Perin aunty hugged me, saying: "We were worried about you darling." Khorshed aunty pressed her lips together and glared at me. We piled into the taxi and drove off to begin our round of afternoon visits.

The first house we went to was Arni's. It was only a mile down the road from the fire-temple. Her family was vaguely related to ours, though I wasn't entirely sure how we were connected. We only saw them once a year, since they lived in Udvada year-round and seldom came to Bombay. Arni's father was one of the temple priests. Even though Arni was several years older than me — she must have been eighteen or nineteen that year — we were good friends. We drove up their dirt driveway, raising clouds of dust.

Mrs. Dustoor stood on the porch in her white sari, calling

out: "Welcome! Welcome! Such a long time since we last saw you!" We got out of the taxi, carrying one of the silver trays of food between us. Since the food had been blessed, no non-Parsi was allowed to touch it, so the servants could not carry it into the house.

My aunts settled down for a long chat while our hostess ordered the servants to bring tea and pastries, and cold drinks for my sister and me. I had brought a present for Arni — a scrapbook of dried flowers I had made for her in school. I pulled it out of my straw handbag. "Mrs. Dustoor, may I go up and give this to Arni?" I asked.

Arni's mother dropped her eyes and wouldn't look at me. "Arni's not well right now," she mumbled; I had to lean towards her to hear her. I saw Perin aunty hide a smile behind her hand.

Khorshed aunty abruptly launched into a loud discussion of the last Parsi Panchayat meeting she had attended in Bombay. Mrs. Dustoor leaned across the coffee table and offered me several sweetmeats from the the tray of blessed food. The moment passed. I remained confused, but Roshan and I munched on, our mouths and attention occupied for the moment.

There was a lot more talk about grown-up matters — navjote ceremonies, Panchayat politics, the difficulty of finding good servants. I was so bored the top of my head was floating towards the ceiling. I tried again. "Mrs. Dustoor, may I please go up and see Arni? I'll be very quiet, I just want to say hello and give her this scrapbook I made for her."

Mrs. Dustoor pursed her lips and raised her eyebrows ever so slightly. Her nostrils flared. She looked at me out of the corners of her eyes. "Ummm . . . I think she's asleep. Better not disturb her. You can see her next time you come." She reached out her hand for the scrapbook. "Here, give me that. I'll give it to Arni when she's better."

I kept a protective hand on the scrapbook. I knew Mrs. Dustoor was lying. Arni wouldn't sleep in the middle of the day! But the rules of polite discourse forbade my pushing the matter further. I sat back in my chair and pretended to believe her. I watched a fly circling her head, quivering towards her ear. She brushed it away, then saw me watching her and said abruptly, "Arni has a headache. She is lying down with a wet cloth on her head." I nodded and make a clucking noise to indicate my sympathy. All the while I kept thinking, Liar!

There was an uneasy silence. My aunts filled it by picking up their purses and patting their saris in place, preparing to leave. As we headed out the door, Mrs. Dustoor sighed and said, "Oh, all right, you can see Arni just for one minute, if you really want."

Khorshed aunty put on her "gracious" voice and trilled, "Oh, it will be so nice to see the dear child!"

Instead of going down the front stairs, Mrs. Dustoor led us through the dining room and out a small door into their back garden. The back garden was mostly full of fruit trees, but in the far corner, almost out of sight of the house, was a small stone shed. Mrs. Dustoor led us to within a few yards of it, and stopped. Its front door was open. The inside was dark. We stood under a mango tree, waiting for Mrs. Dustoor to explain what we were doing there. The same unease that had ruffled my spine when I asked about Arni now made my ears itch.

Mrs. Dustoor raised her voice and called Arni's name. After a moment, Arni's slender figure appeared in the doorway of the shed. She was wearing a printed house-dress and maroon velvet house-slippers. Her hair was neatly combed, her body upright and alert. She didn't look as though she'd been ill or asleep. She stood shading her eyes with her hand. I couldn't see her face, as the overhanging roof cast it into shadow, but I was so happy and excited to see her that I darted off towards her with the scrapbook tucked under my arm. Before I'd taken half-a-dozen steps, Khorshed aunty hissed at me urgently: "No! You musn't go there!"

Perin aunty ran over to me and, grabbing my arm in a grip so tight it hurt, dragged me back to where the others were standing. Bewildered, I looked up at her and asked, "What's wrong? I was just going over to give Arni a hug and her scrapbook."

Mrs. Dustoor pursed her lips and shook her head. Khorshed aunty said, apologetically, "It's the way they are raised. Sorab doesn't hold with the old ways, and their mother . . . well, you know how things are there."

I turned back to look at Arni, but she had disappeared into the shed again. "Can't I at least give her the scrapbook I brought?" Then, seeing the appalled look on Mrs. Dustoor's face, I hurriedly added, "What about a pomegranate? Arni loves pomegranates." I faltered to a stop, aware that I had transgressed some unspoken code, but bewildered about the nature of the transgression. Khorshed aunty looked at me as though I'd crawled out of a hole in the ground.

Mrs. Dustoor smiled grimly at me, a tight stretching of her lips that bared her teeth and sent a shiver up my spine. She said, with quiet contempt, "Arni is unclean. She can't touch sacred food. And you can't touch her without becoming unclean yourself. You should know that by now, a great big girl like you." Then she turned on her heel and marched back into her house.

I was so stunned I couldn't say a word. Perin aunty put a sympathetic arm around me. We walked back to the taxi in silence. Khorshed aunty announced that she had a headache, so, instead of continuing on our visiting rounds, we drove back home. Khorshed aunty went straight to her room. She held her head very high. Her neck was unnaturally stiff, her shoulders pressed back so far I could see her shoulder-blades through the thin white silk of her blouse. I knew she was furious but I didn't know why. I felt guilty, confused, defensive, as I so often did when I was with her. Once again I'd done something dreadful and was too stupid to even know what it was. Perin aunty called for Mangala to help Roshan change out of her good dress. Then she took my hand and led me out onto the verandah.

"Shahnaz," she began. "Do you understand what happened at the Dustoor's?"

I shook my head. "I feel as though I did something wrong but I didn't. They shouldn't treat Arni like a leper. What's she done that's so bad they have to put her out in a shed and treat her like an untouchable?"

"She hasn't done anything, sweetheart. The Dustoors are an old-fashioned family. They follow the old traditions. Arni has her monthly period. You know how I told you about that? How a woman bleeds each month? Well, the Dustoors believe — and other orthodox Parsis feel this way too — that a woman is impure while she is bleeding. So she must stay in a separate place, away from other people, where she won't pollute the house or the other members of the family. She has to sleep on an iron bedstead and nobody may touch her or speak to her until she has finished bleeding."

"But who takes care of her? What about her food? They can't just leave her in a shed like an animal!"

"The servants bring her her meals and leave them on a tray outside her door. She can't come out, and they can't go in, but she's taken care of. When her bleeding time is over she has a ritual bath and goes to the fire-temple to pray. After that, everything returns to normal."

I was so appalled by the unfairness of this, I turned and shouted at Perin aunty through a sudden storm of tears: "How could you just stand there and let them do this to Arni! You should have told me before we went, I would never have come with you to visit those barbarians. Are you going to do this to me when I start bleeding?"

Visibly startled by my outburst, Perin aunty reached out and pulled me to her, saying, in a soothing tone: "Oh Shahnu, of course not. You know our family doesn't believe in these primitive taboos! When your time comes, we'll . . ."

Before she could finish, I yanked myself free of her embrace and ran down the verandah steps, out onto the beach. I pulled off my shoes and tore into the surf. Something sharp and wordless pushed its way from my belly into my throat. A coconut shell, washed up on the tide, slapped against my leg. I kicked it with such force, my foot stung and I almost lost my balance. My dress was soaked, my legs were itchy with sand and salt, and the toes on my right foot felt bruised. The coconut shell bobbed up behind me on the next wave, butting against the backs of my knees. I whirled around and snarled at it in a rage, then scooped it up in one hand and threw it as far as I could. It landed a few feet away, buoyant and undisturbed. I laughed, then, shakily, and began wading back towards the beach.

The waves splashed against my face, their briny foam shocking and cleansing, bringing me clarity. As the waves surged and receded, I tried to sort out the implications of all I'd discovered over those past two days.

So. First of all, bleeding from down there made you a woman. And becoming a woman made you filthy, untouchable. Then when you'd become a woman and you married a man you didn't love, you developed woman troubles. You bled too much so they had to cut out your insides so you wouldn't be hysterical. Then you went crazy.

I shivered as I realized the enormity of what I'd just conceived. How long had I known my mother didn't love my father? I couldn't think about that just then. Next. What came next? Oh. If you did love your husband and he died, you had to throw yourself into a well and spend eternity shivering in the dark like a snail without a shell. Waiting. Waiting for him to come back to you so your life could begin again.

I didn't ever want to grow up. I looked down at my body, which was flat as a board. My father often teased me about being all skin and bone. I hugged myself, wrapping my arms around my ribs, fiercely glad that I still had time.

Chapter 6

The pilot's voice rumbles over the P.A. system: "This is your captain speaking. Well, folks, we're about fifteen minutes from Eugene. It's a beautiful afternoon. The temperature below is sixty degrees. This may be the only sunny day you'll see here this year, so enjoy it while you can! I'd like to thank you for travelling with American Airlines. My crew and I wish you a very pleasant evening. Please extinguish all smoking materials and fasten your seatbelts in preparation for landing."

I surface out of a confused dream in which I was tangled in the clammy embrace of a giant octopus, twisting my body this way and that, struggling to free myself from its tentacles. The pilot's voice, with its exotically American cadences, reaches me like a breath of air just as the creature winds itself dangerously around my throat. I gasp as I wake, swallowing great gulps of dry, recirculated aircraft cabin air as though it were the freshest breeze from the sea.

I've slept through most of the flight from Los Angeles. My mouth tastes stale; my bladder stings. I stand up abruptly. My purse flips off my lap, spilling its contents onto the floor.

Flustered, I crouch down in the tiny space in front of my seat to pick up my lipstick, which has rolled under the seat in front of mine. I drop it into the open mouth of my black leather bag, then begin scooping up the rest of my things: a gold compact with my initials — S. S. — in curly script; a small spiral-bound notebook, slender gold fountain-pen. Handiwipes. My hands are cold. A toothbrush in a blue plastic case. A tube of ayurvedic toothpaste. A bar of dark Swiss chocolate. Impatience makes me clumsy. Wallet, keys, tampons. The envelope my father gave me at the airport. I close the gold clasp of my hand-bag with a snap, and turn towards Shahrukh, who is snoring lightly in the seat beside me. I bend over and rub my cheek against his, murmur in his ear: "Shahrukh! Wake up, love. We're almost there."

His eyes flutter open, blinking against the light. He looks blankly at me, his eyes still veiled with sleep. "Shahrukh, move over. I have to get to the loo. They've got the seatbelt sign on. If I don't make it to a toilet in the next two minutes, we'll have a real mess on our hands!"

Shahrukh grins and sits up, saying, "Hey! Can't let that happen." He stands up and steps into the aisle to give me exit room. We both remember, vividly, the time we'd gone out to lunch at a Chinese restaurant in Calcutta. We'd shared a bowl of wonton soup, greasy and delicious. Minutes later, I'd whispered that I felt ill, needed to get to the restroom fast. Shahrukh urged me wait until we got home. He swore he'd seen a cockroach scuttle across his shoes when we'd entered the restaurant. Unable to hold it in any longer, I had thrown up all over the table, spewing bits of pork dumpling onto the white formica tabletop, on my own lap, on Shahrukh's shirt. I'd mopped up as best I could with the yellowing linen table-napkins. Shahrukh, furious and embarrassed, had paid the bill, leaving an enormous tip. He'd hustled me out of the restaurant, his hand gripping my arm so tightly it hurt. He hadn't said a word to me all the way home. The car smelled of sour vomit despite the rolled-down windows.

Now, the memory makes us both laugh as I edge past him into the aisle. I walk quickly to the restroom, lock the door, pull down my pants and sigh with relief as my bladder empties. Dreamily, my mind still back in Calcutta, I tear off a long strip of toilet paper from the roll at my elbow, wipe myself, zip up my pants. As I stand up, the aircraft hits an air-pocket and I lurch against the sink, hitting my hip-bone hard. I rub it with my right hand, steadying myself with the palm of my left hand braced against the wall. I check my face in the mirror above the sink to see if I've sprouted any pimples in the past couple of hours. Flying plays havoc with my olive skin, which feels dry and papery. There are purple smudges under my eyes. My tongue is coated with a metallic-tasting white fur. I get my toothbrush out of its plastic case, squeeze on a ribbon of toothpaste, brush my teeth. Splash cold water on my face, pat it dry.

Better. Much better. The illuminated sign on the wall of the tiny restroom dings and flashes red: "Please return to your seat." Unlocking the door, I stagger down the aisle, the plane still bouncing around. I squeeze past Shahrukh to sink into my seat. Panting a little, I buckle my seat-belt and grin at Shahrukh. "Made it just in time!"

He smiles and nods towards the window. "We're flying right over Eugene/Springfield. Take a look."

I have to squint against the light flashing off the aircraft's fuselage to see through the small window. The town below is a grid of miniature houses surrounded by neat patches of lawn. White fences enclose a paddock in which toy-sized horses graze. Clumps of dark green trees finger up to the sky. Ribbons of road intersect at right angles. Everything square, tidy, precise.

I close my eyes and squeeze the bridge of my nose between forefinger and thumb. Images of Bombay tumble through my mind. Streets bright with sunshine and brilliant with colour: orange and magenta, red and green and gold, colours as vivid and as hectic as the city's tropic life. Hawkers calling their wares in a variety of tones, melodious or raucous. Mounds of scarlet chilli-peppers and giant green watermelons, yellow cobs of corn and purple eggplants heaped in gorgeous array on the sidewalks.

Taxis honking their horns, pedestrians, handcarts, sacred cows, motor cars jostling for room on narrow streets. Men, women, children, babies, living, bathing, cooking, sleeping out in the open. Birth and death as public and visible as commerce on the teeming streets. Home.

What am I doing here? In this new world, with its mathematical perfection, its peculiar accents, its architectural conformity to a Euclidian ideal? I want to stop this plane, imagine myself barging into the fight-crew's cabin, babbling to the pilot: I've made a mistake. Turn this plane around. I have to go back!

Yet this is what I've wanted. Order, calm, precision. After the murderous madness of Calcutta, with its ten million refugees flooding in from the bloodbath that was the birth of Bangladesh; after the deafening commerce of Bombay, I've dreamed of freedom. Of sweeping vistas and wide violet spaces. Nature. Mountains. A temperate peace. Pastoral calm. Not the chaos that swirls a deadly whirlpool around my mother, threatening to drown us all in its eddies.

Even so. Now that I'm practically on top of the order I've craved, I feel a kind of despair. Maybe this is all my life will ever be, vision outstripping reality at every turn. Maybe this is what it means to be grown up.

I swallow against the fear that opens inside me, and fill its hollow ballooning with spit and resolution. I open my eyes and look once again through the small window. And see the river. A broad sweep of silver that loops and meanders through the landscape below, leaving houses and roads, lawns and ranches to shape themselves to its shifting rhythms. Hope sings in my belly.

The aircraft's engines scream as the big plane lurches and slows on its approach to the runway. The pilot makes a perfect three-point landing, bumping gently onto the tarmac. There is a subdued rustle and hum as people stand up, open overhead bins to retrieve their carry-on bags, collect their coats.

When the cabin doors open, Shahrukh pulls me into the aisle. My feet move forward, but my mind, stubborn as a weed, remains rooted on the spot. I'm not ready! My black winter coat feels hot and heavy on my shoulders. There is a lump in my throat as big as a guava. It chokes me as I nod at the smiling cabin staff on my way out the aircraft door. The heels of my black Ferragamo boots clang loudly on the metal steps. The sun glinting off the windows of the terminal building flashes diamonds at my eyes.

At the bottom of the steps I stop, brought up short by the smell of the air. Under the sharp, oily fumes of aircraft fuel, there is a cool green fragrance that reminds me of Khandala. A whiff of home: the clear sweetness of the hill-station where I spent childhood summers in the shade of mango trees, drowsing and dreaming. I sniff and close my eyes, the better to take in this soft, clear air that flows into my lungs like a benediction. Shahrukh loops his arm through mine, half pulling me across the tarmac. I follow him, reluctantly, into the fluorescent glow of the terminal building.

Inside, the terminal is a single rectangular room, painted in bland monotones — beige, tan, brown. We walk into the passenger arrivals area, which is separated from the main lounge by a low fence. On the far side of the fence several dozen people stand waiting in knots and groups for the disembarking passengers — friends, family, business associates — to come through the small gate. It is so unlike the airport in Bombay that I want to cry. I'm ashamed of myself, giving way to such maudlin nostalgia when we've only just arrived. The voice in my head sounds a lot like that of Miss Lambert, my old school principal: Chin up. That's quite enough, young woman. This is what you've wanted, and now you've got it; so stop snivelling and carry on. I pull up the collar of my coat so Shahrukh won't see my anxiety. We wait quietly, with the other passengers, for our suitcases to come bobbing down the baggage roundabout. Finally, here come our bags; their khaki covers stand out among all the soft-siders and Samsonites.

Shahrukh hauls them off the conveyor belt, straining against their weight, grumbling at me. "I don't know why you had to pack everything we own. Eight pairs of shoes! Who needs eight pairs of shoes? And you've got enough saris in here to pave the streets of Eugene with silk. You don't even wear saris."

Ashamed again, I go off in search of a trolley. I find one and wheel it back through the crowd, dodging people's feet, murmuring apologies as I collide with someone's baggage cart. Shahrukh stands a few yards away, his eyes half-closed and pouchy, mouth a grim line. Looking at him, I feel a pang of contrition. I wheel the trolley over, slide my arm around his waist. "You look awfully tired. I'm sorry, love. I know I've overpacked. It's just . . . What if we need something and we haven't brought it with us?"

"Yeah, like fifty coat-hangers. You don't think they have coat hangers here?" Then, looking at me, he smiles and his voice softens: "It's okay. You're being a turtle, carrying your house on your back. God, I'm so bloody tired! I'll be glad when we get to wherever it is we're going. I'm going to have three glasses of Scotch and sleep for a week." Shahrukh leans over and rubs his chin along the top of my head. "C'mon, let's get this stuff loaded."

We push the heavy trolley through the gate. The arrivals lounge is buzzing with conversations, punctuated by occasional cries of greeting. A small, elderly man on my right reminds me of my grandfather, vulturous in old age. Same S-shaped body, beaky nose, hooded eyes, iron-grey hair. This man is leaning over, trying to lift a small, sturdy little girl in a blue polka-dotted dress. Defeated by the child's weight, he rocks back on his feet. I watch him as he rubs his forehead with the back of his hand and looks momentarily bewildered. He takes the child's hand and they weave their way through the crowd, followed by a train of family members carrying assorted bits of luggage.

I wonder if there's anyone here to meet us. Raising myself onto the tips of my toes, I crane my neck, look around the crowd. "Shahrukh, I don't see anyone who looks as though they might be here to fetch us. They'd have one of those placards with our name on it, wouldn't they?"

Shahrukh grumbles, his voice a tired growl. "You never got a reply from the International Students' Office. And the bloody Housing Office didn't even acknowledge our application for married students' housing. God knows if they got your letter telling them when we were arriving." He scowls at his feet.

"Let's go over there and sit down." I point towards a row of seats against the wall opposite us. "We'll wait till people clear out. Then we'll know if there's anyone left to meet us."

The seats are narrow, uncomfortable. Shahrukh wads his coat against the back of the chair and rests his head on it, his eyes half-closed. He has parked our luggage trolley like a barrier in front of him. I'm too restless to sit. I get up and pace around the lounge, weaving through groups of people. I stop at the row of counters on the far side of the room to look at brochures advertising car rentals, hotels, restaurants in Eugene/Springfield.

Slowly, the crowd thins, as people leave in groups, talking, laughing, jingling keys. The room grows quiet. There's no one left except a lone janitor who empties a row of dustbins into a large canvas container on wheels. My heart hammers a steady beat. I walk over to Shahrukh. I must be frowning, because Shahrukh teases me: "Hey, cheer up. You look like a hawk with a finger up its bum." And then, "What time is it?"

I glance at the clock on the wall behind where Shahrukh is sitting. "It's three o'clock. They may not have received my letter — you know what the mails are like. I think we should take the airport limo to the University. If it hasn't left already."

"No, no. Better stay where we are. They're probably just late, the lazy buggers. Besides, we don't know where to go or anything." Shahrukh's voice edges into a whine.

I can feel the familiar impatience rise inside me. He's a man. He's supposed to handle all these arrangments. Sometimes he acts like a spoiled child, and it infuriates me. I can't rely on him.

My voice is sharper than I'd intended. "For God's sake, Shahrukh, we can't stay here all night. Its pretty obvious no one's coming."

"We don't know that. They might be late."

"We're not little kids. We don't need someone to hold our hands and tell us where to go. Let's just get on the limo to the University. We'll get directions from there."

"You always think you know everything . . ." Shahrukh begins heatedly. Then he shrugs his shoulders: "All right, fine, we'll go. But don't blame me if we end up wandering all over the sodding place."

"We aren't going to get lost. Come on." I grab the handle of the trolley and wheel it out through the automatic doors. Shahrukh follows, dragging his feet. The cold air nips at my cheeks and earlobes. The airport coach is parked in front of us, at the curb, empty. Its driver stands beside its open door smoking a hand-rolled cigarette. The smoke has an odd, sweet smell, which tickles my nostrils and makes me sneeze.

The driver looks up and flashes me a smile: "Gesundheit!" He puts the cigarette out on the heel of his boot and tucks the stub behind his ear. He is young, my age, maybe a bit older. Bright blue eyes, dark grey sweatshirt with a University of Oregon Track Team logo on the front. Faded blue jeans, cowboy boots. His hair is long and silky, dark brown. It hangs down to his waist in a pony tail, and is tied with a brown leather thong. His smile carves deep creases in his cheeks, like elongated dimples. I feel an immediate urge to touch them, feel my body leaning toward his.

"Is that really all yours?" he asks, raising an eyebrow in mock astonishment at our loaded trolley.

Shahrukh frowns, and, without replying, begins unloading our bags onto the sidewalk. I can tell he thinks this young man is impertinent, a chauffeur stepping outside his station.

"Guess you folks are headed for the U of O." It is not a question.

I duck my head, embarrassed by the knowing tone of his voice. "Uh-hunh. That's where we're headed." I find myself mimicking his diction, drawing out the vowels in that sleepy American way. "Can you give us a lift to the campus? Someone was supposed to meet us, but . . ."

"Sure thing. Here. Lemme give you a hand with those."

The driver picks up a suitcase in each hand. He climbs into the coach and begins clattering around inside. Shahrukh follows with the remaining two suitcases, bumping them clumsily up the steps. I wait while they stack the bags in the luggage area at the front of the bus. I can hear Shahrukh making a sarcastic remark about women and their luggage, as he pays the bus driver the fare.

Both men laugh.

I am angry at this conspiracy of men. I stamp awkwardly up the coach stairs, a cabin bag on each shoulder. My purse, looped over my arm, bangs painfully against my knees as I climb. At the top of the stairs, the driver reaches over and unslings a bag from my right shoulder. This throws me off-balance. I stagger and lurch almost into his arms. He steadies me with a hand under my elbow, flashing me another of his dimpled smiles.

Feeling foolish, I drop into the safety of the nearest seat, glare at Shahrukh sitting across the aisle. His long legs are stretched out in front of him; he looks infuriatingly relaxed. He smiles serenely at me, enjoying my confusion. The driver takes his seat and the doors close with a sigh.

As the coach pulls onto the road, I slide open the window beside my head. The cold air chills my cheek, but the inside of the coach is warm, and I unbutton my coat, unwind the scarf from around my neck. I refuse to look at Shahrukh. Instead, I concentrate resolutely on the landscape gliding by.

The earth here is a rich, choclatey brown, moist and fecund — a far cry from the thin red and ochre dust of India. The trees are a dark green, with narrow, vertical trunks and branches which stick straight out, like prickly arms. They flow past in a tall, viridian blur. I couldn't climb any of these trees; their limbs are too thin, spiky and uninviting. Closing my eyes, I think of the sprawling peepuls and banyens which cradled me in my childhood, their broad branches solid as beds, their heart-shaped leaves sheltering me from the sun.

Water purls through a wide ditch alongside the road. I open my eyes. The water is clear, with small twigs swirling in its current. Fans of sharp-edged ferns nod over the edge of the ditch. The air smells moist and swollen with unshed rain. I relax and sink back into my seat, realizing, with surprise, that I'm hungry.

The banks of trees alongside the road give way to occasional houses surrounded by small farms — flat, furrowed fields, fenced paddocks in which horses graze. The horses have grey blankets draped across their backs, which makes them look like stooped old men. The houses are set far from the road; their windows glint in the westerly sun. There are no people visible. Maybe they're all inside their houses, or in the hooded, metal-roofed barns.

This rural landscape soon blends into something halfway between country and town. The houses here are more like large estates, surrounded by towering coniferous trees and situated out of sight of the road. All I can see now are the beginnings of winding driveways, tiled rooftops thrusting up above tall evergreens, the occasional skylight or upper-floor balcony.

Then the scenery changes again and we're driving through town. Wide streets, exquisitely clean. Houses made of — wood? And picture windows like large, unblinking eyes, through which I catch fleeting glimpses of people's lives. A white lampshade. The back of a sofa. Plants on a window sill.

The windows are all closed; everything is hushed, still, as in a painting. Everywhere, immaculate green lawns; rainbow arcs of water hissing across emerald grass. Everything so spacious and cool, the colours so singular, the corners so perfectly angled.

I look down at my black vicuna suit, creased across the width of my hips. I feel rumpled, out of place. Tugging my jacket smooth, I stand up and move across the aisle to sit beside Shahrukh. I bury my head in the hollow between his shoulder and his neck. Shahrukh puts his arm around me. He smells faintly of sweat and deodorant and aircraft air. The collar of his white shirt scrapes against my cheek. But I snuggle in closer, breathing in the musky, familiar smell of his skin.

"Here's the campus." The driver flashes us a cheerful smile. "That there is the Health Sciences Centre. Across the road is Administration; you'll probably have to go there Monday to register." He continues to point out various buildings, most of which look alike to me. Red brick and glass. Horizontal lines. Green open spaces. Trees. He pulls up at the curb in front of a small, two-storey house.

"This here is the Foreign Students' Office. Probably best if you talk to them first. They'll get you set up."

The driver opens the coach doors, grabs a suitcase in each hand and heads down the steps. I follow behind him, a cabin bag slung on each shoulder. As I step onto the sidewalk, Shahrukh bumps down behind me with the rest of our suitcases. By the time he puts down the cases he is carrying, the driver is swinging back up the stairs into the coach.

"Well, folks, it's been good meeting you. See ya around." He smiles cheerfully, waves goodbye and climbs into the coach. The doors hiss shut, and the coach pulls away.

Taking a deep breath, I turn around and look up at the house in front of us. Mock-Victorian, made of wood, with steep stairs leading up to a small verandah. Lots of wrought iron fretwork painted grey and white. I turn back to Shahrukh, who is standing on the sidewalk looking forlornly after the receding bus. Our four suitcases and two cabin bags stand around him like orphaned children. Shahrukh abruptly sits down on one of the suitcases. My watch says 3:40. I look up at the blank windows of the Foreign Students' Office. Squaring my shoulders, I turn and walk up the steps.

76

Before I reach it, the front door opens. A slight, balding man in T-shirt and jeans stands smiling in the doorway. His watery blue eyes swim like fish behind thick lenses. He stretches out his hand in welcome. "Hi. I'm Greg Mays. You look like you've come a long way."

Feeling ridiculously shy, I extend my hand, take his outstretched one. His palm is cool and hard. "Hello! I'm Shahnaz Shroff. That's my husband Shahrukh. We just flew in from Bombay. Well, actually, from Bombay via Los Angeles. I wrote to say we were arriving today. We were worried because we hadn't heard a word from your office." I falter to a stop. It's obvious Greg has no idea what I'm talking about. "Weren't you expecting us? I did write to tell you we were arriving on the 2:30 flight today," I say finally.

"No, I'm sorry. Your letter probably got lost somewhere. We're pretty disorganized this time of year, with all the new students coming in." He adds, as an afterthought: "Its a good thing you got in when you did. We close at four o'clock, for the weekend. If you'd come in a half hour later, you'd've been on your own until Monday."

I am stunned into silence by this information. Unthinkingly, I raise my chin, sight down my nose at him in a gesture Shahrukh would recognize as nervousness.

Greg, however, seems to think he's offended me. His tone is apologetic. "Look, you're here now. Come on into my office. I'll make a couple of phone calls, see if we can't find you a place to stay for the weekend. The Housing office is closed. They pack it in at noon on Fridays, but we'll talk to them first thing Monday. I'm sure they'll have an apartment for you."

Greg keeps talking as he ushers me into his office. He rummages around in his desk drawer, pulls out a Rolodex and ruffles through the cards, which are soft around the edges and dog-eared. He picks up the phone. Dials. Frowns. Hangs up. Ruffles through the cards again. Redials. This time I can hear a woman's high voice on the other end. Since I don't want to eavesdrop, I walk over to the windows and try not to listen to what Greg is saying.

The sun's rays cast a peculiar slanting light that glimmers through the trees outside, gold-green-gold. Light and shadow chase each other across the width of the room as a car roars by. The sky is a delicate blue, with high cirrus clouds. The colours here are pastels, limpid, transparent in their purity. Unlike the violent cobalt skies of India, the overheated glare of its tropical sun. My heart unclenches in this lambent afternoon light.

Greg talks for a few minutes into the phone, smiles, gives me the thumbs-up sign as he hangs up. "That's Ann Carrington. One of our international host families. She's on her way over to pick you folks up, take you to her place for the weekend. She'll show you the ropes, get you settled into your own place on Monday."

What is an International Host Family? Seeing my dubious look, Greg adds hastily: "She's great, you'll like her. She's working on a Master's in Public Admin. Her husband's in the U.S. Army, so she's lived all over the world. She understands about jet-lag and culture shock."

Culture shock? Is that what this is? I feel exhausted, past the point of caring. Everything around me feels strange, wavering, distant, as though I'm seeing and hearing through miles of water. Greg's relentlessly smiling face fades in and out. I feel as though I've landed on the ocean floor, or on some far distant planet. The room sways disconcertingly around me. Dimly, I hear Greg's voice.

"Are you okay? Look, come and sit down in here. I'll go get your husband. Sheer Ook? Is that how you say his name?"

I nod. I haven't got the energy to respond to Greg's kindly concern, to tell him how to pronounce Shahrukh's name. All I want is to lie down in a dark room and go to sleep for a week. I let Greg help me to a small couch, sink gratefully into its billowy embrace. I lean my head on its pillowed arm, curl my body along its length and close my eyes.

I hear Greg leaving the room, then the murmur of voices

78

outside. By the time Shahrukh comes in with the suitcases, I'm too far gone to open my eyes. I drift in a half-dream in which Shahrukh's voice and Greg's rise and fall like the hiss of ocean waves. It's pleasant, floating on waves of sound like a piece of driftwood.

I don't know how long I've drifted like this. But I wake up to Shahrukh's breath warm on my cheek, his arm around my shoulders. He is saying something I don't quite catch. I look up at him, follow his gaze across the room. That smiling woman with the short, blonde hair and red Capri pants must be — what was her name? — Andrea, Arlene. Something with an A.

The woman walks across the room, leans over me. She has a direct, level gaze, a wide mouth lipsticked red, a blunt chin. Her face, framed by short, very shiny blonde hair, is round and thickly freckled.

She takes my hand and holds it in both of her own. Smiling inches from my face she says, "Hi. I'm Ann." Her teeth are large and very white, perfectly aligned. I'm mesmerised by them. Everyone I've seen in this country — people at the airport, the bus driver, Greg Mays, and now this woman, Ann — has perfect rows of white, even teeth. I've never seen so many perfect teeth in my life. I wonder, hazily, if all those teeth owe their perfection to lucky genes, or if there's something in the air of this country that makes everything in it grow cleaner, larger, straighter than anywhere else on earth.

Realizing that the woman is waiting for me to say something, I blurt out: "You're the host family."

Ann smiles again. Her eyes are friendly, appraising. "You must be exhausted. We've got your stuff all loaded in the car. C'mon. Let's get you home. We'll get you something to eat and pop you right into bed."

Exhausted as I am, this woman in front of me looks like a ministering angel: kind, brisk, infinitely competent. My legs feel wobbly as a toddler's as I follow her meekly down the stairs to where her dark blue Chrysler is parked.

79

Chapter 7

I wake up with my head full of fog and my mouth tasting like monsoon mould. The small folding alarm clock that has travelled with me everywhere since I was ten years old glows green on the table beside the bed. It's three o'clock in the morning. Ann's house is quiet. The only sound I can hear is the hum of the refrigerator and the small click when it turns on and off in the kitchen. Now that I'm awake, I can't get back to sleep. I'm so tired I want to crawl into a patch of warm earth and plant myself in it, like a rose-bush.

When my mother was in the throes of her violent, manic phases, I would lie quietly in bed and imagine myself as an animal — a cheetah, or a snow leopard, something sleek, fast and lethal. I would become so still even my breathing slowed until I was barely sipping air. I imagined myself blending into the bedsheets, my whole body paling to a ghostly white, flattening out until there was no trace of me. So that my mother, when she came looking for me with the kitchen knife in hand, would see only sheets. White sheets, smelling of Sunlight soap and the warm salt breezes in which they were dried, billowing out on the clothesline at the side of our house at Juhu Beach. And just as she turned to walk away, I would come leaping out with a great roar, sink my fangs into her throat.

Shahrukh is fast asleep next to me on this springy fold-out sofa bed, which squeaks every time one of us moves and slopes under his body, tilting me towards him. We are in what Ann refers to as her "den." In my present mood, I feel bearish enough, so perhaps this "den" is the right place for me to be. It's four-thirty in the afternoon — tomorrow afternoon — in Bombay. The future here is the past there. My grandmother will be in the kitchen, giving the cook instructions for dinner. My father will be in his office. But no. It's Saturday. He and my mother will be out for a drive, or taking a walk along Juhu Beach, if mum is feeling well enough to leave her room.

I take long, even breaths, willing my body to minimal motion. The quilt on my chest barely moves as I breathe in and out. This quilt is patterned with a vigorous jungle print: green leaves and twisting vines, brilliantly coloured trumpet flowers. Not a restful background to blend into. But deep breathing slows my chattering mind, and I drift into a troubled, shallow sleep filled with dreams of the hunt, in which I am both hunter and prey. In the early hours of the morning Shahrukh wakes me, holding me close, telling me I'd cried out in my sleep. He cradles my head against his chest until I drift off to sleep again, my breath syncopating with the rhythm of his heartbeat.

When I open my eyes again, the small rectangle of window in the room is a pale grey, which lightens, as I watch it, to a mild blue. I sit up in the sagging bed, stretch my arms over my head, trying to loosen the muscles knotted like ropes in my neck and shoulders. My head is foggy with unfinished nightmares and insufficient sleep. I roll over to look at the clock. Nine-fifteen. I really ought to get up, get dressed. Instead, I look around the room.

It's small, no larger than my grandmother's linen room back home. Its walls are panelled in a smooth, fragrant wood that smells sharper, more resiny than sandalwood. There is plush sand-coloured carpet underfoot. A small, high window. A low ceiling textured in some sort of bumpy white plaster. On the wall just above my head there is a framed watercolour of a lop-sided barn in a hayfield. I kneel on the bed to get a closer look — the pale red of the barn's roof, the crazy angle at which it leans into the pastel sky. So not everything in this country is entirely symmetrical after all. The painting is signed, simply, Carrington. I wonder if Ann painted it. Across the room there is a small pine desk with an IBM electric typewriter sitting squarely in the middle of it, two bookshelves overflowing with files and papers and books, a swivelling office-type chair on wheels.

Accustomed as I am to the spacious, white-walled rooms of my parents' house, with their cool, marble floors, high ceilings, banks of open windows and doors, this den seems like a cave. Shahrukh, has crept out of bed, left me. I suppose I'd better get up. Reluctantly, I pull on my dressing-gown, tying its belt in a tight knot at my waist, as I walk towards the bathroom door.

The bathroom is surprisingly spacious and white with steam. Over the hiss of the shower, I can hear Shahrukh singing "Misty" in his off-key voice behind the blue shower-curtain. Seized by an irresistible impulse, I tip-toe over to the sink and turn the hot water tap on as far as it will go. There is a sudden yelp from behind the curtain and a rattling of curtain rings as Shahrukh pulls the shower-curtain aside to peer at me through the film of soapy water streaming down his face. "Hey! Turn that water off. It's bloody freezing in here!" I stick out my tongue at him. "C'mon, stop fooling around. I'm freezing my balls off! Turn that bloody water off."

By this time I'm laughing, standing just out of reach of his dripping arm. "Make me," I challenge him, and prance around in a half-circle, still keeping carefully out of reach as he grabs the air in front of me in wild snatches. But I underestimate him.

"You want to play rough, hunh?" Shahrukh's wet arm snakes out and grabs the belt of my dressing-gown. I brace my bare feet on the wet bathroom floor and hang onto the edge of the sink, but he manages to haul me into the icy shower with him.

The water is so cold it stings like needles on my skin, but we're both laughing so hard, it does little to dampen our spirits.

There is a knock on the door, and ann's voice calls out: "Are you okay? I thought I heard a scream. Did you fall down?"

I'm laughing too hard to answer. I bury my face in my soaking sleeve, trying to muffle my laughter. Shahrukh turns off the shower and attempts to reassure Ann through the closed door. He's having trouble getting the words out. He keeps choking and snorting on the laughter that bubbles irrepressibly in his throat. "We're all right. No worries. We'll be out in a few minutes," he finally manages.

"Oh, okay. Long as you guys are okay. I'll get breakfast ready, and see . . ." Ann's voice recedes.

Limp with laughter, I clutch at Shahrukh for support. We lean against each other, soaking wet and still guffawing. We're at that giddy stage of fatigue where everything — a look, a bead of water on the tip of Shahrukh's nose, the damp, steamy air — seems irresistibly funny. "We're coming unhinged," I say to him, between giggles. And the thought brings on a melancholy against which I instinctively stiffen my body. I shake my head like a wet dog, strip off my soaked dressing-gown and drop it on the floor. "I'm going to take a shower," I tell Shahrukh. "Maybe you'd better wash the soap off yourself first."

Shahrukh is in and out of the shower before I've even unpacked my toilet bag. He towels off and heads into the den to get dressed, leaving me the bathroom. I stand under the generous spray of hot water for a long time, turning around and around so that the aching muscles of my neck and back relax in the warmth; the tightness in my chest eases. Lulled into a dreamy state by the hiss and warmth of water and steam, I watch soap bubbles dissolve against the downy hair on my arms. I remember watching my cousin Zenobia wax the hair off her arms. She said it made her arms look cleaner. She offered to do mine, but I wouldn't let her. It looked excruciatingly painful, and I'm attached to every bit of me, even the hair on my arms. I tilt my head to shake the water out of one ear and then the other, luxuriating in this seemingly endless supply of hot water, a far cry from the bucket-baths of my life in Bombay. My belly relaxes, my bones seem to be turning aqueous. My eyelids droop and I'm only half awake. Everything around me is enveloped in a benevolent, warm fog.

A part of me floats off above my head and watches as I slowly lift my arms, slowly reach the faucets, slowly turn them until the stream of water narrows to a trickle and eventually stops. I stand inhaling the steam, feeling weak-kneed. Then, bending my head forward so that my hair hangs down, I twist it, wringing the water out of it, into a long rope. I love the feeling of my hands — strong, with long, supple fingers. My dad's fingers. I admire them for a moment, hanging them upside down. Then I straighten up, flinging my hair back until it slaps wetly against my neck and upper spine. I step carefully over the edge of the shower, and squelch my toes into the damp, woolly bathmat, relishing the feel of all that soft fur underfoot. I reach for a blue towel which hangs on a rack next to the tub. The towel is warm and thick, and covers me from head to foot like a blanket. I wrap myself in it, using one end to rub my wet hair and head until my scalp tingles. I hum, "Ain't Nobody's Business If I Do" and luxuriate in this feeling of inordinate happiness.

As I head towards the den, I reach back to flip the switch that turns off the bathroom light. The switch is already up. The light is still on. This throws me into sudden confusion; I panic. The light switches don't work the way they should; I'm in a foreign country. I flip the switch the other way — down — and the light turns off.

I close the bathroom door behind me, walk shakily over to the sofa-bed and sit down, pulling the towel around my body. The air in the room is cool, and my hands and feet are cold. I feel vulnerable, defenseless. Shivering, I drop the towel at my feet and bend down to pull a sweater out of my suitcase, which is on the floor beside the bed. My eyes are blurry with tears as

I grope blindly among my clothes, so carefully folded and packed by my sister just three days ago. Eventually my hand finds something that feels woolly and warm. I fish it out of the bag — a white turtleneck cashmere sweater, bought on a trip to Edinburgh with my grandmother two summers ago. I pull it on hastily. The room is too cold to linger in. I finish dressing quickly. Black wool pants, white silk socks, black shoes. Not bothering to go into the bathroom for a look in the mirror, I comb my hair, tying it back in a damp ponytail with a black velvet ribbon. My fingers, cold and wrinkled from the shower, tremble as I hook my pearl earrings into my ears. I walk over to the door and open it.

The small hallway outside the den is lit by a wall-sconce. I look up and down the hall but see no signs of Ann or Shahrukh. Feeling somewhat abashed at having taken so long, I walk down the hall in what I think is the direction of the living room. I was so tired yesterday, when Ann gave us a brief tour of her house, that I'm not certain of the layout. The first doorway on my right turns out to be Ann's bedroom. The door next to that seems to be a sewing room. There is a sewing machine on a table by the window, a small wooden chair in front of it. A long table against one wall holds a small pile of fabric, as well as boxes of sewing implements — scissors, spools of thread, zippers, elastic, and other mysterious things that go (I'm guessing) on the insides of clothes.

I've never seen an entire room devoted just to sewing. Maybe Ann is a seamstress on the side?

At home, the tailor comes whenever anyone wants something made. Mr. Hamidullah is an elderly, obsequious man with yellow, crooked teeth. He bows and smiles and nods as he comes in, dipping and ducking his narrow head like a bird. His little hands are careful never to touch us directly as he takes measurements of the most intimate kind with a long fraying roll of plum-coloured measuring tape. He wears a pencil behind his ear, and licks its point before writing down arcane sets of numbers in a small dog-eared notebook. In this notebook he keeps a record of the changing shapes and sizes of every member of my family, an archive of our bodies' shape-shifting. Each family member has his or her own section in this book, headed with their name and the date on which the measurements were taken. My section begins when I was six weeks old.

I have never seen the tailor actually sew anything. He comes, measures, writes. He pores gravely over the illustrations we tear out of magazines for him to copy. He takes them from us, folds them into minute little packages which he tucks into the pockets of his handspun cotton waistcoat. He folds his hands together in farewell, bows and departs, fabric carefully folded into a large cloth bag which he always carries slung over his left arm.

Several days later he returns with the garments cut and loosely tacked together at the seams. He waits patiently while I, or my mother, my grandmother, or my sister, try on his handiwork. When we emerge from our bedrooms into the small dressing room where we conduct our business with him, Mr. Hamidullah smiles, nods, raises his eyebrows and listens attentively while we tell him what needs to be taken in, what must be let out. He peers at the fabric from underneath the half-moon glasses that slide halfway down his nose. He steps back for a better look, frowns, purses his lips. From the depths of his cloth bag he produces a fat round pincushion, faded red, from which he pulls out several long, straight pins. He places the pins head first between his lips. Then, frowning and nodding, he gets to work. He tucks here, pulls out stitches there; pins a sleeve, a dart, a hem, smoothing the fabric with his long, tapering fingers. He departs, at the end of the day, with a pile of clothes bristling with pins.

The sewing itself takes place unseen. I have never, until now, given any thought to where Mr. Hamidullah does his sewing. I suppose he must have a sewing room too, though his is probably an airless cubicle in a dingy chawl on Mohammadali Road, in Bombay's Muslim quarter. Probably, too, it doubles as living quarters for himself and his extended family. He has two wives, and seven small children (according to Sunder ayah, who seems to know everything about everyone.)

Ann's laugh, loud and musical, rings out from somewhere on the far side of the hall. I'm embarrassed at having blundered into her private quarters. I follow her voice, which trails before me in the hallway like a blithe, guiding spirit. The narrow hall turns a sharp corner and opens out into a large, sunny room which appears to be both kitchen and dining room. There is a long window along one wall, with a row of cactus plants in clay pots growing on the windowsill. Below this window is a pale yellow formica-topped counter with a row of cupboards underneath, bisected by a double stainless steel sink. Ann is standing at the sink, rinsing out a teapot. She is dressed in apple-green pedal pushers, red tennis shoes without any socks, and a short-sleeved red shirt. Her bare arms are freckled, her bright gold hair is tied back with a narrow red ribbon. She looks much younger this morning. My guess is she's in her early thirties.

I seem to have entered midway through a conversation she and Shahrukh are having about a holiday Ann spent in India several years ago. Shahrukh is sitting at a round oak table in a corner of the kitchen, his mouth shiny with butter. He's holding a partially eaten slice of toast over a small plate littered with crumbs. He nods his head whenever Ann pauses for a breath. He has a white coffee mug in his fist, with an American flag decal on the front and FLORIDA written across it in bold black letters. Breakfast is on the table: a jar of raspberry jam, a ceramic butter dish with a tidy rectangle of butter and a crumby smear of leftover butter beside it. There is also a carton of milk, a bowl of sugar, boxes of Cheerios, Rice Krispies, Kellogg's Cornflakes. My stomach gurgles and growls. Ann raises her head, sees me standing in the doorway, and smiles her brilliant smile: "Hi! How are you? Did you sleep well?"

I smile back. Ann's exuberant cheeriness overwhelms me, but

maybe this is just the way Americans are. I haven't met many Americans, other than some of the friends my mother made when she was in the U. S. in the '50's, who would come to visit us from time to time. I manage a reply: "I'm well, thank you. Still a bit jet-lagged, but I'll get over it." Maybe that sounds too abrupt, ungracious. So I add, somewhat lamely: "This is a wonderfully sunny room." Everything I say this morning sounds off-kilter to me.

"Yes, it's great when we get some sunshine. Doesn't happen often enough, around here. Let me get you a cup of coffee. Would you like eggs? Some toast?" Ann Doesn't seem to mind my clumsy attempts at conversation. She puts the teapot down in a dish-drainer next to the sink, walks over to the dining table and pours coffee into a mug. "D'you take it black?"

"I beg your pardon?" I cast about wildly in my mind, trying to guess at what she's talking about, but her words make no sense. Black?

"Your coffee. Do you drink it black?" Then, seeing the bewildered look on my face, she adds, "D'you take cream and sugar in your coffee?"

"Oh! I see. Yes. I mean, yes, I'd love a spot of cream and two teaspoons of sugar, please." I feel like a complete idiot. Black. Of course. Sarah Vaughan singing "Black Coffee" in her smoky voice.

Ann waves the coffee-pot in the direction of the nearest chair. "Have a seat," she says in that excruciatingly loud, cheerful voice. I wish she came with a volume control. I sit down at the kitchen table with the cup of coffee she has placed in front of me. She walks over to the refrigerator and takes out a carton of something called Half And Half. She hands it to me, jutting her chin forward when I don't take it from her quickly enough. "Cream. For your coffee." All her vowels are long, drawn out. She pronounces it "Cawwfee." I take the carton from her and pour some of the liquid into the mug. The cream is cold. I think of Sunder ayah lovingly warming the cream for our tea, pouring it into my mother's silver creamer, sending it in with the bearer on the silver tray which has been in my family for generations. I am stupid with fatigue. Ann chatters on. I nod every time she looks in my direction. It seems to be all the encouragement she needs, because she keeps on talking. Every once in a while her voice rises, questioning. I am grateful to Shahrukh for following the thread of the conversation and responding when a response is called for.

"That would be very nice. Wouldn't it, Shahnoo?" Shahrukh nudges me with his knee under the table. Startled, I agree that yes, it would be very nice. I have no idea what I'm agreeing to. Ann must sense my bewilderment because she looks at me dubiously.

"Are you sure you feel up to it right now? Maybe we should wait a day or two until you've had a chance to catch up on sleep and get settled in." Her voice is still too loud, but there is such kindness in it that I want to cry.

"I'm awfully sorry, Ann. I haven't a clue what the two of you are talking about. I'm so tired, I'm just not entirely here."

Shahrukh laughs. "She gets this way when she hasn't had her beauty sleep," he says to Ann, in a confidential tone. Then he smiles at me as though I'm a recalcitrant child.

Ann remains kind: "Hey, it's okay," she begins. "I should have realized. Lord knows, I've travelled enough. You just take it real easy, and we'll do the tour when you're ready. The Pacific Ocean isn't going anyplace." Then, seeing my blank look, she adds: "I was telling Shahrukh about this great seafood restaurant out on the coast. It's about an hour and a half drive from here. We'll go have dinner there in a couple of days, when you're over the jet-lag."

There is more talk about the University, about our flight, about Ann's husband who is on a tour of duty in Germany. I tune in and out, getting a sentence here, a couple of words there. My coffee goes cold and develops a wrinkled skin on top. I pour myself a bowl of Cornflakes, add milk, stir my spoon around and around in the bowl until the flakes are fat and soggy. Finally, I turn to Ann: "Would you mind terribly if I went back to bed? I know this is very rude of me, but I can't keep my eyes open."

Ann's response is immediate and generous. She pulls my chair back from the table as I stand up. "You go right ahead and sleep for as long as you want. If you wake up and get hungry, just come on in here and help yourself to whatever you like. I won't wake you for lunch, but I'll make you a sandwich and leave it in the fridge. Okay?"

I nod and half-drag, half-float my way back to the den, which is cold. The thermostat on the wall says sixty degrees. I fumble with it, turning it all the way up to eighty. The electric bar under the window begins clicking and ticking as the room warms up. I crawl under the quilt, burrowing into the squishy spring-bed. The last thing I remember is a strand of my hair blowing against my upper lip every time I exhale. I am too tired to brush it away, and I fall asleep with it tickling under my nose.

I am standing on a deserted beach, my bare feet sinking into the wet sand at the water's edge. Small waves hiss and foam over my feet, splash against my ankles. The water is warm, its surface reflecting the brilliant gold of the sun. The sky is bleached colourless by the fierce heat. A moist breeze blows against my body, lifting the hair away from my damp neck and dropping it back again. On either side of me, white sand flows away in sweeping curves, bare except for the wrack left by the sea — stranded jellyfish, curling fronds of seaweed, trees stripped to their bones by salt water and sun. The sand is blindingly white, each tiny particle glinting like glass in this inexorable light. I feel paralyzed, unable to move, my limbs heavy, wavering as if I were drowning.

I startle awake, my fingers clenched hard against my palms, a red pulse beating in my right eye. My cheeks and pillow are wet with tears. The quilt presses down on me, a suffocating weight. I thrash it off and sit bolt upright. Trembling, I try to calm myself, reining in my breath, slowing it from a gallop to a trot. I was dreaming of Udvada, our house on the beach, the sea roaring in my ears. And something else. A metallic taste in my mouth, a twanging alarm along the back of my neck where I can still feel the fine hairs bristle. How long have I been asleep? I turn to the small travel-clock that sits by the bed. Ten o'clock. Morning? Evening? The curtains are drawn. The room is dark. I can't tell whether it's day or night. I look around me. No sign of Shahrukh. Where is he? How can he leave me here all alone in this strange room?

Chapter 8

Overnight, my entire household disappeared. It happened on my thirteenth birthday.

Two weeks before the big day, my mother announced that she was going to throw me a birthday party. I thought she meant we'd have the same birthday celebration I had each year, which I loved because it was the one day of the year when I felt truly cherished by every member of my family. However, I soon learned that my mother had other plans for this birthday.

Usually, the ritual was unvarying. Each year, I'd wake up in the morning astonished to find I'd slept soundly despite the almost unbearable excitement of the night before. I'd have my birthday head-bath with milk and rose-petals and put on the brand new clothes Sunder ayah laid out on my bed for me.

By the time I got out of my bath Perin aunty and Khorshed aunty would arrive, bearing fragrant garlands of flowers which the servants hung ceremoniously in each doorway. Khorshed aunty would turn on All India Radio, which blasted out bhajans at top volume, waking everyone in the house. Meanwhile, Perin aunty would kneel on the marble floor of our front veranda, her sari tucked between her knees, drawing mandalas on the floor to celebrate my birthday.

Perin aunty would scoop up brilliantly coloured powdered lime from a row of tin containers into her small fingers and use the powder to draw exquisite designs of fish, their mouths and tails linked to form wreaths — a symbol of prosperity and long life — at the top of the stairs. She'd repeat these flowing patterns on the floor of our living room, where the Birthday Ritual would take place. The jewel colours glowed red and green and purple in the sunlight, rich as a Kermanshah carpet. Then my aunts prepared the low wooden dais for me, placing it on a coloured mandala in the living room, sprinkling it with rose-water and blessing it with prayers.

The rest of the family — my grandparents, my other aunts and uncles and cousins — would begin arriving soon after and by the time I emerged from my room, the house hummed with laughter and conversation. I'd make my entrance, this year, feeling like a princess in my new yellow dress, flaunting the pointy-toed white shoes with one-and-a-half-inch heels which Perin aunty had bought me after much pleading and persuasion.

Each year my father gave me his arm when I arrived at the doorway to the living room. He escorted me solemnly to the dais, which I would climb onto, right foot first for good luck. My gathered relatives clapped and cheered and my grandmother began the ritual by lighting the sandalwood logs in the silver brazier, then draping a garland of jasmine, lilies and roses, en-twined together with green mango-leaves, over my neck. The garland felt cool and prickly against my throat; the scent of flowers tickled my nose. She sprinkled grains of rice over my head and decorated my forehead with red kumkum, chanting prayers and benedictions in her sharp, quavering voice. Then she hugged me, reaching up on her toes to put her arms around my neck. The velvety cheek she pressed against my own smelled of Yardley's soap and rosewater.

Lastly, she gave me her gift, offered unwrapped on a silver tray. Then she fed me a lump of rock-sugar, so my new year would be blessed with sweetness. I crunched the sugar between my teeth and tried on her gift, which was always jewellery of some kind. Last year she had given me a gold necklace with matching bracelets, earrings and a ring, all in a pattern of little birds, their outstretched wings linked together to form a chain. I wondered what she'd give me this year. Since I was going to be thirteen and had already started menstruating I was no longer a child. I hoped she'd give me pearls, this year. Pearls felt grown-up.

This ritual was repeated as many times as there were relatives, with lots of laughter and exclaiming over gifts in between. So it was often an hour or more before we all sat at the breakfast table, eating the special birthday breakfast of fried vermicelli sweetened with honey and crusted with sauteed almonds and raisins. The smell of it was warmly celebratory, and it was always followed by my personal favourite — cream of wheat browned in butter, sweetened with jaggery, double cream and egg-yolks rendering it a rich yellow, its garnish of rose-petals and paper-thin gold leaves glowing in the morning light. The whole house was suffused with the scents of flowers and sweets and sandalwood, and I'd spend the entire day stuffing myself with food and playing happily with my cousins.

However, this wasn't what my mother had in mind. We had been at the dinner table one evening, a couple of weeks before my birthday, when my mother began talking abruptly in the loud, shrill voice she had begun to use ever since she'd had her "nervous breakdown." It scared me — my soft-spoken mother transformed into this strident stranger who talked incessantly and at top speed, as though trying to outrun her own dreadful thoughts.

Her soft, silky voice grew rough, deep and coarse like a labourer's. Her face, which was rounded and beautiful, hardened into something ugly, deep grooves appearing like monsoon gullies on either side of her nose, her mouth pinched and white, with strange horizontal lines appearing across her lips. Her eyes, those dreamy, toffee-coloured eyes, darkened and flashed like volcanos, their rims red, her lashes almost disappearing in the sudden electric rage of them.

She looked around the table at all of us and hissed. "Now listen. The CIA and the FBI have hidden microphones in our house and out in the garden and we all have to be VERY CAREFUL what we say because they are after me, yes, they are after your mummy so they can steal her brain and use it to power their nuclear plants I tell you THEY ARE AFTER ME AND THIS MAN THIS SO-CALLED FATHER OF YOURS IS IN CAHOOTS WITH THEM HE WANTS TO GIVE ME UP TO THEM SO HE CAN CARRY ON WITH HIS FLOO-ZIES AND HIS DARLING MOTHER AND HIS WON-DERFUL SISTERS AND BROTHERS CAN FEED OFF MY FLESH, isn't that right darling?"

Frightened, Roshan and I glanced at each other and squirmed in our chairs as our mother rushed on, her monologue unabated by the necessity for either breath or response. Roshan dropped her napkin, banged her head on the edge of the table as she bent to pick it up, and began to cry. My father consoled her, then tried to interject, pleading, "Dinshi, jaan, you don't know what you're saying. No-one is trying to hurt you, we all love you . . ." But my mother shrieked on oblivious of everything but the sound of her own voice.

"You think I don't know what I'm saying? I have more brains in my little finger than your whole family put together. HA! I HAVE MY SOURCES AND I KNOW EXACTLY WHAT YOU WERE DOING WHILE I WAS IN AMERICA. EX-ACTLY! YOU SEX-CRAZED FOOL YOU THINK YOU CAN GET AWAY WITH THIS? WELL YOU ARE MIS-TAKEN I HAVE THE WHITE HOUSE ON MY SIDE, YES, AND PRESIDENT EISENHOWER WILL DO ANY-THING I ASK, YOU HAVE NO IDEA . . ."

Then, pausing suddenly in the middle of this sentence whose thread I had long since lost, she turned and looked at me with a puzzled frown as though trying to remember who I was. Her

brow furrowed and cleared, her mind visibly clenching and re-
laxing. "SHAHNAZ!" she bellowed, triumphantly. "Now, about
this birthday party. We'll have it in the garden, after six o'clock,
so it won't be too hot. I'll make up a guest list, and phone that
Goanese dance band Mani aunty had for Cyrus's wedding, they
were quite good, I thought, though not . . ."

She rattled on without pause, but my attention had snagged
on the words "guest list." "What guest list?" I interrupted, my
voice emerging high and querulous although I was struggling
to control it. These vocal flights of hers — the innuendos I
didn't quite understand, the sudden swoops and turns — left
me bewildered and anxious.

"What d'you mean what guest-list? For the party, of course.
Now, I'll get the invitations engraved at Jeejeebhoy Printers
and . . ."

"Mum! We don't need to send our family invitations, they
always come. They know when my birthday is."

She turned her head towards me, her eyes glittering unnaturally. She seemed to be looking, not at me but at something
above and behind my head. She nodded in a familiar way at
whatever apparition she saw in the air behind me, a sudden
grimace etching her face. Abruptly, she dropped her chin and
looked directly at me. There were such depths of implacable
will in those sable eyes of hers, I shuddered and put both hands
between my knees to keep from shaking. She glared at me bale-
fully for a moment.

When she finally spoke her voice was sibilant, menacing:
"This is my party, that I'm giving for your birthday. The so-
called family," — she spat out the word — "is no longer welcome in my house. This party will be for my friends and
colleagues only. And their children, of course."

She pushed back her chair. Standing there in front of me she
seemed unspeakably tall, like those shadows that wavered in the
corners of the house at night when the sweep of passing head-
lights shot across its whitewashed walls. Her mouth and the

edges of her nostrils were pinched and white. She turned and swept towards the doorway, her sari palloo fallen off her shoulder and trailing at her feet. She held her back and head utterly rigid so that I was afraid she'd trip and fall. My father mumbled something placatory in the direction of her receding back, but she did not seem to hear him. As she reached the doorway, she turned her head and looked over her shoulder at me with hooded eyes. "It's time you met some people worth knowing," she said, the contempt in her voice including everyone I knew and loved. Then she stalked out of the dining room.

As soon as she had left I turned to my father, who sat quietly in his chair fiddling with the stem of his unlit pipe. He would not look at me. "Daddy, you can't let her do this! Everyone always comes for my birthday. I don't want a party, I just want our family here. Daddy! Are you listening to me?"

My father smiled absently at me, his eyes on the empty doorway where my mother's imprint lingered, an almost visible shimmer of rage and hate. Patting my hand, he murmured, "Don't worry beta, there is nothing to worry about. Everything will be all right."

"How can you say that? Nothing is all right! She said she won't let our family come here any more. She's ruining my birthday, and you won't do anything to stop her. Why did she have to come back home? She should have stayed in America!"

"Come on, Shahnaz, that's enough. She's ill, she needs our care."

"She doesn't even like us any more, she's ashamed of us in front of her friends. I don't want her here, I hate her!" I flung my chair back and stormed out of the dining room. I ran out into the garden, my face hot and swollen, blood whooshing in my ears. I headed directly for my favourite mango tree, and scrambled up it as fast as I could go. Its rough bark scraped my arms and shins as I pulled myself hand over hand to the high fork that was mine. My arms and legs shook so that I had to stop every few moments to tighten my grip. Eventually I reached the fork I was aiming for. I straddled the thick branch, leaned my head against the sturdy, warm wood.

The sun was low on the horizon, the sky the colour of a bruise. I held my belly and cried as the wind rocked the tree and all around me slender green leaves rustled and murmured. The house was a glimmer of white in the fading light. It had that doomed look of a place where a disaster was about to happen — a mud-slide, an earthquake, something of such earth-shattering proportions that my heart could not assimilate it.

A mynah bird hopping from twig to twig at the end of the branch on which I sat caught my eye. As I shifted my weight and the branch trembled, she cocked her head, looking at me with a bright brown eye, then spread her tiny wings and swooped off. My whole body yearned to follow her. I would never go back in that house, I vowed. My father would be sorry he had not taken better care of me. I wrapped my arms around myself, feeling the slender, curving ribs with my fingers. My newly budded breasts hurt and I began to cry again, helplessly, feeling my world slide away from under me like a mountainside eroding under a violent monsoon.

Some time later, my father came looking for me. He stood at the base of the mango tree, his face turned up to me like a brown flower, pleading with me to come down. I would not.

"Then I'll just wait here till you're ready to come down," he said, his voice sounding tired, forlorn. He leaned his back against the tree trunk. I could see the top of his head, the care-fully combed furrows in his thick black hair. I heard the click, saw the gleam of his gold Dunhill lighter, smelled the moist, brown fragrance of his pipe tobacco. Smoke wreathed the top of his head, floated up toward me.

When he spoke again, his voice was low, careful. "Shahnu, your mother is very ill. We must . . ." His voice struggled, broke. He stopped, cleared his throat, began again. "It's up to us to take care of her now. You and me. I need your help."

"Daddy, she scares me." But he looked so sad and lost, I knew I had to find a way to help him.

I started down the tree-trunk, my shirt snagging on the bark, my hands and shins scraped and raw. I stopped at a fork just above my father's head, leaned over and touched the nape of his neck with my fingertips. It felt warm, sweaty. Vulnerable.

I swallowed the shaky feeling inside me, tried to feel strong instead, like the mango tree. I would shelter my father the way that tree sheltered me. "What do you want me to do, daddy?"

"Just be patient with her, beta. She needs a lot of rest and love and patient understanding. Sometimes she doesn't know what she's saying." Again, his voice slid off down a treacherous slope and wobbled to a stop. I couldn't see his face, but I knew he was crying. I jumped down onto the ground and threw my arms around him, holding his bony waist, feeling the buttons of his shirt press against my cheek as he hugged me hard against him. Under the nutty aroma of his pipe tobacco I smelled the sharp, metallic sweaty smell that reminded me of our dog when he was frightened or alarmed.

As I held my father, I concentrated on being like the mango tree — I imagined myself with roots anchored deep into the ground, a tall, sturdy trunk and widespread, sheltering boughs draped in a canopy of sharp-scented green leaves that miraculously exchanged carbon dioxide for life-giving oxygen. Matching my breathing to his, I breathed in my father's fear and breathed out love and strength and peace. After a while, I could feel the anxiety drain from my father's body, replaced by a gentle calm. His breathing, which had been shallow and ragged, became deep and even, and soon, he said he was tired and went back into the house. I told him I would be in in a little while. My own body felt shaky, again, as though I'd climbed a mountain and exerted every muscle to its limit.

I lay down on the ground then, and stared up at the night sky, which was thickly seeded with stars. I must have fallen asleep, because the next thing I remember was Sunder ayah cradling my head in her lap and smoothing back my hair with her rough-skinned fingers. Her sari was ripe with cooking smells — ghee and goat's meat and spices.

"Come inside and go to bed," she said.

"No. I don't want to. I'm never going in there again."

"What is the matter, baba?"

I told her about the scene at the dinner table, my mother telling me how my family was no longer welcome in our house. I cried. Sunder ayah comforted me. Then she gently urged me, again, to go to bed.

"Come, be a good girl and come inside now. If you put on your pyjamas and get into bed, I will tell you a story."

She knew that was one offer I could not resist. I let her lead me to my room. I got into my pyjamas and climbed into bed. Sunder ayah sat on the floor beside my bed in her usual posture, arms wrapped around her knees, her bare toes curling and uncurling as she wove her magic spell. I don't remember the words she used, but I can hear the love and tenderness in her voice as soon as I close my eyes. This is the story she told me, which still glows like a jewel inside me.

It was a hot, sun-bleached morning in late August, the month of monsoons and sultry rain. But the rains had been delayed by more than two months. The newspapers in the big cities of Bombay, Delhi, Calcutta, were full of stories about people in villages in the hinterland dying of sunstroke, dying of thirst and starvation. Cattle were dying too. Their fly-blown carcasses could be seen from the windows of trains that chugged by fields dry as bone and baked by a merciless sun.

Mud huts lacked their usual covering of cow-dung patties. No rain meant no fodder, which meant no cows; hence no patties, no fuel to cook with. But then there was no food to be cooked anyway, so it didn't much matter. Wells were dry. The earth itself was cracked and parched. Trees withered, their sap shrivelled in the merciless heat.

The government of India proclaimed a state of national emergency. It issued communiques on All India Radio exhorting people to tighten their belts and stand in solidarity with the nation's farmers, whose farms were disappearing into dust before their despairing eyes.

An army of astrologers, priests and pundits descended on the capital city of Delhi, intent on making their fortunes by predicting rain in three days, three weeks, or three years. During this time, they said, famine would stalk the land. The gods would have to be propitiated daily, even hourly, by generous offerings of ghee and gold, if the coming of Kaliyuga — the Dark Age — were to be averted by the prayers of these holy men.

In the tiny village of Gopinagar, which stood fragile and exposed in the middle of a broad plain near the bay of Cambay, the village elders had called a meeting to decide what to do. Nine year old Shantha, cradled half-asleep in her father's lap, listened to the arguments swirling around her late into the night. The men's voices, cracked and bleak, hung in the dusty air under the withered tamarind tree which, in better days, had sheltered many village meetings in its green shade. Now it served only as a reminder of the grim fate that awaited them all.

The crops were gone. The cattle were gone. The well was a dusty hole in the ground. The villagers had eaten the seed-grain that was to have been planted after the monsoons. The children were getting sick. Their eyes were yellow, their faces grey. Their bellies had grown round and protruberant. Their hair turned rusty red from starvation.

There was talk of sending a letter to the local Member of Parliament, begging for relief, but to do that someone would have to walk to the nearest town, some eight miles away, where there was a scribe who would write down their words for a small fee. For a further sum, he would take their plea to the post office and ensure that it went out in the mail. But they had no money to pay the scribe, to pay the post-office; and they were all too weak from hunger to walk the required distance. In better times, they would have ridden their bullock-carts into the weekly market in Midnapore, but the bullocks, too, were dead now. The men's voices rose and fell as Shantha drifted off into a tugging dream.

In her dream it was early morning: that brief half-hour when the dew was still on the ground. The air was cool, the sky pearly with the first rays of the sun. Birds chattered in the paddy fields and preened themselves in the muddy waters of the village pond. She dreamed that, at this hour, before the sun had become fierce and burning, a great bird flew overhead. It wheeled like a hawk — a hawk whose wings spanned the whole sky — directly over her parents' hut. Its wings were the colours of a peacock's plumes, rich and glossy. But instead of an "eye" at the precise center of each feather, there was a round, gold coin which glistened and winked in the morning light. This magical bird uttered no sound. But the great sweep of its wings as it circled the sky made a powerful whoosh-whoosh-whooshing that brought other members of the village to the threshold of their huts to gaze at it, open-mouthed with wonder. As Shantha dreamed on, the bird circled lower and lower, until the shadow of its wings darkened the interior of her parents' hut.

All around Shantha, people were screaming and crying, prostrating themselves on the ground below this mystic bird, this messenger from the gods. They believed that such a messenger could only be the bringer of bad news. Anything out of the ordinary was, in their experience, to be feared rather than welcomed.

In her dream, Shantha was the only member of the village still standing upright, face turned to the sky, following, with her eyes, the spiralling course of this Garuda, this mythical, magical beast. As she watched, it slowed its course until it was completely still, hovering in mid-air a few yards above her head. Then, with a final rush of its wings it swooped down until its great, hooked beak was directly beside her left ear. She felt the touch of it, cold and hard against her cheek, but she was not afraid.

Even as her mother and brothers shrieked and called on their household gods to come to her aid, Shantha felt a great peace.

She felt herself enfolded in a love as supple and infinite as the sky. And she knew, with the certainty of one who is touched by the gods, that this was no ill-fated omen but the great god Vishnu himself: Preserver of that mortal world which was breathed into being by Brahma and which would be destroyed, in its last days, by mighty Shiva, the third face of their holy Trinity.

At that moment, Shantha turned her head and looked into the bird's all-seeing eye. For a long moment, they gazed upon each other, and in that moment much was transmitted, darshan offered and received. And even though Shantha, in her dream, did not know the precise meaning of the knowledge she had thus gained, she knew that the course of her life had been altered forever.

The bird rose vertically, without any visible movement of its wings, and, in another moment, it was gone. Shantha slept on, waking only briefly when her father carried her in his arms back into their hut. The meeting had been adjourned without any decision being made, and the people of the village went to their beds that night wondering how many more nights they had left to live.

The next morning, Shantha woke early; so early that even her mother was still asleep. She felt herself transformed, buoyant as a bird, with a nameless joy which started in the region of her heart and spread its fingers into her belly and out through all her limbs. Into her mind there flashed an image. Before she had time to consider it, she ran out of the hut.

Her skinny legs pumping as fast as they could, she made her way down to the wadi, the dry creek bed beside which their village was nestled. Avoiding the thorn bushes which nipped at her bare feet, she ran down into the middle of the wadi and there she began to dance. She twirled her slender body around and around. She stamped her feet, raising clouds of red dust around her. She wove intricate patterns in the dusty air with her arms and swung her head from side to side. Her long black hair, dishevelled from sleep, swung to and fro to the beat of an invisible drum. Her mouth was stretched wide in a joyous smile.

A moment later, she began to sing. Shantha sang a song no one had ever heard before, in a language she did not know. Its melody was simple and haunting, with a rising lilt and a pronounced beat. It had the same celebratory joy as the dance she was still dancing, as the dance that was dancing her. She went on and on as the sun rose in the sky, untiring and energetic as though she had just eaten a bellyful of dal and rice.

Some of the villagers, waking to this joyous sound, dragged themselves down listlessly to the edge of the wadi. They squatted there in small groups, wagging their heads from side to side as they discussed Shantha's peculiar behaviour. The village headman said she was surely possessed by a demon. He was soon surrounded by a group of villagers who agreed with this diagnosis. One man suggested a fool-proof way to exorcise the Raksha who had possessed the child's body. Tie her to a tree and burn tulsi leaves on her belly, he said. No-no, protested another. Draw a circle of protection around her with chunam. Then read the Bhagavad Gita aloud until the demon, unable to bear the power of the holy words, voluntarily departed. The village midwife suggested rubbing Shantha's head with mustard oil, then placing two lemons and a green chilli on her chest to drive away the evil spirit. This last suggestion was met with derision. Where would they find a lemon, or green chillies? Waah-waah! Such stupidity! An elderly woman maintained the child was merely delirious from thirst and starvation. This hypothesis met with the approval of several other women, who murmured agreement. The village headman sent two of his children to summon Shantha's parents.

Weak from hunger and thirst, Shantha's parents shuffled slowly towards the wadi from their hut. Walking into the circle of their neighbours, they were greeted with much shaking of heads and sober commiseration.

Shantha's father ventured down into the middle of the wadi.

He tried to put his arms around his daughter, pleading with her to return to their hut and lie down in its shade. Her eyes remained closed. The expression on her face was ecstatic. The muscles in her throat rippled as she sang. She danced with her head flung far back, her hair flying in the dusty air. Her father commanded her, in his cracked, hoarse voice, to stop, to return to their hut. Shantha remained oblivious. She danced and sang with a single-minded grace and purity of purpose that excluded everything else.

Meanwhile, Shantha's mother, surrounded by the women of the village, maintained an air of resolute unconcern. The women looked at her out of the corners of their eyes. She ignored their whispered warnings, their damp palms which patted her sweating back and arms. Cradling her elbows in her hands, she kept her eyes fixed on her daughter. A small smile came and went on her sun-chapped lips.

Eventually, the women, rebuffed, left her alone. They gossiped and speculated about her alarming lack of concern for her child. One of them called on the gods and rolled her eyes skyward in automatic tribute. A second later, she gasped. Trembling with excitement, unable to speak, she pointed to the sky. Dark clouds were racing in from the west, obliterating the sun. The women around her cried out, pointed, clapped their hands. Excitement spread like lightning. Within moments, the entire village had forgotten about Shantha and her astonishing behaviour. They were laughing and weeping. They praised Vishnu and embraced each other in a transport of joy. The monsoons had finally arrived.

The first drops of rain were met with jubilant cries and prayers of thanksgiving. The villagers opened their parched mouths and let the blessed rains fall directly down their eager throats. The drops turned into a deluge, and people were squatting on the ground in the rain, allowing its sweet coolness to soak through their clothes and drench them to the skin.

Nobody noticed that Shantha was no longer singing or dancing; that, indeed, Shantha was nowhere to be found among the celebrating throng. Only her mother saw Shantha open her arms joyously towards the sky as though welcoming a friend, or a god. She watched Shantha being pulled upward by an invisible force which bathed her entire body in a blue-green glow before she disappeared, leaving no trace of her passage through the glistening rain.

For many years after, the villagers speculated about what had happened to nine-year-old Shantha in that year of the terrible famine and the magical monsoon. None of them came near the truth, however, because Shantha's mother never spoke to anyone in the village of what she had seen that day. Only in her old age did she break her silence, when her younger sister, Lalita, came to visit her from Midnapore. Late one summer's night, as she sat combing Lalita's hair, she whispered to her the true story of Shantha's disappearance.

For the rest of her life, Shantha's mother placed daily offerings of fruit and flowers at a small shrine she had made near the edge of the wadi, between the roots of a mango tree. The shrine was simple: a flat rock with a natural hollow into which she poured oil and floated a wick. Lighting a lamp for her daughter who had flown away into the sky so that her village and her people might live and prosper.

"So you see, baba, even small girls have the power to save lives, with Vishnu's help." Sunder ayah stroked my hair, her voice a whisper.

I opened my eyes — I couldn't see her face in the dark, but Sunder ayah's presence, her small body hunched beside my bed, gave off a tangible warmth. I was no longer afraid of my mother, or of anything she might do. I felt myself part of a Wholeness in which there was such power, and love, and beauty, that my body relaxed completely. I closed my eyes again and knew, in my deepest self, that all was well, all was as it should be.

Poised in that state of grace, I had a vision of what my life would be. And my mother was an essential part of it; she too loved and served that Wholeness. In this vision, she was infinitely compassionate, a glowing, majestic soul who, out of love for me, had chosen to play a terrible role. One I had asked her to play a long time ago — long before I was born. I saw us all, my father, my mother, Roshan, Sunder ayah, myself, all the people I loved, as living filaments of light, part of a web that encompassed the earth and the sky and stretched across the furthest galaxies. Everything we said and did, every thought and feeling that flitted through our minds and hearts, made the grid glow brighter or broke the links between the filaments, leaving the web of light disconnected and dim.

I turned to Sunder ayah, to thank her for the story, and to tell her about my vision, but she had gone.

Chapter 9

Over the next few days, our house was ominously quiet. My mother took to her bed. My father went to work early, usually before my sister and I were awake. He returned home late, after we had gone to bed. Roshan and I ate our meals alone at the big dining table, with only Sunder ayah and each other for company. By unspoken agreement we stayed home after school, not going out to play with our friends, or to visit Perin aunty or our grandparents. We did our homework, read, played Scrabble or chess together in the living room, keeping a watchful eye on the closed door of our mother's bedroom.

Our father had hired a Mangalorean nurse named Maria to look after our mother. We looked up from our game each time Maria glided in and out of our mother's room, her face a dark oval against the white glow of her uniform sari. We kept our voices low, listening for the soft squish of Maria's crepe-soled sandals on the marble floors, the occasional clatter as she placed a tray of half-eaten food out in the hallway for the servants to take away.

One afternoon, Roshan and I were playing carom in the living room, trying to keep as quiet as possible so we wouldn't disturb our mother and be sent up to our rooms. Roshan looked at me as I flicked the white carom disk and knocked two of her counters into the far right hand pocket of the board. "Shahnu," she began, her voice solemn and low, "what's wrong with Mum? Why are they hiding her away in her room? We never see her."

"I don't know, Rosh. Daddy says she's very sick and we have to be patient and take care of her. Perin aunty told me mum had a nervous breakdown."

"What's a nervous godown?"

I laughed. "Not godown, silly. Nervous breakdown. It means there's something wrong with her nerves."

"Is she ever going to get better? I forget what she used to be like before she got sick."

"She has to get better, Roshan. She's our mother."

"Then why is Maria here? I don't like her. She looks at me as though I smell bad."

I sat back from the carom board and looked at my sister. Her dark hair had come undone from its plait and she looked cranky and sturdy and I realized for the first time how much I loved her.

"Rosh, you know how Dr. Pereira comes every day to see Mum?"

"Yeah . . ."

"Well, Maria has this exercise book in which she writes things. When Dr. Periera comes, she shows him what she's written. I think it's notes on how Mum's doing, or maybe he asks her to observe Mum and she writes down what she observes or something."

"I bet that's what it is!" Roshan's round face flushed with excitement. "If we can find her exercise book, we could read it and it would tell us what's really wrong with Mum, and when the doctor thinks she'll get better!"

"I don't know. When she's not carrying it around with her, she keeps it in her room. Although, she does leave her room to go have her bath every day . . ."

"That's it, Shahnu! We could sneak in while she's having her bath and take a look at the exercise book. Then we'd know what's going on. Nobody ever tells us what's happening with Mum. She's our mother. We have a right to know."

"Okay. But I'll do it. Next time Maria goes out, I'll sneak into her room and look for the book. You keep cavey, and if anyone comes you cough loudly, like this, so I'll know."

With my father away so often, Maria had become our only link to our mother. She was a short, dark, severe looking woman who never spoke to us. She spent the entire day in our mother's room, emerging only briefly to empty a bedpan or carry in an extra quilt, a glass of water, or a pot of tea. At night she slept in the dressing-room adjoining my parents' bedroom.

One afternoon when Maria went off for her bath, I peeked into my mother's room and saw she was asleep. This was my chance. Roshan sat on the couch in the living room, watching Mum's door, ready to call out our signal if anyone came. I tiptoed through my mother's room to the dressing-room where Maria slept. I hadn't been in there since Maria had arrived. The room looked quite different.

My mother's dressing-table had been moved against one wall, and a small cot set in its place. The cot was tidily made up with sheets, a pillow and a blanket. Next to the cot was a round cane stool on which there was a cheap suitcase. The clasps were undone, but the suitcase was closed. I bent down, opened the lid and looked inside. It contained two white nylon saris, two white cotton cholis, a sari petticoat and two white cotton bras with vicious looking metal hooks and buckles. No underpants. I wondered about that. I felt guilty and excited, going through Maria's things like that. But I needed to know what she knew about my mother's illness. I was looking for the exercise book.

Jumping nervously at every sound, I searched through the rest of the room, but found nothing more enlightening than a bible under her pillow. It had black leather binding, tissue-thin pages edged in gold, and a narrow red ribbon keeping her place at John, Chapter 4. I riffled through it and found her name written on the frontispiece — Maria Soares — in a flowing script, along with the date, March 1, 1948, and an inscription: "On the occasion of your Holy Communion, with love from Grandfather Jacob and Grandmother Assunta."

I wondered whether I should risk opening the steel almirah, which was probably where she'd keep her valuables, including her notes on my mother. Before I could make up my mind, though, I heard the bathroom door creak open. Roshan coughed loudly from the sitting room, our signal that the coast was no longer clear. I pushed the bible under the pillows and looked wildly around for anything that might offer me a clue about my mother's illness. I saw several sheets of yellowing paper folded together and tucked underneath a marble paper-weight on my mother's dressing-table. Roshan coughed loudly again, so I grabbed the sheets of paper, stuffed them in my pocket and fled back to the sitting room, where Roshan was lying on the sofa pretending to read The Wind In The Willows.

"Did you find it?" she asked, her face red with excitement.

"I don't know. I found something, but I don't know what it is." I started to pull the papers out of my pocket. "There wasn't much there. Mostly clothes and stuff."

"You should have looked in her bag. She always carries that big black doctor-bag when she goes out. Bet you the notebook's in there."

"I didn't see it. It could have been in the almirah, but the door creaks and makes a noise when you open it. I didn't want to wake Mum." I pulled the papers out of my pocket, and was about to unfold them when Maria entered the room. Roshan flung her book over the papers. The edge of the book's hard cover hit my hand and I stifled an exclamation. Roshan giggled. I held my breath as Maria swept past us and went to her room, closing the door firmly behind her.

"She's gone," Roshan whispered, picking up her book. "Show me what you found."

I unfolded the sheets of paper, which were wrinkled and looked as though they they had been inadvertently soaked, and then dried. My palms were damp with excitement, so I wiped my hands on my dress and handled the pages carefully, holding them by the edges, with my fingertips. The writing, in faded blue ink, was tiny and cramped, with spiky letters bristling across the page. There were no margins; the blue letters extended from edge to edge, as though the writer had been afraid of running out of paper. Only the first few lines were clear — the ink had bled and then faded entirely, across the rest of the page.

"What does it say?" Roshan yanked impatiently at my arm.

"Hold on. I can't read when you do that," I whispered back. I started at the top. The document began mid-sentence, so the page I was looking at was obviously not the first one. It was not numbered; neither were the rest of the pages.

I began reading out loud. ". . . the formations are similar to those seen in the circle of Willis and encompass the following. . . ."

"What's the circle of Willis?" Roshan breath tickled my ear.

"I don't know. It's hard to make out the writing. I don't even know if this is a letter, or a medical report, or something else entirely. There's a whole string of Latin words, and then these things, which look like equations or formulae." I pointed with my finger. "The ink has washed out, so I can't read the rest of it." I flipped through the following pages. "These are even worse. I can't read any of them." I was furious.

"Circle of Willis," Roshan sighed. "Sounds so romantic."

"Come on," I said. I stood up. "I'm going to look it up in the dictionary."

Roshan followed me to my room, and leaned over my shoulder as I opened the Oxford English Dictionary to the letter C. I ran my finger down the page and muttered under my breath. "Circinate . . . Circinus . . . circlage. Here it is, circle." There was a whole column of definitions, and then I found it.

"Circle of Willis. It's named after an English doctor, and it's a circular structure in the brain formed by linked arteries. That must be it, Rosh! There's something wrong with Mum's brain.

Maybe one of the arteries burst, and that's why she's been acting so strangely."

I was so excited about my discovery, that none of the obvious objections to this line of thinking occurred to me. I was convinced we'd stumbled on the reason for my mother's personality change.

Roshan and I talked about it for hours afterwards, speculating on what had happened to mum's circle of Willis and what the doctors might be able to do to fix it, to fix her. We replaced the papers in Maria's room later that evening, when she was out taking a stroll in the garden. We also decided that, at the first opportunity, I would talk to Maria and try to confirm our discovery — without giving ourselves away, of course.

The next evening, when Maria came out into the living room to use the telephone, I asked her, hesitantly, how she thought my mother was doing, and when she might get better. She looked at me coolly, over the tops of her rimless glasses.

"Why you are asking me all these poky-nose questions? Your mother is my patient only. I am not able to be telling you about her health. That is confidential information. You must be asking your daddy only." She waggled her head from side to side and made an impatient tchh sound with her tongue. Then she sailed out through the front door, her black bag held firmly in her right hand, the pleats of her white sari swinging out in front of her with every step.

A week before my birthday my mother was still a sleeping shadow in her bedroom. I kept asking my father about plans for my birthday, but he was vague and preoccupied. When I pressed him he admitted he had made no plans as yet; he was waiting for my mother to get better.

I tried phoning Perin aunty and my grandmother, to get them to help me arrange my birthday dinner, but both of them were uncharacteristically evasive. Perin aunty said she might be going away to Dehra Dun for a holiday — Dehra Dun, in October!

My grandmother sounded sad and old. When I pressed her

for answers, she began to cry. "Dikri," she quavered, "I am too old to fight your mother. She doesn't want us old people at her house any more. Your grandfather and I . . . we must respect her wishes." I cried too, in my bed that night, where no one could hear me.

Four days before my birthday, my mother emerged from her hibernation. The hushed silence of the past ten days promptly gave way to screaming discord. The first thing she did was sack Maria, who left in a dignified huff carrying her cardboard suitcase in one hand and her doctor-bag in the other. Roshan and I weren't sorry to see her go. We had only known her for ten days, and already we didn't like her. But we were worried by the unsettled atmosphere in the house, the feeling that things were afoot that would bring changes we had no way of predicting or controlling.

My mother spent her days on the phone, arguing loudly with caterers, yelling imprecations at my aunts and grandmother, talking to her friends in a bright, gay voice. My father floated around like a ghost.

Late one night when my sister and I were supposed to be in bed, I tiptoed into the living room on the pretext of retrieving my homework. I stood outside my parents' room and listened to them argue. My mother's voice dominated the air, high and strident, clawing through the velvet night. My father's emerged only occasionally, a low, pleading murmur.

"Dinshi, jaan, I'm begging you, don't do this. You are not well, you don't understand what you're doing."

"Me! Me not understand! I am a genius. Who are you to tell me what I understand and what I don't understand, hanh?" Her voice dropped to a hiss and I edged closer to their closed door, terrified, yet intent on hearing the rest. I heard her pace across the length of the bedroom as my father murmured something in that pleading voice that frightened me more than her shouting. Then she shrieked at him.

"Just because I took pity on you and married you doesn't

mean you can come here and tell me I must have this one or that one in my house. I know what you've been doing here. I know what my fine sister has been up to, in my own house, with my own husband. You think I'm a fool? And your wonderful family, your two-faced parents saying, Arre, Dinaz, you are our daughter, when all the while they're thinking Sorab married the wrong sister. They think the sun rises and sets on Perin's arse. As for your sister Khorshed, that dried up old witch would screw you if she had half a chance! Don't think I don't know that. They can go to jhanam for all I care. They are never going to set foot in this house again, you hear me? Never. Not as long as I'm alive."

Her anger, her tone of vituperative malice was unmistakable. She hated everyone I loved most. And she would not allow any of them to come to my birthday. I tiptoed back to my room and crawled into my bed, wondering who would fall under her axe next. Sunder ayah? My father? Anything was possible these days. The unthinkable had become appallingly real.

The morning of my birthday dawned clear and sparkling. I woke up in a burst of excitement and flung open my door only to face an eerily silent house. No bhajans blared from All India Radio, no flower-garlands or sandalwood smoke scented the air. I pulled on my dressing gown and headed for the bathroom, expecting to find Sunder ayah there with buckets of hot water and bowls of cream and rose-petals, ready for my head-bath. The buckets stood upside down and empty. There was no sign that anyone else was up.

I tiptoed out the back door, through the garden to Sunder ayah's quarters. When I was younger, I'd hung around there for hours, playing dressup with Sunder ayah's nine-yard saris. I'd pester her to tell me stories. But I seldom went into Sunder's room any more since my mother had returned home. Mum got furious if she caught me fraternizing with the servants, and Sunder ayah's quarters were strictly off limits.

Mostly, Sunder ayah and I talked in the kitchen, where my

mother would never venture, or out in the garden when she wasn't home. We both felt guilty, though, and the sense of secrecy, of doing something forbidden, made it difficult for us to go back to our old easy way of being together.

Sunder ayah had always been more like a mother to me than my own mother. She had raised me since I was a baby. She was the one who woke up at night when I had nightmares, and squatted on the floor beside my bed, crooning lullabies and stroking my forehead with her rough-skinned hand till I fell asleep. For years she had slept on a bedroll on the floor of my room, her breath warm and reassuring beside me, her loving presence an anchor I had always taken for granted.

Since my mother's return and her subsequent "nervous breakdown," Sunder ayah had been banished to sleep in her own quarters. I'd never known her to sleep in late, though. No matter how early I woke up, she was always up and about, preparing our baths, laying out our clothes for the day, arranging for breakfast to be served at 7:30 am.

As I reached the small one-room cottage at the back of our compound where Sunder ayah lived, I noticed that the door was shut. This in itself was odd. She always slept with the door wide open, so that the salty sea breezes could cool her room. I knocked on the door. There was no answer. I listened for sounds inside, growing increasingly alarmed at the impenetrable silence on the other side. I turned the glass knob and pushed at the door. It opened inward with difficulty, the last monsoon having swollen its aging wood. I called out, "Sunder?" a sudden fear snagging the breath in my chest. No answer. Putting my shoulder against the weathered wood, I forced the door open.

The room was empty. Sunder ayah's bedroll was not on the floor; the low, chipped charpoy on which she kept her oil lamp burning in front of luridly coloured lithographs of the gods Ganesh and Lakshmi, was gone. There was only the clean-swept granite floor, plain white-washed walls. The silk scarf she had

116

made into a curtain for the low window was gone, as was the photo of her daughter. The green tin trunk with fat pink roses painted on it, which had been her pride and joy and in which she had kept her few worldly posessions, no longer stood in the far corner. There was nothing in that room to suggest she had ever lived there, except for the lingering odour of the coconut oil she rubbed into her hair each morning.

Stunned, I stood in that bare room unable to take in the fact of its emptiness. Maybe Sunder ayah was in the kitchen. I hurried out of there, not stopping to pull the door shut behind me. I walked briskly to the kitchen, scolding myself for feeling so upset. Come on now, Shahnaz, don't be ridiculous. She's probably just seeing to breakfast, making sure the cook makes the cream of wheat the way you like it. I was still mentally castigating myself for overreacting when I reached the kitchen, which was housed in a small concrete building connected to the back of our house by a bougainvillea-covered walkway. The door was, as always, open, but there were no smells of cooking, and when I thrust my head in the doorway, there was no one there. The stove wasn't lit, there was no sign of the cook or the bearer.

Confused, I turned back toward the house, thinking perhaps I'd woken up too early. Maybe the cook, Manjushri, and the bearer, Sushil, were still in their quarters and I should go back to bed. But the sun was up, the crows were cawing and the road outside our compound was noisy with traffic.

I entered the house through the back door, and went to Roshan's room. She was still in bed, her long hair tangled and plastered to her neck by the heat, her eyelids fluttering as they did when she was dreaming. I didn't want to wake her, so I sat on the edge of her bed and watched her. She twitched and tussled with her sheets in her sleep, breathing hard the way she did when she was having a nightmare. I thought about waking her, then thought she was probably better off in her dream nightmare than waking up to the reality of this ghostly, empty house. I heard the big grandfather clock in the sitting room strike nine times, so I knew it was eight o'clock. Why wasn't anyone up? What was going on?

By now I was scared. Everything seemed off kilter, this morning. Although the house looked the same, it didn't smell or feel the same to me. Not knowing what else to do, I went to the bathroom and had a cold water bath. Then I put on my new yellow birthday dress and my new socks and shoes and headed towards my parents' bedroom, afraid of what I might find there. I knocked on the door. No answer. I pushed the door open a little, and peered around it. My mother lay curled on her side in bed with the sheets pulled up to her chin. Her eyes were closed and she was breathing gently and evenly. My father's side of the bed had not been slept in — the sheet was still tightly folded and tucked in under the mattress, his white pillow fluffed and undented.

I tiptoed across the room, barely breathing, glancing at my mother every few seconds to make sure I hadn't woken her. When I got to the dressing-room, I pushed the door open and slipped inside. The cot Maria had used during her short stay with us was still there. It was disordered, the sheets tangled and spilling onto the floor. My father's dressing-gown was flung across it, as though he had left in a hurry. Maybe this was where he'd slept.

I tiptoed back through my mother's room. Just as I was about to slip out the door, her voice barked out, "Shahnaz! What are you doing here?" Startled, I whirled around to face her. My elbow hit the Ch'ing Dynasty vase that sat on a small table by the doorway. It crashed to the floor, exploding into tiny shards on impact.

Horrified, I knelt down and began gathering up the pieces with quaking fingers. "I'm so sorry, Mum! It was an accident!" I cried, ducking my shoulders against the expected onslaught.

"Accident! What were you doing sneaking around in my room like that? Who told you you could come in?" she demanded, her voice ringing with righteous accusation.

"I . . . I woke up and I couldn't find Sunder ayah or any of the servants, so I came in to see if you or daddy knew where they were. I'm sorry." I was so mortified I wanted to run out of her room and back to the shelter of my bed. But I kept gathering up shards of the vase, placing them in a heap beside me on the floor. I felt semi-paralysed, the way I did in my dreams when something menaced me and I knew I had to get away but couldn't move. My limbs felt heavy, immobile, even while my fingers gathered up what remained of the delicate porcelain.

I dared a glance at my mother, and saw that she was sitting up in bed, clutching the sheet to her chest. Her face looked angry, implacable, and my spirits sank even lower. There was a peculiar charred odour in the room which I hadn't noticed before. She glared at me and growled, "Get out. Go to your own room."

"I just want to finish . . ."

"I said GET OUT! What are you, deaf? Your father spoils you rotten so you think you can do whatever you like," she hissed, saliva spraying from her mouth, her neck outthrust like a snake. Then, as I dropped the pieces I was holding in my hand and stood up to leave, she added, a sly glee glittering in her voice: "You want to know why your precious Sunder ayah isn't here?"

I nodded dumbly, yes.

"I got rid of her."

I looked up at her, stunned, not knowing what she meant. I had a sudden vision of Sunder ayah's body floating belly-up on the tide. "What have you done to her?" The words burst out of my mouth without conscious volition. They hung in the air between us for a moment. My mother laughed.

"She thought she could take my place, that toothless old woman. Well, I got rid of her. Sent her packing last night, bag and baggage out on the street where she belongs. Good riddance to bad rubbish." She grinned, baring her teeth in a triumphant smile.

"You turned her out in the night?" I felt stupid, as though

I'd been hit on the head. I couldn't think, couldn't put thoughts and words together. "Where will she go?"

"How should I know? It's not my job to find out where the riff-raff who've been running this house go to, once I sweep them out. She can go to hell, for all I care."

"But how can you turn her out? This is her home. She's lived here since before I was born. Before you and daddy were married, even."

"Well she doesn't live here now, so that's that." Her voice was fat with self-satisfaction. Then, in a sudden change of mood, she clapped her hands and shouted gaily, "Don't just stand there gawking at me, go on and have your bath and get dressed. It's your birthday!"

"I'm already dressed," I stammered. "But . . . where are the other servants? Where's Manjushri and Sushil?"

"Gone. All gone!" She laughed, obviously delighted with herself. Then, as I opened my mouth to protest, she added, "I threw them out too. Off with their heads!" She made a sweeping gesture with her arm and smiled beatifically.

"Where's daddy?"

"Oh, he had to fly to Bangalore on business. He'll be back tonight, although I don't think he'll be here in time for the party." Her mood changed again and she frowned. "Baap-re, I have so much to do to get ready. No-one helps me, I have to do everything myself. The caterers should be here soon, to set up the shamiana out in the garden. Now go on, get out of here so I can get dressed." She clapped her hands again, and made shooing motions with her arms.

I turned to go. As I headed through the door, I felt something hit me hard between my shoulder-blades, so hard that all the breath was knocked out of my body and I gasped. Unable to breathe, I clung to the door jamb, my whole body trembling with shock, pain blooming in my back like a flame. Dimly, I heard the sound of shattering glass, and my mother's giggle, rising into maniacal laughter as she shrieked, "Happy Birthday!"

Chapter 10

I hear the Coca-Cola jingle coming from the living room. Shahrukh has discovered television. Ann has a colour TV set in her living room, and ever since she told Shahrukh he can get twenty-four different channels on it, he spends every waking minute with the curtains drawn, downing TV shows like they were masala peanuts.

We've only been here in Eugene one night and a day. So far all I've seen is the inside of Ann's house, and various scenic spots through the windows of her car. We've had dinner (at six o'clock in the evening!) and even though it's dark now, I want to get outside, go for a walk. I'm overwhelmed with the strangeness and newness of this place, and with all that has happened to me in the last forty-eight hours. On Monday, we will launch ourselves into university and our new life will begin in earnest. I need some time alone with Shahrukh right now, to talk, to get at some of what I'm feeling inside, to find out how all this strikes him.

I march into the living room, determined to pry Shahrukh loose from the ubiquitous grip of the television set. He is sitting on the couch, his face glowing angelically in the flickering blue light. He seems rapt, like someone having a religious ex-

121

perience, his full lips slightly parted, head leaning forward, eyes fixed on the screen across the room. His right hand dives into a foil-covered package of potato crisps and carries a fistful to his mouth. He munches noisily, his eyes never leaving the screen. He doesn't notice me standing beside him. In fact, I doubt he'd notice an earthquake right now, unless it was on television. I walk over and slide down onto the couch beside him, snuggling up against him, lifting his arm to place it over my shoulders.

"Shahrukh," I say.

"Mmmm?" he replies.

"Let's get out of here and go someplace where we can talk."

"Sssshhhh!"

He still hasn't looked at me, his eyes riveted to the show on the screen, whose absurd dialogue is punctuated periodically by the sound of an invisible audience laughing.

It's clear to me he isn't going to be parted from the TV, so I settle down to watch the show with him. There is a pause during which the volume swells to a crescendo, and we see a bunch of short advertisements: Irish Spring deodorant soap (featuring fake Irish accents, pastorally romantic scene, laundry billowing on a clothesline, flying green soap); Mr. Clean floor cleaner (bald hulk with bulging muscles, vaguely sexual innuendos as he helps a woman in a cherry red dress achieve an indelible shine on her wooden floor); and Clairol shampoo (meadows, wildflowers, woman and child waltzing barefoot in the grass). I look at Shahrukh, who is as still as Buddha, watching this ridiculous performance and munching cow-like on the crisps.

The show comes back on. I Dream of Jeannie. A not-so-funny comedy about an astronaut who "owns" his own genie; the genie being a silly woman with dimples and a blonde ponytail who lives in a bottle, wears fake harem-gear and calls the astronaut "Master" in a high-pitched girlish voice. Shahrukh's dream woman, no doubt. Blonde, curvy, adoring. Cheerfully subservient. She caters to her "Master's" every whim by magically blinking up an assortment of consumables and gets him into endless trouble with his superiors. I watch Shahrukh salivating over her and am suddenly furious. Sad. I get up and go to bed, leaving him to enjoy the next mindless confection.

I wake up around three o'clock in the morning, my body still resonating to the diurnal rhythms of the Indian sun. Shahrukh isn't in bed beside me. Alarmed, I tiptoe through the house, hear music in the living room rising to a dramatic crescendo, followed by silence and a muffled scream. I run barefoot down the hall. Shahrukh is sprawled on Ann's couch, snoring lightly, while the TV flickers ghostly images across his sleeping face. I curl up at one end of the couch, lifting Shahrukh's legs onto my lap to make room. He sleeps on while I watch half an hour of a rather ghoulish old Bette Davis movie. I leave him sleeping on the couch and go back to bed, realizing, with a pang, that this is the first time since we've been married that we haven't slept together in the same bed.

When I wake up again it's 8:30 in the morning. I shower, do some yoga stretches in the bedroom, dress and go out into the living room, where Shahrukh is still snoring on the couch. Ann doesn't seem to mind; she smiles her cheerful, indulgent smile as she makes coffee and toasts frozen waffles for breakfast. She and I eat together in the kitchen.

Ann has a big research paper due for her Public Policy class tomorrow. "I'm real sorry I won't be able to take you guys out sightseeing today," she drawls, apologetically. "I've gotta get this paper done. We'll go someplace nice for dinner when I'm finished."

"Don't worry about it, Ann. If I can get Shahrukh away from the TV we'll go out for a walk, maybe get a closer look at the campus." In fact, I'm looking forward to spending the day alone with Shahrukh, walking around town, getting the feel of the place.

Just as we're finishing breakfast, Shahrukh wanders into the kitchen. His hair is still wet from the shower, and he smells of the Mysore Government Sandalwood Soap we brought with us from Bombay. He bends down to kiss me, his mouth tasting of toothpaste and sleep. Ann excuses herself and goes off to the university library to work on her paper. Shahrukh pours himself a bowl of Cheerios and milk, and eats it slowly.

"Hey," I say, "let's go for a walk. I have a map of the city; it isn't far from here to the university."

"God, woman, I hate walking. I don't want to go to the university."

"Ah, come on, Shahrukh, it'll be fun. It's a lovely day. Let's walk down to the campus, and potter around there for a bit."

"Forget it. I'm not walking any further than the couch. I'm tired." Then, looking disgustedly at his bowl of cereal, Shahrukh continues, "The food here is bloody awful. You know, Shahnu, Ann's a sweetheart, but she has no sense of taste. That wine she served with dinner last night came in a cardboard box! Who the hell drinks wine out of a box?"

"If you come for a walk with me I'll take you out for lunch," I wheedle. "Ann says there's a great little French restaurant just off campus. We could have lunch there and then take our time strolling back."

Shahrukh looks at me, his expression irresolute. "Hey, I'll even buy you a bottle of their best wine," I promise recklessly, determined to get my husband away from the TV set.

"Okay, you talked me into it." Shahrukh smiles and winks at me. "You could have got me with just the promise of a decent meal, you know. You didn't have to go as far as the wine. One of these days I'll have to teach you the fine art of negotiation."

I laugh and tug at his cowlick. He pushes his chair back and gets up, leaving his bowl and the carton of milk on the table as he saunters off towards the living room. I think about calling him back to put away the dishes he's used, but it seems a petty thing to do, so I put the milk in the fridge, wash his bowl and put it in the dish-drainer. I don't realize how annoyed I am until

I find myself cursing at my boots as I try to tug them onto my feet. How did I end up cleaning up after him?

Fifteen minutes later we are walking arm-in-arm down the sidewalk outside Ann's house, heading towards the University. It is a cold day, the air crisp and fragrant as an apple. My body is confused by the sunshine, expecting the air to be hot and humid, surprised by the snapping chill of it. Rows of copper beeches line the street on both sides. Their branches are mostly bare, a few deep maroon leaves clinging desperately to their twigs, the rest scattered on the ground by the wind, which blows briskly against my ears. Smoke rises from the chimneys of houses, and as we walk by them I sense a whole vocabulary of smoke, its various fragrances distinct as fingerprints. Although I cannot yet identify the different trees whose burning woods give rise to these resinous perfumes, I promise myself I will soon learn their names.

"Mmmm. Doesn't that smell wonderful? Like Kashmiri apples," I say, sniffing appreciatively and squeezing Shahrukh's arm. When he doesn't reply, I look up at him. He is looking around uneasily, a wary expression on his face. "Shahrukh? Is something wrong?"

He looks down at me and frowns. "Shhhh," he hisses.

"Don't shush me. What's the matter?" I'm beginning to feel alarmed.

Shahrukh looks furtively around as though expecting to be ambushed. "We have to go back. Right now." Shahrukh voice is grim as he swerves on his heel, dragging me with him back in the direction of Ann's house.

"Oh come on, Shahrukh. We've barely been walking for fifteen minutes. I'm not ready to go back yet."

"Notice anything?" Shahrukh mutters, bending down to speak quietly into my ear.

"No, what?" I ask, mystified by his peculiar behaviour.

"The streets. They're deserted. No cars, no people, nothing." His face is flushed and, despite the cold, beads of sweat stand out on his forehead. "It must be a bundh. We have to get indoors quickly." He jogs into a half-run, still dragging me by the arm.

I pull my arm away from his and stop, staring at him in amazement. He stops too, but is poised to take off, his whole body leaning impatiently away from me. I shake my head and say, "Shahrukh, there are no bundhs here. This isn't Calcutta, we're quite safe here."

Then, seeing his uncomprehending look, I begin to laugh. "It's Sunday. People are probably still at home, having breakfast with their families. Or getting ready to go to church." Shahrukh flashes me a disbelieving look. I laugh again. "Trust me, love, there's nothing wrong."

"How can there be nothing wrong when we're the only people out on the street?"

"That's just the way it is on Sundays. Even in London, which is a lot bigger than Eugene, you'll find the streets deserted on a Sunday morning." I loop my arm around his waist and hug him. "Come on, let's carry on with our walk."

Shahrukh's face flushes in that familiar way that presages an explosion. Then something seems to shift inside him and I feel his body relax against my arm. He laughs, somewhat shakily. "Bloody hell, I really thought we were going to get shot. Good thing we got out of Calcutta when we did. I'd be ready for the loony bin if we'd stayed there another year." He smiles and holds me hard against him for a moment. "Let's get to that restaurant, I'm starving!" His voice is buoyant with relief.

As we walk on, Sharukh is euphoric, laughing and hugging and twirling me around. "No bloody army tanks rumbling down this street!" he exclaims, joyfully. "No big guns pointed at our bellies!" He is jubilant, exulting. I realize that, in the last two years of living in Calcutta, we've developed an almost unconscious paranoia. It helped us to survive there. Here, it seems ridiculous.

I look around at Eugene's benignly empty streets and my heart lifts too. We walk all the way to the campus, shuffling

126

through piles of dry leaves and giggling like children as they crackle under our feet, our breath emerging in milky little puffs in the cold morning air. I feel my soul expand to meet the space and silence here, touch the rim of this gentle horizon with a grateful heart.

The French restaurant Ann has recommended is closed until 11:30. We're too hungry to wait, so we walk a few blocks further, right to the edge of the campus, and find a pub on the corner across the street from the university bookstore.

Inside, the pub is warm and dimly lit. We slide into a booth near a window, facing each other across the plain wood table. The room is panelled in wood, which makes it look smaller than it is. It's only half-full. Sitting alone at a small round table next to us is a young woman in blue jeans that are torn at the knee and patched along one thigh with red gingham. She is thin and freckled, with wispy reddish hair that glows in the light from the window. She lifts one booted leg and rests it on the chair beside her, intently absorbed in the book she's reading. In front of her is a half-empty cup of coffee, which she lifts to her mouth, sips, and returns to the table without ever removing her eyes from her book. I wonder if some day I'll be able to sit in a pub alone with such insouciance. Back home, women of my class simply don't go to restaurants by themselves. This young woman looks so self-contained, so content, I envy her.

A young man in blue jeans and a U of O t-shirt comes up to our table. He pulls an order pad from his back pocket, a pencil from behind his ear and smiles at us. "What'll it be?" he asks.

"I'll have a pint of bitter," Shahrukh says, surprising me. He doesn't usually drink before evening. The waiter looks a bit mystified. Shahrukh adds, "Beer," and the waiter nods his head and turns to me with an enquiring glance.

"I'd like a cup of coffee, please. And could I take a look at your menu?"

"Sure thing," he says. He reaches back and pulls out a single laminated sheet of paper from the waistband of his jeans. "Here you go. The specials are up on the blackboard. The oysters are fresh, and the clam-chowder's good," he adds, smiling again. He has pale blue eyes and eyebrows and hair so blonde they're almost white.

I order a bowl of clam chowder and a slice of sourdough cheese bread because it sounds good. Even though I've no idea what sourdough means, I can't wait to try it. Shahrukh settles on a grilled bacon, lettuce, and tomato sandwich. "A BLT," says the waiter. "Good choice. You folks new here?"

Shahrukh explains that we've just arrived from Bombay. The young man leans back against the table's edge and says, "Hey, I was there a couple of years ago, on my way back from 'Nam. Great hash there, man," he adds fervently.

Shahrukh and I look blankly at him. "You know, ganja," he says, making a circle with the index finger and thumb of his right hand and miming the action of smoking. Then, seeing our confused looks, I suppose, he shrugs and goes off in the direction of the bar, returning a few moments later with a frosty tankard of pale yellow beer, which he places on the table in front of Shahrukh.

Shahrukh touches the tankard with his fingertips and quickly draws back his hand as though he's been stung. He looks up at the waiter and says politely, "I'm afraid this has been refrigerated."

"What?" The waiter looks bewildered.

"The beer," says Shahrukh, more firmly this time. "It's been refrigerated." The waiter raises his eyebrows, obviously nonplussed. Shahrukh spells it out for him, enunciating each word with insulting slowness. "This beer is cold. Undrinkable. It's been refrigerated. Take it back to wherever it came from, and bring me one that's at room temperature." Then, as the waiter makes a sound of protest, Shahrukh adds, "Also, I asked for a pint of bitter. This is a lager. I don't drink lager." Shahrukh crosses his arms over his chest and looks at the waiter from under his long lashes.

The young man flushes, his face turning red and then white. He opens his mouth to say something, then silently picks up the mug of beer. I can tell he is angry by the way he holds the mug in his fist, his knuckles white, the muscles in his forearm jumping. He gives Shahrukh a long look in return. "In this country we drink our beer cold," he says, his drawl more pronounced than it had been, as insulting in its way as Shahrukh's earlier precise diction. "But you're the customer. You want it warm, I'll get you warm." He turns on his heel and walks away.

"Bloody cheek," grumbles Shahrukh. But I can tell he's relieved the confrontation hasn't gone any further. He likes to play lord of the manor, but he doesn't like having to assert himself. He would rather be deferred to naturally. He turns to me, his lower lip jutting out like a spoiled child's. "Let's go somewhere else. The service in this place is bloody awful."

I shake my head, no. "Let's just stay and eat. I'm tired and hungry. The waiter's already gone to get you your bitter."

"He's paid to take orders and to give me what I ask for. The silly bugger just wasn't paying attention." Shahrukh juts his chin at me, satisfied that he's had the last word.

"You were rude to him, Shahrukh. You embarrassed me. You can't treat him like one of the servants, you know. Not that you'd ever treat a servant that way," I grumble.

We eat our meal in silence after that. The soup and bread are good. The coffee is watery and tasteless. The waiter brings Shahrukh another beer. Shahrukh takes a cautious sip, then wrinkles his nose at it, muttering, "It's still cold. And it's not a bitter; it's some sort of American excuse for an ale." However, much to my relief, he doesn't make a scene.

Shahrukh asks for the bill. He pays it, fumbling with the unfamiliar currency which is all one colour — green — and all the same size no matter what the denomination of the notes. He does not leave a tip.

We return to Ann's, taking a different route this time. The streets are broad and incredibly clean. But the houses here are older, larger, with wide porches and Victorian turrets and gingerbread trim, painted in unusual colours, purple, olive, viridian. Children's toys and old cars litter their driveways. The trees lining these streets are chestnuts, their fruit scattered across the sidewalks. I fill my pockets with shiny brown conkers, finger their satiny coolness as we walk along.

We run into a few other people. A young couple riding bikes bright with chrome, an older woman pushing a blanket-bundled baby in a pale blue carriage, an elderly man raking leaves on his front lawn. They smile at us, say "Hi!" or "How're you doing?" their greeting ending on a surprised, rising note as though they've known us forever and are delighted to run into us unexpectedly like this. There's a friendliness here, an openness that I missed when we lived in Calcutta. I remember it from my childhood, from holidaying in villages and small towns like our beach place in Udvada, or our mountain cottage in Khandala. Places where everyone greeted everyone else, and an encounter with a newcomer was an excuse to stop and chat and make friends.

By the time we reach Ann's we're both warm from walking and very tired. Ann's house is quiet. The garage door is open, and her car isn't in there, so I assume she's still at the library working on her paper. Shahrukh and I take off our many layers of outer clothing: jackets, boots, scarves, gloves, hats. What a lot of stuff one has to wear here, in order to go out into this gelid world. At home, I would throw on a pair of sandals, hitch my purse over my shoulder and walk out the door wearing whatever I'd been wearing when I was inside. Inside and outside were less segregated; life flowed in and around and through without all these intervening layers of insulation.

And yet, it's not a bad thing to be insulated from life sometimes. I imagine this is what television does for Shahrukh. I can think of times when I wanted nothing more than a thick layer of insulation between me and the events exploding around me.

Chapter 11

The afternoon of my thirteenth birthday was one of those events I wanted nothing to do with, so I climbed high up into my favourite mango tree and watched as our garden was transformed.

First, my mother came out into the garden wearing an orange Kanjeevarum sari I had never seen before, looking like a brilliant butterfly against the green of our lawn. She cornered Mr. Subramaniam, the catering supervisor from the Taj. He was a short, dignified looking man who wore a black sherwani buttoned all the way up to his neck, and creamy white trousers which draped over the tops of his shiny black shoes.

"Mr. Subramaniam!" she barked, looking so cheerful and composed that I wondered if I'd imagined the whole scene in her bedroom that morning, when she'd hurled a crystal ashtray at me. But the searing pain between my shoulder-blades remained, a reminder of what had taken place. I watched, fascinated by the way in which she could transform herself from Lady Macbeth to Lady of the Manor in a couple of hours.

"Mr. Subramaniam," she was saying, "I want your men to put up the tent right there, in front of the rose garden. Now. You know where the banquet tables go. I want the head table to have a Mughal theme. There will be important people, friends from the U.S. State Department and the U.S. Embassy here tonight, and I want to show them what we Indians can do when we set our minds to it."

Mr. Subramaniam, who was a head shorter than my mother, peered up at her through his round, gold-rimmed glasses and nodded deferentially as she changed her mind and then changed it again, demanding first that a red carpet be laid from the wrought iron front gates to the tent, then deciding it would be better to have rose petals strewn across the gravelled path instead.

She wanted a Rajasthani theme for one of the banquet tables, and declaimed at some length on the exact details of the central floral arrangement for that table, the ice sculpture of a horse and its rider, the tablecloth to be covered with Rajasthani tapestries of yellow and red. Then she decided Rajasthan had been overdone and Khajuraho would make for a more impressive conversation piece.

"Americans like those erotic sculptures from Khajuraho. I want an ice-sculpture of Shiva-Parvati — you know the one I mean — and the flowers can be like the ones carved in the temples, lotus blossoms floating in gold bowls, champa and jasmine and so on."

Mr. Subramaniam took notes with a gold pen in a small, black, leather-bound notebook. He smiled. He bowed. Then, when my mother went back into the house, he walked over to where the workmen were setting up the big green striped tent. He spoke to the foreman in a low voice, waving his hands about to show where he wanted the dhurries placed, where the hanging tapestries were to go.

The tent was huge. As big as a sideshow tent in a circus, it was made of green canvas that billowed and flapped in the wind. It took sixteen men to hoist it up and peg it down. They heaved and hauled, the ropy muscles straining on their bare brown legs, sweat standing in large drops on their torsos and faces. I felt bad that they were doing all this work for a party I didn't want.

Then, caterers from the Taj Hotel brought in round tables, which they set up in the tent and covered with colourful tribal tablecloths reflecting the theme of each table. Huge vases of flowers — tuberoses, gladioli, lillies, lotuses, roses — decorated the centre of each table. Then there were the ice sculptures, sweating in the heat. I'd never seen ice sculptures before. These had Indian themes, but would never be seen in any self-respecting Indian home. Sculptures from the temples of Khajuraho — ancient and venerated by generations of Indians — were imitated here, an obscene display carved in glittering ice.

The workmen brought in and assembled a semi-circular raised bandstand in one corner of the tent. I had a splendid view of it from my mango tree, which stood across the garden from the tent's V-shaped opening. Then more men came in carrying speakers and microphones and cables and lights. They put strings of lights inside the tent as well as all through the garden, even in the rose bushes and the trees. All except my mango tree — I shooed them away when they came near me.

After a while, the band members arrived. They set up their instruments and practised for a while before the party. There were eight of them, all Goanese, slender men with slicked-back, brilliantined hair. They wore white shirts and skinny silk ties, black trousers that looked shiny from being ironed too often, and black western-style jackets which they slung on the backs of their chairs. They set up a huge drum-set — not tablas, but a Gene-Krupa-type drum set with four drums, gleaming gold high-hat cymbals and a foot-operated drumstick. The band's name, "Canguna Beach Swingers," was painted on the side of the largest drum in glittering gold paint. It looked tacky, and exciting, and as odd, in our garden, as if the Statue of Liberty were standing in that tent all decked out in coloured lights.

The rest of the band consisted of guitar and bass players, two saxophone players, a trumpet and a piano. The last to arrive was a woman singer — the only female in the lot. She wore a shiny silver ankle-length dress, cut very tight and low over her considerable bosom. Her face was covered in a thick layer of make-up. I could see her false eyelashes, their edges lined in glittering diamonds which I assumed were fakes. They ran through a couple of their tunes — I recognized "In The Mood" and "Beale Street Blues" and "Moonlight In Vermont."

While the band practised, more workmen arrived to lay out a dance floor next to the bandstand — a round, polished wood floor, which they dusted with powder, I suppose so people's feet could glide around more easily.

All afternoon, workers came and went, carrying tables, chairs, lanterns, china, silverware. I stayed in my mango tree hideout and kept watch. My mother never appeared again. Maybe she was resting for the party.

Roshan came looking for me at tea time. She stood under the tree where I was hiding and called my name. "Shahnaz! Shahnu, where are you? Come out, pleeaase!"

I didn't want to come down, ever. But she sounded close to tears, so I climbed part way down. "I'm here, Rosh. What's the matter?"

"I'm hungry," she wailed, "and there's nothing for tea. I haven't even had lunch, I can't find Sunder ayah or anybody."

"Mummy sacked them all last night. They've all left," I replied, grimly noting her dishevelled hair, her unironed dress. "Did you dress yourself?" I asked.

"I couldn't find Sunder so I got a dress out of my drawer and put it on. It's clean," she added.

"It's all wrinkled, Roshan. Come on. Let's find you something else to wear."

"But I'm hungry. I don't care what I wear. I haven't had breakfast even, and now it's teatime!" Roshan looked up at me helplessly, waiting for me to tell her what to do.

"Go and see if the car is in the garage. If Mum hasn't sacked Mukesh, we can have him drive us to Perin aunty's. I'll go phone her and tell her we're coming for tea."

I scrambled down the tree and hugged Roshan. She clung

to me, wrapping both arms around my back, inadvertently pressing on the sore spot between my shoulder-blades. "OWWW! Let go, let go!" I yelled, pulling away from Roshan. She stared at me, her eyes wide and round, her mouth hanging open.

"What? What's the matter?"

"Nothing. My back hurts. Mummy threw an ashtray at me when she caught me in her room this morning."

"Let me see." Roshan walked around behind me and, standing on tiptoe, peered down the back of my dress. She screamed, startling me so that I jumped. "Oh my God, Shahnu, there's a big cut on your back. Blood and everything. It looks awful!"

I twisted my head, trying to look over my shoulder, but I couldn't turn far enough to see anything. My back stung, my skin chafed against the lining of my dress and felt raw. "How much blood? Is it dry or still oozing?" I demanded.

Roshan gingerly pulled at the back of my dress. "It looks sticky, your dress is stuck to it. I can't see."

"Oww! Don't pull, it hurts. Come on, let's go to the bathroom."

Roshan scratched her calf with the toes of her right foot, her face puckering.

"What? Come on Roshan, I need you to help me with this."

She began to cry. Noisily. I tried to shush her, to pull her into the house away from the workmen who were looking at her with open curiosity. But she seemed to have reached some limit inside herself and wouldn't budge. She stood there and sobbed as though she'd lost the whole world and would never be able to recover it.

"Roshan, stop being such a big crybaby. I'm the one who's hurt. What're you crying about?" I took her sticky, sweaty hand in mine and pulled her towards the house. "Come on, sweetie, it's okay. We'll phone Perin aunty. She'll come and get us, okay?"

Roshan nodded between sobs, and let me lead her back to my room. I sat her down on my bed and went into the sitting room to use the telephone. I dialled Perin aunty's number, but there was no reply. I phoned my grandparents' house. The butler answered, but said my grandparents and Khorshed aunty had gone out shopping. He wasn't sure when they'd be back, but they had ordered dinner for seven o'clock, so he felt certain they would be home by then.

I sat down on the couch in the sitting room, trembling. I wanted Perin aunty to come and take care of me, bandage my back, get us something to eat. But Roshan was in the bedroom waiting for me to come up with something.

I considered my options. I couldn't reach my father; he was still at his business meeting in Bangalore. My grandparents and aunts were out and might not be back until dinnertime. None of the servants were around. I picked up the intercom phone that connected us to the garage and rang for the chauffeur, Mukesh. The phone rang and rang, but there was no answer. Probably my mother had made a clean sweep of it and sacked him along with all the other servants.

That left my mother. Or Roshan. Of the two, I'd have more luck with Roshan, even though she was only ten and a crybaby. My back burned. If I didn't do something about it I could get tetanus and die — then they'd all be sorry they hadn't taken better care of me.

On the other hand, I might just end up with a permanent scar, like the one I had on the bottom of my chin from the time I was skipping in the bathroom and slipped and split my chin open on the tiles. There'd been lots of blood that time too, and it had hurt, but I hadn't died or anything. I got up and headed off for my bedroom.

I found Roshan still sitting on my bed, where I'd left her. Her sobs had quieted down to occasional sniffles, and she had the hiccups. She looked up, when I came in, and sniffled some more. She's only ten, I thought. She's probably scared to death. I was scared too.

I sat down on the bed beside her. "Rosh," I began, "there's

no one home. Perin aunty's out, Sheroo Mumma and Soli Pappa have gone shopping with Khorshed aunty. You'll have to help me get out of this dress and clean up my back."

Roshan began to cry again, quietly this time, her chest and back shuddering, tears running down the sides of her nose. She shook her head. "I can't . . . You need a doctor. Perin aunty or someone."

"There's no one else here. Only Mum." Roshan must have heard the despair in my voice because she reached up and touched my arm.

"I'll try, Shahnu. But don't blame me if it hurts."

"I won't. I promise. I just need you to do this for me now. Please. Come on. I've seen Perin aunty do this a zillion times, I know what to do." I led her to the bathroom we shared. It was a big room with a tiled bath area at one end, a steel almirah, an old dressing table and a stool at the other end. I sat down on the stool, and got the First Aid box out of the bottom drawer of the dressing table. In it was a pair of scissors. I took them out and handed them to Roshan.

"Here. Unbutton my dress and pull the lining away from my skin as much as you can. Just cut around the part that's stuck to my skin. Okay?"

"But it's your new birthday dress! It'll be ruined," Roshan cried.

"It's ruined any way. My whole birthday is ruined." I grimaced as Roshan finished undoing the buttons and began sliding the top of my dress down my arms. I could feel the patch that was stuck to my back. It tugged at my skin, and felt as though the skin would come off with it.

"Careful, Rosh! You're hurting me."

"I can't help it, it won't come off." She took the scissors in her hand and maneouvred herself behind me again. I could see her in the dressing table mirror, her head bent, her tongue sticking out between her teeth. The scissors made a snicking sound as she carefully cut the cloth around the wound in my back.

"There." Roshan was panting with the effort. "I got it." She pulled the rest of my dress off. Suddenly shy, I crossed my arms over my nubby little breasts.

"You did that like an expert, Rosh," I said. "Maybe one day you'll be a doctor, like Perin aunty." She beamed at me in the mirror. I sent her to get me a towel, to wrap around myself, and a hand-towel, which I had her wet under the tap and use to sponge the rest of my dress off the cut in my back.

"Euuugh! Big mess," she said, wrinkling her nose, dropping the bloody piece of cloth in the waste-paper basket. I felt such a surge of love for her in that moment I leaned forward to hug her. Then realized I couldn't move my arms that far or my towel would fall off. My brave little sister. Instead, I got out the white First Aid box, soaked a square of gauze in iodine and handed the smelly square to Roshan. "Here. Put this on the cut."

She did as I asked. The iodine felt cold and burned. Roshan taped a piece of plaster over the gauze, pressing it lightly down against my back. It was only then, when it was all over, that I began to cry.

My body ached and throbbed. My head hurt. I cried soundlessly, no breath left in me to give voice to all the fear and grief inside. Roshan stroked my head for a while, then began to cry too, and we held each other, huddled on the small stool in the bathroom, and wept and wept.

I don't know how long we sat there clinging to each other. I was comforted by her warm, moist breath mingling with my own, her smell of sweat and sandalwood soap, her round nose pressed against my throat. Our pulses beat together, her wrist on my inner elbow. The salt of her tears ran down her cheeks and into my mouth. In the distance, I heard my mother's voice calling our names.

We both became very quiet, barely breathing when we heard her enter my room and shout for us, and then scream a few obscenities. Her voice and footsteps receded and the only sounds were those of the workmen outside, setting up their preposterous tent for my birthday party.

By six o'clock I had had a lukewarm bucket-bath, being careful not to get my bandage wet. I found the sky-blue shimmery dress I was to wear and dressed myself in it, easing the scratchy taffeta lining down my back. I pinned my hair in a clumsy French roll — the first time I'd ever tried to do it myself. I put on my new white high-heeled shoes. I felt burning hot and icy cold, angry and sad, furious with my mother one minute, and in the next, devastated, aching for my lost family.

Roshan needed help. I dressed her, combed her thick, curly hair into two fat plaits and tied them with ribbons in a lopsided bow. We could hear my mother outside, greeting the first guests. Her voice through the open windows was high-pitched, laughing, charming the men and women she had invited to my birthday party. People I had never met before.

As I walked down the stairs with Roshan, I was scared. My skin felt wide open, as though every pore was a doorway through which any passerby could walk uninvited into my soul.

Standing in our round marble hallway, I saw fifty or sixty people out in the garden, most of them Westerners with pink-and-white skin. They were taller than most Indians, and their hair was bright gold or brown. One woman even had red hair like a carrot. They had broad, meaty shoulders and necks as stiff and wide as their heads. Even the women looked brawny, as though they ate raw meat every day.

The women wore pastel chiffon or silk dresses down to their calves, and thin, high-heeled sandals. One or two wore saris, the elegant silk folds hanging awkwardly around the thick bodies and clumsy rolling gait of women unaccustomed to the precise, delicate movements a sari requires of its wearer. The men wore tropical suits made of raw silk or linen, silk ties, and polished leather shoes. I got an impression of foreign bodies, foreign clothes, a blur of subdued colours, a chatter of voices, some deep, some shrill, wafting smells of foreign perfume.

The members of the band were still tuning their instruments when my mother spotted me standing at the front door. She turned towards me, smiling, gesturing with her hand that I should come out into the garden. I walked over slowly, to where she stood tossing her head gaily at the man standing next to her. "Here she is, my daughter Shahnaz! The birthday girl. Young woman, I should say, she's thirteen today."

The man beside my mother was very tall and cadaverously pale. He bent over and murmured something in her ear. She laughed, a high, tinkling laugh that reminded me of shattering glass. She stepped toward me, holding out her hand, palm up, beckoning me closer. "Shahnaz, come and meet my guests."

She introduced me to the tall man. His name was Graham something. He didn't smell musty, like an Englishman, but he smelled foreign nonetheless. The stink of meat overlaid with a spicy cologne that was like too-strong perfume. He shook my hand. He had an American accent, broad vowels slurred out in a slow, deep voice. "Happy birthday, Shurnaaz," he said, mispronouncing my name, smiling and showing his broad, white teeth. He winked at me as I stood there, flustered, and handed me a square package wrapped in shiny paper and tied with a huge red ribbon.

Before I could say thank you, my mother whipped the package out of my hand and walked over to a nearby table, where there were a number of other packages similarly wrapped in gaily coloured paper, bedecked with ribbons and intricately tied bows. She put Graham's package down beside the others, then caught my hand and pulled me close to her. Putting her mouth next to my ear, she whispered, "These presents are all mine."

I looked at her, bewildered. She was smiling brilliantly, waving to some of her friends. "But I thought he said it was for me, my birthday present."

My mother stopped and glared at me, her mask of smiling ease suddenly turned to an angry frown. "They're my friends, and they've given you these things because of me. Ergo, the gifts belong to me. Q.E.D.," she hissed, triumphantly.

140

I was furious. I didn't want her friends' gifts, they meant nothing to me. But before I could protest any further, she grabbed my hand in hers and pulled me over to introduce me to a group of her friends.

She was scintillating, witty, sparkling like a star, so high-strung I wondered when she'd implode. But no one else seemed to notice anything wrong, so I followed along beside her, meeting people, answering their condescending questions, nodding, smiling till my cheeks ached. "Thank you for the lovely gift. Thank you for coming."

I kept listening for my father's car, kept waiting for him to get home, to put an end to this interminable evening. People ate, and drank. I sat at the head table with my mother and Graham, the American consul and his wife, and the American ambassador to India, who had just flown in from Delhi. When the last course had been cleared away by the uniformed waiters from the Taj, Graham unfolded his long body and stood up, towering above the table. He tapped his wine glass with a teaspoon, making the glass ring until everyone stopped talking and looked up at him.

"Ah'd like to propose a toast," he announced, looking down at my mother's upturned face as tenderly as though he were looking at a newborn. "To our exquisite hostess and my dear friend, Dinaz."

The rest of the people murmured, "To Dinaz," and clinked their glasses together. My mother glowed like a golden flower, her eyes riveted on Graham's cadaverous face as they touched glasses and smiled at each other, oblivious to anyone else.

Then Graham raised his glass again, and in that slurry accent, proclaimed: "Ladies and gentlement, let's drink to the young woman whose birthday we're celebrating tonight." He turned to me and, putting his large, sweaty hand on my arm, pulled me up until my feet almost left the floor. "I give you Shahnaz!"

Everyone clinked glasses again, and clapped and cheered as

though I were a cricket player who had hit for six. Some of them were even vulgar enough to whistle at me. I wanted to sink under the table and disappear! I sat down in my chair, and then everyone began proposing toasts to everything: "To India!" said one portly gentleman at the table next to us, his fat belly bouncing as he raised his glass high. "To the U.S. of A." shrieked a woman who seemed drunk and had one breast half falling out of her red gown. The American ambassador was very quiet, smiled politely and didn't say anything. When he finally did get up — because the band suddenly burst into "Stars And Stripes Forever" — I was astonished to see how very tall he was too.

After that, the band played song after song, taking requests from the guests. "Autumn Leaves," "Stardust," "Misty," "They Can't Take That Away From Me." The singer had a good voice — strong and loud and musical — but her Goanese accent sounded bizarre wrapping itself around these American songs. People got up and danced. I recognized some of the dances — cha-chas, the jive, the tango — from American films I'd seen. I felt as though I was in a film myself, the unreal glitter of fairy-lights, the atmosphere of sophistication and heightened sexuality.

After a short break, the band swung into "All Of Me." My mother got up with Graham. They walked side by side onto the dance floor; she looked achingly beautiful in her burgundy and gold sari. She held out her arms to him. I realized, with a shock of dismay, that the sleeves of her silk choli were very short, and her arms were smooth and bare except for the gold bangles she wore. Graham wrapped his huge hands around her back and swept her across the floor as though she were a silk doll.

I had a round, red headache. My back hurt and I felt like throwing up. I went looking for Roshan, who had been seated at a children's table, but I couldn't find her anywhere in the tent. I walked out into the garden. The sky had deepened to a velvety dark, but the stars seemed very far away, dimmed by the garish light of the coloured lanterns that winked around the garden. The music from the tent rang and clamoured in my head. I couldn't stand it any more, couldn't bear my mother floating like a doll in a foreign man's arms while my father stayed in Bangalore and my family stayed away, banished from our home by my mother.

I went back into the house, upstairs to my room. I closed the windows even though that made my room hot. I had to get away from the din of the party.

I lay awake for a long time, thinking about all that had happened that day, wondering if I would ever see my family or Sunder ayah again. I felt a fearful sadness, as though nothing would ever be the same, yet I couldn't tell what my life would be, from here on. I just knew that it was altered forever, and the world of my childhood was gone, washed out, like the stars, by this new order of party lights.

Chapter 12

Our life in Eugene is about to begin. I have, clutched in my hand, the following: a photocopied map of the Housing Complex, with a big red X marking the site of our apartment — 7A; brochures praising the high academic quality and informal friendliness of the University of Oregon campus and displaying coloured photographs of smiling students strolling across impossibly green lawns; Tourist Bureau maps of Eugene, Springfield, and Lane County, a grid of black lines on a pink background with the Willamette River snaking through, marked in blue; a map of the campus with the Psychology Department, where I will be studying, marked with another red X, the handiwork of a helpful clerk in the Housing Office.

Dangling from the index finger of my right hand are keys to our new apartment. Despite the prosaic nature of the maps and brochures, I am so excited I feel ready to burst as we hurry across campus to Registration and sign up for our fall semester courses. Beginnings thrill me, learning thrills me; this new campus, with its massive trees and emerald vistas, is as exciting to me as my first day in Mrs. Green's kindergarten class when I was three years old.

Classes have already begun. We're two weeks late, thanks to

the delay in getting our visas from the American embassy in New Delhi, but both of us have managed to get into the courses we wanted, and we start tomorrow.

Ann has appointed herself our chauffeur and guardian angel this morning. She takes us to the University Bookstore and helps us find textbooks and notebooks and new, wondrous supplies. I now own half a dozen brightly coloured pens with felt tips.

We load brown paper bags sagging with books and binders and pens into the trunk of Ann's car and drive out to our new apartment. I try to memorize the route, since I'll be walking it every day once we move in. We drive down the main street leading away from the bookstore and turn left at a set of lights onto a broad boulevard lined with trees. The boulevard has wide sidewalks, a few houses set back behind broad-leafed trees, several low commercial buildings tastefully painted in muted colours, trying to look as though they're something other than offices.

Ann says, "We're getting pretty close to the apartment complex now."

On our right is a long, grassy field with a running track laid out with shredded tree-bark along its perimeter. On our left is a low brown building with a sign that says "YMCA" in blue letters. "This is it!" calls Ann, flicking on her turn signal and turning right onto a narrow street. There is a large sign in front of us that proclaims "University of Oregon Married Students' Housing Complex. Welcome!" Someone has inked in a smiling round face beside the "Welcome!" Next to the sign is a large painted map of the complex, which seems to be divided into alphabetically labelled sections, with clusters of numbered apartments in each section.

We drive into what looks like a small village. Tiny, single-story houses, all identically tacky, their once-white paint now moulting in great leprous blotches, flank both sides of a narrow street. Each house has two front doors set side-by-side, each door with a black metal number nailed about a third of the way down from the top. Flimsy houses, about as substantial as the dolls' houses my sister Roshan used to play with. The air is redolent with cooking smells and the sharp green scent of wet grass. I look at the map in my hand. Our apartment should be near here somewhere.

Shahrukh spots it first. "Hey!" he exclaims, excitedly. "There it is, that's 7A." Ann backs up the car and stops beside a peeling front door. 7A indeed. There is a low flight of rickety wooden stairs, painted white. These lead up to a small landing, at the end of which is our new front door. I look at its unpromising exterior and fight a sudden urge to bury my head in Ann's lap and beg her to let me live with her forever. Squaring my shoulders, I step out of the car.

The apartment key sticks in the lock and won't turn. I struggle with it while Shahrukh and Ann carry on a running conversation about the housing complex. "These are all prefab houses, you know," says Ann. "They built 'em for the war vets who flooded into universities on the G.I. Bill in the late forties and early fifties. They were only meant for temporary use, until the administration could build something more permanent. These were built in Canada, I think. Floated south down the Columbia river on big barges, then on the Willamette river all the way to Eugene."

I curse the jammed key under my breath. Ann sounds like an annoyingly perky tour guide. Shahrukh asks, "Is that why they all look as though they've been cut out of cardboard?"

Ann laughs. "Yeah, they're kinda grim looking, aren't they? Actually, the adminstration's been talking about tearing them down for years, but there's such a shortage of cheap student housing, they can't afford to take these down."

Shahrukh laughs. "They look as though they were built for Genghis Khan and his short but mighty hordes, back in the Dark Ages. They're puny!"

Ann shrugs her shoulders. "Well," she says, "the University Housing Department built a brand new condo complex a coupla years ago. It's real nice, but it's miles away. You pretty much have to have a car to live there, and the rents are twice as high. So not many people want to live there. Meanwhile, believe it or not, this dump has a waiting list. You guys are lucky you sent in your housing application back in the spring, or you'd end up having to live way out in condo-town."

All this while I've been jiggling the key back and forth, trying to get it to turn in the lock, or, failing that, at least to get it out in one piece. Now, suddenly, it turns with a click. I twist the doorknob and try to open the door, which seems to be jammed too. Shahrukh puts his shoulder against the door and pushes hard. The door creaks open reluctantly. A whiff of pine-scented disinfectant strongly flavoured with mildew wafts into our nostrils. I sneeze. Shahrukh wrinkles his nose in disgust and pushes the door inward with his foot.

The first thing I notice, as we step inside, is the ceiling. It is low, its contours sagging miserably, like the belly of a very fat man. I can stand on tiptoe and touch it with my fingers, and I'm only five foot five in my flat-heeled boots. It seems to hover mockingly above me, a reminder of all the spacious, elegant rooms I have left behind. It leers at me, daring me to befriend its grease stains and call its peeling yellowed paint my home. I burst into tears.

The rest of the apartment is not as completely dreadful as I had supposed. Once I've had a good cry — as my Perin aunty would put it — I am able to appreciate the wide windows along one wall of the living-dining-kitchen-all-purpose main room. They let in lots of light as well as a draft of icy cold air, and overlook a grassy playing field. Under the windows is a preposterous little couch covered in tweedy mustard fabric, flanked by two mismatched chairs. Hanging grimly over it all are a set of bedraggled flowered curtains that look as though they may have begun life as bedsheets.

Ann is bubbling about, opening kitchen cupboards, peering into closets, chattering away enthusiastically. Shahrukh has

147

found the bathroom, which seems to be where the mildew smell is strongest. He calls me over.

"Hey, Shahnaz! Take a look at this. How the hell am I supposed to take a crap in a loo like this? If I sit down on that toilet seat my knees will hit the wall! This is pathetic!"

I walk over to the bathroom and peek in past Shahrukh's bulk. He's right. The bathroom is as long and narrow as a coffin, with a tiny ochre toilet at the far end, a shower just inside the door, and a small, cracked yellow sink between the two.

"Hey, Shahrukh," I tease, "now I can use the bathroom without getting up at the crack of dawn to beat you to the loo." Shahrukh hogs the bathroom each morning; it's a sore point between us.

Ann calls from the kitchen. "Hey, you guys, we should go over to Albertsons and buy you some cleaning stuff. You know, mop, broom, dustpan, that sort of thing. There're no carpets in here, so you won't need a vacuum cleaner."

"In a minute!" I call back. "I just want to take a quick look at the bedrooms, then we can go."

I open the door to one of the bedrooms and poke my head in. It is tiny, a square cubicle with the ceiling sagging overhead like a lowering cloud. It contains a single bed, a small, battered-looking wooden desk, and a plain wooden chair. A desolate little room, icy cold — I can feel the cold air seeping in through the paper-thin walls.

The second bedroom is only marginally bigger — same blank white walls, low ceiling, one tiny window. Dark. Mouldy. Cold.

I hear the hyperactive blare of a TV announcer's voice burst out in the living room. Shahrukh calls out, "Hey, there's an old black and white TV in here."

Suddenly, I can't wait to get out of this apartment. "Ann," I call, "let's go get whatever it is we need from Albertson's. We can pick up our bags from your place after we've finished shopping."

I turn away from the bedroom door to find Ann standing right behind me. She puts her hand on my shoulder, and gives it a little squeeze. "Hey, you know, you don't have to move in today. You can wait until you're ready; I've got lots of room."

I smile at her, grateful for her offer, but shake my head. "I think we ought to settle in as soon as possible. I want to start classes tomorrow." Then I think, dolefully, I want to go home!

Ann opens the front door. Shahrukh is sitting on the mustard couch, looking like a large baby. His big brown eyes are fixed on the tiny TV set, his chin resting on one dimpled fist. He has the sated look of an infant who's found his mother's nipple. I call him, but he doesn't hear me.

Chapter 13

I sat on the bench outside Miss Lambert's office, waiting. The corridor in that wing of our school was quiet, except for the rumble of traffic outside the school walls. There were no classrooms on the upper floor, only the principal's office, the staff dining room, a conference room, and the school library. My watch said 2:05. I'd been here for fifteen minutes, but I didn't mind waiting. We were in the middle of a maths test when the monitor had stopped by with a summons from the principal. I was in no hurry to get back to class.

I wondered what Miss Lambert wanted. I hadn't done anything wrong, so I couldn't be in trouble. Besides, she liked me, in her rather grim, English way. She'd known me since the day I was born. My mother and she were friends. Or they used to be, before mum became ill and we stopped inviting people over to our house. Miss Lambert hadn't visited us for ages.

When I looked up my eyes were level with the top of the giant peepul tree that stood in the middle of the hockey field. Its heart-shaped green leaves rustled in the slight breeze which stirred the sultry afternoon air. A dog barked somewhere in the distance, and, with a rushing of wings, a flock of parrots fluttered upward from the branches of the tree. The birds spread their green wings, uttering harsh cries as they wheeled off into the sky. I followed them with my eyes, into the blue vault of the sky. I stood up and leaned over the parapet to catch the small breeze on my face.

I was hot and uncomfortable. The laundry had put too much starch in my white uniform pinafore. It chafed against the burn on my shoulder where my mother had thrown a bowl of hot dahl at me, a few days earlier. Dr. Joseph had put Burnol on it and bandaged it for me, but the bandage rubbed against my skin, and my starchy uniform made it worse.

"Shernaz!" I heard Miss Lambert call my name. She gave it a pronunciation all her own. I turned around. "Come in, child. Don't stand there day-dreaming; I don't have all day."

"I beg your pardon, Miss Lambert." I hurried past her into the dim coolness of her office. She followed, closing the door behind her. "Sit down, Shernaz," she said, sounding brisk and impatient. She settled herself behind her desk, which was massive, and polished to such a high gloss that I could see my face reflected in it. I lowered myself into a chair, keeping my knees and ankles together, placing my hands in my lap. Miss Lambert made me nervous. I knew I hadn't done anything wrong, but I felt guilty and anxious. She looked at me appraisingly, her face stern, her pale blue eyes nailing me to my seat.

"How are you, Shernaz?" she asked.

"I'm very well, thank you," I replied, wondering where this would lead.

"And how is your mother?"

"She . . . she's been unwell."

"I see. What is the matter with her?"

I didn't know what to say.

"Well? Go on."

"Uhh . . . she's had a nervous breakdown."

"Indeed. And what does that mean?"

"She spends a lot of time in bed."

"Yes . . . ?"

"And she sometimes gets quite agitated, upset."

"Hmf. What does your father say to all this?"

"He's away at the moment. In Delhi. On business," I stammered.

"Ah. How long has he been away?"

"He . . . he has a flat there. He comes home when he can."

"So he's living there, is he?"

"Not exactly. He still lives at home, it's just that he has a lot of work in Delhi and . . ."

"When was the last time you saw him, Shernaz?"

"Last month." I felt my face flush. "He's very busy. They've opened a new office in Delhi. He's just there to get it established, then he'll come home."

"Last month did you say? In October?"

"Yes. He was home for three or four days."

"And now it's the end of November."

"Yes, Miss Lambert."

"Who looks after your mother while your father is away?"

"I do. And Dr. Pereira looks in on her each morning."

"And who looks after you?"

"I take care of myself. I don't need anyone to look after me."

"I see. Stop wriggling, child. What is that untidy bulge under your uniform? On your right shoulder."

"Oh, that. It's nothing. I hurt myself. I have a bandage on. I'm sorry."

"Have you had it seen to by your doctor?"

"Yes, it's quite all right."

"Hmf. Your teachers tell me you haven't been submitting your homework on time lately. What have you to say for yourself?"

"I'm sorry Miss Lambert."

"Shernaz, you are a very bright young woman. This is your last year of school. It's important that you pay attention and do well in your A Levels. Have you thought of what you might like to do, once you're finished?"

"No. I suppose I'll go to college."

"Righto. But where will you go to college?"

"I . . . I thought St. Xavier's, or Elphinstone perhaps."

"Hmm. They're both fine colleges, but rather parochial. You've had the very best education, here at Queen Anne's. I'd like to see you carry on and make something of yourself."

"Yes, Miss Lambert."

"Have you thought about going to university abroad?"

"Abroad? You mean, to England?"

"Yes. I went to Trinity College, myself. Rather a good school."

"I . . . I'd never given it a thought."

"Well, give it some thought now. You don't have much longer to go before you sit your A Levels."

"Thank you, Miss Lambert."

"I haven't finished yet. Now. Miss Merriweather seems to think you have the makings of a rather good thespian. She has just returned from her annual furlough in England and she's asked me to speak to you about a jolly interesting proposition." Miss Lambert paused. I looked at her mutely, my mind racing with new possibilities. Could I really go to university in England?

"Shernaz!" Miss Lambert's voice was sharp.

"Oh, sorry, Miss Lambert."

"Pay attention, young woman. Miss Merriweather spoke to some people about you, while she was in England. She has an offer for you. A fellowship to study acting for three years at the Bristol Old Vic Theatre School. You will, of course, have to get a First Class on your A Levels."

I stared at her blankly.

Miss Lambert's ice-blue eyes glimmered with a hint of warmth. "You really must pay attention, child. Did you hear what I just said?"

"Yes, Miss Lambert."

"We shall have to speak to your father, of course."

"I . . . I don't think he'll let me go all the way to England."

"I shall speak to him myself. Write down his Delhi telephone number for me. I will ring him this evening." Miss Lambert pushed a pad of paper across the desk. She took a pencil from her drawer and leaned forward to hand it to me. I took it from her. My mind was as blank as the sheet of paper in front of me. I couldn't remember my own name, let alone my father's phone number. Miss Lambert had that effect on me.

She looked at me with that stern expression that made me quail. But her voice, when she spoke, was gentle. "Go on, child, write down your father's telephone number. Then I'd like you to go to the sick bay, and let Miss Chacko take a look at that shoulder. We don't want it to get infected."

I scribbled my father's name and phone number on the piece of paper, pressing so hard in my anxiety that I broke the lead of the pencil. I flushed and muttered an apology, but Miss Lambert dismissed me with a brisk nod of her head.

I walked slowly towards the sick bay, my head filled with new possibilities. I could leave. Just go. To England.

My father telephoned me that night. I was brushing my teeth when the phone rang. Wiping my mouth on the sleeve of my nightgown, I ran to answer the phone before my mother could pick up. My father sounded upset. Miss Lambert had rung him up and given him a tongue-lashing about leaving me alone at home with Mum.

"What did you say to her?" he asked.

"Nothing, daddy. She wanted to know what was wrong with Mummy. I told her she had a nervous breakdown."

"Shahnaz, you shouldn't be talking about our family's business with outsiders." He had that disappointed tone in his voice that made me want to crawl under my bed and hide.

"She asked me. I didn't know what to say."

"And what's all this nonsense about going to England?"

My breath caught in my throat. "Miss Meriweather arranged for me to study at the Bristol Old Vic Theatre School. Daddy, that's a real honour. I'd learn so much if I went; its the best Shakespearean repertory company in the world."

"It is out of the question, beta. Your mother is not well. I am in Delhi. Someone has to be there to take care of her."

"Why can't she go to Delhi with you? Or live with Perin aunty? I want to go, please, daddy! I'll work hard, I'll do well in my A levels, please?"

"You're not even fourteen years old. That's too young to go all the way to England by yourself. Besides, I can't afford to send you to England for three years. It is just not possible."

"But I'll be fourteen by the time I finish my A levels. And you won't have to pay for it, Miss Lambert said there was a fellowship."

"It's out of the question. When Mummy is better I'll take you there for a holiday."

"I don't want to go for a holiday. I want to go and study there. I could be a good actress, Miss Meriweather said so."

"Actress! That is not a profession for a Parsi girl. It may be all right for Westerners, but . . ."

"You always said I could be whatever I wanted. Now I have the chance to do something I really love!"

"We'll discuss this when I come home."

"You're coming home? When?"

"Miss Lambert wants to have a meeting with me next Thursday. I will fly in on Wednesday afternoon."

"You're really coming home? How long can you stay?"

"Only two days. I have a big case to prepare for, and I have to be back in Delhi as soon as possible. This is a very inconvenient time for me to leave here."

In the end, my father refused to let me go. I cried and pleaded and sulked, but it was no use. He had made up his mind. I was to stay in Bombay with my mother.

Chapter 14

The first time I meet Patrick, he is sitting in his office with his feet on his desk, talking on the phone. He has been assigned as my graduate advisor by the psychology department. I had phoned him earlier in the week to set up an appointment, and am standing nervously outside his office door, waiting for him to get off the phone. He is swivelling around in his chair, chatting, his big feet in their hiking boots arcing back and forth across his desktop. He glances up and sees me, then motions with his hand for me to come in. I look for someplace to sit, but every available surface of his office is covered in books and papers. He leans over, holding the phone between his shoulder and his neck, and lifts a pile of papers off a chair. He drops them on the floor, pulling a rueful face, and gestures for me to sit. I smile, sit down, and try not to listen to his end of the phone conversation. It sounds as though he's making arrangements to play basketball this evening.

I look at him out of the corner of my eye as he talks on the phone. He doesn't look like any professor I've ever met. His knees stick out, bony and awkward, where the legs of his blue jeans are ripped. I think of my psychology professor back at Elphinstone college, who always dressed in three piece Harris tweed suits with an Oxford tie, and wonder if all the faculty dress like hobos here. Patrick's jeans are hiked up over his ankles, his long legs encased in coarse grey wool socks, folded over brown leather hiking boots. He reaches across his desk to grab a pencil, and I notice the right sleeve of his sweater is unravelling at the wrist. He grins and winks at me, then finishes his conversation and hangs up the phone.

Leaning forward precariously in his swivel chair he sticks out his hand and says, "Hi! I'm Patrick Wells. You're my new graduate student?"

"Yes. I'm Shahnaz Shroff." I shake his hand, which is large and dry and warm.

"Where're you from, Shahnaz?" He pronounces my name with the exact intonation I've given to it, which impresses me more than I care to acknowledge.

"Bombay. We've only been here a few days," I reply.

"Far out! Must be an exciting place, Bombay. I'm from Boston, back on the East Coast. Oregon's new to me too; I've only been here a year. What brings you here?"

"My husband and I applied to a number of American graduate schools. U of O was the first to offer both of us a place," I say.

"I'll be damned. You came all the way from Bombay to go to university here? Either you really wanted to be in the United States, or you couldn't wait to leave home. Which was it?"

A window opens in my heart. "A bit of both," I say. "My mother spent a couple of years in Washington, DC, when I was a child. I decided, back then, that I would come here some day."

"And?" he prompts.

"And I wanted to get away from Bombay," I admit, reluctant to go into the reasons why. I open my bag and take out a file folder. "I have some ideas here for a thesis topic. I'd like to go over them with you. Perhaps you could suggest some topics too?"

"Changing the subject, huh?" Patrick smiles, his voice teasing.

"Maybe when I know you better I'll tell you more," I reply, smiling back.

157

"Tell you what. Let's go get some lunch at the pub around the corner. I'm starved, and they make a mean Reuben."

I am flustered by this sudden invitation to lunch, but have no way of knowing what passes for normal in this very strange country. "Yes, that would be fine," I reply, trying to imagine what a Mean Reuben is.

We walk down to the pub, Patrick in his parka and tattered blue jeans, with his knapsack slung across one shoulder, me clicking along beside him in my black wool dress and knee-high Bally boots. Patrick greets the waitress by name, and asks her if she's managed to get into all the classes she wants. They chat for a couple of minutes while she clears a table for us by the window. The pub is noisy and packed with students. There are parkas and knapsacks and open books at every table.

Patrick orders a Reuben and a cup of coffee. I request a bowl of clam chowder. He asks me about my family; about Bombay, school, my friends, my views on everything from American food to Indian politics. I am shy, at first, and uncertain of how to behave with a man who is to be my thesis supervisor, but Patrick is as friendly as a puppy. The more I talk, the more questions he asks, probing with an insistence that leaves me feeling uncomfortable, but curiously relieved. Somehow, his openness about himself, his eagerness to know me, makes it okay for me to be open too.

We end up talking for a couple of hours, oblivious of the time, until Patrick slaps his forehead in mock dismay and says, "I've gotta go. I have a date!"

I look at my watch and realize I've missed my Marriage and Family Therapy seminar. We walk back together to the Psychology department building, and as I collect my things from my locker, I find myself smiling.

On the walk home, bits of our conversation drift through my head. I've made a new friend.

Chapter 15

Our house was hollow with silence on my fourteenth birthday. There was no one left to remember, or help me celebrate. Most of the rooms were closed, the high ceilings cobwebbed, the furniture swathed in white canvas dustsheets. Everything smelled of monsoon mildew, and of the napthalene mothballs and tobacco leaves Perin aunty had laid over the upholstery to keep it from being ravaged by moths.

My mother and I had been living alone in the house for nine months. We lived like two ghosts, side by side, in adjoining rooms. When she was depressed, she seldom spoke to me. I would look in on her each day before I left for school. I'd bring her her breakfast of fruit and curds, toast and strong Nilgiri tea. When I returned home in the late afternoon, she'd be in bed, huddled under the heavy winter quilt, curled up like a snail in its shell. Most days, her tray of food lay untouched on her bedside table. She would not get out of bed to eat or bathe or do anything other than go to the loo. Her hair remained unwashed, her body smelled as musty as the rest of the house. She would not let me open the windows in her room.

My father's law firm opened a branch office in New Delhi that year. He was away for up to three months at a time, returning for a couple of days before flying out again. I remember the precise moment when he told me he was leaving. It remains embedded like a thumbprint on my brain. We were eating breakfast, just the two of us, at our long dining table built to seat twenty four. My mother was in one of her depressive phases then; she hadn't emerged from her room in days. My sister was away at boarding school.

It was a Saturday morning. My father suggested we go and see an exhibit of Mughal miniatures at the museum that afternoon. I smiled at him, sleepy and replete with happiness at having him all to myself for an entire day. I reached into the fruit bowl and picked up a ripe guava, sinking my teeth into its juicy flesh, savouring its cardamom fragrance.

That's when he turned to me and said, "I have to go to Delhi for a while, Shahnu." He glanced at me out of the corners of his eyes, then looked down at his plate.

"Why?" I demanded, blurting the word out. Realizing I'd been rude, I backtracked quickly. "I mean, why do you have to go?"

"We're opening a branch office in Delhi. You know your Fali Kaka has been travelling there and back several times each month. But since he had his heart attack he hasn't been able to keep up. We need someone on the spot to handle our business in the North."

"But . . . what about mummy? She's sick. Who will take care of her?" I felt suddenly nauseous. My throat was stiff; the guava stuck in my throat, the skin too fibrous, the flesh too blatantly fragrant to swallow. I pushed my plate away.

"Beta, this is a very difficult time. There is a lot of pressure at work; it is necessary that I go. You've always been my strong girl. I must rely on you now to take care of your mother while I'm away." My father looked down at his plate again, and would not meet my eyes.

"How long will you be away?"

"I don't know, Shahnaz. I have to find an office, hire staff, arrange for someone to handle renovations and furnishings and so on. Also, it takes a long time to get permits from the government. It is very difficult to say." He looked at me then, his eyes watery, like fresh curds, behind the thick lenses of his glasses. He took a forkful of omelette into his mouth and chewed. I could hear my own breath loud in my ears.

"When will you leave?"

"Tomorrow. My plane leaves at three."

"Tomorrow! But . . . who's going to take care of mummy and me? I have school. I can't stay at home to look after her. What if she starts getting angry again, what will I do?"

My father took off his glasses and slowly polished the lenses with his handkerchief. He looked so vulnerable, his eyes blinking against the light like the eyes of some nocturnal animal.

When he finally spoke it was in a slow, trailing voice. "Beta, someone has to earn money to take care of this family. Your mummy's treatments are very expensive. Each time she sees Dr. Pereira, it costs me fifteen hundred rupees. That's over seven thousand rupees weekly, only for doctor's fees. Then there are medicines she has to take. They come from Switzerland. They are very expensive also. And the shock treatments. She goes into the hospital for three, four weeks, I get a bill for half a lakh, sometimes more. On top of that, I have to pay Roshan's school fees, and . . ." His voice trailed off. He rubbed his eyes, pressing his thumb and forefinger into the inside edges of the sockets.

I had never heard him talk about money before. I felt sick, hot and shivery all at once, the way I did when I had chicken pox. "Are we in trouble, daddy? Are we going to be poor?"

"No no Beta, nothing to worry about. I just have to pay more attention to my business. I have been so preoccupied with your mummy's illness, that the business has suffered."

"I'm sorry. I'll manage here 'till you get back. You are coming back, aren't you?"

"Of course, Shahnu. You are my life, Beta. Where would I go without you? I'll return as soon as I can. But I won't be able to stay here for long, I'll have to leave again. Your Dina aunty is looking for a flat for me in Delhi."

161

"You mean you'll be living there, and we'll be here? I want to come with you. Don't leave me here alone with Mummy, please! I can go to school in Delhi; I won't be any trouble, I promise."

My father smiled and shook his head. "You are never any trouble, my jaan, but I can't take you with me. Someone has to stay here with your mother. The gunga will come every morning, to clean the house. I've already talked to Mahrukh Antia about sending meals, so all that will be taken care of."

I opened my mouth to protest, but he continued in a rush: "And Dr. Pereira will be here. He'll see your mother daily. I will leave his home phone number right here next to the phone, in case there is any problem on the weekends."

I could see he had already made up his mind. There was no use arguing.

My father spoke again, in that grave voice that made me want to cry. "Shahnaz, I will leave money with your mummy for the household expenses. But you should have some money too, just in case."

I shook my head. I didn't want to think of a "just in case."

"Beta, look at me. Come, now. You are my brave girl. Here." He reached into his briefcase, which was standing beside his chair, clicked it open and pulled out a thick package of hundred rupee notes. He tore open the paper band that held them together and, licking his thumb, counted off ten of the purple notes. They smelled of fresh ink and new paper, crinkled crisply in my hand. I stuffed them into my pocket, pushed my chair back and ran from the room.

We didn't go to the museum that afternoon. I hid in my mango tree while my father called and called my name. When I returned from school the next day, he was gone.

My little sister, Roshan, was in boarding school in Simla that year. She wrote me long letters on grubby scraps of ruled paper smudged with whatever she'd been eating at the time. She was very homesick. I hadn't seen her for several months, although she would be home soon for the rainy season holidays. In her last letter she said she'd become chubby as a jackfruit. The other girls teased her, calling her Fattyface and Jellybelly. She said she hated boarding school. The food was awful. They served custard that looked like baby poop for an after-dinner sweet every night. She couldn't wait to come home for the holidays and would I please send her a big tin of Cadbury's chocolates in her next parcel of tuck.

I wrote to her every week. Long, rambling letters, telling her about school, and the play I was rehearsing for, and who was wearing what in Bombay that season. I bought her treats with the money my father had given me, and sent her a parcel of tuck every couple of weeks. I never told her how it really was at home, that she was better off in Simla.

Since my mother had sacked all of our servants, we'd had a succession of ayahs and gungas and cooks. None of them stayed longer than a few days or a couple of weeks at the most. Either she fired them for crimes and misdemeanours that existed primarily in her paranoid imagination, or they quit. Some left because she refused to pay them. Others were terrified and ran away when they woke to the sight of her leering face hanging moonlike over their bedrolls, or saw her brandishing a kitchen knife and then laughing madly as they scampered away to safety.

On one of his brief visits home, my father told me that Ali, a Muslim cook who had worked for us for a couple of months, had threatened retaliation for the insults and chappals which my mother had hurled at him before she sacked him. For several months after that the wrought-iron gate at the end of our driveway was locked, and we had a chaprassi who patrolled the grounds of our house at night. I would fall asleep to the thumping of his stick against the ground, as he marched up and down around the perimeter of our compound. It comforted me to know he was there.

Eventually, though, my mother quarrelled with the chaprassi and sacked him too. So for nine months we had been alone, just the two of us.

We made do with meals catered by Miss Antia. My father paid her handsomely to cook for us in the safety of her own kitchen. Our dinners were delivered in hot aluminum tiffin carriers by a boxwallah, who brought them to our back door shortly after I returned home from school each evening.

My school was called Queen Anne's. I had been there since kindergarten, so all the teachers and staff had known me since I was four years old. Each morning I put on my pleated white uniform — delivered by the laundry man at 7 a.m. — tied my maroon woolen sash around my waist, and pinned my School badge and House badge to my chest. I laced on my white canvas shoes, combed my hair in two thick braids and tied the ends with black satin bows, hauled my satchel over my shoulder and went out onto the front porch to wait for my grandmother's car.

I was in my last year of high school. My best friend Dilly always waited for me in the morning, underneath the peepul tree which stood in the middle of the hockey field. We'd have a half hour to talk before the first bell rang. Dilly'd tell me about what she and her family had done the night before; I'd tell her about how my mother had kept me up all night, how she had found the money my father had given me and taken it away from me. Dilly became the repository of all my sadness and loneliness. She took it like a trooper. She'd hug me, listen patiently as I sobbed out my latest heartbreak. Then she'd wipe my tears with her handkerchief and we'd walk up the broad teak stairs to our classroom.

After school I'd walk with Dilly to her house, which was just across the railroad tracks, a few blocks away from the school. We'd spend a couple of hours together, talking, doing homework, playing Scrabble or chess until my grandmother's chauffeur came for me and I had to go home.

I loved Dilly's family. I wished they'd adopt me. I wanted to live at her house. I wanted her mother to be my mother.

Dilly's house was suffused with happiness. Her father was a handsome, balding man who played tennis with her mother several times a week. They'd come in flushed and laughing in their tennis whites as we sat at their dining table having an after-school snack of bhelpuri. Dilly's dad joked and teased the way my father used to do before my mother's illness. Her mother was a grey-haired woman with a serene face and smiling, honey-coloured eyes. She was several years older than Dilly's father, who openly adored her. They'd sit close together on the living room sofa, shoulders and hips touching. They were the only married couple I had ever seen holding hands.

Dilly's brother, Rohinton, was her same-egg twin. They used to look exactly alike when they were younger, but by the time they turned thirteen both of them had changed in so many ways that they no longer looked like identical twins. Rohinton went to Cathedral Boys' School. He came home in a green school bus with his school's name painted in white on the sides. He'd walk in the door, drop his satchel on the floor in the entryway and head straight for his room. A few minutes later, we'd hear him tuning his violin. Then he'd play for an hour or more — exquisite, tender music which made me want to laugh and cry and twirl about. Drawn by the music, I would stand, entranced, in the doorway of his room. He played with his eyes closed, his body bending into the music like a reed leaning into the wind, an expression of such joy on his long, narrow face that I wanted to stay there forever.

At five-thirty on the dot, my grandparents' black Daimler arrived to pick me up and take me home. I'd open my book and read all the way from Dilly's house to mine. My grandparents' chauffeur, an elderly Parsi gentleman named Mr. Manek, was an old-fashioned man who would not let me talk to him or ride in the front seat with him. I'd look up from time to time and see him crane his head this way and that as he negotiated through the honking, seething traffic. The back of his neck was brown and wrinkled, his large head pinkly bald under his peaked cap. He would pull into our gravelled driveway, stop the car and come around the back to open my door for me. Then he'd hold his uniformed arm courteously akimbo to help me out of the back seat. I'd stand and watch him as he drove away. I'd walk through our ruined gardens for a while, kicking at the pebbles on the paths, reluctant to go inside and face whatever fresh hell my mother had cooked up for the day.

Perin aunty had told me, on one of the few visits I had with her that year, that my mother had a disease with an actual name — manic-depressive disorder. She explained that this was what caused my mother's moods to go up and down. I was too embarrassed to tell her about the circle of Willis and the theory about brain damage that Roshan and I had devised to explain my mother's behaviour. But I was also excited by the information Perin aunty gave me — somehow, I felt that if Mum's illness had a name, it was less mysterious, maybe even curable. Eager to know more, I asked Perin aunty a lot of questions. But she didn't want to talk about it and was in a hurry to get back to her clinic.

I looked up manic-depressive in my Encyclopedia Brittanica. The disease, it said, was caused by an as yet unidentified imbalance in brain chemistry, which could be corrected by giving the patient lithium carbonate, a chemical compound derived from an alkali metal group that had been used for years in industrial applications. There was some evidence that the disorder might be hereditary. Your chances of getting it were greater if your parents or close relatives were affected.

For days after I read this, I went around looking at myself in mirrors, wondering if, under my smooth skin and clear brown eyes there lurked a monster, waiting to devour me. I could almost see its face, green and warty — long yellow teeth bared in a vicious grin, drool dribbling down its pointy chin. It lay coiled, cunning as a snake, waiting for me to relax my vigilance and fall asleep. Then it would come roaring out, and destroy my life.

Meanwhile, my mother was getting stranger every day. She slept all day when she was depressed. When she was manic, there was no telling what she'd do next. There was the time she went out on the street in her nightgown and tried to drag a bewildered beggar into our house. The poor man was hunched over on the front porch, clinging to the railings, while my mother yanked at the back of his dhoti with both hands, determined to get him inside. When my father and I drove up, she was shrieking at him, in English, telling him the White House had sent her to bring him back where he belonged. As we got out of the car, the fellow jabbered wildly in Marathi, his eyes rolling in terror, paan juice dribbling down his chin. He took advantage of the momentary distraction provided by our arrival, and scuttled away from my mother. He ran down the driveway, clutching his dhoti and calling out to his gods to save him from the mad woman.

One of these manic episodes took place at my school. I thought I'd never live it down.

From February until mid-April of that year, I was busy with rehearsals for our school play. We were performing Julius Caesar. I played Mark Antony. I had a purple toga which Mr. Hamidullah, our tailor, had made for me out of one of Perin aunty's old silk saris. My hair was cut very short, Roman style, in preparation for our opening performance.

Three weeks before opening night, my mother began pestering me for tickets to the play. I tried to talk her out of coming and told her it would bore her because the play was long and tedious. But she was adamant. She wanted a ticket. I got her one, but kept forgetting to bring it home from school. I hoped that, if I left it long enough, she would become obsessed with something else. But the longer I stalled, the more determined she became. Eventually, she rang up the school and got a ticket from the principal's office.

Opening night arrived. The auditorium was packed with teachers, students and their families. The curtain rose. I looked, from the wings, for my mother, but her seat was empty. I almost laughed out loud with relief. I went on, played my part, became absorbed in Mark Antony's complex game.

I was in the middle of my first big soliloquy — in the middle of Act 3, after Caesar's murder — when she walked into the auditorium. She made a lot of noise coming in. She banged the door behind her, and stumbled in the dim light of the auditorium. I looked up and saw her. My whole body flushed hot with shame. She swept down the aisle wearing a pink negligee which she had brought back with her from America. Underneath, she had on what looked like her gold brocade wedding sari. She wore so much gold jewellery that she jangled as she walked to her seat, which was in the very first row, right in front of the stage. I froze for a moment, and turned to run offstage. But that would have ruined the play, so I made myself turn back. Shakespeare's lines flowed from my mouth like water from a tap.

> Blood and destruction shall be so in use,
> And dreadful objects so familiar,
> That mothers shall but smile when they behold
> Their infants quartered with the hands of war
> All pity choked with custom of fell deeds . . .

And all the while part of me drifted up to the ceiling, looked down on the scene below. A sibilant susurration floated up from the audience. People turned to stare at my mother, craning their necks and whispering amongst themselves.

Somehow, I made it through to the end of Act Three. When the curtain came down, I fled to the bathroom and sat shaking on the toilet. By the time I returned to the stage for the opening of Act Four, my mother was no longer in her seat, which remained empty for the rest of the evening.

An even more bizarre incident happened a few months later. It started one evening, when I got home from school. My mother wasn't home. At first, I was relieved. But when it became dark and she hadn't returned, I grew worried. Frightened about where she might be, or what might have happened to her, I tried ringing my father first, but the lines to New Delhi were down and the operator could not tell me when they would be repaired. I was scared.

I phoned my grandparents. My grandmother said she was sure my mother was all right and would come home in a while. She couldn't leave my grandfather, who had had a stroke recently and who got upset if she left his side for more than a few minutes. I was not to worry, but should go to bed as usual, and phone her in the morning.

Next, I rang Perin aunty, who had been away for a week. She told me to hang up the phone. She would try to contact my father and would ring me back.

I did as I was told. As soon as I rang off, the phone shrilled, startling me. It was the duty officer for Air France at Bombay's Santacruz Airport; a Mr. Dasgupta. I had never met him, but he knew my parents. He said my mother was creating a scene, holding up a flight to Paris which she insisted on boarding. She had no passport or papers with her. He said she had urinated in her clothes and was giving away her jewelley to passersby. He needed someone to come and get her. I told him I was trying to reach my father. He sounded worried, but told me he would take my mother into the staff room and keep her there. He asked me to try and get someone to collect her as soon as possible.

I hung up and a few moments later, Perin aunty phoned back. She hadn't been able to reach my father either. I told her about the phone call from Mr. Dasgupta. She sighed and said she would ring Dr. Pereira. She'd arrange for him to go out to the airport with an ambulance. He would admit my mother into his clinic for a while.

That night I was completely alone in the house. I couldn't sleep. I switched on my bedside light every time I heard a noise. Once it was a lizard rustling along the wall. Another time it was something crawling through the bushes outside, a field mouse, or a rat. The night seemed very long. I was relieved when morning came, and I could go to school.

In between her depressive and manic phases there were a few days when my mother was almost normal. She did ordinary things like bathe and eat and sleep. She didn't scream and throw things across the room, or whimper in bed in the fetal position. She would read, go for walks in the garden, do the Times of India crossword puzzle. Sometimes she even talked to me.

We had had several relatively calm days together. I found myself holding my breath when I was around her, waiting for the inevitable manic phase to begin. One afternoon I returned home from school later than usual, having spent a couple of hours at my friend Dilly's house. I walked in through the front door of our home, alert for sounds or smells that might tell me my fragile peace was about to end.

When my mother swung into manic mode, she became louder, noisier, a boastful, swaggering caricature of her previous self. And she smelled — a peculiar, musty smell that resembled nothing so much as a dead mouse. This smell permeated her skin, seemed to come from deep in the recesses of her body. It surrounded her, a deadly aura I had learned to take note of and avoid.

As I walked in the front door that day, I could smell her particular smell, even in the hallway. The house was very quiet. My whole body became alert, all of me one great listening ear, trying to sense her presence: which room was she in, what mood dominated that day? Nothing. I couldn't sense where she was. This made my skin crawl. The backs of my ears turned hot with anticipation and dread.

Cautiously, I set my satchel down on the hall table. I took

off my shoes and socks and walked in my bare feet to peer into the living room. She wasn't there. I tiptoed into the dining room, although I really didn't think I'd find her there either. I was buying time, avoiding the inevitable. I began climbing up the curved wooden staircase, holding onto the banister, listening for sounds upstairs.

When I got to the top of the stairs, the door to her room was open. The smell of dead mouse invaded my nostrils, and I swallowed hard against the bile rising in my throat. Padding quietly to her door, I looked in. Her bed was unmade, her room a mess. Clothes lay tossed on the floor, piled on her high, four-poster bed, strewn across the chaise longue that stretched underneath her window. Her dinner from last night had congealed and lay uneaten on a tray on the floor. My foot caught the edge of the tray. The silence was shattered by the clanging of silver and china. A cluster of brown cockroaches scurried across the floor to disappear under the bed. I screamed when I saw them, ran out of the room down the hall to my bedroom.

My mother was sitting on my bed, holding my diary open on her lap. She looked up, a triumphant smile on her face. Her eyes glittered in a way that made me tremble.

"So," she began, calmly enough, raising her eyebrows at me. "You think I'm crazy."

Picking up my diary, she put on her glasses and began reading out loud, her voice rising unnaturally, as though she were reciting from a poem or a play: Mummy scares me. Last night she came and woke me, shaking me hard until I surfaced from sleep. Her eyes were wild, and she kept laughing like a maniac. She dragged me, half-asleep, to her room. She had pulled all her clothes out of her cupboards and drawers and thrown them all over her room. She told me I had to sort them out and put them back. I told her she was crazy, it was two o'clock in the morning and I had school in a few hours. Then she went completely berserk, slapping me and calling me a whore and screaming at me as she dragged me around the room by my hair. It hurt so much I finally begged her to stop and said I would do whatever she wanted me to. I hate her so much I wish she'd die!

I looked down at the floor as she read, my face burning with shame.

"So this is what you think of me. You think I'm crazy. I gave birth to you. You owe me your life, you ungrateful whore. If it weren't for me you wouldn't be here."

I felt my face flush with anger. I lifted my head to look at her. "Don't speak to me that way. That was private! My private diary. You had no right to read it! Its mine."

"I have every right. Nothing in this house belongs to you. You did not earn it. Everything here is mine, do you hear me? MINE. I am taking this disgusting diary with me. I'll show your father what his precious daughter has been up to, when he comes home."

With that, she stood up and swept past me, carrying my diary in her hand. I turned and watched her as she left my room, my heart beating hard and hot in my chest, my own fists curled in fury.

I closed the door to my room and sat shaking on my bed. Tears crawled down my cheeks, their salt stinging my skin. I had no one to help me, no one who would protect me from her. My grandfather was too sick, my grandmother too preoccupied and afraid to do anything.

Perin aunty, who was not afraid of my mother, was avoiding me. When I phoned her she was always happy that I rang, but it was hard to talk about what was happening to me at home. She wouldn't exactly change the subject, but when I started telling her about my mother, I sensed she was uneasy. She asked no questions, did not advise or sympathize. She just listened very quietly until I'd finished, and then made no comment at all. She had changed, somehow. Had removed herself from me, from our family. I felt it in my bones, though I didn't know what caused it. It was as though she had decided she couldn't help my mum, and so talking about it made her uncomfortable. Whatever the cause, this was one subject I could not discuss with her. It left me feeling lonelier than I'd ever felt before.

None of my friends would come to our house any longer. Dilly had stuck with me — spending the day with me on weekends, or staying over whenever her parents would let her — long after the rest of the girls I knew had been scared away by my mother. But after what Mum had done to her a few weeks earlier, her parents would no longer allow her to come to our house.

It had happened on a Sunday morning. Dilly was coming over to spend the day. She usually got there around 9:30 or 10:00, so at 9:00 I went into my bathroom to have a bucket bath. My room was upstairs, at the back of the house, so when Dilly knocked on our door, I didn't hear her. My mother opened the door. As soon as she saw Dilly she began screaming at her. "Saali-mooi badmaash, why are you always coming here? Like a pye dog, you are, always sniffing around Shahnaz. Get out!"

Dilly was a tall, athletic girl, captain of our school hockey team. She was not easily intimidated. And she loved me, so she stood her ground. "Shahnaz invited me over to spend the day, Dinaz aunty," she said politely. "Could you please tell her I'm here?"

My mother went berserk, grabbing Dilly by the bangs of hair that hung over her forehead. She yanked her into the hallway. Caught by surprise, Dilly grunted and fell. My mother stood over her, screaming. "So Shahnaz invited you, did she? Well, she's not here. I know why you want her. It's your brother you're pimping for, don't think I don't know. I saw him the other day, all decked out in a shirt and tie. He came all the way to Juhu in the car to drop Shahnaz off. Now why would he do that? Hunh? Answer me that riddle, now!" Then she laughed. Dilly told me later my mother's laugh was the scariest thing she'd ever heard.

Dilly sat up, frightened and angry, and tried to explain. "Rohinton was on his way to the airport to meet my father's 'plane. Roshan's grandmother couldn't send her car to pick up Shahnaz because it had broken down, so my mother told our driver to drop Shahnaz home on the way to the airport."

But the mention of my grandmother seemed to inflame my mother even more. She shouted at Dilly, spit flying from her mouth. "GET OUT AND STAY OUT. DON'T COME BACK HERE. THIS IS MY HOUSE. SHAHNAZ HAS NO BUSINESS INVITING GARBAGE IN HERE."

Dilly turned and fled. She ran next door to our neighbour's house and telephoned her parents from there. I didn't find out what had happened until the doorbell rang, shortly after I'd emerged from my bath. I went to answer the door, and there was Dilly, flanked by her mother and father. I was so surprised to see her parents that it took me a minute to realize something was very wrong. They were both grave, unsmiling, their voices clipped and curt as they asked to speak to my mother.

I ushered them into the sitting room and offered them tea or a cold drink. They refused, politely, but in that same curt tone that puzzled and dismayed me. I flashed a questioning look at Dilly, who rolled her eyes at me to indicate she couldn't talk with her parents there. I went to fetch my mother.

I knocked on her door. She called for me to come in. She was sitting at her dressing table, calmly brushing her hair. I told her Dilly's parents were downstairs and wanted to speak to her. She nodded. "Tell them I'll be there in a minute. Give them tea or a Goldspot something."

"What's going on? Do you know why they want to talk to you?"

"Oh yes," she replied, and smiled cryptically. Clearly, she wasn't going to tell me.

I turned and went back downstairs. Dilly had slipped out into the hall, and was waiting for me there. She followed me into the kitchen.

"Dilly, what happened? Why're your mum and dad here?"

"Oh God, Shahnu! What a morning!" She rolled her eyes and

174

shook her head. "I didn't know they were going to react like this, or I wouldn't have phoned them."

"Phoned them? What are you talking about?"

"You want the whole story or just a summary?"

"Dilly! What's wrong? Your mum and dad are here looking as though somebody died."

"Ah, you know parents — always getting hot and heavy about little things." She filled me in on the events of the morning, acting out her part as well as my mother's, making light of the whole thing.

My eyes filled with tears. "Dilly, I'm so sorry. I was having a bath. I didn't know you were here."

She hugged me. "It's okay. My parents will give her what-for. No harm done."

I got cold drinks out of the refrigerator, poured them into glasses, put them on a tray. Dilly filled bowls with chevda and biscuits. I carried the tray back into the sitting room.

My mother was there, neatly dressed, smiling and talking to Dilly's parents, who seemed bewildered, but wary. She looked up as we came in. "Ah there you are, girls. Dilly, you naughty child! Telling your mummy and daddy such stories. They were so worried about you."

Dilly's father wrinkled his forehead and raked his hair back with one hand. "Dilly, Mrs. Jeejeebhoy says you were very rude to her this morning when you arrived."

"She what?" Dilly pulled herself up to her full height, glowering down at her seated parents and my mother. "I told you what happened. You're not going to believe anything she says, are you?"

Dilly's mother flushed. "Darling, that was very rude. Now I want you to apologize to Mrs. Jeejeebhoy." Turning to my mother, she said, in a voice mild with distress, "I don't know what's come over her. Please do excuse my daughter. We didn't raise her to behave this way."

"Mummy!" Dilly exclaimed. "I'm not going to apologize to her, she's the one who should be . . ."

175

"Dilly, that's enough!" said her father.

My mother smiled graciously. "Oh, it's all right. Shahnaz has been quite horrid lately too. I think it's their age, don't you? Perhaps," she added, looking shrewdly at Dilly's mother, "Dilly and Shahnaz ought not to spend so much time together? They seem to egg each other on. Just for a while," she said, turning to Dilly with a beatific smile, "until the two of you can behave in a civilized manner."

"You don't understand," I burst out. "She's lying. She's done this to my other friends and now they don't come over any more because of her." Tears of rage and frustration rolled down my face.

Dilly's father looked at me sternly. "Shahnaz," he began. But my mother interrupted.

"Perhaps it would be best if you took Dilly home," she suggested, in that insinuating voice.

Dilly's mother seemed relieved. They stood up, apologizing all the way to the door. As they were leaving, Dilly's father turned to me and said, "I think it would be best if you and Dilly had some time away from each other."

"No!" Dilly exclaimed. "You can't do that."

"She's lying," I shouted, "don't you see? She doesn't want me to have any friends. She's trying to . . ." But they just shook their heads and left, pulling a protesting Dilly behind them.

Dilly told me at school the next day that her parents knew, by the time they left our house, that my mother wasn't telling the truth. But they could not shame her, and wanted only to get away. They said they would speak to my father about the incident the next time he came home. Meanwhile, while they understood my mother was ill, they simply could not allow Dilly to come over any more. They also felt it would be best if I stayed away from their house, since my mother seemed to object to my spending time there. At least until my father came home and they had had a chance to talk with him.

I went home that evening, bereft. I lay down on my bed, hugged my pillow against my belly, and cried myself to sleep.

I woke up in the dark gasping and choking. My mother's body pressed down on the edge of my mattress beside me. Her hands circled my throat with a deadly grip, squeezing my neck as though it were a tube of toothpaste. The smell of dead mouse was overpowering. I could not breathe. I tried to cry out, to beg her to stop, but her hands had closed my throat and no sound would come.

I was shaking so hard, I could feel my teeth against my tongue as the blood roared in my ears and surged behind my eyes. I struggled against her grip, tried to twist my neck this way and that to get away from her. She pressed her fingers into my throat harder, wringing my neck as though it were a wet towel. I pulled desperately at her arms, trying to break her hold, but in her manic state she was strong, her fingers steely and tenacious. She chuckled genially, and squeezed with an iron grip. I felt myself slipping away from my body, slipping sideways into a sliver of time. I thought to myself: this is it. I'm going to die.

The only sound, besides my own blood whooshing in my head, was the uneven, jagged noise of my mother's breathing. Darkness spread like a stain inside me. I rolled, a fish, a fetus floating.

She grunted. Let go. Air rushed cold in my throat. My throat burned. Fire. I gasped. Swallowed gulps of sweet air.

She touched my hair. Gently, with her hand — the same hand that had just tried to strangle me. I opened my eyes; they were blurry with blood. Moonlight flooded my room, silvering my mother's face. She was leaning over me, her eyes screwed shut, her mouth wide open, as if she were screaming, but she made no sound. Tears streamed down her cheeks.

Then she rose, a silent shadow, and slid away.

Chapter 16

I am home with the flu, huddled under a blanket on the living room couch, trying to read Kuhn's *The Structure Of Scientific Revolutions*. My head hurts, my nose drips, my throat is raw. I have to squint to see the thermometer I've just taken out of my mouth. The silver line of mercury stops at a hundred and three degrees. My eyeballs feel as though they've been boiled in oil.

The clock on our wall strikes eleven when I hear the mailwoman's familiar triple knock. I divest myself of book and blanket and shuffle over to answer. She stands at my door, smiling cheerfully. The tip of her nose is red with cold, and so are her cheeks. Despite the cold, her blue jacket is unzipped; it flaps open as she hands me a stack of mail. She tells me she hopes I feel better soon and waves as she hurries back down the stairs. I close the door behind her, flip through fliers and bills which I drop unopened on the kitchen counter, and see the blue airmail envelope from India. I sit down on the living room couch to read it. The room is cold despite the noisy efforts of the wall-mounted space heater, and my fingers are stiff as I slit open the bulky envelope with a butter knife. I unfold the wad of limp, Indian airmail paper. It smells of Perin aunty's

178

Chanel No. 5 perfume. Perin aunty writes in a doctor's impatient scrawl, which I've had years of practise reading. If I hold the paper at a slight angle, I can make out most of what she says.

I skim, first. "Your mother has just come out of the hospital, after an operation to treat a detached retina. She has lost all vision in one eye. The other eye is going too."

What will she do if she can no longer read? It's almost the only thing she has left.

I skip a couple of pages. ". . . his name is Jal. I've known him for many years; we did our MBBS together. We lost touch after college, when he went to England to do his FRCS in opthalmology and I moved to Nagpur. A few weeks ago I ran into him at Delna Petit's wedding — his mother was a Petit before her marriage . . ." I blow my nose, which stings from being blown so much, and flip back to read her letter from the beginning.

She's met someone. My aunt, who I thought would never marry, who's been more of a mother to me than my own mother, has met a man. Most of her letter is about Jal Mehta. He's handsome, sophisticated, a good dancer, a few years older than her. They went to a BMSO concert together; he loves Beethoven's string trios as much as she does; he took her sailing on his yacht.

"He's such a lovely man! He reminds me of your father, so intelligent and honest, and I can hardly believe this, Shahnu, but he loves me!"

I've never known Perin aunty to use so many exclamation marks; she sounds over the moon about this guy.

"We share so many interests! He wants a family, but I had to explain to him that I cannot have children. Still, he wants to marry me. Everyone tells me it's best not to rush, but Jal is emigrating to Australia and he wants me to go with him."

Australia! She's supposed to come here, to visit me. She promised she'd come during spring break and stay until the summer. I need her here.

"We will have a small wedding, just family and a few friends. I wish you could come. I can't imagine getting married without you here. But you must be busy with your studies. I know you'll do well; we are all so proud of you. I have so much to do to get ready: I need a passport, visas, exchange permits — your daddy is helping me with all that."

She's really going. I can't believe she's leaving India with this Jal person. What does she know about him? So he's good looking, and an opthalmologist? That's no reason for her to go traipsing off with him to bloody Australia. I've heard it's a tough country for women to live in, and inhospitable to non-whites.

"I have to find a buyer for my house too, although, if it doesn't sell before we leave, your father has kindly offered to arrange for an agent to handle it. My friend Dina is going to take over my practice. I've never been outside India and now, imagine, I'm going to live in Perth with my husband! He already has a partnership there, with a friend from Cambridge who is a neurologist. I will have to pass the Australian Medical Board exams to practice in Perth . . ."

I blow my nose again, hard. Why is she going all the way to Australia? I'll never see her again.

"Jal has done the operations on your mother's eyes. He says he could have saved her vision if she had come in sooner, when she first began experiencing difficulties. I feel very bad about that. She's been complaining about her eyes for months, but how were we to know this wasn't just another of her attention-getting tricks? She is deeply depressed. I don't know what will happen to her. She will never recover the vision in her right eye, and she has only twenty per cent vision remaining in her left eye."

My mother must be devastated. For all her craziness, she's a fiercely independent woman. To lose her eyes would be to lose what's left of her life, a cruel paradigm shift.

"If you could see her now you would pity her. She paces up and down in her room, from the time she wakes up until she goes to bed. She hates it that she can't go for walks by herself any more. We have to lock her in her room to keep her from running off. I go over to see her at least once a day, to give her her injections and sit with her for a while. She is very angry and lonely, I think. Your father's still in Delhi much of the time, and there is only a manservant here to take care of her. I don't know how she will manage once I leave for Perth."

I see us all as if from a great height, as if I were on board the Sputnik circling the globe. My mother is at the centre of this scene, savage and caged. The rest of us are walking away from her on our separate trajectories: my father, and I, and Perin aunty. We are free to walk away. And yet, I don't feel free, despite the oceans and continents between us.

We carry the seeds of our destruction in the cells of our mortal flesh.

When Shahrukh comes home from school, I show him Perin aunty's letter. He reads it without comment.

"I feel as though we've all abandoned her," I say. And yet, that isn't exactly what I mean. I struggle to find words, but am too confused to articulate what I feel.

What I want, more than anything else, is to have Shahrukh hold me, to be comforted. I want him to tell me I'm safe; his love will keep me safe. I put my arms around him, and rest my burning cheek on his chest. He pats me cursorily on the back, then pulls away, saying, "Don't get too close; I don't want to catch your cold."

Chapter 17

I didn't close my eyes, the rest of that night my mother tried to strangle me. I lay in bed after she had left, watching, through my window, the stars glimmer in the sky. Crickets chirped; an occasional lorry whined as it drove by. I listened for sounds from my mother's room, which was just down the hall from my own, but I heard nothing. The moonlight faded into dawn. As the rectangle of light in my window turned silver-grey, I crept out of bed. I opened my door, trying not to make a sound.

The upstairs hallway was quiet. I tiptoed down the stairs to the sitting room in the semi-dark, stumbled over a lamp cord and held my breath, afraid that she'd heard me and would come downstairs. Long moments passed before I dared to breathe again. There was still no sound from her.

I sat on the chair by the telephone, picked up the heavy black receiver, dialled Perin aunty's number. My fingers shook so much, I had to hang up and dial over again. The phone rang. There was no answer. Then the operator came on and said the number was disconnected. I hung the receiver back on its cradle. Of course. Perin aunty had just moved to Nagpur, less than two weeks ago. I had her new phone number in my desk upstairs. I wasn't thinking clearly. I took a deep breath and dialled the operator. Talking as softly as possible, I asked for a trunk call to Delhi.

"What number madam?" the operator asked, in a nasal, Marathi accented voice.

I gave her the number and prayed that the call would go through before my mother woke. Sometimes it took seven or eight hours to get a trunk call through.

"Sorry madam, Delhi lines are all busy. Would you like to book a trunk call for later?"

I didn't know what to say. If the call came through later and my mother heard the phone ring, I didn't know what she might do to me. On the other hand, it was the only way I could contact my father.

"Thank you, operator. Please ring me when a line becomes available." I hung up the phone and sat beside it, scarcely breathing, willing it to ring. For half an hour I sat absolutely still, staring at its mute black face. My neck was stiff and painful, my shoulders were hunched near my ears. I stood up, stretched, rubbed my eyes, walked over to the window and looked out at the garden. The ground was damp, and shrubs and bushes glistened with dew in the early morning light.

The phone rang, startling me. I dashed across the room to pick it up before it could ring again and wake my mother. I stubbed my toe, tears prickling my eyes, then lifted the receiver to my ear.

"Your party's line is ringing, madam."

"Thank you." I could hear the double ring of my father's phone at the other end of the line. Please let him be home!

"Hullo?" The voice was deep, but it wasn't my father. The line crackled and hissed like hot tar in my ear.

"Is Mr. Jamshedi there, please?"

"Sahib no here." It must be one of my father's servants.

"Do you know where he's gone?"

"Hanh?" More hissing and crackling.

"Where has sahib gone?"

"Sahib go out. You leaving message please?"

"Tell him to phone his daughter in Bombay."

"What name, memsahib?"

"Shahnaz, his daughter." I tried to remember the Hindi word for daughter, but my mind was blank. "Home. Ask him to ring home."

"Sahib not home."

"I know that." I took a deep breath, trying to stifle my frustration. I talked slowly, enunciating every word. "Tell sahib to telephone his house in Bombay. 202-9966. Can you write that down?"

"Yes-yes, I writing. Two oh two nayen nayen ashix ashix."

"Right. Thank you."

"Accha, bye-bye!"

I hung up the phone. My hand was numb from clutching it so hard. I prayed my father would get the message and ring me before my mother woke.

As I turned to climb the stairs to my room, I heard my mother walking across the floor overhead. I froze. For what seemed like an eternity, I heard her footsteps thump across the length of her room and back. She paced like that for hours sometimes, during her manic episodes, as though demons in her body propelled her forward against her will.

I forced myself to move. I crept up to the heavy front door, undid the latch, froze again when it clicked. As I turned the door handle, I heard the footsteps overhead stop. Then a quick muffled series of sounds flupfflupflup out to the upstairs hallway. I imagined her heading out of her room, down the stairs. I opened the front door and ran out in my bare feet — down the broad front steps and across the gravelled driveway.

The gravel was sharp and cut my feet. I veered onto the garden path, slipping every now and then in the red mud, which was damp with early morning dew. The rim of the sun appeared over the tops of the casuarina trees that lined the edge of our compound, touching the treetops with gold and blinding me momentarily. A breeze blew cool against my face as I ran without looking back; my throat and neck ached from the night before, my pyjama legs whipped against my ankles. The wrought iron gates at the edge of our compound seemed very far away. I thought I heard my mother call my name. I ran faster, my heart beating high in my chest, the cawing of crows punctuating my stride.

Once I'd slipped through the gate and was outside the walls of our compound, I paused to catch my breath. I couldn't think what to do next. I couldn't go left. There was nothing there except a row of hole-in-the-wall shops that sold paan-beedi, eggs, vegetables, flour, pakoras, sticky sweets in flyblown glass cases. Most of these shops were still closed, their shutters drawn, their owners probably asleep on the premises. Beyond the shops was an Irani restaurant and bakery. I had never been inside, though I'd passed it often enough driving by in our car. I could see its fluorescent lights glaring in the distance, but I couldn't go there unaccompanied and in my pyjamas. On my right was a vacant lot. Next to it was the house of our only neighbours, the Ambedkars. I had been there a few times with my parents and my sister Roshan. I didn't like going to their house, but had no choice. I needed to use their telephone.

I ran from the shelter of our wall across the filthy sidewalk, trying to stay close to the bushes that lined the street. I reached our neighbours' front door panting and out of breath, with a stitch in my side from running. I knocked on their door, waited impatiently as I heard various bolts and latches sliding open inside. Ayamma, their servant, opened the door and peered near-sightedly at me.

"Ayamma, it's me, Shahnaz. From next door."

"Ayyayy, baba, what is happening that you are coming here in your pyjamas only?" she asked, wagging her head from side to side and clucking in disapproval.

I threw my arms around her, burying my face in her neck, which smelled of eucalyptus oil and night sweat. I cried and

185

cried, great sobs shaking my body, my heart banging against the wall of my chest as though it would force its way out and fly away. I cried for Sunder ayah, and for my lost childhood; for my father, my sister, Perin aunty. For all the losses of that year, and all the loneliness that engulfed me.

Ayamma must have been completely bewildered. I'd never so much as touched her before. But she patted my back, cradled my neck in her small hand. She stroked my hair and made soothing sounds until the ache in my chest had eased and my heart grew lighter. As I lifted my head from her shoulder, she wiped my face tenderly, with the corner of her sari palloo, and drew me inside the house.

Ayamma walked me into Mr. and Mrs. Ambedkar's sitting room. Mr. Ambedkar was an engineer with Air India. He had grey hair, slicked back with Brylcreem, and close-together eyes in a bony, pock-marked face. He was short and skinny and smelled of snuff, which he put on the top of his curled fist and sniffed vigorously into each nostril every few minutes. Roshan and I avoided him on the few occasions we were at their house. He hugged us a little too closely, and, although he'd never tried anything else, his embrace lingered long enough to make us both feel uncomfortable. He was a creep with sticky fingers.

We both felt sorry for his wife. She was a shy, plain woman who kept her head covered with the palloo of her sari and, like a good Hindu wife, never referred to her husband by name, calling him "Ji," or "himself" when she had to mention him at all. They had moved next door to us about four years ago. We didn't see them much. Mrs. Ambedkar was often away visiting her married daughter in Poona. Mr. Ambedkar and my father did not move in the same circles.

Ayamma went off to the kitchen to make some tea. The sitting room was hot and airless, its windows all closed tight. It smelled of stale cooking and dead flowers. I looked around. Every horizontal surface in the Ambedkar's sitting room was crowded with framed photographs of their daughter, son-in-

186

law and grandchildren. A large hand-tinted wedding photograph of Mr. and Mrs. Ambedkar hung in an oval brass frame above the sofa. To my right was an altar with an oil lamp which hadn't yet been lit that morning, and a framed, sepia-toned photo of a fat, smiling baby. The photo was hung with a garland of jasmines which had turned brown in the heat. I knew this was a picture of their son, who had been born with a hole in his heart and who had died before his first birthday. I stood up and bent over to take a closer look. Someone's hand touched my shoulder.

I jumped and screamed with fright, smelling the snuff at the same moment as I turned to see Mr. Ambedkar standing right behind me, smiling his oily smile.

"Oh, Mr. Ambedkar. You gave me a fright." If he touches me, I thought, or tries to hug me, I'll scream again!

Much to my relief, he did neither. Instead, he gestured with his hand towards the sofa and said: "Sit down, please. To what do we owe the honour of this visit?"

I sat down dumbly, exhausted, not knowing how much he knew about my mother, or what I could safely say. The room was swimming strangely around me and Mr. Ambedkar's pock-marked face kept moving in and out of focus. I heard him say something, but he sounded far away, as though I was underwater and he was talking to me from from a distant shore.

They told me later that I'd babbled something about calling my father, and then fainted. I suppose the combination of heat, exhaustion and fear caused me to black out. When I came to, the first thing I heard, before I opened my eyes, was Mr. Ambedkar hissing: "It is none of our business. She cannot stay here."

Then Mrs. Ambedkar's soft voice, sounding surprisingly firm: "Ji, look at the marks on her neck. Her mother is a crazy person; we cannot send the child back. If anything happened to her it would be on our heads only."

"Then we must ring up her father and ask him what to do. He must come and take her home."

I opened my eyes then. Mrs. Ambedkar helped me up, handed me a cup of sugary tea. "Drink this, Beti, it will be making you feel better."

I detested tea — for years my sister and I had had to drink it right after a weekly dose of castor oil, which, my father believed, was good for the constitution. But I drank it down because Mrs. Ambedkar was kind, and without her protective presence her loathsome husband would have sent me back to face my mother alone. Putting the cup back on its saucer, I asked, timidly: "Could you phone my father for me? I tried earlier but the lines to Delhi were down."

"Yes-yes, we are phoning this very minute," Mr. Ambedkar boomed, wrinkling his sharp little nose. "I will ring up, you take care of the girl," he said to his wife.

"Okay, Ji. I will take her to lie down in the spare bedroom. Come, Shahnaz." Mrs. Ambedkar placed an arm around my shoulders and, with the delicacy of someone who has known suffering, helped me to my feet .

I stood up, suddenly realizing I was still in my pyjamas and bare feet. Embarrassed, I tried to explain as Mrs. Ambedkar led me to a bedroom in the back of their house. She listened intently as I gave her a hesitant, jumbled version of the night's events. Her dark eyes filled with tears. Then she hugged me and drew back the covers on the bed, saying: "You go to sleep now, Beti. Your father will be coming soon-soon. Nothing to worry, all right?"

I nodded, knowing I would never be able to sleep. But I closed my eyes as she left the room, grateful for the thick curtains that shaded it from the sunlight.

After she left, I lay on the strange bed with the covers pulled over my chin. I tried to calm myself by breathing as my yoga teacher had taught me, seven breaths in through the right nostril, out through the left; paying attention to the moment of stillness between in-breath and out. But my breath was ragged. My throat hurt; my head felt hot and shivery. My body ached as though I had been run over by a train, great thuds of pain surrounded by a yawning numbness. Under my closed lids I saw my mother's face, twisted with rage, swollen with a monstrous pity. And I saw myself through her eyes, neck meekly bent, irresistibly vulnerable; my naked need sucking at her flesh. A leech, which had to be peeled off her and squashed with her bare hands.

I wondered what would happen to me now. I knew I could not go back to live with her. I wondered if the Ambedkars had managed to reach my father. If my father would come. If Perin aunty would come. After that, I must have dozed off. I know I dreamed, but I don't remember details, just a chaos of sharp light and harsh sounds, like the cries of seagulls, but wilder, more lonely.

I woke up to find my father sitting on my bed, stroking my hair. I sat up and burst into tears, burrowing into the safety of his chest, his heartbeat thudding reassuringly in my ear.

"Daddy, you came!"

"Of course, Beta. As soon as Mr. Ambedkar rang me, I took the first flight out. How are you feeling?"

"I was so scared, I thought she would kill me. I thought, this is it, I'll never see you or Roshan again, never finish school or go to college. But then she stopped squeezing. I don't know why." I snuffled and wiped my nose on his shoulder.

My father held me close. "I tried to telephone home, but the phone was engaged. Maybe your mother left it off the hook. I took the first flight. Mr. Ambedkar was waiting for me at the airport. We came straight here."

"Daddy, she almost killed me. I was so scared!"

"Ssshhh, it is all right, Beta, I am here now. Come on. Let us go home and see to your mother."

"I'm never going back there. Never."

"It will be all right, Shahnaz. Dr. Pereira will come. He will give your mummy an injection. She will calm down."

"No!" I pushed away from him, feeling furious and betrayed. "You can't make me go back there. I'm not going to live with her, ever again."

"Beta," my father pleaded, "you must not behave like this. She is not well."

"I don't care. I hate her, I don't care any more how ill she is, I am not going back to live with her." I began to cry again, furious with myself for not being able to stop bawling, outraged that my father would care more about her than he did about me.

"Okay, Beta, okay. Don't cry. I will telephone your grandmother. You can go and stay there for a while until I can think what to do." He looked defeated, suddenly old. I felt a pang of guilt, seeing the corners of his mouth droop, the lines on his forehead deepen.

My father left to go and deal with my mother. Mrs. Ambedkar brought me a dressing gown and helped me put it on. Then she sat me down in a chair in their guest bedroom while she oiled and combed my hair into two plaits, fastening them with elastic bands. Her touch was light and soothing.

My father returned an hour or so later, with a small suitcase full of my clothes, and my school-books in my satchel. He handed me the suitcase, and put my satchel on the floor beside the bed.

"Did you find Mum?"

"Yes, darling. Dr. Pereira is with her now." He hesitated. His eyes, wide and melting behind his thick glasses, were filled with tears. "She was curled up in the bottom of the cupboard. Her knees were pulled up to her chin. She was naked. She kept screaming that the CIA was after her, the FBI was after her."

"What did Dr. Pereira say?"

"He gave her a Thorazine injection. She is sleeping now. They have taken her to his clinic. He wants me to consider a frontal lobotomy."

"What is that?"

"They would cut out the front part of her brain."

"Why?"

"He says it would calm her, she would not be violent any more."

"Daddy, you can't do that. She would never forgive you."

"I told Dr. Pereira: just now I can't, but I will think about it." He looked at me with despair. "I promised your mother I would never put her in an institution. This would be worse. For her, a living death. But I don't know what is the right thing to do."

"Why don't you talk to Perin aunty?"

"I rang her up. She says if I let Dr. Pereira do the operation, it may be a chance for your mother to have some peace, but she would never be the same again."

"Don't do it, Daddy."

My father began to cry. Brokenly. Sobbing. I began to cry with him. We held onto each other, and wept.

Later, I got dressed and went downstairs, and thanked Mr. Ambedkar, who looked at me greedily as though I were a prime laddoo. Mrs. Ambedkar pressed a large amber bead in my hand, for good luck. I clutched it in my fist as we said goodbye, waving to them from the front seat of my father's Humber. My father drove me to my grandparents' house.

My grandmother greeted us at the door. She looked so frail, I was afraid to hug her too hard in case I broke her bones. Her hands fluttered about my face, stroked my bruised throat. "Darling, I am so sorry," she said. And to my father, "Come in, come in. Soli Pappa is sleeping. He has had a bad night." She sighed, and led us into the house.

She and my father went out to the back verandah for tea. I ran upstairs to the room that Roshan and I always shared when we stayed with my grandparents. My collection of seashells, acquired during various trips to Udvada, was still there, glowing whitely on top of the dark teak dresser. The ornate teak desk still had our initials carved under its lip — I traced them with my fingertips, S. J. + R. J. I felt a pang of sadness. Roshan was far away at boarding school. The house felt suddenly dark, mournful, its shutters closed like tight-lipped mouths against the day's oppressive heat.

I went out to the verandah and sat next to my father, holding onto his arm as he and my grandmother talked. My grandmother sat quietly while my father told her that Dr. Pereira wanted to do a frontal lobotomy on my mother. Her nostrils flared slightly, whitely. Her eyes looked troubled. She asked questions in her silvery voice. How long would it take? What changes would it bring about in my mother? Then she shook her head, her eyes widening. She looked at my father as if seeing him for the first time. "You are considering this?"

"I told him I would think about it."

"It would solve many problems," my grandmother said dreamily, picking Arrowroot biscuit crumbs from her lower lip with the tip of her little finger.

"Then you think I should give him permission?"

My grandmother stared off into the distance. "You know how your brother Behram has been these many years. Do you think we should consider this operation for him?"

"No!" my father gasped.

"So," said my grandmother, and stood up, brushing crumbs from her sari.

My father stood up too. I realized, suddenly, that he was leaving and I was not going home with him. I clung to him, wanting him to stay with me, wanting his tobacco-scented warmth, the safety of his arms. He gently disengaged himself from my clinging body, gave me a slight push towards my grandmother.

I went upstairs to my room, fell on my bed and cried for a long time.

A few days later, my grandmother and I went to visit my mother at Dr. Pereira's nursing home. Her room was white. White walls, white ceiling, white metal furniture. White-silled window with white metal grating. My mother lay huddled under a white sheet, her head pink and bald against the white pillowcase. Her wrists were tied to the metal sides of the bed with lengths of white gauze.

My grandmother ushered me closer to the bed. My mother looked up at me from under swollen eyelids. She looked at me without recognition or interest, her eyes blank, her face pale and puffy. They had shaved her head for the shock treatment, my grandmother explained. She looked like a soul in purgatory. I trembled inside, knowing I had brought this punishment upon her. She was here because I had told my father I would not live with her any more. The guilt rose up in nauseating waves.

My mother never spoke or gave any sign that she knew us. When my grandmother stroked her hand, she turned her face away. The back of her head was a bumpy terrain of skin and stubble, a field of bone.

Chapter 18

Sunder ayah went to live with Perin aunty. Perin aunty had sold her house in Bombay and moved back to Nagpur, and Sunder ayah went with her. She did not have her own kholi there, as she had had in our compound. She slept in a small room behind the kitchen and took care of Perin aunty as she had taken care of our family for so many years. I missed her fiercely.

One Saturday afternoon, shortly after I had moved to my grandparent's house, Sunder ayah came to visit me. She stood in the doorway to my room, holding a cloth bag in one hand. She looked frailer than I remembered, a small, sad-looking figure with thinning grey hair pulled back into a bun. Her feet were bare, as always, the heels cracked from years of walking barefoot in all kinds of weather. She had lost weight; her skin, soft as blotting paper, curved into hollows at her cheeks and around her eyes. I jumped up from my desk and ran to her, hugged her. My chin rested on top of her head. She seemed to have shrunk since we'd last seen each other. I brought her over to my bed and sat beside her, hugging her to me, inhaling the familiar smell of her skin, of the coconut oil she used in her hair.

She cradled my head on her shoulder and told me in her soft voice that Perin aunty had come to Bombay to attend to some business, and that she, Sunder ayah, had come with her. They

194

were staying in Bandra, with a friend of Perin aunty's, and Perin aunty had given Sunder ayah the day off, so that she could come and visit me. Sunder ayah had taken the bus from Bandra to Juhu, then walked all the way to my grandparents house to see me.

She asked me how my mother was doing, although I sensed that she already knew. I told her about that nightmare night, when my mother almost killed me. My mother sitting on the edge of my bed. Her hands around my throat, squeezing. As I talked, my body began to shake uncontrollably. My teeth chattered so I couldn't speak. Sunder held me close, and listened quietly. I began to sob and couldn't stop.

"I want to die, Sunder, I don't want to live any more. I don't know how to live like this, all alone. My grandmother is at Soli Pappa's bedside all day. I never see her. I haven't seen daddy for two months. Take me with you. Let me come with you to Nagpur, please!"

Sunder ayah held me and rocked me, the way she had when I was a small child. I cried until there were no more tears left. Tenderly, she wiped my eyes and nose on the corner of her sari palloo. Her own eyes were troubled, cloudy with grief.

"Baba," she said, "I am an ignorant old woman. I don't understand. How can a mother harm her own child? It is against Nature's law."

She stroked my hair; her mouth trembled as she added: "But there are worse things in this world. If it is our fate, we must accept. No matter how terrible the suffering, we must accept."

"How can you say that? If I were your daughter, you would protect me!"

Sunder ayah's face crumpled like an old handkerchief. Her arms went limp. She looked a hundred years old, her eyes dim and far away. As if in a dream, she began speaking. At first, I didn't know who she was talking to. She seemed to be looking inward, talking to a ghost.

"I could not protect her; my own child. I could not protect her."

She closed her eyes and I felt her despair in my belly. I clung to her, willing her back. Her mouth twisted as though trying to shape words, but for a long while, no words came. When she finally spoke again, it was in a voice I didn't recognize as hers.

"Mothers do terrible things to their daughters. I too made a mistake. My daughter paid the price."

Then she told me the story.

"My daughter Nirmala was sixteen and was soon to be married. On the full moon of Vesak; a most auspicious day. It was a very good match for my Nimmi. The boy, Raju, was twenty-two years old, his father's oldest son. He was quite dark, compared to my Nimmi, but he was strong and had good teeth. His family owned their own paan-beedi shop in Poona. They could have done better for their son than a servant's daughter, but at least we were of the same caste and clan. And their horoscopes were a perfect match."

Bewildered, I opened my mouth to ask why she was telling me this now. But Sunder ayah hurried on.

"I wish my husband had been there then. He would have known how to deal with my daughter's in-laws-to-be. As it was, they knew I was alone, a widow. They took advantage. When the matchmaker first approached them about my Nimmi, he showed them a photo of her, wearing my mother's green silk sari and looking like a champa blossom with her wheat-coloured complexion and her beautiful long hair. The boy's parents approved of her looks: fair skin, light eyes, shapely figure. She had broad hips too, good for delivering babies. Of course, the matchmaker did not tell them she could read and write, that would have brought down her value. No-one wants a daughter-in-law who is educated. It gives a girl ideas above her station. I gave the matchmaker fifty rupiah to keep quiet. He tucked the folded notes into the waist of his dhoti and swore on Ganpati he wouldn't say anything.

"When the groom's family made their first dowry demand, I was in despair. They sent me a list with the matchmaker: one steel Godrej cupboard with built-in safe; two full sets of new clothes for each member of their family, including silk saris with gold zari-work for the mother and the old grandmother, and kurta-pyjama or ghagra-choli for the nine children; six tolas of gold jewellery; a mangalsutra for the mother; gold kurta buttons and a stainless steel wristwatch for the groom; a complete set of stainless steel pots and pans; twelve stainless steel thalis with bowls and tumblers; one primus stove; one gas stove with two gas cylinders. Plus all wedding expenses, including a horse for the groom to ride in the wedding procession, a brass band, a feast with one hundred guests, payment for the pujari, and so on. Hai Ram, I beat my breast in despair. I was only earning sixty rupiah a month. Even though I had saved almost my whole salary for fifteen years just for that, to get my Nirmala married, I would never have enough money to pay what they asked. Sadly, I admitted to the matchmaker, I could not meet their demands.

"The matchmaker told me I was a fool. I would never get a better offer for my Nimmi. The family was well-known in their bustee. They had a good business. I shook my head, feeling the tears well in my eyes. I turned to go back in the house, just as Perin bai came out into the courtyard. She saw I was crying. She has a tender heart."

Thinking of how Perin aunty had all but disappeared out of my life since my mother's illness, I said, "Sometimes Perin aunty is not so nice. Sometimes she . . ."

"You must not talk that way." Sunder ayah said.

"But she left me all alone when Mummy went crazy. She knew what was happening and she wouldn't do anything to help me. She . . ."

"You are just a child. What do you know?" Sunder ayah had never spoken to me so brusquely before. She scowled at me, and half-raised one hand. "Perin bai has a kind heart," she repeated, firmly.

Then she continued with her story.

"Perin bai called out to me: 'Sunder! What is the matter? Is this man bothering you?' She glared at the matchmaker, who was salaaming and smiling his one-toothed smile and wagging his head from side to side. 'What are you grinning at, you fool?' she demanded. 'If you are making trouble for Sunder, you better know she has bai-seth who make it their business to take care of troublemakers like you.'

"'No-no bai,' I said, 'he is not making trouble. He is only a matchmaker.'

"'Who's getting married?' she asked.

"'I am trying to arrange a marriage for my daughter Nirmala.'

"'Nimmi? But she's only a child!'

"'No, bai, she is sixteen years old. It is time to get her married.'

"Perin bai looked at me with troubled eyes. 'How old were you when you were married, Sunder?'

"'I do not know, bai. Once my monthly bleeding time began, my mother found a husband for me.'

"'And Nirmala is sixteen. Hm. That is still very young. Who is the boy?'

"The matchmaker spoke up eagerly. 'He is very good boy, bai. He is standard-ten pass. His parents own a paan-beedi shop in Poona. Very good family.'

"'If he is such a wonderful match, why are you crying?' Perin bai demanded. She has a sharp tongue sometimes, but I did not take offense. I knew she had my welfare at heart.

"I was ashamed to say anything, so I looked down at the ground. The matchmaker spoke up: 'Bai, groom's family has given dowry demand. It is not so much. The girl is servant's daughter, but boy's family are prosperous. Very good tradespeople. Own business and everything. It is a good match for this girl.'

"'Let me see that.' Perin bai held out her hand. The matchmaker reluctantly handed her the piece of paper with the list of dowry items. She read it quickly, frowning. 'You know, this is completely illegal. Dowry has been abolished by law!'

"'Yes, bai, that is for educated lok like your good self,' the matchmaker began, in his wheedling voice, waggling his head and raising his palms flat to the sky like a kathakali dancer. 'But you see, for us poor people, it is most necessary. If we did not demand dowry for our sons, how would we get money to marry off our daughters?' He looked delighted with this argument. 'These people are not bad. Some ask for lot more. Furniture and whatnot. Bajaj scooters, even. This request is most reasonable.'

"'What, reasonable? It is absolutely outrageous! How is this poor woman to come up with so much money? Besides, Nimmi is educated, she has just passed SSC. She could get a job as a government clerk, or even get her nursing diploma. That should count for something.'

"'Tobaa, that is big problem, bai.' The matchmaker looked around, then leaned closer and whispered, 'Groom's family not knowing girl is reading-writing. If they know, they will say No marriage.'

"'You people!' Perin bai exclaimed in disgust. 'Sunder, is this what you really want for your daughter?'

"'It is a good match for her bai. She will have a husband and family to take care of her when I am gone.'

"'If you're sure this is what you want, I will talk to Sorab seth. We will come to some arrangement to help you with the money.'

"I knew daddy would help you," I said, hugging her.

But Sunder shook her head, and squeezed the bridge of her nose between her thumb and forefinger. "How could I have been so foolish? I should have listened to Perin bai. It is all my fault, stupid old woman that I am . . . "

"You're not stupid! And you're not old. Come on," I coaxed. "I'll get you some tea. I want to tell you what happened between me and Mummy."

Sunder ayah squinted as though the light in the room hurt her eyes. She gave another slight shake of her head, then continued with her story.

"So we went ahead. Once I said yes, they wanted to meet Nirmala and me. That went very well — my Nirmala so beautiful, her head bent under the overhanging palloo of her sari. I had never seen her so pliant, so docile. Like a chameli blossom. They told the matchmaker they liked her.

"Then came the headaches."

What headaches? Feeling suddenly impatient, I got up from the bed and walked over to the tea-table which stood in one corner of the room. I wanted to talk about mother and me. I couldn't understand why Sunder ayah insisted on telling me a long, boring story about her daughter's wedding instead.

I poured Sunder ayah a cup of strong Darjeeling tea, adding lots of milk and two teaspoons of sugar. I brought the cup back to the bed and touched her shoulder to get her attention. She opened her eyes. I offered her the cup. She took it from my hand without looking at me, poured some tea into the saucer, and slurped it down. Then, wiping her mouth with the back of her hand, she set the cup down on the bedside table, shook her head, and continued.

"Everything with those people was arguments, arguments. They wanted malai-pethi, they wanted goat's meat curry, they wanted jasmine garlands only, marigolds won't do. Want, want, want. I began to wonder if this was such a good match. Boy was good, no doubt. My Nimmi saw his photo and liked him. She said he looked happy. What did she know? I told her, happiness doesn't fill your belly. But she was still a child. It was up to me to think of her future. The boy's family was well settled; they lived in a pukka chawl above their shop. Nimmi would have enough to eat, pukka roof over her head and all. That was good enough for me. But would it be good enough for her? Maybe I had done wrong by letting her go to school, and pass SSC exams. She was thinking too much. All that reading — she got big-big ideas in her head. Take that nursing business, for example. Silly girl wanted to be a nurse, and Perin bai encouraged her. What rubbish was that? Who would marry her if she did such a thing? Only Goanese and low-caste people do such work, cleaning other peoples' dirty wounds, wiping up their shit and blood. I thought, better marry her off before she spoiled her chances.

"Matchmaker came knocking on my kholi door. When I saw him, I would get headaches only. Even before he opened his mouth, I knew there would be trouble.

"'So, what is it now?' I asked him.

"'Nirmala's mother, they are saying they cannot let their boy go so cheaply. They have received a better offer. You must give them Hindustan bicycle for groom and one thousand rupiah cash, or wedding is off — khatam.'

"'Hai Ram! I have used up everything I had. Even my kholi in Khandala is sold to pay for Nirmala's wedding. Go, tell them there is nothing left.'

"'If you don't give them what they want, they will marry their son to another girl. Your daughter's reputation will be mud. No man will look at her to marry. Her life will be ruined,' the matchmaker said.

"'They can't draw water from an empty well. Tell them I have nothing. If I could sell my flesh pound by pound I would, but who would want it? This well is dry,' I replied.

"'Speak to your bai and seth,' he urged. 'Maybe they will help you.'

"'They have already given me so much money,' I said. 'How can I ask for any more? Hai Ram, my child is ruined!'

"'Maybe the moneylender, then?'

"'No. I promised my dead husband I would never let those bloodsuckers in our house. Better I should speak to my seth about a loan,' I told the matchmaker."

Sunder ayah paused and looked at me. "Are you listening?" she demanded, her voice high and querulous.

I squirmed in my seat and nodded, wondering when this interminable story would be over, so I could talk to her about what had happened to me. "Yes, yes. Go on. You were going to ask Daddy for a loan."

"Seth was troubled, when I talked to him about a loan. 'It is not the money, Sunder,' he said. A worried frown made sharp lines in his forehead. His eyes were cloudy like a monsoon sky. 'These are not honourable people. They made a contract, and now they are blackmailing you because they know they can. Two days before the wedding they suddenly demand more. How do you know they won't keep on demanding, even after the wedding? You cannot give in to blackmailers.'

"'Seth,' I said, 'I am a poor, simple woman. Only I want my daughter to be settled. Then I can die in peace. I know these people are greedy. But this is the way of the world. How can I fight? If I refuse, my daughter will be soiled goods. Her chances for marriage will be zero. Who will take care of her after I am gone? I beg you, I will work like a slave for you for the rest of my life. Only lend me this money so my Nimmi can be happy.' I knelt down and touched his feet.

"Seth pulled away as though a scorpion had stung him. 'What are you doing?' he shouted. 'Don't ever do that.' Then, seeing the fear in my eyes, I think, he made his voice softer. 'I am not so different from you, Sunder. You may think: oh, he is a big seth and I am just a servant, but we both have children we love. I have known Nirmala since she was a baby. I will do what I can, for her, as though she were a child of my own household. But I must tell you, I have grave misgivings about this family, this marriage. Are you sure you want Nirmala to marry into such a clan?'

"'The wheel of fate has been set in motion, seth,' I said. 'Neither you nor I can turn it back. What's done is done.'

"'If you are sure, then tell these people we will pay what they ask.'

"'May Vishnu shower blessings on you. I will repay every rupiah. I will work,' I promised him.

"And so the wheel turned. My daughter was married. I returned by Deccan Express from Poona. Nimmi cried when I left. Her young husband comforted her. I waved from the window of the train until I could no longer see even a speck of her. My beautiful dove had found a good home."

Sunder took a deep, sighing breath, and rubbed her eyes with the back of her hand. I was frightened. She looked like a sleep-walker. I touched her shoulder tentatively, afraid to bring her out of her trance, but needing reassurance that she wasn't crazy, that she knew who I was and where we were. Her eyes focussed briefly on me. She tried to smile, but something was wrong with her mouth; it drooped and seemed to slide down her face. She began speaking again, in a strange, singsong voice.

"I woke up in the middle of the night; big-big noise, so much tamaashaa! Telegraph boy was banging on seth's door. What happened? I ran out of my kholi in my night sari; I saw the red Urgent Telegram in seth's hand. Something bad had happened, I knew. Two nights earlier, chaprassi killed a big king cobra, long as my whole body, no lie. I told him, you must not kill this holy snake, the gods will be very angry. But Dinaz bai was shouting kill, kill, so what could the poor man do? He put the snake in the fire and burned it. I thought: for this deed fire will come down on our heads. I covered my head with my sari palloo and prayed: Hai Ram, keep my seth and bai and Shahnaz baba and Roshan baba safe."

Sunder ayah's face puckered. She made a harsh, guttural noise in the back of her throat. The tea in her cup smelled like smoke. She turned to me, her eyes flat and empty of light. Unwrapping her arms from around her knees, she raised her hands and placed them on either side my face. I could feel the callouses on her palms as she squeezed my cheeks between her hands.

"I never thought the fire would come for me. My Nirmala, my flower! Her father died when she was still in my belly, a stone from the quarry crushed him. They scraped his body onto a blanket. They brought it home to me. Bundle of blood and broken flesh. That same night she was born. Such a beautiful child, golden like a champa blossom. I put kaajal in her eyes and amber beads on her wrists to save her from the evil eye."

I shuddered and tried to hold still under the pressure of those hot, hard hands. She was looking into my eyes without seeing me.

"Seth read the telegram to me. 'NIRMALA DEAD ACCI-DENT STOP. CREMATION NINE AM TOMORROW STOP.' Her father-in-law must have gone to letter-writer to write, to GPO to send. Such a message he should not have been sending. My Nirmala! Sixteen years old. Only married seven months. What jealous fate snatched her away so soon? I am a selfish old woman. I should be rejoicing, she is dancing now with the gopis in Vishnu's garden.

"How? How am I to bear this world without her?

"But enough foolishness. You are a silly old woman, I thought. I had to pack my bedroll. Praise the gods for my seth's kindness. He was taking me to Poona in his car. No train 'till the next morning, and I had to be at her father-in-law's house before nine o'clock or she would burn without me, my heart, my Nimmi. How she used to humour her old mother! She would press my legs for me, massage my head with coconut oil, tie my hair into a long plait at night with her small fingers. She was to me like monsoon rain blessing the cracked and broken earth. There will be no more springtimes in my life.

"Seth was waiting for me in the car. I went out. The pleats of my white nine-yard sari flashed in the moonlight. I wore that sari when my mother died. Seth was sitting in the drivers' seat, waiting for me. Driver had gone to his muluk, for his youngest grandson's wedding.

"And that was the last time I saw her, my Nirmala, at her wedding. Her face hidden in her sari palloo, her hands red with mehndi. So solemn and beautiful, sitting by her husband on the dais while the pundit chanted slokas and poured ghee on the fire. Her head bent so meekly.

"She was always laughing, full of mischief, curious as a mongoose. As a child, she pestered me to send her to the village school. She wanted to learn to read and write. As if a girl of our desh needed such things. But seth gave me school books, for her. I took them to her when I went to see her each Diwali, at my mother's house in Lonavala. We would spend my one-month holidays together. When the day's work was done, she would bend over those books by the light of the kerosene lamp; I can still see her, squatting on her bedroll on the floor of my mother's jhopdi. She would follow the lines on the page with her small finger, her face shining with joy. Her eyes as black as night, Her face bold and bright like the full moon.

"Was she happy at her in-laws' house? I was waiting for her to tell me she was with child; then I would have gone to see her, I would have found some way to go. Now I will never hold her children in my arms, I will never hear her laughing voice."

Sunder ayah's voice rose to a wail. She turned away and hunched over like a turtle. Her voice was muffled, but she kept talking, as though the words would bring her daughter back to life. I wanted to comfort her, but did not know, in the face of her grief, what to say.

205

"I was sitting in the back of the car, like a bai. Seth was driving. The car twisted this way that way like a snake on those winding roads as we climbed the Western Ghats. In those mountains, the sky was so close I could reach out with my hand and caress the stars the way I used to caress my Nirmala's hair at night until she fell asleep. We had been driving for a long time, the car engine whining on the steep mountain roads. We passed through Khandala, where her father and I lived in the kholi we built together. Where Nirmala was born. I wanted to shout, go slowly-slowly seth! I did not want to reach her in-laws' house, or see her body on a funeral pyre. I would have died for her, my raat-ki-raani. This old body is useless, I would have gladly given it to Yama in exchange for hers.

"Khandala, Lonavala. The mountains slipped silently by and my head went round and round as the road twisted and turned. The inside of the motor car smelled of petrol. I had eaten nothing, but I felt as though I must vomit. I held my face to the open window. A cold mountain breeze blew grit against my skin.

"Seth drove in silence. What could he say? The back of his head was full of white hairs. Yet I remembered when he had no hair at all. I was there when he was born, my mother was his mother's ayah. I was only a girl myself, but I fed him and dressed him. I played with him until he went away to school. And when he married, I went with him to Mumbai to take care of his children, leaving my own child behind. Oh my Nirmala, how I wept with loneliness those first few years. Leaving her and my mother behind.

"Seth's face had crumpled, his hair grown white like his own father's, since Dinaz bai came home from phoren. So much suffering he had seen since then, Hai Vishnu! And still he was always asking me how Nirmala was doing. Each year he gave me money for her, so she could go to school in our village. In the old days, before bai came back from Amrika, he let me go to my muluk three, four times a year to see her. He would write

206

her letters for me any time I asked; I never had to go to a letter-writer.

"Now he was taking me to her for the last time, my Nirmala, my child.

"He tried to warn me. I didn't listen.

"Her blood is on my head."

I could not bear it. I put my arms around Sunder ayah, rested my cheek on her hunched back and held her as she huddled into herself. I could feel her anguish — it electrified the back of my neck. If I could have swallowed her pain, absorbed it into my own body, I would have. But I could do nothing except hold her and listen, while she talked in a choking, strangled voice.

"Railway chawls rushed by in the dark. We were just outside Poona. Her father-in-law had a paan-beedi shop in the old city. Her in-laws' family lived in a pukka tenement room above the shop. And she lived there all those months with them. So far away from me. I was only there once, for the wedding.

"Did Nirmala's husband treat her well? She only wrote to me a few times after her wedding. That was proper, as it should be. She belonged to their family once she was married. But I cried for her, selfish woman that I am. Our dharma kept us apart our whole lives. I had to live far away in the city so I could earn a living for her and her grandmother. So she could grow up strong and healthy in our village. I've learned to live with loss. But this loss? My soul longs to tear free of this worn-out body and fly to her."

My whole body went hot with pity and shame. She had given up everything to take care of our family, to take care of me. And, with a child's self-centredness, I had taken all her love and care for granted, never asking what she wanted out of life, never questioning the cost of her presence in mine.

"Seth was driving through the narrow streets of the old city, trying to find her in-laws' house. He stopped, and leaned out of the car window. He asked a chaiwallah, who was just opening up his shop, for directions. I was confused by the dreaming streets. I did not know where we were. Seth turned the car around. He craned his head through the window to see behind him so as not to run over people sleeping on the street.

"He drove in silence. And I looked out wearily at this world just waking from sleep. A world with a hole in it, shaped like her, my Nirmala. Those streets looked familiar to me. Did she walk down this alley? Stop in that grocer's shop for methi-bhaji? Did her feet feel the broken edges of the potholes on that street? Her eyes rest on this chawl every day? I did not know her world, what she saw, where she went, what she ate. So I could not imagine it, her married world.

"Seth stopped the car. I looked up and saw her father-in-law's shop. The shutter was drawn, the window in the room above was dark. They should have lit a lamp for her. Her young husband should have sat beside her body, praying for her spirit through the night. Maybe they had taken her to the crematorium already. But how could that be? They must have known I would come. It could not be.

"Seth turned to me, and said: 'Sunder, this is the address. But there doesn't seem to be anyone here, or else they are still asleep.'

"He climbed out of the car. I left my bedding on the floor in the back and climbed out too. My old legs were stiff from the long drive. We looked up at the darkened window. Seth knocked on the narrow door leading up to her in-laws' chawl. It was once painted blue, but the paint had blistered and darkened where many hands had touched it. Did her hands rest here? And here, where I rapped on the wood with my knuckles?"

As she said this, Sunder ayah knocked on the wooden edge of the bed. The rapping sound and sudden movement startled me,

208

but before I could say anything, she had curled into a ball again. Her voice was raspy by then, worn thin at the edges.

"No answer. But as we looked up again, a woman leaned out from the window next door. An old woman. Her hair was wispy and grey; she wore a dirty white sari. Its palloo was wrapped around her head. She called down in a hoarse, loud whisper: 'Nirmala's mother?' Her voice raised the hair on my arms.

"'I am she,' I replied. 'Where is the family?'

"'Gone in the night,' she said.

"'Gone where?' asked seth. Irritation made sharp lines in his forehead.

"The woman withdrew her head. We heard her coming down the stairs. She opened the door and looked at me with eyes milky with cataracts. Then she glanced at seth and looked shyly down at her bare feet. When she spoke again it was in a frightened whisper. I leaned close to hear her. I could smell her old woman's smell of paan and hair oil and stale sweat. 'If you have come for your daughter's cremation, it is too late.'

"My heart slammed hard against my chest. 'They cannot have taken her so soon!' I wailed.

"Seth cleared his throat. He pulled some money out of his pocket and thrust it under the woman's nose. 'Look here,' he said, 'can you tell us where they have gone? We have come a long way.'

"The woman shook her head. 'Blood money. May the gods strike me where I stand if I profit from that poor child's death,' she hissed. 'Her bhoot will haunt me forever. I do not want your money.' Then, drawing back into the shadows of the stairwell she beckoned with her hand. 'Come inside, come.' She held a finger against her lips. 'Her father-in-law has many friends. Come quietly before everyone wakes.'

"We stood in the stairwell. The walls were stained with paan juice, the stairs rose steeply behind the woman's hunched body. There was a smell of old, fried food and the sharp stink of

209

urine. She knew something. Did she know my Nirmala, see her every day, this toothless old woman with the paan stains on the edges of her mouth?

"'Please, take pity on a mother's grief. What do you know? How did my daughter die?'

"Seth's deep voice echoed mine: 'How did the child die? The telegram said an accident.'

"The woman waggled her head from side to side. 'I have seen "accidents" like that before,' she said slyly. 'But not on our street, not since . . . But that is neither here nor there.'

"I wanted to shout at her, to shake her till the few teeth left in her mouth rattled like dried peas in her head. 'What are you saying? What happened to my Nirmala?'

"'Ssshh,' the old crone hissed. 'A few months ago, your girl was washing dishes at the tap in the courtyard. A glass slipped out of her hand and broke. Her mother-in-law slapped her and screamed abuse at her; she made so much noise, the father-in-law came running out. She began shouting: Look, look at your worthless daughter-in-law, only been here a few weeks and already she is bringing destruction upon our house. Chop off her hands!'

"'They dragged the girl inside; we heard her screaming. Such terrible screams. After that, she did not come out to wash clothes or dishes any more.' The old woman's voice was very low, and I had to lean forward to hear.

"'I saw her only once, a few weeks later,' she continued. 'Her hands were cut off at the wrists. The wounds were full of pus, and the poor child looked white as a bhoot; her eyes were red and wild. I went downstairs to talk to her, but I am slow, my old legs don't work so well any more. By the time I reached the landing, her father-in-law came out and dragged her back inside their chawl.' The woman bowed her head

"'My God, what kind of people are these? Even animals treat each other better!' My seth burst out angrily. I could feel nothing, only look at the blood-red paan stains splattered on the wall and think: So this is why you never wrote to me.

"The old woman looked warily around, fear dilating the pupils of her eyes. She pulled her sari palloo over her mouth and whispered: 'Two nights ago there was a fire. Not here. In that empty lot behind our building.' She pointed behind her. I could see nothing, only a filthy window at the back.

"'She was burned? This fire. . . .' Oh my Nirmala, did her tender flesh burn?

"Seth spoke, his voice hard, like stones. 'Were the police informed? Did someone take her to the hospital?'

"The woman laughed. 'Seth, who takes people like us to hospital? She was careless with the primus stove, they said. The palloo of her sari caught fire. Who cooks dahl-bhaat in the middle of the night, I ask you? And her with no hands! There was another quarrel; we heard them shouting at her. But they were always shouting at her. We did not interfere. I live with my son next door.'

"Seth's voice rumbled, the old woman's voice quavered in reply, but I heard no more. My nostrils were filled with the smell of burning flesh.

"No! No. This could not be so. I could understand if I had not given them the promised dowry, but I gave them everything they asked for, more than fifteen years' savings. I borrowed money from seth and from Perin bai when her in-laws asked for more on the eve of her wedding.

"I gave it to them. I wanted her to hold her head up high among her new family.

"Oh my Nirmala, they cremated her alive! With the stove I bought for her dowry they burnt her like a pye dog.

"I would tear the hair from my head, the flesh from my bones to keep her from harm. And I chose them. Me! I gave her to them, my treasure, my life! What have I done?"

Sunder ayah's voice was a rising flame. She sat down suddenly on the floor.

"Seth touched my arm. It shocked me to my senses. 'Sunder, we must go to the police,' he said. 'I will demand an investigation.'

"The old woman wagged her head. 'Police are paid by this man, seth. He is big ShivSena supporter. He is protected.'

"'We'll see about that,' said seth.

"I sat down on the paan-stained stairs. My legs would not hold me. This was my fault, my Nimmi, my heart! I should have known when she didn't write. I should have made enquiries. Her flesh, her sweet flesh!

"My bones were on fire.

"My hair burned.

"My eyes were filled with smoke.

"Flames licked my belly, my belly where she once lay curled and sleeping. Fire wound around me like a snake, hissing, burning.

"Her death was in my mouth, my flower, bitter ashes in my mouth."

Sunder ayah was panting as though her lungs would burst; her eyes looked charred. She glanced up at me, not seeing me, but she let me stroke the hair back from her face.

When she spoke again, her voice was rusty and slow.

"I woke up with a jolt as seth braked the car to a stop in front of the big house. I had slept most of the way from Poona back to Mumbai. I dreamed about her, my Nimmi. A small child, her hair in two pigtails sticking out behind her ears, jumping up and down with joy when she saw the sweetmeats I had brought her from the bazaar. Her eyes shone like coals. She and her questions, her demand: why? how? show me!

"I climbed out of the car, my legs like two sticks, stiff, unbending. You and Roshan baba stood at the front door. When you saw me you came running down the steps, and threw your arms around me. I could not bear it. You were the child I had raised instead of my own, standing there with tears in your eyes.

212

You were saying something. I could not hear. Standing there healthy and strong.

"My girl was dead. I had no heart left. My heart was burned to ashes. I pushed you away. Picked up my bedroll. Walked towards my kholi."

I put my arms around Sunder's waist, laid my head on her shoulder and held her unyielding body. She sat as still as a corpse, her face a mask, her eyes uncomprehending.

Chapter 19

I'm standing in the doorway between the living room and the kitchen, trying to talk to Shahrukh: "Okay, I've got everything off the floor. Can you help me move this dhurrie into the bedroom? We'll have to roll it up and pile it on the bed."

Shahrukh grunts and carries on reading. He is sitting on the couch in the living room, where he has spread his text books out on the coffee table and is working on his first assignment for the semester.

"Shahrukh! Come on! I'm not going to wash these floors by myself. I've done all the work so far, while you've sat there doing nothing. Get up and help me!" I am tired, and cranky, and my voice is beginning to rise in a way I hate, but can't seem to help.

"I'm coming, have some patience. I have to get this assignment done or Professor Dalen will have my balls for breakfast," Shahrukh grumbles.

"I have assignments due on Monday too, but this floor isn't going to clean itself."

We have been living in our tiny flat in married students' housing for six weeks now, and the floors are so dirty our shoes make squelching sounds and stick to the floors when we walk. Among the household essentials Ann had helped us buy when we moved in are a large red plastic bucket, a bottle of Lysol cleaner, and a long-handled mop with a small strip of green sponge at one end. It is Saturday morning, and we've agreed to tackle the floors today. I get the bucket, Lysol and mop out of the closet, and put them in the middle of the kitchen floor. I read the instructions on the Lysol bottle out loud: "It says here: For floors, countertops, sinks, and bathroom fixtures, dilute 8 ounces of Lysol in four gallons of water. Shahrukh! How much water do you suppose this bucket holds?"

Shahrukh stands up and comes ambling into the kitchen, scratching his bottom through his pyjamas. His hair sticks up in a cowlick at the back of his head, and he has a two-day stubble that looks like mould growing on his cheeks and chin.

"How the Hell should I know? I've never had to measure water in a bucket before." He picks up the bucket by its metal handle and looks inside it. "Looks like there are measurements marked in here, but they're in ounces. How many ounces to a gallon?"

"I don't know. Ah, never mind. Let's just measure out the Lysol and then fill the bucket. Or maybe just half-fill it. It is rather big." I eye the bucket dubiously. "Pass me the measuring cup from that cupboard behind you, would you?"

Shahrukh reaches behind him for the cup and hands it to me. I open the bottle of Lysol and pour the yellow liquid carefully into the cup. It looks like urine and has an overpowering smell that resembles nothing I've ever encountered before. It makes my eyes water.

"Eight ounces hardly seems enough to do this entire flat," I say, frowning at the cup of Lysol in my hand. "Maybe I should put in twice as much and fill the bucket all the way to the top."

"Just get on with it Shahnu! I want to get back to my assignment. Here!" Shahrukh grabs the cup from my hand, spilling the smelly liquid all over my sleeve.

"Now look what you've done!" I snatch a kitchen towel off the refrigerator door and dab at my sleeve and my hand, which feels slimy and stinks of chemicals. "Ugh! Here, why don't you fill this bucket with warm water, and I'll go change my shirt."

I hand the bottle of Lysol to Shahrukh and escape into the bedroom. Lately, we seem to argue over just about everything. It worries me. I strip off my shirt and put on a short-sleeved t-shirt, then return to the kitchen. Shahrukh has filled the red bucket with water, and is pouring Lysol directly from the bottle into the bucket. He turns to me.

"Voila! One Lysol and water, stirred, not shaken. Now what?"

We look at each other, realizing, simultaneously, that we have no idea what to do next. I've seen floors being washed, of course, but back home the ayah puts phenol in a tin bucket and mops the floor by squatting on her haunches, swabbing away with a large wet cloth while she scoots across the floor like a crab. I've never paid the least attention to the mechanics of how she does it. I pick up the bottle of Lysol, our sole guide to the mysteries of floor-cleaning, but it has nothing further to say on the subject. I shrug. "I suppose we just . . . empty the bucket onto the floor."

"Righto!" says Shahrukh, and matching deed to word, tips the bucket over. The foamy water splashes onto our feet, soaking my shoes. It rolls in a glistening wave across the kitchen floor, flowing into corners and to the edges of kitchen cupboards.

"Looks promising," says Shahrukh, "but we'll need more water to wash the whole flat." He begins filling and emptying buckets with great gusto, moving from the kitchen to the living room, the bathroom, the bedrooms. Eight buckets later, the Lysol bottle is empty. A swaying tide of yellow water rolls across the living room, its foamy current slithering under the legs of couches and chairs and tables. I watch, fascinated, as it flows sinuously into the tiny entrance hall, where it surges back, its onward progress momentarily stayed by the closed front door.

"Hey! We did it!" Shahrukh's voice is jubilant. I look around the flat. There is a miniature sea lapping gently at the walls of

216

the living room, streaming into the bedrooms and bathroom, sloshing and rocking by the front door.

"Not quite," I say, drily. "We still have to mop this up. Where's that mop Ann got us?"

Shahrukh splashes his way into the kitchen, leaving a rippling wake behind him. He returns with the mop. Holding it sponge-side up, he hands it to me with a sweeping bow and a flourish, saying: "Here you are, madam. Your sceptre of power!"

I giggle and take the mop from him, then look dubiously at the tiny rectangle of green sponge. "It looks awfully small, Shahrukh. How on earth are we going to mop up that . . . that torrent with this? I feel like King Canute." I turn the mop sponge side down and jab it into the water swirling at my feet. When I lift it up it drips pathetically, making ripples in the pool of water on the floor.

"I think you're supposed to use that little plastic handle to squeeze the water out of the sponge," Shahrukh says, helpfully. "Here, I'll show you." He takes the dripping mop from my hand and presses down on the lever, smiling gleefully as the mini-ature sponge squeezes a tiny rivulet onto the mass of water at our feet. "Hey! It works!"

"No, you idiot!" I cry. "You're squeezing it right back into this mess. Why don't you squeeze it into the bucket?"

"Of course! You're right," Shahrukh beams. He hands me the mop and wades into the kitchen again, returning, this time, with the bucket. We work in silence, for the next few minutes. I dip the ineffectual sponge into the rising waters and empty it in dirty little dribbles into the red bucket which Shahrukh holds for me.

After about ten minutes of dipping and bending and squeez-ing I turn to him and say, "This is not working. It'll take us for-ever to get the water off the floor at this rate." I'm trying not to panic.

Shahrukh plunks the bucket down, creating a big splash which soaks my trousers. He puts his hands on his hips, tips his head forward and peers at the water all around us. "Hmmm," he says, after a moment. "You're right. This isn't working."

He wades towards the couch and sits down, holding his feet up off the floor. His shoes drip onto the water below. He picks up his textbook and begins to read. I stare at him in amazement.

"Shahrukh, what the devil do you think you're doing? There's a great bloody mess here. We have to clean it up."

"Hey, you said yourself there's no way to clean it up with that little mop, so why worry? I'm going to get on with my work." Shahrukh shrugs with infuriating nonchalance, and, licking his index finger, turns a page. I look around the room. I'm standing with water seeping into my shoes, while my idiot husband reads a book. Why did I ever leave home? I feel a great wail rise in my chest, but press it resolutely back. Thrusting my hair off my face I march over to the front door and fling it open so hard it slams against the wall.

"What're you doing? Its bloody cold in here. Close the door!" Shahrukh yells.

"I'm letting the water out," I yell back. And it's true, the tide is beginning to turn. The water nearest the door flows out onto the landing and down the stairs to the concrete driveway below, a sinuous, soapy river that has its headwaters in our flat. I grab the useless mop and use it as a sort of broom with which to push the water out. It sloshes against my legs, but obeys the laws of gravity and flows, reluctantly, at first, then faster, through the only outlet available to it.

I push the water furiously, all the pent-up frustration and fear, loneliness and doubt of the past two weeks fuelling every stroke. I will not drown here in my flat because no one taught me how to mop a floor; no one told me I would ever need to know how to do these things. I am livid. I don't know who I'm angry at — my parents? Myself? Shahrukh? But the anger feels cleansing, exhilarating. I'm finally doing something for myself instead of sitting and waiting for someone else — Shahrukh, or my father or the servants — to handle this.

Hot with exertion, I stop a moment to lift my hair off the back of my neck and twist it into a knot. Shahrukh has pulled on a thick wool sweater and is absorbed in his textbook once again. There is still an inch or two of water on the floor. I go into the bathroom, run cold water in the small sink and splash it on my flushed face.

I hear a knock on the front door and then Ann's voice calling out, "Yoo-hoo! Anyone home?" I squish my way back to the living room. Ann is standing in the doorway looking in amazement at the flood. "What happened?" she asks, her eyes rapidly skimming the floor, darting from Shahrukh's face to mine.

Shahrukh laughs and shrugs. "Ahh, it's just Shahnaz. Silly bint had the brilliant idea of washing the floor by dumping buckets of water all over the flat," he says. "So now we have our own private lagoon. Like it?"

I open my mouth in furious protest, but close it again. I won't show him up in front of Ann. But I throw him a narrow-eyed look that means he'll catch it from me later. Ann's jaw is hanging open in a caricature of astonishment. I smile tentatively, feeling hideously embarrassed, ashamed. The idiot immigrant.

"It doesn't say, on the Lysol bottle, what you're supposed to do once you've diluted it to the right proportions," I begin, defensively. "I've never washed a floor before."

Ann looks at me, then her eyes crinkle and she begins to laugh. After a moment I begin laughing too, uncertainly at first. But her laughter is so cleanly joyous, so unadulterated by any malice, that soon I am laughing as hard as she is, holding onto the walls for support as I whoop and gasp for breath.

Shahrukh looks at us both as though he thinks we've lost our minds. He goes into the bathroom and comes out with a stack of towels, which he tosses onto the floor. He scoots them around with his feet, mopping up some of the remaining water. Soon, though, the towels are sodden, and there is still enough water on the floor to form a small, shimmering lake.

Ann squishes her way across the living room and begins mopping with the tiny mop.

Still breathless from laughter, she gasps, "I guess I'm gonna have to take you two in hand. C'mon, let's finish cleaning up this mess and go down to the Excelsior for lunch. My treat."

At the mention of lunch, I realize I'm starving. Neither Shahrukh nor I have ever learned to cook, so we've been eating at the McDonald's just around the corner from our flat, ever since we moved in here. I'm sick of greasy burgers and fries.

"The Excelsior sounds wonderful," I sigh, so soulfully that both Ann and Shahrukh laugh.

Ann looks at me appraisingly: "Hey, you look even skinnier than you did when you first got here. Are you guys eating okay?" Then, spotting the look that passes between Shahrukh and me, she adds, "Okay. We've gotta have a heart-to-heart here. D'you guys know how to cook?"

I stare glumly at my sodden shoes, wondering why I feel guilty when Shahrukh seems completely unaffected. After all, it's no more my job to cook for us than it's his. Is it?

Ann looks at us thoughtfully for a moment, then continues: "Hmmm. I thought so. Tell you what we're gonna do. After lunch, we'll go to the supermarket and buy you some basic foods for your kitchen, okay? Then we'll swing by my place and pick up the Betty Crocker Cookbook my momma gave me when I first moved away from home. It won't teach you how to make curry, but it'll get you started." She smiles. I feel about ten years old.

We end up using the last of our towels and all our sheets to mop up the rest of the water. Ann looks at the mound of wet linens and, turning to me, asks: "Have you figured out how to do laundry yet?"

I shake my head, too humiliated to reply. She smiles and pats my shoulder. "Why don't you go get some trash bags for this lot. Oh, and bring the rest of your dirty laundry too. We'll stop at the laundromat on Alder, it's just a block away from the restaurant. I'll show you how to work the machines. We can get it all into the dryers before we go shopping."

I plod glumly into the kitchen and pull out several green garbage bags, handing them to Ann, who begins stuffing them with wet sheets and towels. I gather up our laundry, which is overflowing out of two large white baskets in our bedroom. We load everything into the boot of Ann's car. I sink into the plush blue seat in the back, feeling mutinous, ungrateful and ashamed. I want to kick something.

When we get back to the flat later that afternoon after a splendid lunch of grilled salmon washed down with a light Oregon Moselle, I'm feeling distinctly better — well-fed, nurtured and determined to tackle the task of learning how to cook. Ann has managed a minor miracle, bringing order into our lives, which were beginning to disintegrate under the pressures of the quotidian. Now, sheets and towels are clean, dry and folded. I won't have to go out and buy more underwear. Best of all, I know how to do laundry. I'm feeling inordinately proud of myself for this minor accomplishment.

My mind drifts to a conversation I'd had with my father when I was about eight. It had dawned on me that my mother never cooked. And unlike the mothers of my friends, she didn't supervise the servants or order meals or take charge of household accounts. Our housekeeper did all that. I asked him why. He smiled, put his pipe down on his desk and said: "You know, Shahnu when you die, no one's going to sit around at your funeral talking about how clean your house was, or how well you'd trained your servants. People will remember you for the work you did, how you contributed to your culture and society. Your mummy does important, creative work. She doesn't need to spend her time taking care of a house and servants."

Now I've come half-way across the world to get away from the subtle tyranny of servants, and unless Shahrukh and I can learn to take care of ourselves tout de suite, our lives will be dominated by the more immediate vissicitudes of dirty laundry and inedible food.

"Shahrukh," I begin. "I think we'd better learn how to cook." Shahrukh is back on the living-room sofa, reading PERT Charts for Organizational Development. He glances up at me.

"What?"

"We must learn how to cook. We can't keep eating at McDonald's. The food is disgusting. It's making me ill."

"Okay," Shahrukh mumbles, his attention on his book again. "You pick something from that cookbook Ann gave us, that Betty Boop or whatever it's called. We'll work on it after dinner."

"I was thinking we could try making something simple for dinner instead of going to McDonald's. You know, hard-boiled eggs and toast, or something."

"Fine, whatever you like. Just leave me alone right now so I can finish this." Shahrukh goes back to his book, chewing his lower lip between his teeth, his face scrunched into a frown.

I look at him and realize, with sudden surprise, that he's worried about his studies. He's enrolled in the MBA program at the U of O. His father wants him to come back to India when he's graduated, and work in his business. It has never occurred to me that Shahrukh might be feeling pressured by the course-load he's taking. "Shahrukh, are you worried about your classes?"

He looks up at me warily. "No, not worried exactly. But you know, I'm used to being smarter than everyone else. All the way through high school and then at IIT, I was The Brain. In fact, till I met you, I was the smartest person I knew." He grins as he says this, and then continues, "Here, though, I'm sort-of high average. Better than most, but not as good as some."

"But that's the beauty of it, don't you see," I respond excitedly. "After years of coasting we're finally in a place where we can really learn something." Then, seeing his skeptical shrug, I add, "Come on, Shahrukh. Don't tell me you weren't bored silly by those ancient instructors at IIT droning out twenty-year old lectures class after class, nothing to stimulate your mind or make you think. You said yourself it was driving you crazy."

"Yah, but . . . I don't like feeling second-rate," he blurts out. Then blushes and turns back to his book.

"You're not. You're a brilliant, capable man and you'll do well at this, you'll see."

"You're just saying that because you love me. You don't know how competitive it is in the Business School. They expect so much work from you, I don't know when these buggers find the time. Half of them are in intramural basketball or some other neanderthal sport, and they all seem to work as well as go to university. I don't know how they do it."

"They're used to it, I suppose. We aren't. It'll just take us time. Look, why don't I have a go at making dinner while you finish your reading. I can do my assignments later tonight." I kiss Shahrukh on the top of his head and walk into the kitchen.

Eggs. I'll boil eggs and make toast, and we can have that with tea. After all, how hard can it be to boil an egg? I get out the long-handled stainless steel pot and fill it with water. I turn on the stove, glad that I'd swallowed my pride this afternoon and got Ann to show me how the various knobs worked. I watch the element on the stove slowly turn from black to glowing red, then I put the pot on to boil.

I open the refrigerator, which, until now, has had nothing in it except for a cardboard carton of milk and a drawer full of apples. Annhas helped us stock it with what she considers essentials. We have a carton of eggs and a fluorescent orangey cheese, pre-sliced, each limp slice wrapped in its own little bit of plastic. Salad ingredients — Ann insisted we buy these, although, like most Indians, we seldom eat uncooked vegetables for fear of cholera or worse.

There's a loaf of sliced, fluffy white bread, a carton of butter, a jar of bright red strawberry jam. I haven't tried any of these yet. The jam looks unreal. And there's sliced ham, pink and wrinkled under a tight seal of plastic; a jar of mayonnaise and bright yellow mustard in a squishy plastic bottle. I stare at this cornucopia of foods in their unfamiliar, lurid wrappings, while my face chills in the cool refrigerated air.

I take out the carton of eggs and close the refrigerator door. The carton is fluorescent pink, made of a squeaky plasticky substance that feels soft against my fingertips. I take out four eggs and lower them carefully into the pot of water, which is still barely lukewarm. This could take a long time! I go to the bedroom and get my textbook on Human Sexual Behaviour, then sit reading it on the tall stool in the kitchen, waiting for the water to boil.

Just as the water in the pot is beginning to sing a little, Shahrukh wanders in. He peers at the eggs rattling so whitely in the bottom of the pot. "Hey," he says, "did you find a recipe for boiled eggs?"

"No, I couldn't find one in Ann's cookbook. They've got all sorts of egg recipes, but nothing about how to boil eggs."

"I know you have to boil them a long time," Shahrukh says, with brisk authority. "I remember my mum yelling at our cook once because the eggs were still wobbly. She said he hadn't boiled them long enough."

"So we'll boil them a good long time. How long is long enough?"

"I don't know. An hour? Maybe ninety minutes, just to be on the safe side. Ninety minutes should be plenty of time, no?"

"I suppose. I didn't think this would take so long. I'm getting hungry."

"Me too," Shahrukh replied. "Hey! Let's walk down to that little cafe we saw on the other side of Hunter — it's only seven or eight blocks past McDonald's. Change of pace. We can leave the eggs boiling and have them for breakfast tomorrow."

"Okay. I want to wait till this water's boiling, though, so I can turn the temperature down a bit before we go — this coil is glowing so red it looks as though it might explode."

"Don't be silly, its not going to explode. That's just the way electric cookers are."

"How would you know, Shahrukh? When have you ever used an electric cooker?"

Shahrukh grins sheepishly, shrugs his shoulders, then adds, "All I know is, if we don't go soon it'll be dark by the time we get back. So let's go now."

The water in the pot is rolling and steaming splendidly by now. I turn the knob from Max. to 8, but the coil continues to glow red-hot. I peer at it, worried that it's going to burn the bottom of the pot. I stand in front of it shifting impatiently from foot to foot while Shahrukh clomps off into the bedroom. I can hear him opening and shutting drawers, going into the bathroom, flushing the toilet. He comes into the kitchen again holding my coat.

"Hey, come on, let's go. You don't have to stand there and supervise it for it to boil."

I take one last look at the coil, which seems to be gradually cooling from bright red to a marginally darker, less frightening colour. The water is still sputtering and boiling; the eggs rattle against the sides of the pot. I put on my coat, grab my hat and gloves and head through the front door, waiting out on the street while Shahrukh locks up.

The evening is clear and cold, the sun low over the playing field across the road from our apartment, where two men in shorts and U of O t-shirts are jogging around the track. My breath steams in the crisp air and I wonder if these men are just better acclimatized than I am to the weather here or if they have a different metabolism altogether. My blood is so chilled, it's like melted ice in my veins. My nose is numb with cold. I pull my hat down over my ears and smooth on my black leather gloves, which make my hands feel as though I'm wearing a tight and uncomfortable second skin. Shahrukh runs down the stairs and loops his arm in mine, pulling me around the corner and onto the sidewalk. We walk arm-in-arm down the road to the El Sombrero Cafe.

The food at the El Sombrero was unexpectedly good, our first introduction to Mexican cuisine. After my initial surprise at chicken with chocolate sauce, I'd savoured the flavours and textures of this new world of food, and we had sauntered home in the gathering dusk, sated and happy.

"Hey, that was really something; great beer, and those Mexicans know how to cook!" Shahrukh belches and beams at me as he fumbles with the keys to our apartment. There is a shrill alarm beeping frantically somewhere in the vicinity. I try to ignore its annoying shriek. This country is full of sirens, day and night. Police, ambulance, fire-trucks, car alarms, who knows what else.

"I'm glad we went out there. It's wonderful food," I say to Shahrukh, wrapping my arms around his waist. And then, sighing at the thought of all the work I still have left to do, I add, "Now if only this term-paper would write itself, I could crawl into bed and sleep like the dead for the next twelve hours."

Shahrukh fumbles in his pockets some more, finally manages to find the right key, and unlocks our front door. As he pushes it open, we are greeted by a thick gust of smoke and an unspeakable stench of something burning. The alarm is much louder now, a high-pitched ditditdit. The eggs!

My eyes tear as I race into the kitchen. I can hardly see, for all the smoke. I grab a towel hanging on a hook next to the sink, and yank at the handle of the pot, trying to get it off the stove. The handle is so hot it burns my hand right through the towel. I scream and drop the pot, which clatters loudly at my feet. There are no flames, but the water in the pot has completely evaporated. The eggs have exploded and burnt to cinders and the whole inside of the pot is covered in a thick, viscous black crud. The bottom and handle of the pot are red hot. The stove element glows dully, an evil, sullen red. The smell is unbelievable — acrid, sulphurous.

I turn around to find Shahrukh right behind me, his handkerchief clamped around his nose and mouth. "What's going on?" he yells, above the thin shriek of the alarm. "Don't tell me you burnt the bloody eggs?"

"Me! You're the one who said they had to be boiled for ninety minutes!" The smoke is searing my lungs and I'm coughing so hard I can barely speak. "Why don't you do something useful instead of blaming me, Shahrukh. Open the kitchen window. I'll turn off the cooker."

I reach over the top of the stove, where the metal from the bottom of the pot seems to have partially melted and is sizzling and stinking on the element. I turn off the dial. Shahrukh stumbles silently to the kitchen window and tries to open it. It has been painted so many times that it's sealed shut. He rattles it harder and harder, trying to force it open. I hear the tinkle of breaking glass.

Shahrukh yelps and swears: "Bloody hell! Sodding window cut my hand." He grabs the towel I'd dropped and jams it against his palm. His forehead is beaded with sweat and he is breathing hard. The smoke has left sooty streaks on his nose and cheeks. Bits of glass glitter in the hair on his arm. "Look at this. I'm bleeding like a bugger. Go get me a bandage for God's sake!"

I realize I've been standing there, stunned, while the blood from Shahrukh's hand has soaked through the small kitchen towel and is beginning to drip onto the floor. Shahrukh is mildly haemophilic; I've always known that, but this is the first time I've actually seen him bleed. I run to the bathroom, grab a thick bath towel and pull the First Aid kit out from underneath the sink, silently blessing Ann for insisting that we buy it. By the time I get back to the kitchen, Shahrukh is pale, his face contorted with pain. I press the larger towel hard against the heel of his right hand, where a deep gash is welling dark red blood. Shahrukh screams and pulls his hand away.

"I'm sorry, I'm sorry," I say. He holds out his hand gingerly, and lets me examine it. A sliver of glass is embedded in the cut. I clamp it between trembling fingers and slowly pull. There is a gush of blood, bright and festive, which stains his sooty hand and mine. I throw the sliver into the sink, and, getting out the bottle of disinfectant, pour some onto a large cotton swab, dab at the cut, trying to get it clean. The blood keeps coming, the alarm keeps shrieking. I pack the gash with a wad of cotton gauze, and tie it tightly with a roll of gauze bandage, which is soaked with blood almost as soon as it's on.

"Shahrukh, I can't get this bleeding to stop. We'd better get you to the hospital." My voice quavers even though I'm trying to sound calm, collected. "I'll call Ann, she'll take us there. Come on, let's get you to the couch. You can lie down until she gets here."

Shahrukh is uncharacteristically quiet. He lets me steer him to the couch, obediently lies down as I plump the cushions under his head. His meekness scares me even more than his pale colour and wide eyes. I run into the bedroom and lift the big quilt off the bed, drag it into the living room, cover him with it. My teeth are beginning to chatter and I have to clench them together to keep them from rattling.

The living room is full of smoke, although it isn't as bad as the kitchen. I throw open the only two windows that do open, in the living room, letting in a gust of freezing air. I open the front door too. The smoke drifts out through the open door in lazy wisps that float up towards the ceiling. The alarm abruptly stops shrilling.

I pick up the phone and dial Ann's number. The phone rings and rings. It had never occurred to me that she might not be home. I hang up, coughing, and redial, holding the phone to my ear, listening to that single ring pealing in the distant dark of ann's house. No one there.

The light has bleached out of the sky in the half hour or so since we got home and the living room is full of shadows, drifting smoke and shadows. I feel as though my bones have turned to smoke, insubstantial, incapable of holding me up. I know I should look up the number of the hospital, call a taxi or an ambulance, but I can't move, can't stop the futile tears clogging my nose and trickling stupidly down my cheeks.

I don't know how long I've been sitting here in the gloom, holding the phone to my ear. Shahrukh seems to have drifted off to sleep, and the apartment is very still. I'm startled into an awareness of place by a knock on the open front door. Looking up, I can just make out the figure of a man in the light from the street-lamp outside. He knocks again, and calls out: "Hi! Anyone home?"

I stand up and turn on the lamp beside the couch. In its sudden illumination, I see that the man at the door is young, but older than me. He has stringy brown hair and a moustache that flows along both sides of his mouth. He's wearing blue jeans and a dun-coloured parka, holding what looks like a rolled-up newspaper in his right hand.

"Oh, hi! I'm sorry, I didn't hear you at first."

"I'm your neighbour, in 16B, across the street?" His voice is deep and rich. I can feel my hearbeat slowing down. "My name's Tom." He sticks out his hand. It takes me a minute to realize I'm supposed to shake it. I get up off the arm of the couch and cross the living-room floor to the front door. I shake his hand, which is large and dry and warm.

"Hi, I'm Shahnaz. Won't you come in?" The habits of hospitality die hard.

"Nah. My wife and I were wondering what was going on. The smoke," he adds, his voice aggressively loud. "We saw your front door open, and all this smoke . . . What'd you guys do, set the place on fire?"

"Oh, God, I'm sorry. We . . . I was trying to cook eggs, and we went out for dinner and left them on the cooker and by the time we got home everything was burnt. My husband's hurt his hand opening the window and he's bleeding. He's got haemophilia and I can't make it stop. I need to get him to the hospital." I recognize, dimly, that I'm babbling but I can't make myself stop.

Tom looks angrily at me. "Well do something about it, will

229

ya, before you burn the whole complex down? I'm gonna call the fire department." He turns on his heel and clomps down the stairs.

I watch him, stunned, as he walks across the street to his own apartment, opens his door and disappears inside.

As soon as he is out of sight, panic rolls over me like a cloud. I run to Shahrukh. His eyes are closed, his breath comes in long, shuddering gasps. He is very pale. I feel his forehead with my hand. It is cold and clammy, but then so are my hands. I can't tell if this coldness has any significance. I feel stupid — ignorant, useless and utterly alone. I stroke his cheek with my hand, which is papery and dry from the cold. His eyes flutter under his lids, his impossibly long lashes, of which he is so vain, make tender shadows on his cheeks. "Shahrukh," I whisper, "I'm so sorry, love, I'm so, so sorry. I'm going to get you to the hospital, as soon as I can phone an ambulance. Please, please be okay."

The fire-truck arrives before the ambulance, a flaming red beast of a truck, so massive it barely has room to turn onto our narrow street. Four firemen loom like shadows in the smoke-filled doorway of our living room, dressed in yellow raincoats and helmets. They introduce themselves in gravelly voices, and set to work, moving cautiously about our tiny apartment. Two of them check the kitchen to make sure the fire is out. The third talks on a crackling radio-phone in cryptic acronyms, while the fourth, a jowly, older man, turns his attention to Shahrukh.

I have improvised a tourniquet with a kitchen spoon and a twisted towel, but there is blood all over the couch, on the quilt that covers Shahrukh's body, on the towel. Blood has dried on his arm; dark clumps congeal on the hairs of his wrist. The fireman measures Shahrukh's pulse, checks his pupils by pulling open one eyelid and then the other, into which he shines a small torch.

Kneeling on the floor beside Shahrukh, he unties my crude tourniquet. He fishes a flexible rubber tube out of a white metal box he's carried into the living room, and ties it tightly just above the gash on Shahrukh's wrist. Then he gets out a pair of tweezers and gently begins removing slivers of glass from Shahrukh's hand, dropping each one onto the glass-topped coffee table with a small clink. I watch in silence. The smoke is beginning to clear, though the air in the apartment still reeks, acrid and sharp.

"Is he going to be okay?" I ask, my voice dim in my ears.

"His pulse is irregular, kinda slow. And his body temperature's dropped 'cause he's lost so much blood. Can you tell me what happened here?"

Hesitantly, I outline the events of the evening. I feel embarrassed. Frightened. The fireman listens without comment, his grey eyes fixed on mine, his lined face expressionless as I falter to the end of my story.

"My husband has haemophilia," I add, after a pause. " I told the woman who answered the phone when I called 911. She said they'd send an ambulance." I look at him, wanting him to tell me everything will be okay.

The fireman who has been speaking on the radio-phone calls across the room: "I've just talked to them, ma'am, they're on their way." Turning to the older fireman, he adds," They've been out answering a call near Springfield." The older man presses his lips together and nods, the two of them exchanging a cryptic look which I cannot decipher. I feel an exhaustion so deep I want to curl up on the floor and and sleep for a week. It has been years since I've felt so much like a child in an incomprehensible world of grownups.

It seems an eternity before the ambulance arrives, although my watch tells me it's only ten minutes later. Two paramedics in white uniforms run up the front steps and in through the open front door. They nod to the firemen, greeting them abruptly by name.

One of the firemen leads the paramedic to the couch where Shahrukh lies, pale and immobile. They talk in low voices while the other firemen and the second paramedic go out to the ambulance. They return with a stretcher and what looks like a white plastic picnic cooler.

The firemen leave, the older man raising his hand in a silent goodbye.

Meanwhile, a paramedic kneels beside Shahrukh. He takes his pulse, straps a black cuff onto the arm that isn't bleeding and checks his blood pressure. Shahrukh's eyes flutter open.

"Shahrukh, love, are you okay?" He tries to turn his head in my direction, but then his eyes roll upward, only the whites showing. His lids close. The skin under his eyes looks purple and bruised.

The paramedic glances up at me. "He's lost a lot of blood," he says, "but your husband's gonna be okay." He calls out to the other paramedic: "We need to start a line here."

The second paramedic has flaming red hair and freckles that stand out on his pale face in the smoky light. He opens the cooler and lifts out a bag of blood, while the first paramedic fumbles around in his case, emerging with a sealed plastic bag. He slits the bag open with his teeth, then he pulls out an IV tube and needle, much like the ones I'd seen hooked into my mother's arm whenever she spent time in Dr. Pereira's clinic. He ties a rubber tube tightly onto the upper part of Shahrukh's arm, then slides the silver needle expertly into a vein near the crook of his elbow. He attaches one end of the IV tube to the bag of blood, the other end into the top of the needle, fiddling with a nozzle to start the blood flowing into Shahrukh's vein. I hold my breath for long moments while the two of them work.

The red-haired paramedic turns to me, saying, "We'll have to take him in to the hospital."

I nod, overwhelmed at the thought of what this might mean. "I'll get my purse. May I come along with you?"

"Sure thing," says the first paramedic, who is skinny with dark eyes and skin browner than my own. "Don't forget to bring your husband's health insurance papers."

I go into the bedroom, pull open the chest of drawers in which we keep our passports and other documents. I can hear the paramedics talking in the living room. One of them grunts as they lift Shahrukh onto the stretcher, then I hear the stretcher's metal legs click into place.

Unsure of what I'll need at the hospital, I grab the manila envelope that holds all our documents and stuff it into my purse. Then I slam the drawer shut, right onto the tip of my index finger. I yelp, pain searing through my body.

By the time I get back to the living room, Shahrukh is already out in the ambulance, and the skinny paramedic is waiting impatiently for me in the doorway. I lock the front door, pulling on my coat as I climb into the back of the ambulance. Shahrukh lies in the back, strapped onto the narrow stretcher. He looks like my Framroze uncle looked on the day of his funeral, his face waxy, his body very still. All that's missing is the smell of incense and the white muslin cloth with which they'd covered the body.

We speed through the deserted streets of Eugene to the hospital. I hold Shahrukh's hand, which is limp and cold as a pomfret. His eyes are closed, though his eyelids flutter from time to time. I keep talking to him, but I don't think he hears me.

The ambulance pulls up at the Emergency Room entrance and the paramedics wheel Shahrukh into a large waiting area brightly lit with fluorescent overheads. The place smells aggressively clean, a mixture of disinfectant and floor cleaner. One of the paramedics points past some benches and plastic chairs along the walls, where people sit waiting, to a counter marked "Admitting."

"You'll have to go there and fill out a bunch of forms," he says, and turns away.

"Aren't you going to take him in to see a doctor?" I ask.

"No ma'am. We have to head out on another call." Then, seeing my anxious look, he adds, "They'll take care of you here, once you fill in the proper forms."

I watch him as he walks over to the red-haired paramedic, who has wheeled Shahrukh into an L-shaped alcove of the waiting area. They confer in low voices for a minute or two, then turn and leave through the front doors.

The woman at the front desk is talking on the phone and ignores me. She is plush as a sofa and black — the blackest woman I've ever seen, darker even than the darkest South Indian. She keeps talking, laughing loudly, her teeth large and yellow in her mouth. I find myself gritting my teeth as she carries on her conversation, oblivious to my presence. Her hair is teased up into a big ball around her head, squished down in the middle by a black telephone headset. She wears dangling red earrings, and a small gold cross on a chain around her throat, which moves up and down as she talks. I want to grab her by the chain and yank her towards me, force her to pay attention, but of course, I do no such thing. She finally rings off, glances at me, seems about to speak. But then the phone buzzes again and she is quickly embroiled in another conversation. I clear my throat and lean forward over the counter, but it becomes obvious that I'll have to interrupt her if I hope to get Shahrukh treated.

"I do beg your pardon for interrupting," I begin, then repeat, louder this time, "Excuse me." She looks up at me, her thin, pencilled eyebrows raised, and keeps talking on the phone. I am mortified, both by her rudeness and by the necessity of having to be rude myself.

"My husband is lying on a stretcher over there, bleeding. He needs someone to attend to him," I say firmly, clutching my purse in my hands to keep my voice from quavering.

"I'm on the phone here. Don't you people know enough to wait?" She looks me up and down, contempt written on every curve of her cushioned face. "Go sit down in the waiting area. I'll get to you when I'm done." She turns her attention back to the phone.

"Hey, Bo," she says into the phone. "So what time d'you wanna meet?"

This is too much. I look at her badge, which states her name in block letters: "Lavinia Prine."

234

"Miss Prine," I begin, taking a deep breath and drawing myself up to appear as imposing as possible. "If you don't get off that phone immediately and admit my husband for treatment, I will personally speak to the director of this hospital and have you removed from your position here."

Lavinia glares at me, but I have her attention. I sail on, thinking, it doesn't matter now, she already considers me a bitch. So I continue: "If my husband suffers because you are too busy socializing on the phone to attend to your duties, my solicitors will commence immediate action against this hospital."

Lavinia throws me an evil look, bares her teeth at me and grumbles her goodbyes into the phone. Pulling a bunch of forms out of her desk drawer, she slams them onto the counter in front of me.

"Here. Fill these out and show me proof of medical insurance."

I move aside from her window, my arms and legs trembling. Look at the forms. See a blur of black on white. Wiping my eyes surreptitiously on my coat sleeve, I take out my pen from my handbag and begin filling them in.

There are 168 questions, numbered, and in sections. Some are relatively easy to answer — name, address and so on. Pages 2, 3 and 4 ask a lot of questions about Shahrukh's family's medical background. I can't answer most of them, so I skip ahead. The questions on the pages 5 and 6 are even harder. I don't understand the terminology, which refers to social security numbers and other arcane bits of Americana which mystify me. Panicked, I think: I have to come up with the right answers or they won't admit Shahrukh. He'll bleed to death here and it'll be my fault.

My hand is shaking so hard, I have to stop and sit down in order to finish filling in the forms. I invent wildly, trying to remember what I little I know of his family history. I write that his grandmother has diabetes and his father high cholestrol; I make up a family history of kidney disease and heart attacks. I keep expecting someone to clamp an authoritative hand on my shoulder and drag me off to jail for lying. Finally, under next-of-kin I put down Ann's name, address and phone number. We have no one else within 14,000 miles of here.

I take the forms back to Miss Prine, along with Shahrukh's medical card, which is one of the first things we had received from the University after registration. She holds the card between her fingertips, peering at it skeptically, as though it might be forged. She glares up at me, then looks down at the card again. Wrinkles her nose. She riffles through the forms, frowns, yawns, fluffs her hair with the tips of her long red nails. Then, with a show of reluctance and a practised pout of her thick, purple-painted lips, she gets up from her chair and growls at me to follow her — the doctor will see Shahrukh in Room 208.

The doctor turns out to be a friend of Ann's. A stocky, broad-faced man with bright gold hair. His blue eyes are blood-shot and watery at this hour of night. We've met once before, at a dinner party at Ann's house. I try to recall details of our dinner-table conversation as he hovers over Shahrukh, checking his vital signs.

Harry. That's his name. From Nebraska. He'd told me he worked at the University Health Sciences Centre during the week and moonlighted at the Emergency Room on weekends. He is reassuring, friendly, in a loud-voiced, American way, and lets me stay while he examines Shahrukh. I watch him anxiously as he checks Sharukh's pulse and respiration. Then he rings for the nurse, has her bring in bags of blood. He gives Shahrukh a local anaesthetic before he cleans and sutures the cuts on Shahrukh's palm and wrist. I wince each time the needle punctures Shahrukh's flesh, feeling the bite of it as though it were piercing my own skin.

"His blood pressure's returning to normal. He should be in good shape by morning." Harry puts a reassuring hand on my shoulder

I let go of the breath I've been holding, feel some of the tension melt from my jaw and neck.

"I'd like to keep him overnight, for observation," Harry continues, sounding apologetic. "We'll give him something to keep him comfortable while we replace the blood he's lost." Then, looking at my haggard appearance, he adds, "Why don't you give Ann a call and have her come get you? You look like you could use some sleep."

"I tried ringing her earlier. She wasn't at home," I reply. "I'd really rather stay here. I don't want Shahrukh to wake up alone."

"Hey, no problem. There's a coffee machine in the lounge if you need it. I've gotta go see other patients, but I'll stop in later."

I settle into a chair beside Shahrukh's bed, curling my feet up under me. The room is cold. Bleak. My coat feels tight and uncomfortable under my arms. I hug my purse to my chest, close my eyes for a moment, to rest them.

When I open my eyes again, the clock on the wall says 6 a.m. Shahrukh has always teased me about being able to sleep through anything. My eyes feel grainy, as though I've been walking through a dust storm. My neck is stiff; I can only turn my head one way. Shahrukh sleeps with a beige hospital blanket pulled up to his chin, stretched tight across his body, tucked severely under the mattress. Oh Shahrukh, we should have stayed at home. He looks like a corpse, in the blue-green aquarium glow.

Chapter 20

Moonlight floods in through the small window on the wall behind our bed, filling our icy bedroom with cold light. Despite the noisy space heater which rattles in one corner, the window-frame has ice on the inside. Shahrukh and I are huddled under a down quilt, two thick wool blankets, and a large wool comforter. We have spent the day with my friend Sheila and her family, eaten a massive dinner complete with turkey and dozens of accompaniments, all of which, Sheila assured me, were essential to the Thanksgiving meal. So Americans have holiday foods too! Sheila's husband, Bob, drove us home a couple of hours ago, both of us groaning at the fullness of our stomachs and the lateness of the hour. We went to bed soon after, but sleep eluded me.

"Shahrukh, are you awake?"

"Who can sleep? I ate so much, I feel as though my stomach is going to explode."

I burrow my head into Shahrukh's warm shoulder and tuck my arm around him. "It was nice, being at Sheila and Bob's."

"Yeah, I had fun."

"They've been married for twenty-five years."

"Hmmm."

"Do you ever wonder what we'll be like in twenty-five years?"

"I'll be bald — a paunchy old fart like my father. You'll be skinny and gorgeous and you'll run away with a Yankee millionaire."

I giggle. "Of course. His name will be Marshall or . . . Pierpont, and we'll sail the South Seas on his ninety-foot yacht. If you're very good, you can come along as our bartender."

"Oh, I'll be good, I promise ma'am!" Shahrukh says, in a high-pitched breathy voice that sets me laughing.

"Don't you wonder where we'll be in twenty-five years?"

"No. I have enough trouble figuring out where I am today."

"I'd like us to be like Sheila and Bob. Still friends, still in love after all those years. They have the nicest kids."

"No kids," Shahrukh says, his tone wary, his shoulder tensing under my cheek. "I told you, I'm not bringing any brats into this world."

This is a sore point between us. Shahrukh is adamant about not wanting children. He says he hated being a child; he felt miserable and powerless and has no intention of inflicting such a state on any human being. My own childhood was frightening, painful, but I believe we could provide our children with the love, safety and acceptance we ourselves never had. But we've had this argument so often, I know it's useless to bring it up now.

"Okay, forget the kids. It's just — Bob and Sheila are so happy together. They do things together."

"Like what?"

"They travel, they just hiked the West Coast Trail on Vancouver Island. They go camping . . ."

"You don't seriously expect me to sleep in the jungle in a bloody tent!"

"No. But it would be nice to do something together once in a while."

"Aaahh, we will, don't worry."

"Shahrukh, do you still love me?"

239

"Of course. I'm here, aren't I?"

"Half the time, even when your body's here, your mind's somewhere else. Like right now. What're you thinking about?"

"I'm thinking I want you to get your freezing cold hands off my ass. What do you want from me, Shahnu?"

"You never talk to me any more. You shut me out. I miss you."

"What more do you want? I came here because you wanted to. I was happy in India."

"Don't give me that: I came here because of you. You were miserable in India too. You complained about your parents, your job, the mess, the heat, the flies. You were always going on about how the damn country was going to the dogs."

"It may be going to the dogs but at least it's my country. I'm not a bloody 'resident alien' there. I had a place there, people looked up to me."

How did we get into this argument? All I want is to feel close to him again. I lean forward to nuzzle his cheek, but Shahrukh is bristling with indignation, all edges and angles; he crosses his arms over his chest. I draw back to my side of the bed.

"Shit!"

Shahrukh's tone is sharp, angry. "I'm fed up with all this bloody talking!"

He picks up his pillow, pulls the blankets off the bed and thumps off to the living room. I hear the creak of the sofa, the click of the TV set being turned on, then canned laughter.

I lie awake for a long time, the hours limping by like beggars at a deserted midnight bazaar. Two a.m. Three fifteen. Three forty-five. I feel lonelier than I've ever felt before.

Chapter 21

I get home from school the next day to find a stack of mail waiting for me on the kitchen counter. There is a fat manila envelope from Perin aunty, a postcard from my father, and a letter from Dilly. I read the postcard first. My father is laconic as always: he's fine, the Delhi office keeps him intensely busy, Roshan is doing well in school. Not a word about mum.

Dilly's handwriting is clear and round, and I smile as I read her letter. She is excited about her studio classes at the J.J. College of Art, and has made friends with people she works with at the art gallery. She also has a boyfriend, an oil billionaire from Dubai who comes to Bombay from time to time, and who wants to marry her. She says she'll never marry him — he already has three other wives — but she enjoys his company, and is having fun being the only woman not in purdah at the sheikh's parties.

I weigh Perin aunty's letter in my hand. The envelope is plastered with stamps, the letter as heavy as a manuscript. What on earth has she sent me? I'd written to her a while ago, telling her how angry and frustrated I felt about Shahrukh's addiction to TV, his refusal to do his share around the house. I feel ashamed now, complaining about Shahrukh like that, but Perin aunty will understand. I slit open the manila envelope and pull out her letter — a great stack of blue airmail paper folded in half. Curious, I unfold the pages, smooth the creases with the palm of my hand and sit down on the couch to read. On the first page is a scribbled note: *I sent this to you earlier but had the wrong address, so it was returned to me. You'll have got my letter about Jal and Australia by now, but I wanted you to have this, so am sending it again. Love, P.*

On the next page, her letter begins:

Bombay, India
September 28, 1972
Dearest Shahnu:

I was so happy to receive your letter, and so sorry to hear that you and Shahrukh are having problems. It must be difficult for both of you, adjusting to a new country and climate, being so busy with your school work. Is it really necessary for you to work at a part-time job too? I understand that you want to be independent, darling, but you know if you're having difficulties with money you only have to ask. My cousin Mani's daughter is coming from New York for a holiday. She will be here for a month, then she returns home. I can send whatever you need with her.

You are probably wondering why I've written you such a long letter. There are things I've wanted to tell you for some time, but I wanted to wait until you were old enough to understand. I'm not ashamed of anything I've done, Shahnaz — although, in hindsight, I would probably have done things differently if I had been wiser, and better acquainted with myself. I hope that, by sharing my experiences with you, I can offer you some insight that will help you in your own situation with Shahrukh. Things aren't easy for women in our culture, and we must help and support each other.

Do you remember the year you turned twelve and we went to Udvada for our summer holidays? You and I and Roshan and Khorshed. We stopped in to see the Dasturs, and Arni Dastoor had her period. It was the first time you had ever seen a woman confined to the women's hut during her menstrual period; you were so upset and angry.

You were such a tomboy then, happiest when you could run around in pants and an old shirt. You hated wearing dresses even though they were cooler, in that heat. You always said they got in your way. Your mummy insisted on buying you dresses: for all her independence, she felt that pants were not ladylike. Sorab, on the other hand, saw nothing wrong with you wearing trousers. He always wanted a son and he treated you as though you were a boy rather than a girl. I think the way you dressed then — in pants, and a short-sleeved shirt — suited you. After all, what was the harm? You would only be young enough to dress that way for another year. After that, you would have to conform like all the rest of us. You were active and skinny, like your father and tall like him too. Only twelve years old and already you were taller than me!

I used to weigh and measure you girls each month, check your eyes and ears and throats, make sure you had no infected insect-bites or boils or prickly-heat. I gave you your innoculations against cholera and typhoid every six months. So many people died of endemic diseases each year that you couldn't be too careful. You and Roshan were the closest thing I had to children of my own. And what was the use of being a doctor if I couldn't use my skills to keep you, my darlings, happy and healthy and free from harm?

This is a terrifying world, when you have children. I remember, that day we visited the Dustoors, Coomi Dustoor was telling us about her husband's cousin's baby, who was stolen out of his cradle from the verandah of their house in Poona. Right out of his cradle, in the middle of a quiet afternoon. The ayah was supposed to be taking care of him, but she disappeared too. Coomi thought the ayah was implicated in his disappearance, but the poor girl was only sixteen years old. She'd been raised her whole life in her employers' home, so where would she go? No, whoever stole that child took the ayah too. And this terrible thing happened even though the family lived in the army cantonment, not in the city, where such crimes were routine.

When I heard stories like that, I became so frightened for you girls. This child's father was Brigadier General Rustom Antia, Chief of Staff at the armed forces hospital in Poona. The whole army base was out searching house to house. But once these people snatch a beautiful baby boy like that, one of our fair Parsi babies, they just disappear into the bustees. Who can find them? They sell the boy, or cut off his arms and legs and use him as a beggar, to get money from people like his parents. They never did find him. His mother died of grief.

As for the ayah — she probably ended up in Bombay's red-light district on Foras Road, where these poor women were kept in cages and hired out to a dozen men every night. My God it made me want to keep you girls right under my nose, but who can lock up a child day and night? I'm glad Sorab sent you to school in the car, and that your school was completely surrounded by high walls topped with spikes of broken glass. You hated those walls, and the chapprassi with a rifle standing guard at the gate. But in Bombay, they were what kept you safe.

When we were children growing up in Poona, life was safer. Poona was a medium-sized town then, not a big city like now. In the Cantonment area, where we lived in our grandfather's house, we knew everyone on our street. Our family was poor. My father was a very minor government clerk. We had little money, but the Parsi Panchayat helped us with clothes and food and school fees. My mother's father left her his house when he died, so we always had a roof over our heads in the good part of town. Sorab and his family lived about five miles away, near the race-course. His father used to breed racehorses as a hobby. They are distant relatives of ours, on my mother's side, so we used to visit them on holidays. They had a big house, fifteen bedrooms! They were the wealthiest Parsi family in Poona but your grandmother, as you know, is a wonderful woman, who never puts on airs. Always dressed in simple mulmul saris, even then; no ostentatious jewellery or anything. She was very devout. Always giving to Parsi charities, making sure no Parsi family was deprived of necessities. She used to send their horse-drawn tonga for us every morning, to take us to school. My two sisters and I went to school with Sorab and his brothers and sisters. Sorab, as you know, is four years older than me, so he was already in standard four when I started going to kindergarten. But he looked after me. I had no brother; he wouldn't let anyone tease me. He protected me.

I wished I could have done something to protect you that day when you saw Arni isolated in the women's cottage because it was her monthly time. Of course you had never faced anything like that before. Your father had sheltered you from the limitations we women face every day. He made you believe you could do anything you set your mind to and it didn't matter that you were a girl. I know he wanted to believe that, he wanted you to have everything. He even called you "maaro dikro" — my son. But you can't make a son out of a daughter. At that time you were young enough that it didn't matter so much, but soon you began having your periods and your childhood was over. You had to get used to the limits placed upon us.

Look at me, for example. I'm thirty-five years old and I've never married. I have no children. I had my chances, but I passed them up because I wanted more than I was offered. And now I will never know the happiness of having my own family, my own little ones. I will always be just Perin aunty; no one will ever call me "Mummy."

When I was eighteen, my mother wanted me to marry Hoshi Daruwalla. She kept telling me what a "good match"

245

he was, but I refused. He had a round chin like a soup-ladle, buck-teeth and no hair, and he lived with his widowed mother in Shapur Baug. I couldn't stand that woman, never mind having to live with her. She totally ruled his life — he wouldn't go to the bathroom without asking her first. Besides, in those days, I had my own ideas.

Back then, when I was fifteen, sixteen years old, I still dreamed that one day Sorab would want to marry me. I was just a silly girl — I had a crush on him. I would practise signing my name with a flourish, over and over — Mrs. Perin Jamshedji —the three words sounding so absolutely right together. Of course I never told anyone how I felt about him, but I would go over to his house whenever I could persuade Dinshi or my mother to take me along. There I would sit and talk to his mother or play carom with him and his sisters. If he was in a really good mood he would take me riding. He was always busy. He was captain of the cricket team and sometimes I would go with his brothers and sisters to the cricket club to watch him play. He looked so handsome, dressed in his cricket whites, with that thick, dark hair springing straight back from his wide forehead, his eyes so clear and direct. He carried himself well — tall and straight, like a young mango tree.

He is a proud man, although not in the usual way. He doesn't care about wealth or status or class — any of the things that matter so much to most people. I suppose, growing up as he did, he just took those things for granted. But he has a lot of ideals about truth, integrity, honour, strength of character, loyalty. Perhaps because he has such high principles he cannot admit that he needs help or that he might have made a mistake. But in those days I was in awe of him and all I wanted was for him to notice me. However, he treated me with the absent-minded kindness of an older brother, nothing more.

Then he fell in love with your mother, my sister. I don't

blame him. Dinshi was so beautiful in those days, a real jewel. So fair, people thought she was a foreigner, Italian or Portugese. She had beautiful eyes, big and brown, full of dreams. And curly brown hair, like a waterfall, down to her feet. She was so — ethereal almost, an angel, with that pale skin and soft brown hair. People always wanted to protect her, even though she was really completely selfish and, like most selfish people, could take care of herself perfectly well.

And she was brilliant, I have to admit that. A true genius. A mathematician and a theoretical physicist. Gold medals and full scholarships all through university, always top of her class. She worked on her PhD dissertation with Satyendra Nath Bose, the nuclear physicist who, with Einstein, worked out the behaviour of the boson particle. After she finished her PhD, she wanted to go to Cambridge to do her mathematical tripos. She was admitted to the postdoctoral program, but there was no money for her to go abroad.

That's when she finally said yes to Sorab. He had the money, you see, and he promised her if she'd marry him, he would send her to England. He'd been courting her for three or four years, by then. He used to write her poetry and send her love-letters every day when she was at university in Bombay and he was still in Poona. He even moved to Bombay, and bought a house close to his family's compound in Juhu Beach, to be near her. I saw them once, sitting on our verandah. She was stretched out in a longchair pretending to read a book. Sorab sat on the small cane settee facing her and pleaded with her to marry him.

"I love you more than my life, Dinshi. I'll do anything you want, anything to make you happy. Marry me and I will take you wherever you want to go. We can travel, have children . . ."

His voice faltered, when Dinshi finally looked up from her book. She sounded troubled as she replied: "Sorab, I don't want children. I'm a mathematician. What do I want with babies and diapers? I don't want to marry you. I only want to do mathematics."

He shook his head, and looked at her with melting eyes. I saw them. I heard them. I was just inside the house, sitting not ten feet from them but they didn't know I was there. Sorab kept pleading: "I would never do anything to keep you from your work. I know you are much more brilliant than I will ever be."

My sister looked down at her book, then raised her chin and looked directly into his eyes. "Sorab, I don't love you. I don't know if I love anyone. I look at my parents, and my sister, and I can't imagine how I came to be related to them. Do you know what it's like, to understand things that no one else can follow? It's lonely but I've come to terms with it and I've made up my mind. I won't compromise my intellect to become a housewife."

"My darling, I would never ask you to do that. Don't you see, my family has connections. And," here his voice dropped low, "you know there's enough money for you to do whatever you want, go wherever you need to go for your research."

I can give you freedom." He stopped, then continued, "I have enough love in my heart for both of us. Marry me, Dinshi. Please. At least think about it."

It broke my heart, listening to him talk to her that day. I realized then that he would never love me the way he loved her. But I could not remove him from my thoughts or my heart.

When she wouldn't listen to his proposals, he came and talked to me. He sat on our verandah for hours, telling me how much he loved her, how he couldn't live without her. I would listen, or, if truth be told, only half-listen. Mostly, I'd watch his mouth as he talked, and imagine . . . Well, I could daydream, couldn't I? Sometimes he would read me poems he had written about her, comparing her to the moon and the stars. His poems were so flowery and sentimental I barely recognized Sorab in them, but I listened, and praised his poetry, and soothed his wounded ego. He would ask me to talk to her, to try and persuade her to see him, to give him a chance. I tell you, it broke my heart.

But I couldn't bear to see him unhappy so I did as he asked. If things had turned out differently, you and Roshan could have been my children. Mine and his. But of course that's all in the past now. Once they were married, I had to accept; God works in His own way, and it is not for me to question why.

I was lost for a while after they got married. Luckily, I had an eccentric old spinster aunt, my mother's aunt, who was a fabulously wealthy and deeply reclusive woman. One day she sent her chauffeur to our house with a summons for me to come to tea at her place the following weekend. She sent her card, with the invitation scrawled on it in royal blue ink, a demand I could not refuse even if I had wanted to. I had never been invited to her house before. In fact, I had only ever met her once, at my grandfather's funeral, which had taken place when I was five, so I had very little memory of her. Feroza aunty was invited to my Navjote ceremony, of course, but she didn't come. Instead, she sent me a gift — a magnificent gold necklace with an intricate ruby and pearl pendant. The necklace was so large that when I put it on the pendant covered my belly button! That was the last time I had heard from my great-aunt.

So on that March morning, the Sunday after my twentieth birthday, when the chauffeur arrived with the invitation from Feroza aunty I was beside myself with excitement. It was like being invited to tea with the Queen Mother. I wondered what she was like; I was dying to see her fabled house; I couldn't imagine what she wanted with me.

On the afternoon of the Great Day, my mother made me wear her best ivory silk sari and insisted I do my hair up in a bun, even though my hair is so curly the pins kept slipping out and the bun kept sliding down my neck. She made me wear the Navjote necklace Feroza aunty had given me, added her own wedding pearl earrings and bracelet, and tucked her ivory silk handbag into my hand. She would have made me wear her high-heeled satin shoes too, except her feet were much bigger than mine. I felt silly, getting all dressed up as though I were going to a wedding, but Mummy stated firmly that her Feroza aunty was very formal about these things and I must be properly dressed, so as not to shame my family in front of her.

By the time we got to Feroza aunty's house on Malabar Hill, I was a nervous wreck. I'd wracked my brains to think why she'd invited me but couldn't come up with a scenario that made any sense at all. The road leading up to her place wound round and round the steep hillside until I was dizzy and was afraid I would vomit all over the back seat of her Bentley. Finally, though, the interminable ride came to an end and the driver pulled up under a portico at the end of a long, curving gravelled driveway. He got out, helped me out of the backseat and up the marble front steps of Feroza aunty's house. There her bearer met us and escorted me into the sitting room, inviting me to sit on an enormous Victorian sofa covered in green silk damask. There was a faintly medicinal smell in the room — could it be formaldehyde? And no sign of my aunt.

The bearer left through the dark mahogany double doors, his starched white uniform and cockaded red pugree gleaming in the hallway outside the sitting room. I looked around. It was the strangest room I had ever been in. For one thing, it was gigantic, like a great hall, with a high, corniced ceiling. Couches and chairs, tables and lamps were arranged in groups across the room, and all the furniture was made of black Burma teak with heavy, ornately carved arms and legs. Green velvet drapes were half closed over tall, narrow windows that looked out over the harbour, casting a peculiar underwater gloom across the room. I gasped as I realized my feet were resting on a bearskin rug, complete with a leering, long-toothed bear's head. That's when I looked up at the walls and noticed that every available inch of wall space was covered with dead animals stuffed and mounted, their glassy eyes glittering and following my every move. So that's where the smell of formaldehyde came from! I shuddered and tucked my feet close together, smoothing the folds of my sari and telling myself there was really nothing to be afraid of.

Despite my best efforts I was entertaining thoughts of fleeing out the front door, when the butler returned, silently placing a heavy silver tea-tray on the low table in front of me. I turned my head towards the door, moved more by instinct than by any sound. My great-aunt stood in the doorway, tiny and regal in a plain midnight-blue silk sari. The only jewellery she wore was a large Burma ruby ring on the third finger of her right hand; it glowed richly in that strange green light. She walked across the room and sat down on an overstuffed chair in front of me. I realized then that she was very old. Her face was the colour and texture of a mango seed. Her hair was white, swept back in a smooth bun. She had our family's characteristically long nose and slanting, walnut-coloured eyes over which arched thick white eyebrows. She dismissed the bearer with a glance and a nod, and he glided out of the room as silently as he had come into it. Then she turned her attention to me.

Her voice, when she finally spoke, was rusty and abrupt, as though she had grown unused to talking. "So. You're Perin. Ratan's little one."

I didn't know how to respond, so I smiled and nodded.

"You are my god-daughter. Did you know that?" she asked, abruptly.

Startled, I replied, "No. No one told me."

She seemed pleased with my answer. At any rate she smiled, displaying yellowed teeth, and began to pour tea from the heavy silver teapot into fragile white teacups. She added milk and two spoons of sugar to both cups, and handed me mine. She reached for the gold-rimmed eyeglasses that hung by a chain around her neck, put the glasses on her nose and looked at me for a long time without saying another word.

Whatever she saw in my face seemed to satisfy her, because she sat back in her chair and took a long sip of tea. Then, placing her cup carefully down on the table, she said, "I suppose you're wondering why I've asked you here."

"Well, yes. I . . ."

"I want you to go to medical college and become a doctor. I will pay all your expenses, including an allowance to your parents to make up for the income you bring into the family." Then, seeing my startled face, I suppose, she added, "I have my sources. You work at the Parsi Panchayat office. I had a word with Nergish Godrej and she offered you the job. It doesn't pay much but I know the money you earn helps out at home. If you go to medical college, I will replace that income so it doesn't affect your parents."

I sat dumbfounded through this entire speech. Of course I'd dreamed of going to university like Dinshi. But I knew my limitations. Unlike her, I wasn't brilliant enough to get scholarships. Also, someone had to help my parents. My father had just retired and his tiny pension wasn't enough to cover our basic living expenses. But medical college? I wasn't smart enough, I'd never get in. I could feel panic fluttering in my throat.

"Well, girl, what do you have to say for yourself?" my great-aunt demanded, her chin rising along with her tone.

"I . . . I don't know what to say," I stuttered. "It's a very generous offer, but my sister's the smart one, I think you probably mean her." I was stumbling over my words and groaned inwardly at my ineptness.

Unexpectedly, Feroza aunty smiled. A wide smile of such sweetness that I saw she was a beautiful woman still, despite her great age. "I know exactly what I'm doing. I've heard all about your sister. And met her too. She'll do very well without my help. She knows precisely what she wants and she'll get there because she won't allow anyone to stand in her way. Now you. Do you know what you want?"

I was beginning to relax. "I suppose I want what everyone wants. A home, a family. Love. Companionship."

My aunt looked keenly at me. "And I suppose you have a young man in mind who will provide all this for you?"

Shamefaced, I admitted, "Not exactly. I mean, there is someone, but he . . . he's not interested in me."

"So. You don't really know what you want." I opened my mouth to protest, but she continued, "I never married. Didn't have to. I was an only child and my father left me everything. Which, as you can see, is a great deal." She glanced around the enormous room and smiled again, turning the ruby ring around and around on her finger. "He loved me, but a man's love, even a father's, can be a terrible, binding thing. He could not bear to be parted from me, even for a day. My mother died when I was an infant, you see, so I was all he had." She paused, and looked at the backs of her hands, which were small, with thick blue veins like canals crisscrossing them.

"He gave me whatever I wished for. But the one thing I truly wanted, he could not give me. I would have been a great surgeon. I had the head and heart and hands for it, and blood doesn't scare me. I went hunting with my father all over India. Bagged as many trophies as he did, until one day I realized I wanted to heal instead of kill." She coughed, and took a sip of her tea. My own was getting cold, I realized, and I drank it down hastily, my eyes never leaving her face.

"I should have gone to England to take my medical studies. I had the marks for it. But in my day it was difficult for

253

women to be anything other than nurses, and my father didn't want to let me go. So I stayed with him, and took care of him until he died. No regrets. My choice."

I was fascinated by her story but repelled at the same time. "So you want me to become a doctor instead? To make up for what you missed?" My voice was edged with the slightest hint of anger.

Feroza aunty looked wearily at me. "No. I'm neither that selfish nor that stupid. I told you, I have no regrets. I have lived a fuller life than most people my age. After my father died, I travelled all over the world. I learned to fly an aeroplane and got my pilot's license." She grinned at my obvious surprise. "And I learned to paint and sculpt, in Florence. My hands understood marble and stone. They are trustworthy materials, durable, honourable. Some day I might show you some of my work." She trailed off and looked bewildered, for a moment, as though she'd forgotten what she'd planned to say.

She pulled herself upright with a visible effort and continued: "You, young woman, are going to have to make your own way in the world. You'll inherit some money from me when I die, but most of my inheritance is tied up in a complicated trust which will go to the Parsi Panchayat Benevolent Aid Society." She grinned at me. "So. The question is, are you going to be poor and wait for some man to marry you so you can live a respectable middle-class life, or are you going to take your destiny into your own hands and make something of yourself?"

"I'd never really thought of it that way. I don't think my marks are good enough to get me into medical college. It's very competitive and there are so many applicants for each position," I said.

"I know that. I'm on the Board of Trustees at Nagpur University. You'll have to complete your pre-med courses and pass the entrance exams, but you're a bright girl, and if you put your mind to it, you can do it. I guarantee you admission won't be a problem, if you do your part. What do you say?"

"Could I think about this for a few days? I need time to talk to my parents."

"I've already spoken to your mother. They'll do whatever you want. But you take some time to think over my proposition. Give me a ring when you've decided."

Feroza aunty stood up. The interview was over. I thanked her, collected my silly ivory purse, and was escorted out to the car by the bearer.

And that's how I became a doctor. It was not easy for me. I'm not good at studies, and I failed twice before I finally got admitted to Nagpur Medical College. Even after I got in, I had to work hard to get through all the exams and graduate. But I stuck it out until I was finished. I'm stubborn that way.

Feroza aunty sent me five thousand shares of Tata stock as my graduation present. I didn't know it at the time, but that stock became the cornerstone of my financial independence. It grew exponentially in value. When I finally sold some of the shares several years later, there was enough money to buy myself a small house and clinic in Bombay and I was still left with most of the shares she had bequeathed me. They provide me with a freedom I would not otherwise have had.

I never saw Feroza aunty again after that afternoon when she made me that extraordinary proposition over a cup of Darjeeling tea. She died about a year after I graduated from medical college, of pancreatic cancer. I wonder, now, if she knew she was dying when she summoned me that afternoon. She changed my life and I will always remain grateful to her. She gave me a vision of what an independent woman could be, how a woman's life could be rich and fulfilling all on its own. That vision has helped sustain me through some very bleak and lonely times.

After I got my MBBS I stayed in Nagpur. I worked in a private clinic treating fat old Marwari women, most of whom were as healthy and tough as old water-buffaloes. They were too rich to do any useful work and too old to be interested in children, so they were bored. They would come to see me every day, complaining: "Arre doctor bai, such pains in my stomach, I am telling you! Too-too big headache also I am having. You must give me injection only." They all insisted on injections. I tried to tell them it wasn't necessary but then they thought I wasn't doing anything for them. So finally I gave up, just gave them all glucose injections and immediately they would feel better.

They praised me to the skies, and told all their friends I was Sarasvati's incarnation come to bless them for their former good deeds. They were so grateful to have a doctor who actually listened to them that when I was offered a better job in Calcutta, they quickly got together and raised enough money to build a brand new clinic for me. The Chief Minister of Maharashtra himself came to the opening ceremony. After that, how could I leave? They gave me a house, a car, a driver with a uniform. All the things my parents could not afford, I finally had. And they didn't come to me through marriage, they were mine. I had earned them.

But I was lonely there in Nagpur. I missed my family and my friends. Most of all, I missed Sorab and you children. By then, Roshan had also been born. Did you know that I was the one who delivered you? I was on holidays, visiting your parents, when it happened. Dinshi was in the last weeks of her first pregnancy and having a very difficult time. She'd been frail ever since she'd had a childhood bout of typhoid fever, and right through her pregnancy she was pushing herself hard, working till late every night, not eating proper meals or taking proper rest. She went into heavy labour just before dinner. There was no time to get her to the hospital. So I delivered you. Right there on their big four-poster bed.

When I cut the cord you looked straight into my eyes. Such a look, I felt as though I was falling into the sky. I forgot everything — the scissors in my hand, your mother lying on the bed. You could have been mine, Shahnu. You could have been mine.

When your mother got sick, you kept on asking me about her. What could I tell you? That she was sick from selfishness, from a withered heart? She was sick because she loved no one — not you children, who adored her, not her husband, who would give her the sun and the moon right out of the sky. She was angry; she felt cheated because she never went to Cambridge. She became pregnant with you in the first few months of marriage, and could not go. But whose fault was that? And who would give up such wonderful, passionate, intelligent daughters, such a handsome, loving husband and a beautiful home, for mathematics?

She would.

In 1956, Dinshi chaired a UNESCO conference on nuclear physics in New Delhi which was attended by leading scientists from all over the world. The conference was highly successful and several scientific papers were published as a result of it. Dinshi received a lot of very favourable attention for her work, as well as a promotion at her job with the Indian Atomic Energy Commission. The following summer she was offered a job by the U. S. Department of National Defense. She would be working on a top-secret project. She wouldn't tell any of us what it was, I don't think she's even told Sorab to this day. When any of us asked her about it she just smiled a tight-lipped smile and said she had signed an oath under the Official Secrets Act or something.

Well, I may not be as brilliant as her but there was no doubt in my mind that what she was doing was helping the United States become the biggest, most powerful nuclear power in the world. As though we needed more weapons, more bombs like the ones that destroyed the peaceful

257

populations of Hiroshima and Nagasaki. Women and children and old people, vulnerable innocents, reduced to cinders by the work of physicists like your mother.

She was gone for two years — two years! No thought for her family, her small children growing up without a mother, her husband lonely and surrounded by women only too happy to console him in her absence. But she never thought of these things. She came back with a whole steamer-trunk full of scrapbooks and photo albums all featuring the great Professor Dinaz Jamshedji. Newspaper articles and interviews about her in the Washington Post, the Boston Globe, the New York Times, the San Francisco Chronicle — "visiting mathematician and physicist from India . . . exotically beautiful . . . mapping the mysteries of the universe . . ." that sort of thing. As you know, there are hundreds of press photos in those albums. Even pictures of her at the White House wearing that violet and gold sari Sorab had had custom-made for her on their first wedding anniversary. Do you remember that White House photo, the one your daddy had framed which always sits on his desk? She is smiling, holding a wine-glass in her hand, and sitting at a long table having dinner with President and Mrs. Eisenhower. She looks happy.

When her work in America was finished, she didn't come straight home. She travelled through Europe for six more months, from England to Scandinavia and all the way south to Greece and Italy, all by herself. Or so she says. I sometimes wonder who took all those photos of her in front of Notre Dame and the palace of the Doge, posed beside Norwegian fjords and standing on the steps of St. Peter's in Rome, her hair tucked into a knitted cap, her hands tightly wrapped in black leather gloves, her eyes serene.

When I think about it, though, I have to admit it's an amazing achievement. My sister — who grew up never eating breakfast on school days because our parents could only afford one daytime meal and it would not do to go to school without a packed lunch, everyone would talk — my sister has eaten caviar and drunk champagne at the White House. She has been received by the Queen of England in the gardens of Buckingham Palace. She has the pictures to prove it.

But eventually, she had to come home.

When Dinshi first left for America, I sold my home and my practice in Nagpur and had bought a small bungalow not far from your house in Juhu. After all, someone had to look after you children while she was away. Sorab couldn't do it by himself.

Those were happy days. I came to your house every morning, gave the cook orders for breakfast, made sure you girls got dressed in time for school and saw you off in the car. Then Sorab and I sat in the garden under the guava tree at a white wrought-iron table, drinking endless cups of the strong Nilgiri tea your daddy likes so much, and talking.

We talked about everything. He asked me what I wanted out of my life, whether I would return to medicine. I told him how much I wanted children of my own some day, how I dreamed of setting up a small clinic next to my home once I had a family, so I would always be close at hand for my children and my husband. But, I added, laughing, I was already an old maid and getting set in my ways. Maybe it wasn't in my karma to have the blessings of marriage and children, in this lifetime.

Sorab looked at me then as though he'd never really seen me before, a long look that made my belly warm and my head feel hot and shivery. His face was open and vulnerable when he said, very quietly, "Any man would be lucky to have you for a wife, Perin. You'll make some man very happy one day." He looked so sad as he spoke, I wanted to take his head and stroke it, hold it tenderly between my breasts.

Ah, I wanted to. But instead I laughed, to hide the shiver

that ran through my body. I teased him, saying he'd have to find me a good man to marry; it was his duty as my brother-in-law. I remember that morning distinctly. How the wind suddenly picked up and began blowing so hard it whipped the table cloth right off the tea-table, and we had to go back indoors immediately.

A few days later, Sorab and I were out in the garden again drinking our tea when the bearer brought him the day's post along with a letter opener on a silver tray. Sorab picked up the thick stack of letters and went through them while I sipped my tea. He stopped at a blue aerogramme. I recognized Dinshi's handwriting scrawled across the front of the thin envelope. He set it aside unopened and we continued talking. It was going to be Navroze soon and we were planning a family dinner. Sorab seemed ill at ease, distracted. I stopped in mid-sentence when it became obvious he wasn't really listening to what I was saying.

"Sorab," I said, "why don't you go ahead and open your letter? I have to go in and make a telephone call. I'll be back in a few minutes."

He smiled absently and nodded his head. I stood up and before I'd turned away he was already slitting open the envelope. The tissue-thin airmail paper rustled as I walked away. I looked back at him when I got to the doorway of the house. He was scanning the letter quickly, turning the pages as though looking for something. I went inside the house and sat down on a chair in the hallway, tears springing into my eyes. Dinshi had been gone almost six months and he missed her every day. I wanted him to reach for me as eagerly as he had reached for her letter. My body ached for him and I didn't know what to do about it.

Since I had said I was going in to make a phone call, I made my way to the telephone to ring Feredun, my accountant. He handled all my finances, invested my money for me, and did my taxes. He wanted to marry me. He had asked me many times but I always said no. I could not imagine being married to anyone else when my heart belonged to Sorab.

That day, as I dialled Feredun's private line at his office, I wondered what I would do if he should ask me again. Seeing Sorab with Dinshi's letter made me realize that he would never love me with the kind of passionate, desperate love he had for Dinshi. No matter what she did, his love burned steadily, an unwavering flame. More than anything, I wanted to be loved like that. But in this world one cannot have everything. Maybe it was time for me to be sensible and say "yes" to Feredun after all. He was a kind, caring man. His parents were both dead, so there would be no in-law problems. He was wealthy and cultured and, although he was neither as tall nor as good-looking as Sorab, he had a reassuringly solid presence. He made me feel safe and cared for.

As I was musing on these things, Feredun's voice rumbled in my ear saying, "Hello." I was flustered; I had forgotten that I'd dialled his number. He said "Hello!" again, a bit more sharply. I took a deep breath and began.

"Feredun, this is Perin."

"Perin!" His voice rose in a glad lilt and my spirits rose with it. "How are you my dear? I haven't seen you at any of the Musical Society evenings lately. Have you been away?"

"No, no, nothing like that. I've just been very busy. With my sister away I am taking care of her family and the children seem to take up a lot of my time."

"How is Dinaz? And Sorab and the children? They are managing all right?"

"Fine, fine, everyone is fine here."

"Perin, is everything all right? Is there anything I can do for you? You know you just have to ask."

"I . . . I've been thinking about your . . . proposal, Feredun. I know I've always said I would never marry, but . . . " I didn't know how to continue.

261

"Perin, sweet, are you saying you've changed your mind?"

I laughed, a short little bark of a laugh. "Well, if the offer still stands . . ."

"It stands. Believe me. Would you like to come over here? Shall I send the car for you? We can go to the Taj and have tea and talk about it."

He sounded so eager, so happy, I wondered, for a moment, if I was up to this. Then I thought about all the years I'd waited for Sorab to notice me. I thought about him sitting outside in the garden right at that moment devouring his wife's letter as though it were food and drink for his starved spirit. I made up my mind.

"Yes, Feredun. Send the car. We'll go to the Taj. We'll talk. Now, I'm not promising anything yet, mind you, but . . ."

Feredun had always been very dignified, courteous, courtly. Now he let out a whoop of joy that made me laugh. He chuckled into the phone: "This is my lucky, lucky day. Maybe we should go to the race course and bet on a horse while we're at it. Thank you, Perin. I'll make you happy, I promise."

We talked some more, and there was such sweet joy in hearing his loving words, and the tenderness in his voice, all for me. Even though it was not the voice I wanted to hear.

Feredun had clients booked until lunch-time, so we agreed we'd go to the Taj for lunch. I hung up the phone. My hands were trembling and my pulse was very fast. I took a few deep breaths to calm myself. Part of me was excited about the decision I had made. Part of me was in despair. I composed myself, patted down my hair, and smoothed the folds of my sari with both hands before going out into the garden where Sorab was still sitting, sipping his cup of tea. Dinshi's letter was nowhere in sight, although the rest of the mail lay opened on the table next to him.

He looked up as I came down the steps. Something about his demeanour alarmed me. He usually sits very straight, spine upright, shoulders back, head high. But now his whole body was rounded into a C, his head held gingerly on his neck like a burden too heavy to bear. I quickened my steps, trying to hide the sudden surge of fear that gripped my throat. When I reached him, he put out his arms, wrapped them around my waist and pulled me to him. He buried his face in my belly and began to sob.

I was so shocked, I didn't react at all for a moment. Then my own arms went around his shoulders. I cradled his head in my hands, stroking the short, bristly hairs at the nape of his neck with my fingers, soothing him as I would you or Roshan. My belly felt hot and moist with his breath and I wanted to hold him there forever.

He sobbed, great shuddering sobs that wracked his body and shook my own. He held me tightly in his arms as though he were drowning and I the only upright spar left in his world. I had never seen him cry before, although the men in both our families are an emotional lot, as you know, and cry at weddings and funerals and other occasions where feelings burn hot and intense. I stroked his back, feeling the ridges of his vertebrae, the curved bow of his ribs. His tears soaked my bare belly and I wept with him, joy and sorrow mingling in the salt of my tears.

After a long while his sobs slowed to a quiet shuddering, his body softened and relaxed like a sleepy child. He drew his warm cheek away from my belly, wiping his face with the back of one hand, drawing his white tobacco-scented handkerchief out of his pocket and blowing his nose vigorously. He looked up at me, his eyes so nakedly vulnerable I wanted to cry all over again.

"Sorab, what is it? What's wrong my darling?" The endearment slipped out before I could stop myself. I flushed, and looked down at my feet.

He spoke, his voice drained and hollow: "Dinshi wrote. She's been offered a permanent post in Washington. She's thinking of taking it. She . . . she doesn't want the children or me to come there. She says she's happy. She wants us to remain good friends, she says. Good friends." His voice broke, and when he spoke again it was tremulous, uncertain. "She doesn't say there's any other man. That's good, isn't it? She likes living there, her work is going very well. It's just . . . she doesn't want us...she prefers to be alone . . ."

I was so angry with my sister. If she'd been in front of me at that moment I would have slapped her face till my hand turned red. Selfish, self-centred woman. No woman at all, so willing to abandon all that God had given her. Leaving this broken-hearted man who loved her so much he wasn't even angry with her. Any other man would have demanded that she return to her family immediately, would have taken steps to bring her back where she belonged. She had obligations, commitments. Who did she think she was, just dropping everyone and everything and flying off to America like that?

I bent down so that my eyes were level with Sorab's. "What are you going to do, Sorab?"

"What can I do? She is free to choose whatever she wants. And she does not choose me."

His voice was infinitely sad. Hopelessness curved his neck, lowered his eyes so all I could see was the shadow of his long lashes on his cheek. I felt my breasts rise with anger, and with something else which I had no time to think about. I made a decision; I stood up abruptly. Grasping his hand in mine, I pulled him up from his chair. He rose slowly, looking at my face and seeing something there that caused him to straighten his back. He looked down into my eyes, his pupils wide and distended in his amber irises. Slowly he drew me to his side, wrapped his warm hand around the curve of my waist. I did not look away; I pressed my own hand on top of his, and pulled him closer to me. Without saying another word, we walked across the garden and into the house, our hips bumping together, my womb melting as we climbed up the stairs to the guest bedroom.

When Feredun's driver came to take me to the Taj for lunch, I sent a message saying I was indisposed.

I made a choice in the heat of passion, and the course of my life was irrevocably altered. Feredun rang me up at home that evening and demanded an explanantion.

"What happened, Perin? You were fine just an hour or two before lunch, then suddenly you were indisposed? If you've changed your mind you could at least tell me so yourself, instead of sending me a message with the driver. I'm not some mooning schoolboy, to be treated so dismissively."

"Feredun, I'm sorry. I never meant to hurt you, it's just . . . circumstances have changed. No, I can't explain. I'm sorry. You deserve better. No, I can't have lunch with you tomorrow to talk about it. There's nothing to talk about. I'm very sorry." I hung up, feeling as though I'd either made the worst mistake of my life, or had pulled myself back from the brink of a terrible disaster.

For the next year and a half, Sorab and I lived virtually as man and wife. We were discreet, of course. I never spent the night at your house, although we did manage to get away from time to time for a brief holiday to Dehra Dun or Ooty, without you children. Once we even had a whole week together in Paris, where we stayed at the Georges Cinque and never left our room except to go for a walk each evening in the cool Parisian dusk. Sorab had business there and I simply told everyone I was going to Nagpur to visit an old friend.

Then one day, about a year after the first time we had been together, I discovered I was pregnant. I knew it almost as soon as I'd conceived, a feeling in my womb of tenderness and fullness, as though the moon were ripening inside me. I didn't tell Sorab for four weeks, until I was absolutely sure. He was in shock; he had never imagined such a thing might happen. He pulled back, then; he did not ring me up or come to see me for several days.

But I was so happy, nothing could dampen my spirits. I told myself he just needed time to adjust; there was such a thing as divorce. His wife had deserted him, no one would blame him. As for the two of us, we belonged together. We could go and live abroad, far away from wagging tongues. We would take you girls with us, and our new baby, live in England or Switzerland or even in France. I daydreamed, and planned a small, intimate wedding.

As I'd predicted, Sorab finally came around, though it took him longer than I'd expected. I didn't see him or speak to him for almost three weeks. By the end of that time I was ready to give him whatever he wanted, an abortion, an elopement, whatever he wished. He drove up the gravelled drive-way of my small whitewashed bungalow — I was outside, watering my champa bushes. My belly was beginning to bulge gently and I had had to loosen the string of my sari petti-coat. I put down the heavy watering can and stood there smiling at him as he stepped out of his red Morgan. He came to me, put his arms around me, and told me he loved me. I was so happy. He said we still had time, we didn't have to decide anything right away, but in another month or so, be-fore I began to show, he would take me back to France. He would get a small house for us in Provence, I would have the baby there. He would write to Dinshi, and ask for a divorce.

But the gods have ways of levelling the scales. A couple of weeks later I was in my kitchen making a batch of sutherfeni, which you used to love when you were a girl. It was a warm day and I had the kitchen doors and windows open to catch the morning breezes. I leaned over to put some ghee in the frying pan when I felt a massive cramp, as though a giant hand had seized my belly and was squeezing it be-tween iron fingers.

266

I knew at once what it was, of course. I turned off the stove and went to my bedroom to lie down before the next cramp came, and the next. I was hot and cold and kept pulling my quilt over myself and then tossing it off as my uterus contracted and squeezed until my sari and bed were covered in blood. I knew I should ring the hospital, but I was afraid. I didn't want anyone to know; I didn't want my good name to be ruined. It took two and a half hours before my body finished its bloody work, cramping and squeezing until the little snail of life clinging to my womb had been expelled in a last gush of blood. I lay there, shaking, unable to get up for another hour. Then slowly I climbed out of bed, walked to the bathroom, and cleaned myself up. I washed and washed myself until my skin was raw and I was shivering with cold. I took the sari and petticoat, the wet towels and bloody sheets and stuffed them into a gunny sack from the godown. My legs and arms trembled, my womb burned and ached. I felt as empty as an abandoned house.

I rang Sorab. Told him. Heard the relief and pity in his voice. He wanted to come right over. I said no. I needed to be alone; I couldn't bear to see his ambivalence face-to-face.

Later that afternoon, I rang my gynecologist, a colleague whom I knew from medical college and who I trusted to keep my secret. Daulat came over, examined me and admitted me immediately to Bombay Hospital. She put me under general anaesthesia, as they did in those days, intending to do a D & C to clear out any residue from the miscarriage.

When I emerged from the fog of the anaesthetic, I was back in the recovery room. Daulat sat on the side of my bed, holding my hand. She explained that my uterus had ruptured, probably as a result of my miscarriage. She had been forced to remove it altogether, to prevent me bleeding to death. I should be grateful to be alive, she said, but I would never be able to have children. Her eyes were full of pity. I turned my head to the wall, too exhausted and grief-stricken to weep.

Eighteen months later, your mother returned from America. She did not explain why she was back, any more than she had explained why she'd wanted to stay in that cold land. But she was back, and everything changed. Sorab turned to her like a flower to the sun. Turned away from me. It was as though he and I had never been together, never loved each other. For a while, the current had flowed both ways, but now, it had turned back.

Sorab and I only spoke of it once after she returned. We were in your living room waiting for Dinshi to come downstairs. All three of us were going to his parents' house for dinner. He looked at me from across the room, his eyes shadowed. His voice was hesitant, ashamed. "She needs me, Perin. She is not strong, like you."

Before I could sort through the hot words that sprang to my lips, Dinshi swept into the room. She was as beautiful as a peacock in a blue and gold Benarasi silk, her long hair cut in the fashionable chin-length bob she had acquired in America. Her eyes were luminous; she seemed to shine with a light brighter than that of any mortal — a star fallen from the sky.

A few weeks after she returned home, Dinshi made it clear she did not want me to come to her house uninvited any longer. Me, her own sister, who had been in and out of that bungalow every day for two years, supervising her servants, making sure you girls did your homework, taking care of your birthday celebrations, ordering your clothes, doing the million and one things that had to be done so her household would run smoothly. Somehow, she knew I had betrayed her. And my own guilt was great enough that I did not protest.

Yet I was angry. And so hurt by Sorab's desertion that if I ever let myself feel the full depths of it, I think I would go insane. I would tear him apart with my bare hands — and her. I did not know I had such rage in me. I hated him for being so weak, for going back to her like a dog to its master. I hated her for pulling him to her so casually, tugging at his leash with the barest show of interest. She did not really want him, of course. But he was hers, and she did not ever let go of her possessions, whether she wanted them or not. He was hers.

Well. I don't go where I'm not welcome. I waited for Sorab to invite me to your house but the invitations rarely came. Months would go by without my seeing you children, let alone Sorab or Dinshi. I kept myself busy. I founded a free Women and Children's Clinic at J. J. Hospital and volunteered there three days a week. I went out to dinner parties at the homes of friends, and visited with relatives. I was voted chairwoman of the annual fundraising dinner for the Bombay Musical Society Orchestra. Under my leadership we raised eight lakhs of rupees, more than had ever been donated before. I am good at these things.

Then one day, when Dinshi had been back about six months, Sorab telephoned me at home. He said he was worried about her. He wanted me to come and stay for a few days, observe her, and see if I could diagnose her.

When I got out of the car in your parents' portico that Sunday morning, the place seemed unnaturally quiet. Usually on a Sunday your daddy's house was full of people: you girls would have friends or cousins spending the day; Sorab's parents always came over with Khorshed. Sorab's brothers and sisters and their families came too, and quite often there would be fifty people sitting down for Sunday dhansak lunch. That day, though, the only cars in the driveway were your daddy's Humber and his little red Morgan.

Sunder ayah opened the front door for me when I rang. When she saw me she bowed her head and said, in a choked voice, "Bai, it is good you have come. Seth is having too much difficulties. Maybe you can help him with burra-bai."

She ushered me in, calling out to the other servants to bring in my bags from the car. I went straight to the back of the house, to Dinshi and Sorab's bedroom. Usually, it was such a bright, airy room with its view of the garden and the sea. As I stood in the doorway that day, I could hardly see anything. All the shutters were closed. There was a strong scent of Eau De Cologne which didn't quite succeed in masking the sharp ammoniac smell of a sickroom.

I waited until my eyes had adjusted to the gloom. Then I walked over and sat on a small chair beside the bed. Dinshi was curled up like a fetus under the heavy winter quilt, although it was only October and still quite hot. I felt her forehead. It was cool and clammy. Her pulse was strong and regular, which was a relief, but when I opened my bag and took out my stethescope, she made a mewing sound and buried her head entirely under the quilt. When I tried to pull the quilt aside, she resisted me fiercely. For all her apparent fragility, my sister has a powerful grip.

I put my stethescope away and went in search of Sorab. I found him in his study, sitting at his desk staring blankly at a newspaper. His eyes looked yellow, and pouchy, and there were deep grooves on both sides of his mouth. I was shocked to see how much he had aged in just a few months. When did his hair get so grey? I shook him gently, by the shoulder.

He looked up at me and smiled. "Ah, Perin! Good to see you. Thank you for coming." He added, in a low, pained voice, "I know I have neglected you shamefully since Dinshi got back; I'm so sorry, my dear."

"It's all right," I replied, busying myself with my bag until I could control my own trembling. "Now, what is the matter with her? How long has she been in bed?"

Sorab sighed. "Two and a half months." Shocked, I opened my mouth to protest, but Sorab continued, in a weary drone I barely recognized: "At first, I thought she was just exhausted from her travels. I thought all the strain of the past two years was finally catching up with her, so I encouraged her to rest. She slept all day and all night. Then she refused to eat, and now for the past few days she won't even get up to go to the bathroom. She . . . she soils her bedclothes and the ayah has to come and clean her up. I don't know what to do." He rubbed his forehead hard with the knuckles of his right hand, a gesture of bewilderment I recognized from when we were children. My heart wept for him. I had to take a deep breath to keep my voice steady.

"Have you called Dr. Joseph? Has he examined her?"

"I telephoned him two months ago, when it became apparent her condition was due to something more than fatigue. He came at once, of course. He examined her and ordered an ambulance to take her to Breach Candy Hospital where they performed all sorts of tests. ECG's, EEG's, CT scans, the works. He says neither he nor any of the specialists he's consulted can find anything organically wrong with her. He suspects she may be having a nervous breakdown. He referred her to a psychiatrist — a Dr. Pereira — do you know him?"

"Yes. He's the head of psychiatry at Breach Candy Hospital. Very well regarded in his field, but Sorab, psychiatry is such an imprecise science. What did he say?"

"He didn't tell me much. He's been seeing her daily, though he only comes by for a short while in the morning and sits with her while she turns her back to him and pretends to be asleep. He says she must be given mood elevators, to help her overcome her depression. But she also gets agitated and disoriented, so he gives her other medications for that."

"My God, these psychiatrists! They think they can fix everything with this medication, that medication. What is he giving her?"

"He's prescribed Elavil, three times a day. When she gets agitated she's supposed to stop taking the Elavil and take Thorazine instead, but when she gets excited and high strung she refuses to swallow anything. Here. I'll show you her medications. You can probably make more sense of them than I can."

Sorab reached into his desk drawer and took out two vials of pills, which he handed to me. His eyes were troubled. "Dr. Pereira says that if she doesn't respond to the medications soon he wants to hospitalize her and give her electric shock therapy." He rubbed his forehead with his knuckles again and sighed. "I don't know what to do. I don't like the idea of giving her shocks, but nothing else seems to be working."

"Sorab, has Dr. Pereira explained to you what happens when you give a patient shock treatment?"

"He says it will calm her down, and help her get over her depression. Right now, the Elavil makes her quite agitated, and then she becomes violent." He stared down at the back of his right hand, which, I noticed for the first time, was bandaged.

"What happened to your hand?"

"She bit me — severed a small vein. I had to have stitches and tetanus shots."

"Sorab, you can't let Dr. Pereira shock her. Basically, shock treatment is an electrically induced seizure. They call it a controlled seizure, but the truth is, they have no way of telling how it will affect her brain. She could lose her memory."

Your mother's whole life had been dedicated to mathematics and physics. What would become of her if she lost her intellect? She had no other resources to fall back upon. She had never wanted anything else, never had the least desire for anything but her work. Angry as I was with her, I could not leave her unprotected; I could not allow her to be subjected to such a risky procedure. She could lose everything that mattered to her. There had to be a way to reach her inside the dark cocoon she had spun for herself.

For the next two days, I sat beside Dinshi's bed. It reminded me of times when we were children, when we had shared the same bed, and had stayed up nights talking. Only now I talked and she ignored me. I explained over and over that if she did not make the effort to come out of her depression she faced something far worse. She kept her eyes closed and refused to talk to me. But she did begin eating.

I had the cook make her arrowroot kunji and clear chicken broths, to build up her strength. Gradually, she came out of her depressive stupor. The pale, slack look left her face and her skin acquired some tone and vibrancy. She refused to take the Elavil. I told her I was sorry to do this, but her health was more important and so I injected her with the required dosage of her medication. I did this three times a day, gradually lowering the dosage so that, as she began to surface from the depths of her depression she did not immediately swing upward into an elevated mood and agitation.

It worked, for a while. Then her own brain chemistry seemed to push her towards a full blown manic psychosis. She had all the classic signs. She was aggressive, delusional and paranoid. She ranted and raved. One morning, she refused to let me give her her injection. She grabbed the syringe from my hand and, holding it in her fist like a dagger, tried to stab me with it.

"Saali-mooi!" she screamed, her face contorted with rage. She thrust her mouth so close to my face I thought she was going to bite me and instinctively backed away. Her saliva sprayed my cheek as she hissed, "You think I don't know what-all has been going on here while I was away? I know what you've been up to with my husband. You thought you could take my place?" Here she laughed, a rising, manic laughter that frightened me more than her screaming. "You fool!" she shouted. "He's mine. I hold his life in the palm of my hand and I can crush him just like that!" She clenched her fist, still holding the syringe, and made a feinting jab at my throat with it.

"Dinshi, you're imagining things. These hallucinations are typical of your illness. Now give me that syringe and let me take care of you, or you're going to end up in a mental hospital." I used my best physician's manner, keeping my voice very calm, steady, authoritative. I kept a close eye on the sharp needle she held in her hand.

She wasn't having any of it. She hurled the syringe at me; the needle just missed my eye. I ducked and turned to leave. She followed me, screaming: "Yes, yes, run, Perin, run. You've always run after what was mine. You'll never have it. Everyone hates me. The CIA, the FBI, they are all trying to capture me, to steal my brain. Even Eisenhower. Even my own sister. GET OUT OF MY SIGHT! DON'T COME HERE ANY MORE! You don't belong here. This is MY home, and MY family. GET OUT!"

After this incident I told Sorab it would be better if she was treated by some other doctor, since she seemed to get more agitated when she saw me. He told me that Dr. Pereira wanted to put her in a psychiatric nursing home but he had promised Dinshi he would never do that to her. He begged me to stay for a while longer, to help stabilize her.

I stayed with you all for three weeks. I wondered if one of the servants had seen me with Sorab, back in those days when we were together, and told Dinshi about it. Or if her suspicions were simply a combination of intuition and mania. You children were confused, and often terrified by your mother's raging psychosis. I found myself slipping back into that role of surrogate mum that had become so familiar to me while your mother was away. But I was not your mother, and this time, I did not let myself forget that fact. You and Roshan clung to me because you needed me. But once Dinshi got well again I would revert to being your Perin aunty whom you seldom saw and who appeared only on the distant rim of your young lives. So I protected my heart as best I could, helping as needed without letting myself long for what would never be mine.

Your letter made me think about my life. None of us knows how long we have on this earth and if I were to die tomorrow there would be no one who would miss me much. Oh, you girls would, for a while, I know that. But eventually you would forget. The intimate things — the smell of my skin, the sound of my voice — would vanish from your minds. I'd be a photograph in the family album, a name, a dimly recalled face. Probably you'd remember my stories and songs long after you've forgotten your Perin aunty. Yet I would not miss one moment of my time with you. You are my treasure.

You have always asked more difficult questions than anyone I know. As a child, your favourite word was "Why?" You always demanded the truth, no matter how terrible or painful. Nothing else satisfied you. So I make you the gift of my story now. There isn't much more I can give you, darling. I hope it helps you understand something about me, and something about yourself.

All my love,
Perin

I sit, stunned, unable to take in what I've read. My father. Perin aunty. All those years and I knew nothing about it. I thought I knew my father, but the man Perin aunty describes — weak with yearning for a woman who despises him; a man who had an affair with my aunt and abandoned her when she miscarried his child — I do not know this man. All his talk about honour and responsibility was just that — talk. I am sick of talk.

So this is why Perin aunty disappeared out of our lives.

It's too much. I can't think about this right now. I want to kick something.

275

I toss the letter on the couch and pull on my boots, grab my hat and coat, and head down to the river.

The river is swollen; its brown waters swirl and tumble and roar past my feet. I stand on the pebbled edge of the river-bank, the toes of my boots darkening as water trickles over them. A muddy tangle of twigs and dead leaves churns about in an eddy near my feet. I bend down, pick up a small stone, and throw it as far as I can, into the middle of the river. It dimples the water, swirls in the current for a moment, then sinks, leaving no trace. I pick up another, and another, throwing further each time. I hurl stones into the river until my shoulder and arm ache and I can't throw any more. Then I pick up a fallen branch and poke at the clot of twigs and leaves near my feet, until it loosens and the debris is carried swiftly downstream.

I feel calmer; my heartbeat slows to the deeper rhythm of the river. I sit down on a rock, and scoop up a fistful of pebbles; they feel cool and smooth and nubbly in the palms of my hands.

Somehow, I must make sense of what Perin aunty has told me. I knew about my parents, of course. I knew my mother did not love my father, just as I knew my father loved her hopelessly, almost against his will. I just never let myself think about it.

If I let my mind drift, I can remember — not specific events, exactly; rather, a feeling of joy, an effervescence that sparkled through our house, and fizzed and bubbled around Perin aunty and my father for a while. I remember hearing whispers and low laughter from the living room, after Roshan and I had gone up to bed. Glances whose significance I sensed, but could not read, at the time. Perin aunty's fingertips lingering delicately on my father's arm as he helped her out of the car after they'd been on an evening drive, her hair tousled, stray curls framing her flushed and smiling face — I'd thought she looked that way because she'd been riding in my father's Morgan with the top down.

What else did I miss?

I shiver as I realize how my life echoes my father's, and Perin aunty's. I too love a man who doesn't love me. My mind goes dark when I acknowledge this; Shahrukh doesn't love me.

Chapter 22

Winter in Eugene. The grass is wet and squishes under my boots as I begin my walk to school. I slip on a patch of muddy ground. My feet suddenly slide out from under me. I grab the edge of a fence, hold on trembling for a moment until my pulse slows. Long, bony fingers of trees shiver in the wind, claw at the sky. A fine, drizzling mist softens the outlines of houses, gentles the somber mass of evergreens that stand erect as gurkhas at the end of our street. Water purls through a culvert by the side of the road. The air is soft with moisture, a chilly caress against my cheek. A robin hops along the edge of the playing field behind our apartment, pecking at the ground, hunting for food. It's early, 7 am by my wristwatch. The street is quiet, except for the wind humming in my ears, then the tapping of a rhododendron bush against the window of a house.

I love this time of morning. A verdant peace, its green melody scenting the air with the astringence of juniper and pine, the sky thin layers of grey silk shifting and changing as the wind reshapes the clouds. Serene. It is unlike the dense, sullen silence that glowers between Shahrukh and me. We fight each other desperately, for our very lives, it seems. As though we each believe we'll lose what matters most if the other one wins.

I lie in bed at night, listening to the mutter and roar of the TV set in the living room. Loneliness fills me like a chill, and I can't get warm, no matter how many blankets I pile upon myself. I want my Shahrukh, my friend, my lover. I miss snuggling in bed with him, talking about all that's happened during the day. I miss his warm feet on mine, rubbing my chilly toes.

He was asleep on the living room couch, this morning, the TV set burbling on as I tiptoed about the kitchen getting myself a bowl of Applejacks, trying not to wake him.

A man in a grey sweatsuit jogs by, and raises an arm in silent greeting. People run for exercise here. I don't know how they do it, dressed in just a sweatshirt and pants, in this creeping cold. I pull my scarf close around my throat and walk faster, to stay warm.

My friend and thesis advisor, Patrick, is meeting me for breakfast at the little cafe near campus. As I turn the corner, I can see its sign: Lee's Cafe. Chinese, American. Early-bird breakfast. The words are hand-lettered on a white stand-up sandwich board. I smell the greasy odour of frying bacon a block away.

A clot of students stands chattering on the sidewalk. They smile and say "Hi!" as I edge past them through the cafe door. The owner is Chinese, a small, energetic man in a stained white uniform. He is standing on tiptoe, spraying the glass door phsstphsst with Windex and wiping it vigorously with paper towels. The Windex makes my eyes water. He greets me with a nod and a flash of gold-filled teeth, and stops what he's doing long enough to let me through.

Inside, the cafe is half-full, and steamy with kitchen smells. I recognize a woman from my Marriage and Family Therapy seminar sitting on a tall stool at the red formica counter. She has her books spread out in front of her and is sipping coffee from a thick, white ceramic cup. She doesn't see me. I walk down to the far end of the cafe, away from the cold air near the open door. My reflection stalks beside me as I walk, flashing in the mirror that lines the wall. My face looks pale, but my cheeks and nose are flushed with cold.

I slide into the booth that's closest to the kitchen, pull off my wool cap and gloves, shake my hair loose. I can hear the owner's wife somewhere in the back, arguing with someone in Chinese. She comes out of the kitchen door, looking harassed, her face shiny with sweat. She wipes her hands on her apron, takes down a menu from the shelf behind her and thrusts it at me with a distracted frown. I order coffee, eggs, hashbrowns and toast. It's taken me a while to figure out how to order eggs, but I've finally learned the nuances of sunny-side-up and over-easy.

The owner's wife brings me a cup, pours me coffee from a glass carafe. I add several tiny plastic containers of cream and two paper packets of sugar, stirring them into my coffee. I sip the coffee. It is hot, and surprisingly good. I unbutton my coat and wriggle out of it. Then I open my bag, take out my research proposal and begin reading through what I fervently hope is the final draft.

I'm working on a treatment protocol for chronic pain. Once I've developed it, Patrick and I will do a double-blind research study to test the protocol, initially with a group of geriatric patients in a local nursing home. If that works as I hope it will, then we'll incorporate it into a self-administered treatment manual for people who suffer from chronic pain. It's a complex project, one that will form the basis for my graduate thesis. If the project works, it will empower people to heal themselves; they won't have to rely on a therapist, or on pain medications which dull their senses, to help them manage their pain. I'm excited about the possibilities. If this approach works with chronic pain, we could go on to develop self-administered treatment manuals to help people deal various forms of suffering; everything from insomnia and anxiety, to eating disorders and depression.

I rummage in my bag for a pen and am startled when one is thrust under my nose. I look up to find Patrick looming over me, grinning his gap-toothed smile. "Hi!" he says. I smile back at him. He's tall, all angles and gangly limbs, like an Irish setter. I feel a sudden rush of affection for him as he dumps his backpack onto the seat across from me and shrugs off his parka. He has masses of sandy brown hair which curls wildly around his head, giving him the look of a young Albert Einstein. And grey-green eyes changeable as the sea.

Patrick slides into the bench seat of the booth, pushing his backpack closer to the wall. His dimples deepen as he smiles at me across the table. I feel my heart lift. He cocks his head to one side, trying to read the pages I have spread out on the table. "What've you got there?"

"I've just about finished this proposal. I have to check a few more references, and type up the bibliography, but I'll complete that this afternoon."

"Far out! Bring it by my office when you're done. We'll go over it and make last-minute corrections. Meagan's typing up my NIMH grant application right now; she'll make a clean copy of this and attach it. The deadline's Friday — a week from tomorrow."

"Oh that makes me nervous, Patrick. What if you don't get your funding because my proposal isn't solid enough?"

"Are you kidding? It's brilliant. They're going to fall all over themselves giving us money to implement it," Patrick says cheerfully.

"No, seriously. We're asking for a lot. This is a big project. I just don't feel the proposal's ready for submission yet. I haven't . . ."

"It's great. You're great. Trust me, this is going to breeze right through the committee. NIMH is really big on client-centred care right now. They're looking for practical, clinical applications to fund. They're going to love the whole self-administered treatment angle."

I look at Patrick dubiously. I need more time. There's so much riding on this proposal that I want to be absolutely sure we have enough documentation to back it up, before we submit it to the grants committee.

A young waitress with very blonde hair done up in dozens of tiny plaits brings my plate of eggs and hashbrowns and slides it deftly from her tray onto the table in front of me. She sets down a small plate of buttered toast beside it and turns to Patrick: "What'll it be?" Then, "Oh hi, Professor Wells."

"Hey, Cindy," says Patrick. "Did you find that article on the Gonzaga study you were looking for?"

"Nah, it's on two-day reserve for a fourth year psych course. Every time I check with the reserve desk at the library, it's out."

"I've got a copy in my files somewhere. Check in with me later. I'll dig it up for you."

"Thanks, that'd be great. What're you having?"

"Oh, a cup of coffee and a danish. I'm not real hungry."

Cindy smiles and darts off to get his coffee. I take a bite of egg and toast and chew slowly, still worrying about the research proposal.

Patrick turns to me. "So we're still on for dinner on Saturday?"

"What? Oh. Yes. Seven-thirty."

"What can I bring?"

"Mmm, nothing, just yourself. It's going to be very casual. You already know my friends, Sheila and Bob. There'll be a few other people there."

"Hey," Patrick says, touching my arm gently with his hand. "You okay?"

"Hmm?"

"You seem distracted."

"I'm worried about this proposal. And I have a major research paper due for Jim Taylor's Family Therapy seminar on Monday. What I really need to do is spend the weekend in the library, working."

"So cancel dinner and do what you need to do."

"I can't. Shahrukh's dead-set on having this dinner party on Saturday."

"Then let him do the cooking; you go to the library."

"Unh-unh; I know just what'll happen if I do that. I'll come home at six, the apartment will be a shambles, there'll be no food in sight, and Shahrukh will still be in his pyjamas watching TV."

Patrick laughs and shakes his head. "You know, you should join a women's consciousness raising group. It'd do you good."

"I haven't got time. This is my new mantra, Patrick: I haven't got time, I haven't got time. Anyway, Sharukh will help me on Saturday. He doesn't have anything else on this weekend. We'll have a marvellous meal all ready for you when you arrive."

"Far out! I can't wait."

Cindy returns with a glazed apple danish on a plate, a cup for Patrick, and a carafe of coffee. She fills both our cups. "How're those eggs?" she asks me.

"They're very good, thanks."

"Great!" She drifts off.

I look at my watch. "Oh lord, Patrick, I have to run. I'll see you later?"

"I'll come find you in the library around noon. Lunch at the pub?"

"Right." I scoop up my papers and stuff them into my bag. It's awkward getting my coat back on in the cramped booth, so I slide out of the booth with one arm stuck in my coat-sleeve. Patrick laughs as I wiggle into my coat, pull my hat down over my ears and smooth on my gloves. "You're dressed for Alaska," he teases. I swat him with my bag, then head for the cashier to pay my bill.

As I hurry down the sidewalk towards the library, I bump into my friend Sheila. She's headed for the library too, to work on the paper we both have to turn in on Monday. "Shahnaz, hi!" she exclaims, sounding out of breath. "Listen, I have a new book for you." She digs around in her bag, fishes out a book by Kate Millet: *Sexual Politics*. "It's fabulous, you'll love it," she says.

"Sheila, I haven't got time!" I wail.

"Keep it, it's yours. I bought two copies, one for me and one for you. Mine's all marked up, already."

"Thanks. I'll see you Saturday."

"Yeah, I'm looking forward to it. We'll bring the wine."

Sheila is in her mid-forties, a compact redhead with a delicate, freckled face, pale green eyes, a wide smile. She is funny, bright, outspoken. I feel as though I've known her all my life, even though we've only been friends for a couple of months. We share a similar sense of humour, and we love to read and talk and walk together. Last Monday, after our Family Therapy seminar, we drove out to her turn-of-the-century house overlooking the Willamette River. There, she made us an exotic Mexican meal out of chapatti-like flour tortillas, beans, grated cheese, something called sour cream, which tastes like curds, only thicker and less sour, and a pear-like fruit with a dark green rind called avocado, which is shipped here from California. Her two teenaged daughters came flying in with a bunch of friends, just as we were finishing lunch. Her husband Bob followed a few minutes later, and soon the kitchen, which is as big as our entire apartment, was full of people. Sheila's Siamese cat, a somewhat hysterical feline with narrow blue eyes and a crooked tail, jumped on top of the refrigerator, spooked by all the noise, and meowed furiously when she discovered she was too high up to get down by herself. The afternoon ended amidst laughing commiseration, as Bob sweet-talked the cat into letting him lift it down from its perch, and was rewarded for his pains by the cat peeing on him.

That was the first time I'd ever seen a pet cat. My cousin Hoshi had brought back a pet panther once, from Shillong. I was in high school at the time. It was just a baby when he got it. He kept it in his mother's flat under an upturned baby crib in the living room until the beast grew so big it scared people when he took it out for walks on Marine Drive. He ended up having to fly it back to Assam, where he released it into the jungle. I've often wondered if that panther survived. It was a wild animal raised in a Bombay apartment and ate its meals out of a stainless steel basin. Had its instincts atrophied in that hothouse environment?

My friend, Eileen, who is also coming to dinner on Saturday, has two cats, fluffy white Persians with pug noses and disdainful expressions. Eileen is my age, an athletic, big-boned woman who towers above me. She takes fencing classes with me. She's studying architecture at the U of O, but is from Los Angeles, where her father directs films, which she calls "movies." She invited us to her parents' place for Thanksgiving, but Shahrukh refused to go, so we ended up at Sheila and Bob's instead.

I don't know what to do about Shahrukh. He's always been lazy, but now that we have no servants and must do everything ourselves, he seems to take a perverse pleasure in doing absolutely nothing. Sheila says he's a male chauvinist pig, and that I'm at least partially responsible because I let him get away with it. Maybe the potential for his pigginess has always been latent within him, like a fungus which sprouts only during the monsoons, or whenever the climate is right. Well, if he wants to have this party on Saturday, he'd better help me prepare for it.

Saturday morning. I wake up to the shrilling of the small travel alarm clock that sits beside my bed. It is 5:30 am. I can hear Shahrukh snoring in the living room. I slide out of the warm bed into the chill of our bedroom, shivering as I pull on my dressing gown. I knot its belt tightly around my waist and head to the bathroom to pee, brush my teeth and have a scalding shower to warm me. After, I head back to the icy bedroom, where I pull on my clothes as quickly as my numb and wrinkled fingers will allow.

When I go to the living room to turn up the heat, I find Shahrukh lying on the couch in his underwear, one end of a blanket clutched in his fist, the rest sliding off his body onto the floor. I pick up the blanket and cover him with it, tucking it in behind him. He looks so young, his eyelids brown and smooth as sea shells, his long lashes downswept. I kiss him lightly, on the top of his head. He stirs but doesn't wake.

I turn off the TV and decide to clean the bathroom first, then move to the kitchen. I'll leave the vacuuming for later, so as not to wake Shahrukh. He likes to sleep in on weekends. The bathroom takes longer than I'd expected. The shower walls are green with mildew, which builds up quickly in this wet climate, and the sink is full of soap scum and little hairs from Shahrukh's razor.

Once I've finished with the bathroom, I take my pan full of cleaning supplies into the kitchen. There is a tottering pile of dirty dishes in the sink, pots encrusted with dried-up food on the kitchen counter, something pink and sticky on the kitchen floor. Ketchup has dried in a dark red streak on the refrigerator door. This week it's Shahrukh's turn to do the dishes and clean the kitchen, my chore to cook, and to clean the rest of the house. After our last big fight, I wrote out a schedule of daily, weekly and monthly chores and entered them on the First National Bank calendar which hangs on our kitchen wall. We each wrote our names against a roughly equal number of tasks and agreed that we would take responsibility for those which bore our names. So here is Shahrukh's signature, under kitchen cleanup for Friday, and the kitchen is a mess.

Suddenly furious, I take all the dirty dishes out of the kitchen sink, banging and clattering as I go. I rinse them and stack them on the counter. Squirt lemon Sunlight into the sink and turn on the hot water, watching the liquid soap bubble and foam as the sink fills. I breathe in the warm, lemony steam, load the dishes into the sink, pull on the yellow rubber gloves Ann helped us buy just three months ago. While I wash and dry the dishes, Shahrukh snores softly from the living room.

Next, I tackle the pots. The encrusted food is impossible to scrape off. I soak the pots in hot, soapy water and go to the bedroom to tidy up there and make the bed. As I'm tucking in fresh sheets, I hear the squeak of the couch as Shahrukh gets up. I hear him click on the TV and turn the dial until he finds a channel that sounds as though it's showing reruns of the summer Olympics. Angrily, I finish making the bed and walk out into the living room with the dirty sheets bundled in my arms. Shahrukh is sitting on the edge of the couch, still in his underwear. His eyelids droop, there are purple pouches under his eyes. He is brushing his teeth dreamily, apparently hypnotised by the TV. A thin foam of toothpaste dribbles down his chin. The Soviet national anthem blares as Olga Korbut bows her head to receive the gold medal for gymnastics.

Something in this tableau makes me want to cry. I feel as though I've lost my husband and am living, instead, with a willful, fractious child. Shahrukh is utterly absorbed in the spectacle before him. I put the bundle of dirty sheets in the laundry hamper and take a deep breath as I turn to Shahrukh.

"Shahrukh," I say, "we have to talk."

His eyes never leave the screen. "Not now," he mumbles.

I walk over and stand in front of the TV. I have his attention. "What're you doing?" he says. "Get out of the way, I can't see."

I turn around and switch off the TV. He glares at me, mean-eyed and stubborn as a two-year-old. I want to smack him. "We have eight people coming for dinner tonight," I say. "I've been up since five-thirty this morning, cleaning this place and getting things ready. I want you to help prepare for tonight's party, or we can simply cancel it."

"What the hell do you want from me? I just woke up. Quit nagging."

"I'm not nagging. I want you to get off the couch and help me clean this house. Or, if you prefer, you can walk down to Albertson's and pick up the groceries while I clean. When you get back, we can both cook."

"Forget it. I'm not walking all the way to Albertson's to get groceries. Why didn't you buy them yesterday?"

"Me? What about you? I was in class all day. I didn't get out of the library until ten last night, and then I walked down to the laundromat with that stupid cart thing and spent two hours doing our laundry. Yours and mine. You had only one class yesterday morning, you were finished by lunchtime. You could have picked up the chicken, at least, on your way home. It would have been defrosted by now."

"Not my job," Shahrukh mumbles.

"What did you say?"

"Nothing. I didn't say anything."

"Whose job is it, Shahrukh? You think it's my job to do all the work around here? What am I, your ayah?"

"I'm not saying that, I'm just saying I'm busy with school. I don't have time to do bullshit stuff like cooking and cleaning."

"Hey. I'm busy with school too. In fact, I'm busier than you are. I'm taking six courses to your four, working fifteen hours a week at the psych clinic, and doing ninety percent of the housework. This isn't fair, Shahrukh, you have to start doing your share around here."

Shahrukh gets up without another word, picks up his book from the floor beside the couch, and stalks off to the bathroom. I hear the lock click as he locks himself in. I stand in front of the TV set, seething, wishing I had the guts to toss the bloody thing out into the trash.

An hour later Shahrukh is still in the bathroom, and no amount of banging on the door gets any response from him. I finish vacuuming, tidy and dust, water the plants, take out the trash. Then I pull on my coat and walk down to Albertson's alone.

I am glad to get out of the apartment, away from Shahrukh and the angry words which shimmer in the air between us like a heat mirage. Walking calms me. As I move through the field behind our apartment, the air smells of woodsmoke and wet, mouldering earth, a rich, dark fragrance of decaying leaves and things germinating underground. I pull the collar of my coat close around my throat and thrust my hands into my pockets to keep them warm.

In Albertsons, I run into Patrick — quite literally run into him, our carts colliding with a metallic clatter as I round the corner to the dairy aisle. We laugh and greet each other with hugs, but the collision has startled me and I find myself on the verge of tears. Patrick narrows his eyes and frowns at me: "Hey, what's up?"

The concern in his voice does me in. I shake my head, my throat swelling with unshed tears.

"Come on, let's get out of here," Patrick says, "I'll buy you lunch."

"I can't. I've got all this stuff for tonight's dinner party. I still have to get home and cook."

"I'll drive you home after we eat. You look like you could use a break." He smiles, his dimples deepening into shadows.

"I'm okay, just . . . Thanks, Patrick. Lunch would be nice. I don't usually get so emotional. I'm sorry."

"Don't be. Come on, let's check out these groceries, then we can go some place and talk."

We wheel our carts to the checkout counter. I pay for my groceries. Patrick puts his single bag in my cart along with my four bags of groceries and wheels it out to the parking lot, where his yellow VW bug is parked. The car is tiny. We unload the groceries into the boot and squeeze ourselves into the front seats. Patrick starts up the car. A thin stream of cold air from the vents sets me shivering. The VW has no heat, the windows keep fogging up. Patrick drives down the street peering through a small arc of glass which he keeps clear by wiping the inside of the windshield with his gloved hand. I'm so cold I have to clamp my teeth together to keep them from chattering like monkeys.

Patrick drives us out to what looks like an old house near campus. It turns out to be a Mexican restaurant. It is a beautiful place, all dark wood panelling and high, coved ceilings, plants everywhere. The maitre d' leads us to a table by a fireplace, where a great log crackles and burns, scenting the air with the fragrance of apples. My body relaxes as the heat from the fire slowly warms me. Patrick orders a bottle of wine, a dish of green chillies large as bananas and stuffed with cheese, for me, and pork in a bittersweet chocolate sauce, for himself. The wine is a light Chablis; the food, unlike anything I've ever tasted, is utterly delicious.

Patrick raises his wine glass. "A toast," he says. "To good friends, good food, good wine."

"Now there's a toast I can honestly drink to," I laugh, raising my own glass.

"Okay," he says, gently. "Now, what's going on? You going to tell me what's wrong?"

"I . . . It's Shahrukh . . . me and Shahrukh. We used to argue about things from time to time, when we were home in India, but we always managed to sort things out. We could always talk to each other. We used to be good friends."

"And now?"

"We fight about everything. He won't do his share of the housework. He doesn't see why he should have to shop or cook or clean, since he never had to do any of these things in India."

"Who did the housework when you were back home?"

"We had servants. Now, Shahrukh seems to think I should do it all. I can't do anything right in his eyes. He thinks the courses I'm taking are worthless; he doesn't like any of my friends; he's rude to them when they come over or call. He sulks like a baby every time I go anywhere without him, but he refuses to go anywhere with me. We don't do anything together any more, other than fight."

"You're both in a new country, facing big changes. I'll bet it's hard, learning to live in a culture that's not your own."

"It's hard, sometimes. But not as hard as what's happening between us. Sometimes I feel he's so far away he might as well be on the moon."

"He's busier than he used to be?"

"No. Well . . . we're both busier, but it isn't that." I hesitate, feeling disloyal, talking about Shahrukh with Patrick.

Patrick looks at me with gentle eyes. "But . . ." he says, waiting for my answer.

"He's avoiding me. Take the bloody TV, for instance. He's completely absorbed by it. He turns it on as soon as he wakes up in the morning. It's still on when I leave for campus, it's on in the evening when I get home, it's on all night. He falls asleep on the couch watching TV. He . . . he hasn't slept in our bed in months."

"Hey, I can't tell you how many people I've heard complain about that."

"About their partners watching TV ?"

"Yeah. It's a major problem for lots of couples."

I stare at Patrick. "I thought Shahrukh was obsessed with it because he'd never seen it before. I thought . . . I thought he'd get over it once he'd watched enough of it." I look at Patrick in dismay. "You mean he might never get tired of it?"

"I don't know him well enough to predict that. Do you think he's depressed and doesn't know it? People will often zone out on TV — or get into booze or drugs or some other addictive behaviour — as a way of dealing with depression."

"I don't know. He won't talk to me, or let me talk to him. He won't turn off the TV long enough for us to have a real conversation."

"That must be hard for you, of all people."

"Is that a nice way of saying I talk too much?"

"No. You're a very articulate woman. I love that about you."

"So why doesn't Shahrukh want to have anything to do with me? The harder I try to reach out to him, the more he pushes me away. I feel as though I've lost him."

"Have you told him that?"

"I've tried. He said uh-huh, nodded and kept watching the football game."

"What do you want, Shahnaz? From Shahrukh, I mean."

"I don't know. I want us to be friends again. I want . . . I want him to care about me."

"You think he doesn't care about you?"

"He treats me as though I'm one of the servants. He doesn't see me, he doesn't hear me. He leaves all the housework for me to do and refuses to do his share. It's as though . . . he doesn't care what I do. Last week, when you told me my paper had been accepted for publication in the APA Journal, I was so excited! I ran home in the middle of the afternoon, to tell him about it and to take him out to celebrate."

"Go on . . ."

"Is this weird, Patrick? Me talking to you about this?"

Patrick leans across the table and puts both his hands over mine. "We're friends, Shahnaz. You can tell me anything."

"Well, he was so strange. About my paper, I mean. I waited to tell him my news until there was a commercial on TV, because I really wanted him to listen. When I told him about it he gave me this frigid stare, as though he'd never met me before. Then he said: Anyone can get a paper published in psychology. It's not a real discipline. And he went back to eating potato crisps and watching TV. I felt as though he'd slapped me."

Patrick looks at me curiously. "Shahnaz, he's jealous."

"Jealous of what?"

"Of you. You're the smartest person I know. Even I get jealous of you sometimes."

"But that's ridiculous."

"I don't know how to respond to that."

"I mean, it's ridiculous that either of you should be jealous. Shahrukh is brilliant. And so are you. All I want is for him to love me. What's wrong with me that he can't love me?" I'm crying now and can't seem to stop. Am I going crazy? The restaurant and everything around me darkens and recedes. I am alone with this well of pain deep in my belly, everything I ever loved slipping through my fingers.

My mother's face hovers over mine, her eyes full of hate, her mouth twisted with rage. It's your fault, she hisses. If it weren't for you I would have been free. You ruined my life. I cry and cry. I never asked to be born, why could you never love me . . . ?

Patrick sits quietly holding my hand. I feel empty, fragile as an eggshell. Patrick leans across the table, looks into my eyes. His own are narrowed, fierce. "Whatever is going on in Shahrukh's head right now, it has nothing to do with you. You are a bright, beautiful, desirable woman. If he can't love you, the failure is his, not yours."

I hear his words, but his voice sounds far away, as though there's a desert wind in my ears.

I shake my head. "You don't understand. My mother didn't love me either. She was ill, I know, but she never loved me. What does that say about me?" I'm crying again, and Patrick's face becomes smaller and smaller, as though I'm looking at him through the wrong end of a telescope. He dwindles and disappears into the surrounding shadows.

Dimly, I hear the clatter of dishes and china, see the gleam and flash of firelight reflected in my wineglass . Then everything recedes into the encroaching dark, and I'm standing on the rim of a great desert; its sands stretch out endlessly to the distant horizon, glittering under a white-hot sky, pitiless, burning.

Patrick takes my hand in both of his own. "Go ahead and cry, Shahnaz. I'm here. I won't leave you."

I can hear his words, but I cannot see or feel him. There is nothing but this burning emptiness, this vast desolation inside and all around. I clasp my arms around my knees and bury my head in my lap. I rock and mourn. Mother, why did you leave me?

I'm a baby. I am old as sand dunes glittering in the sun. I am empty, an abandoned clamshell. I am overflowing, a tidal wave of sorrow. The sun scorches my skin until it melts off my bones, my face is melting, my arms dissolve into pools, I can smell my flesh burning, I am dying . . .

Spumes of smoke rise in the crystal air, drift heavenward.

The desert flows and ebbs, a bright, deadly tide.

Then the clink of silver on china, the murmur of voices, and the burning desert heat gives way to the log-fire's patient warmth; the sun's scorching rays become the exquisite weight of Patrick's hand on my back. I'm returning from a long journey. I raise my head from my lap, release my aching arms from around my knees, lower my feet to the floor. The white linen tablecloth, inches from my eyes, is a snowy landscape, its warp and woof the hills and valleys of a foreign land. I look up, see tears in Patrick's beautiful eyes. Are you crying for me, Patrick?

I must have spoken out loud, because Patrick smiles and wipes his eyes with the sleeve of his sweatshirt. He reaches out and wipes my eyes too, dries the tears off my cheeks.

"I'm sorry," I say. "I don't usually do this kind of thing. I'm sorry."

Patrick shakes his head and smiles tenderly at me." Come on," he says, "let's get out of here." He signals to the waiter, and asks for the bill. We look at each other in mute wonder.

Then we are walking through the parking lot. Patrick's arm is wrapped around my shoulders, his cheek laid against the top of my head. We find his little yellow VW bug; its windows are frosted over. He unlocks the passenger door and helps me in. He leans in closer, and a warm, furry animal breathes in me, a sleek, silky half-wild animal like my cousin Hoshi's panther, returned to the jungle. Its breath visible, milky puffs in the cold air. Untamed. Vulnerable. Dangerous. Like Patrick's mutable, sea-green eyes which look into my own with such love I want to cry.

Love. Freedom. Small kernels of words that stand for something big enough to encompass the earth, to include India and America in one embrace. Patrick and me. That include this silky animal stretching and brushing its fur inside my belly. Its sweet breath fills my chest, expands outward in concentric rings like ripples in a pond. Embraces the chilly afternoon and Patrick and the grey, wintry world outside. Embraces them in an animal's tender warmth, licks them with an animal's rough, moist tongue.

And somehow, in that moment, Patrick's tongue is in my mouth, a warm, rough tongue, and sweet, moist breath mingling with my own. A tender kiss, in that cold, cold car. And grey-green eyes changeable as the sea, with depths within their depths. I rise into the warmth of that animal pelt, that animal breath, and find myself home.

Chapter 23

When I was sixteen Shahrukh entered my rather nunnish existence with the uprooting force of a monsoon. He had come to collect his sister Zenobia and me after a late-night rehearsal at our college. Cigarette in hand, Shahrukh waited for us in the college parking lot, leaning against the hood of his parents' big black 1948 Cadillac. The tip of his cigarette glowed and dimmed. The moon was full-bellied and bright in the sky that night; his face was in shadow. As we walked up to the car, Shahrukh flicked his cigarette to the ground and called out: "Come on you guys, it's late."

He opened the front passenger side door for me, held my elbow, and I ducked in. He smelled of shaving soap and a citrusy cologne. Zenobia let herself into the back seat, and introduced us: "Shahrukh, this is my friend Shahnaz, whom I've told you so much about. Shahnaz, this is my good-for-nothing brother, Shahrukh." Shahrukh grinned and raised one perfectly arched eyebrow in ironic salute. In the dim light from the dashboard, I could see only that he had a round, slightly chubby face. He settled into the driver's seat. His hands on the steering wheel were slender, with neatly trimmed nails and dimpled knuckles. He leaned towards me to offer me a cigarette; his hazel eyes were flecked with emerald chips. My heart did a small somersault. Then he swivelled around to talk to Zenobia.

"Hey, shorty! Make yourself scarce when we get home. I want to take Shahnaz out on the town tonight."

I raised my eyebrows at his peremptory tone, at his suggestion. I had never been to a nightclub before. Zenobia just laughed. "It's midnight, you dummy. Where are you going to take her?"

"To Gaylord's, for a drink." He looked sideways at me from under his long lashes. "Coming?"

I had never tasted alcohol; I wanted to go. No one had ever offered me a drink before. Shahrukh started the car and backed out of the parking spot.

"No problem," Zenobia said cheerfully. "I'm going to bed as soon as you drop me home." She yawned and stretched her arms over her head. "Just don't try any funny stuff," she added, looking at Shahrukh. "Remember, she's my friend."

"Yeah, yeah, I'll treat her like the bloody Queen Mother, not-to-worry."

We drove to their apartment in silence. Since our rehearsal ended so late, I was to spend the night at their place. Zenobia lived just a short drive away from the college, in her parents' penthouse apartment on Pedder Road. Once we were there, she got out of the car and waved goodbye as she disappeared into the lobby of their building. Shahrukh pulled out with a squeal of tires, the car swaying like a howdah on an elephant. He drove with one hand, punched the buttons on the car radio with the other, scanning the dial through All India Radio, the BBC World Service, and various Hindi film music stations before finally settling on Radio Ceylon, which played Western pop music and rock and roll. The Beatles came on with Please Please Me. Shahrukh sang along in a tuneless voice, beating time to the music with the heel of his palm against the steering wheel, and bobbing his head up and down.

The car's soft American suspension made it seem as if we

were floating a few inches above the surface of the road. The car cornered like a dirigible. I felt a tingle of excitement and alarm. He was driving too fast, and I had never been alone in a car with a man who wasn't a member of my family.

That night, above the din of a jazz band that started out loud and fast and later mellowed into a series of slow, bluesy numbers, we talked for hours. We danced on the tiny dance floor packed with couples leaning dreamily against each other and moving their feet to the music.

Shahrukh pulled me closer to him. His body was warm, slightly sweaty, and smelled of cigarette smoke. I could feel his belt buckle against my belly; the stubble on his chin burned my forehead. A giddy, half-guilty excitement caught me by surprise when he began playing with the zipper at the back of my dress, unzipping it a few inches, tracing arabesques on my back with the tip of his finger.

The band crashed through the last few bars of "Satin Doll." As we walked back to our tiny table, I felt hot and floaty.

We sat at the rickety table and stared at each other. Shahrukh gulped his scotch-and-soda and ordered me a Brandy Alexander, which arrived in a snifter and looked like a milkshake. I took a cautious sip and grimaced. It tasted like the medicine Perin aunty gave me for a fever. I put my glass down, hoping Shahrukh hadn't noticed. He seemed oblivious; he leaned across the table, his eyes fixed on mine, and talked.

"The whole time I was growing up, we moved around like nomads," he said. "Every bloody year to yet another army base. I was always the new kid in school, at the bottom of the heap. By the time I'd figured out how to survive in one place, my old man would get transferred and we'd move to another.

"My parents packed me off to boarding school when I was twelve. I didn't know what was going on, I'd never been away from home before. That school was a bloody charnel-house. The masters were the biggest bunch of frigging sadists this side of the Gulag. They'd cane you every chance they got; down with your pants, stick out your bare bum — that's how they got their jollies, you know."

I didn't know, but nodded sympathetically.

"The prefects were the worst. Those bastards . . . " He tossed back the rest of his drink, choked and spluttered. A group of women dressed to the nines in silks and jewels edged past our table. They looked appraisingly at Shahrukh, dismissed me with a glance. He did not see them, was intent on his story. "You don't know what-all happened at that place," he continued. "My first week in the dorm, the bloody dorm prefect . . . " He looked down at his drink, his face darkening, his cheeks flushing a sullen red.

I didn't understand a lot of what he said. He talked so fast, with a savage intensity that burned off him in waves of heat, his eyes compelling me not to look away, his body leaning toward me as though I might get up and leave if he didn't keep me anchored there by his look, his story, his naked need. I wanted to hold him, to absorb his pain into my own body until it melted away.

"I wrote to my old man and told him what all was going on. I went outside school grounds into Dehra Dun village to post the letter. Everyone knew the school authorities opened and read your mail; the bastards wouldn't send letters that contained anything they didn't want your parents to know. I begged my father to come and get me. You know what my parents did?"

"They took you home?"

"No, you've obviously never met my parents. My mother wrote back saying she missed me and she was glad I was doing so well at school."

"Seriously? Maybe she hadn't read your letter."

"Oh no. She read it all right. They had just returned from a holiday in Ooty, she said, and she was so happy to see my letter waiting for them when they arrived home. She sent me a parcel of burfi and chocolate-covered biscuits. A bribe; a bloody consolation prize for being raped by a prefect."

How could a boy be raped by another? I knew about pain; pain inflicted, pain denied. But I couldn't picture the mechanics of this. What would fit where?

"Oh Shahrukh, she probably didn't understand what had happened to you! She couldn't have."

"The Colonel did his pukka sahib thing and told me to keep my chin up, not to let the side down. Stiff upper lip and all that, you know."

The smoke and the noise in the nightclub were giving me a headache, but I didn't want to interrupt Shahrukh. I didn't want this fragile intimacy to end.

"Those prefects were bigger, but I was smarter. I made friends with the junglis: you know, those kids who're so dumb they repeated ninth standard God knows how many times. Big hulking guys with no necks and tiny foreheads. I did their homework for them, and they became my goondas."

People began to leave in laughing, drunken groups. The band packed up their instruments. Our waiter hovered at our table, obviously waiting for us to leave too. I put my hand on Shahrukh's arm, feeling timid and bold at once.

"Shahrukh, we should go. This poor waiter's probably been on his feet all night."

"Aah, it's his job. But if you want to go, we'll go."

Shahrukh asked for the bill, paid it with a wad of cash from his pocket. He chatted cheerfully with the waiter, and left a large tip. The waiter ushered us out with smiles and salaams.

Outside, the palm trees in the Oval Maidan cast long shadows across the moonlit street. The dust of the day had settled, the air was clear and warm and suffused with the tart fragrance of an October night. A single traffic light blinked red at the Churchgate intersection. The streets were deserted except for the usual people asleep on the sidewalks, huddled underneath their shawls. Shahrukh put his arm around my shoulders and smiled, a smile so tender it filled me like sweet water. "Hey, you want to go for a walk down to Nariman Point?" I nodded, happy just to be with him.

We sat on the rocks at the Point, the sea crashing against the concrete tetrapods at our feet. I rested my head on Shahrukh's shoulder. He turned my face to his, and kissed me. His lips were warm and dry, and then moist when he pressed his tongue inside my mouth. My body responded with longings for which I had no name. Shahrukh stroked my back, my arms, my neck. His face was rapt in the moonlight, his lips so soft I wanted to disappear into their softness.

A long while later, he pulled away, still keeping a warm hand on the back of my neck. He looked into my eyes, his voice so quiet I had to lean in to hear him. "We're going to get married," he said.

I laughed, not knowing if he was joking.

Shahrukh held my face between his hands, the pressure of his palms insistent against my cheeks. "I knew the moment I met you that I would marry you," he said.

My heart flipped backwards and forwards, but I smiled and joked: "Do I get a say in this?"

"Yeah, sure, as long as you say yes!"

We both laughed, but there was an uneasy feeling in my diaphragm as I replied, still in that joky voice: "But I don't know you. I don't know anything about you."

"Ask me. I'll tell you anything you want to know. I love you. I'm going to marry you." And then, "I warn you, I always get what I want."

He said this solemnly, as though making a vow. I shivered, and sat on my hands. He kissed me again, and stroked my breasts through the thin fabric of my dress. Where his fingers touched me my skin felt wide awake, all the pores open and yielding to his hand.

Abruptly, he groaned, and pulled away, huddling over himself in a crouch, his face contorted as if in pain.

"Shahrukh? What's wrong?"

He shook his head and rocked forward, clutching his knees with both arms.

"Are you all right? Shahrukh?"

He shook his head again, and when he spoke his voice was muffled. "It's just . . . blue balls."

I had no idea what he meant, imagined beach balls, ping pong balls, volleyballs, in cobalt, cerulean, Prussian blue. He turned his head to look at me then, and grimaced. And said, through clenched teeth, "I want you so much it hurts down there."

I blushed, and felt inexplicably guilty.

And so it began.

A year later, we were married in my grandparents' rose-garden. Shahrukh's parents were there, and his sister Zenobia, looking very grownup with her hair piled on top of her head and wearing a gold tissue sari. But he seemed to have no extended family — no aunts, uncles, cousins, grandparents. The four of them, Shahrukh, his parents and Zenobia, seemed less like a family than a group of unrelated individuals. They circulated in their separate orbits during the reception, never speaking to or acknowledging one another. This lack of family connection disturbed me; it made him seem singular and feral, as though he had sprung from the earth fully formed and raised himself to adulthood. He seemed not to know that anything was missing.

Chapter 24

Shahrukh and I went out together almost every day after our first, impromptu post-rehearsal date. Usually, he'd meet me in the college parking lot after my last class, and we'd drive out to the Hanging Gardens or Cuffe Parade, where we'd stroll along holding hands. Or we'd sit on a bench in the shade of a tree and talk. I was still living at my grandparents' house, so I had to be home, most evenings, by seven o'clock. Our courtship was conducted under the constraints imposed by the fact that we could only meet in public places, and even our innocuous hand-holding gave rise to streams of raucous comment and suggestive jeering from the ne'er-do-wells who hung out on street corners and in the parks where we sought refuge. Eventually, we took to going to the matinee shows at the Regal or Eros cinemas, seeing a movie six or seven times and remembering none of it. At least there, when the house lights went down, we could kiss without attracting a crowd.

One Sunday afternoon Shahrukh invited me to lunch at the Bombay Gymkhana to meet his family. I was nervous. Shahrukh's sister Zenobia, who had introduced us, had become curiously distant and avoided me whenever possible on campus. And the stories Shahrukh told me about the rest of his family did not inspire confidence. So it took me an hour to get dressed that morning. I put on my usual outfit of cotton pants and a short-sleeved shirt, but they seemed too casual for the occasion. I pulled them off and tried on a succession of dresses, skirts and blouses, until my bedroom looked like the changing room in a department store. I was close to tears.

I threw myself across my bed and closed my eyes, trying to imagine what this meeting would be like. I indulged myself in daydreams about Shahrukh's mother, imagined a second chance at being the kind of daughter I could never be with my own mother. In my fantasies, Shahrukh's mother would embrace me with delight, exclaiming that I was the daughter she had always wanted; I was her moonchild and she loved me. We would do the things mothers and daughters of our class did together in Bombay of the 1960's — go shopping, get our hair and nails done at the Oberoi beauty salon, exchange saris and gossip, have tea and pastries at the Taj. I tried to piece together a picture of her from the bits and pieces Shahrukh had told me about her. For her, I would learn to play cards and put on makeup; I would set aside my books and my drawing pads, and take up the sitar or learn to love whatever it was she loved.

My sister Roshan, who was home from boarding school for the October holidays, brought me back to reality by bouncing on my bed and exclaiming, "It's almost twelve o'clock and you're not even dressed! Shahrukh's going to be here any minute."

I made a last, desperate search of my wardrobe, and finally settled on a two-piece suit — an ivory linen skirt and short-sleeved jacket which I had worn to a fundraising breakfast for the BMSO. They made me look older — at least twenty — and lent me a false air of confidence. I combed my hair and took a careful look at myself in the mirror, trying to see myself as Shahrukh's family might see me. Was my skirt too short? I'd bought the outfit in London, at a boutique in Knightsbridge. Maybe the neckline was too low for Bombay. My hands and feet were too big, but there wasn't much I could do about that. I slipped on my shoes, put my wallet and keys into a matching handbag, then turned around to make sure the seam of my skirt was straight in the back. I was just tugging it into place when I heard Shahrukh honking for me from our driveway — his characteristic manner of announcing himself, which exasperated my grandmother greatly. She clucked and shook her head and told me no gentleman would call for a lady in such an uncouth fashion. I stuck my head through my bedroom window and called out that I'd be right down. Then I hugged Roshan for luck and ran downstairs to meet Shahrukh.

He teased me about my outfit of course. "Hey, you look like Her Britannic Majesty! All you need is a flowered hat and white gloves and a couple of corgis. And wave, like this." I hit him with my handbag and threatened to exit the car at the next stoplight if he didn't shut up. He smirked and sighed and rolled his eyes — then he began humming "Rule Britannia." By the time we got to the Bombay Gymkhana my armpits were damp with sweat and my carefully blow-dried hair had flopped down and died in the heat.

Shahrukh's family waited for us in the dining room. His father was a short, portly man with a beautiful bald head, a wide, subtle mouth and eyes like honey. He shook my hand, smiled and offered me the seat next to him, chatting all the while about how he had once seen my father play for the Indian XI at the MCC finals.

At this point Shahrukh's mother half-rose in her seat, grabbed me by the arm and shoved me into a chair at the far end of the table. "So!" she said, baring her teeth in what was meant to be a smile, but which looked more like a display of barely restrained fury. "You're the girl my Shahrukh keeps on talking about, hanh? Shahnu this and Shahnu that. He thinks the sun rises and sets on your head only!"

Startled, I could say little beyond murmuring how pleased I was to meet her.

"Hanh, hanh, of course you are pleased. I am his mother, no? So what?" She was a tall, pig-faced woman, her features broad as a peasant's, her eyes black and narrowed into slits. Her complexion was unusually ruddy, the colour and texture of mud-bricks. She saw me looking and announced, in that loud, imperative voice: "I am taking hormones for the menopause. It is making my cheeks red all the time like Kashmiri apples only. Why for you are staring like a jungli? Your parents, they have not taught you the proper way to meet elders, hanh?"

I blushed and apologized, but her attitude towards me from that day on was one of teeth-clenching dislike which she took pains not to conceal.

The harder I tried, the more she hated me. I gushed and doted; she withdrew, hissing, behind narrowed eyes. She found fault with my choice of servants, the furniture I bought, the china and silverware we used, the food I served at our Sunday evening family dinners. She criticized the fact that I worked, the amount of money I spent, the time I "wasted" reading, and the books I chose to surround myself with. My skirts were too short and my hair belonged on a boy's head, she said. I didn't drink, I had no small talk, I loved jazz. I did not go to the fire-temple on feast days. I did not touch her feet in reverence when she entered the room. I seemed insensible to the magnitude of the gift she had bestowed upon me by allowing her son to marry me.

In retrospect, much of her attitude toward me was probably the result of simple envy. My father came from one of the oldest Parsi families in the country. They had been wealthy for generations, their position in the community remained unassailable despite my mother's notoriously bad behaviour.

Shahrukh's mother, Najoo, was a tailor's daughter who had married "up" — her husband, Shahrukh's father, eventually became a lieutenant colonel in the British (later, Indian) army. When he retired, in his early forties, he became one of the new breed of CEO's who flourished in post-Independence India, as the Indian government began nationalizing key industries and creating an exodus of old British India hands back to the mother country. He took over the reins of a large British steel manufacturing company, with all the accoutrements of wealth and the almost feudal power that went with that position in the impoverished, not-yet-politicized Bombay of those days. Najoo finally had what she'd wanted all her life. But she had no idea how to handle herself in her new postion of authority, no concept of nobless oblige. She was vicious towards her servants, bullying and beating them when they did not meet her demands quickly enough to stave off her always simmering fury.

With those above her on the social ladder, she fawned as extravagantly as any other arriviste. Upper crust Parsi society looked down upon her and treated her with devastatingly polite distaste. She never understood why they did not accept her and tried harder, wearing flashier jewellery, saris stiff with gold zari-work. She made her husband buy her a box at the Mahalaxmi Racecourse and membership in the exclusive Bombay Gymkhana Club. With each step, she reinforced her reputation as someone impossibly vulgar.

In me, she found the perfect target on which to wreak her revenge against this society which had closed its ranks against her, and to which I belonged by simple right of birth.

One afternoon, shortly after our wedding, Shahrukh's mother and I were having tea together in her living room. We had been chatting about friends of ours when suddenly she reached across the tea-table and gripped the tip of my ear tightly between her thumb and forefinger. "Such beautiful earrings!" she said. "Why for you are wearing these beautiful diamond studs with ugly blue jeans? You should keep them in the vault only. Otherwise goondas will come and snatch from your ears."

"My father gave them to me. He hasn't seen me wear them yet, and I'm going to visit him later this afternoon, so I thought I'd put them on," I replied, trying to wrench my ear free of her grasp.

"What for he is giving you diamonds at your age? I am an old woman, but you see anyone giving me diamonds? Your daddy is spoiling-shoiling you, nah?" She grew teary-eyed. "My husband has never given me diamonds even. One diamond ring only I am wanting, but no. All of you think of yourselves only, nobody thinks of me." Her face was swollen with grief.

I reached up to unscrew my earrings. "Here, take these. I almost never wear them. They would look much better on you."

"Thooo! I am not wanting your earrings. You are spoiled like a besharam. Everything you want your daddy gives to you, or your aunty brings, or your Mumma and Puppa send." She looked like an angry, baffled child.

When Shahrukh and I were in bed that night, I told him about this conversation. He was unsympathetic. "She could go out and buy herself a ring, but then she wouldn't be able to torture us all and play the martyr. Just ignore her," he said, turning off the bedside lamp.

"Shahrukh, she's your mother!"

"So?"

"So she's really hurt about this. It's important to her; she thinks none of us care about her. I think we should buy her a diamond ring for her birthday."

"Forget it. She can kiss my arse if she thinks I'm going to buy her a bloody ring."

"Why are you so mean about this?"

"You don't know my mother, Shahnu. She doesn't want a ring; she just wants us all to feel guilty. It's what she lives for."

"You should have seen her eyes, she was like a wounded child. I feel badly for her, Shahrukh. I'm going to take my diamond earrings to the jeweller and have him make them into a ring for her. I'll give it to her for her birthday."

And that was what I did. I got Zenobia to smuggle me one of her mother's rings, and took it to the jeweller so he could size it. Since my earrings were a carat apiece, I chose a very simple, elegant design and had them set in platinum. I picked up the ring the morning of her birthday. It was beautiful. I was excited and happy, imagining her joy when she opened the red box lined in dark blue velvet.

We had been summoned to a birthday dinner at Shahrukh's parents' house that night. There were no other guests, just Shahrukh, his mum and dad, Zenobia, and myself. We had a splendid meal, with Najoo's favourite Linzer torte for dessert. After my mother-in-law had cut the cake, we all brought out our gifts, piling them on the table in front of her. She opened them one by one and exclaimed delightedly over the silver tea service, gold Longines wristwatch and bottle of Dior perfume from Shahrukh's dad, the silk sari and beaded evening purse from Zenobia. Shahrukh had not bought her anything, so the only gift left was the small package containing the ring, and a card which I had signed with both our names. She opened the card, read it, smiled at Shahrukh and said, "Thank you, son. First time ever you have given me a card! Now what is in this package, hanh?"

"Open it," I urged.

She unwrapped the box and clicked open the lid. Her face darkened, her lips twisted downward. "What is this?" she demanded.

"It's for you; it's a diamond ring," I replied.

"I can see, I'm not blind. Where from you have got this ring?"

"I had it made for you, from those earrings you admired."

She glared at me, her eyes as hard as the stones. With the back of her right hand she swept the ring in its box onto the floor. "I don't want this. Give it to Zenobia!"

I schooled my face to indifference so she wouldn't see how much she'd hurt me. No one else said anything; they kept their heads bent and shovelled cake into their mouths. I looked to Shahrukh for help, but he was busy eating too. Finally, Zenobia bent down and picked up the ring from under the table. She took it out of its box, slipped it on her finger, turned her hand this way and that so the diamonds flashed in the light from the overhead chandelier. "It looks good on me, no?" she asked. No one replied.

Finally, Shahrukh's mother pushed her chair back and stood up. "You all go now. I am having a too-big headache."

She left the room.

I sobbed in the car all the way home. I was angry with Shahrukh for not standing up to his mother on my behalf; he couldn't understand why I was so upset. "I told you what she was like, but you had to go and make a grand gesture."

"But I thought it would make her happy," I wailed.

"Face it, Shahnaz, she hates you. Until you came along, she hated me too. She used to beat the piss out of Zenobia and me when we were kids. I don't know why you insist on spending time with her."

I was chilled by his anger towards his family. I redoubled my efforts to please.

But it was like trying to embrace a thorn-thicket. Shahrukh's father usually treated his wife with contempt, his son with derision, and his daughter with a kind of benign despotism — all cushioned by large infusions of cash. In the face of this parental treatment I expected Shahrukh and his sister to form a solid bond, to help and support each other as Roshan and I did. But they couldn't be in the same room together without quarrelling. I felt desperately sorry for their family: they seemed the unhappiest people I had ever met.

They provided no shelter or sustenance for each other, and they had none to offer me. Not even when my grandfather died of a massive stroke, six months after Shahrukh and I were married. I was devastated by his death. He had been ill for a long time, but I could not imagine a world without him. My in-laws didn't even attend the funeral. Shahrukh's father was too busy, and Shahkrukh's mother said she was having hot flashes and needed rest.

A week after the funeral, Shahrukh's mother invited herself over for lunch. She sat across from me at our round dining table, cracking a bone of mutton with her strong teeth and sucking out the marrow with obvious relish. She stared at me, her jaws still working, and said: "You know, Shahnaz, if you don't stop all this crying-shying your husband will get fed up only and leave you."

I didn't respond.

She shrugged and added: "If you're not going to eat that kebab I will have it. No sense wasting food." She speared it expertly off my plate and popped it into her mouth.

Chapter 25

Shahrukh is asleep, sprawled on the couch fully dressed, smelling ripely of booze and stale sweat. His eyelids flutter. I wonder what he dreams about.

When we lived in Bombay we used to stay up nights talking, weaving words around our dreams until they became so real we could reach out and touch them. Shahrukh said what he wanted most was to get the Hell away from his family. He didn't really want to move, but if he could put an ocean or two between himself and his parents, he'd be happy. We were lying in bed when he told me this, the air conditioner juddering loudly at the far end of the room.

"I just want to be free," I told him. "I feel as though I've lived my whole life in a box, doing what everyone else wants me to. I don't even know what I'd want to do, if I were free to choose. But I want to find out."

"I know what you mean. Rules for everything, including how to take a shit. It makes me want to join the bloody Naxalites and blow something up."

"We could do what we wanted, in America. We could emigrate."

"How? It costs a bloody fortune. And foreign exchange

312

permits and visas take years to get. We'd be old farts before we could leave."

"If we really wanted to go, we could find a way."

"What way? My old man wants me to stay here and go into business with him. He wouldn't do a bloody thing to help us."

"There're always my parents."

"You think your dad would help us get away? He knows enough people; he could pull strings to get us visas and foreign exchange."

"Not my dad; I'm talking about my mum."

"Righto. She'll get the CIA to fund our trip, the next time they beam in on her antenna."

"Don't be an ass, Shahrukh. My mother left money in America for me. Perin aunty told me; she found a Bank of America passbook when she was cleaning out my parents' closet. Twenty thousand dollars! Mum told her it was for me, so I could go to university there some day. If we want, we can go."

"It just seems so far away; I can't imagine it. When I hear America I think cowboys and Indians — the other kind of Indians. Why don't we go to England?"

I shook my head. "England's worse than India. Class-bound, racist. They don't like Indians. I've been there, I know."

I scrambled around in the drawer of my bedside table and brought out a sheaf of photographs. "Here, take a look at these. That's Manhattan. And this is Times Square."

"Your mum took these?"

"She used to send me snapshots from all these different places. I have boxes of them. Here's one of my favourites. This was taken in Colorado."

It was a picture of my mother standing alone on a snow-covered mountain. Her head was thrown back and she was laughing, squinting against the sunlight reflected off the snow. She looked beautiful in her red coat, happy and carefree and vivid as a poppy.

"I want to climb the Rocky Mountains too, be part of all that space and beauty."

"It looks bloody cold."

I laughed. "I want to taste snow."

I had my first taste of snow last night, after our dinner party. The party was a staggering success. Our guests ate all the food and drank all the wine and talked and laughed, and had such a good time that no one made any move to leave.

Patrick and I hardly spoke to each other all evening, afraid that whatever had been born between us the previous day would be visible to everyone. All evening I knew exactly where he was, my body drawn by the centripetal pull of his presence. Patrick's voice purled like a sun-warmed stream, his melted-chocolate laugh, his tall, rangy body.

Long after midnight Shahrukh, drunk and laughing, scrambled up on the dining table and showed everyone how to dance the bossa nova, using the broomstick from our kitchen cupboard as his partner. He swerved energetically and fell off the table onto the linoleum floor. He lay there giggling, hugging the broomstick, until Bob helped him up. Sheila put on a pot of coffee and pretty soon everyone was drinking tall mugs of coffee spiked with cognac and topped with whipped cream.

The party broke up around three in the morning. I stood by the front door waving goodbye as our guests straggled out into the night. Patrick brushed my cheek with the back of his gloved hand, murmured my name. I wanted to turn my face up to his, lean against him, kiss him goodnight. Instead, I let my hand rest on the sleeve of his jacket for a moment, then went back inside.

The apartment was a mess. Chicken-bones and half-eaten food lay congealed on plates; a broken glass, its pieces neatly piled together, stood in one corner of the living room. Champagne dripped from the ceiling — the result of a too-vigorously opened bottle — and there was Shahrukh, his face upturned, his eyes closed, catching the falling drops like manna on his tongue. I pushed back the sleeves of my sweater and began piling glasses and plates and dirty pots into the kitchen sink. The windows steamed up as I ran hot water and scrubbed dishes for the next hour.

It had just begun to snow. I wiped the last of the dishes, dried my hands, and, pulling on my coat, went out into the street. The snow was delicate, a soft, cold caress that tickled my nose and melted like sugar against my eyelids and cheeks. I tried to catch it; it left my palms damp and empty. I stuck out my tongue; the taste of snow was sweet, like well water.

When I came back inside, Shahrukh was asleep on the couch. I went to bed, but my mind rattled and spun all night.

A sweet roundness settles in the air with the weight of apples. I'm falling in love with Patrick. It reminds me of a game we used to play as kids. I'd close my eyes and rock back on my heels until I lost my balance. My friend Dilly would stand behind me and catch me, her body braced to take my weight. Excitement and fear and letting go were all part of it. The giddiness of surrendering to gravity, the delight of knowing I had a best friend who would catch me as I fell.

And yet, I'd thought I loved Shahrukh. I married him. I sit here in the living room watching him; his body in sleep moves me. He sleeps like a child, fiercely intent, frowning. His fist is curled against his cheek; the pulse in his throat flutters as he breathes.

He knows the world I come from. Patrick is as new to me as winter, as irresistible as this silent snowfall.

The world I've known is giving way. The field and the cedar trees and the entire world outside my window are transformed by snow into a rounded, undulating blessing. But I don't trust the suddenness of love, the way it alters and reshapes the familiar landscape of my life into something bewitching. When I step on this snow-covered ground, will it hold firm under my feet? I'm afraid it's only a fragile crust that will give way under my weight, plunging me into danger.

Shahrukh moans in his sleep. He stirs, rolls over, buries his head in the high back of the couch. The chain of vertebrae at the nape of his neck is slender, precisely articulated. I know the shape of these bones; I've held my hand close against them. I can't make the decision to leave him, to follow blindly where my heart leads me.

Maybe I should go and visit Silloo aunty in Florida over the Christmas holidays. Get away from Shahrukh and his delicate cervical bones and his stubborn refusal to be more than his father's son. Get away from Patrick too, so I can think what to do.

The air here is clear, cold, full of promise and alarm.

A heart is an untrustworthy organ, after all, full of slippery fluids and pumping chambers that open and close in an uncontrollable rhythm. What do I really know of Patrick? What do I know of myself, when I can love one man, resolve to spend the rest of my life with him, and then fall in love with another?

The telephone rings, startling me. Shahrukh reaches out blindly with his hand, and picks up the receiver. He mumbles, "Hello," is quiet for so long I think he has fallen asleep again. But then he says, "When?" and a few seconds later, "Yeah, okay. I'll ring you after I've talked to Shahnaz." He hangs up, rolls over and buries his face in the back of the couch again.

"Shahrukh? Who was that?"

He mumbles into the couch. I walk over and sit down beside him. His body is warm and sweaty. I shake him by the shoulder. "Shahrukh, wake up. Who called?"

"My bloody father."

"What's wrong? Are they okay?"

Shahrukh sighs and sits up. He looks a wreck. His eyes are bleary, his hair is wild, and the tweed pattern of the couch is imprinted on his cheek. "They're fine. Zenobia's getting married."

"That's great! Who's she marrying?"

"Cyrus Tata. Filthy rich; textiles and tea. My father calls it a merger."

"He would. How did they meet? Did she fall in love, or did your parents set it up?"

"Bit of both I think. Knowing my dad, he manipulated her into thinking it was her idea. My sister, of course, never thinks, so she won't have any second thoughts about this."

"Oh, come on, Shahrukh. You're such a cynic!"

"They want us there for the wedding. Third of January. Dad'll send us tickets; he wants to know how long we can stay."

"In Bombay?"

"Yeah, they've got a whole big wedding and reception planned at the Mahalaxmi Racecourse Club. My mum was yelling over my dad's shoulder trying to tell me all about it."

"So you'll go?"

"Of course. We'll both go. Exams are over next Friday; we can leave right after."

"I don't want to go to Bombay."

"What?"

"I don't want to go back. I'm afraid I'll get stuck there and never get away again."

"It's only for a few weeks. We'll go celebrate Zenobia's wedding and come back in time for the January semester."

"I don't know, Shahrukh. My family's no longer there; there's no reason for me to go."

"Your mum's still in Bombay."

"I know. I don't want to see her."

Shahrukh frowns. "You can't avoid her forever you know."

"I can't go back." I feel a panic I can neither explain nor ignore.

"She can't hurt you any more, Shahnu, you're all grown up."

I know I'm being ridiculous, but my throat is beginning to seize up. "I still have nightmares about being trapped in that house," I say, half-choking on my own words. I begin to cough and cannot stop.

Shahrukh thumps me on my back, harder than necessary. "That's silly," he says. You told me yourself she's on Lithium now. She's not violent any more. Besides, we won't be there for long."

"If I went to India at all, I wouldn't go to Bombay. I'd fly to Delhi to spend the time with my dad."

"You and your precious dad. He abandoned you, Shahnaz."

"That's not true! He loves me."

"He left you alone with your mother. Can't you see what a coward he is? He gets everyone else to do his dirty work for him."

I cover my ears with my hands and shake my head violently. "I'm not going to India."

Shahrukh pulls my hands away from my ears. "It's my sister's wedding. We should be there. Both of us."

I shake my head. The thought of seeing my mother again makes it hard to breathe; I want to crawl into bed, pull the covers over my head. "I can't stand your mother," I say. "She drives me crazy."

"Yeah, and I just love being with her," Shahrukh retorts. Then he adds: "This isn't our country, Shahnaz. I know you like it here, but I'm not sure I want to stay."

He looks so unhappy as he says this, I reach over and stroke the back of his neck, caress the small ridge behind his ear. "I'm sorry."

We argue until we're both exhausted. "I'm not going," I say. "We only just got here. I can't face going back so soon. Besides, I want to work on my research project over the Christmas break."

In the end, he says, sadly: "I can't make you come with me, but I'll ask my dad to send two tickets, in case you change your mind."

Over the next few days Shahrukh is affectionate, talkative, more animated than he's been since we came here. The prospect of this visit home has kindled a spark, returned to him some of the warmth and humour that drew me to him in the first place. He sings in the shower, emerges damp and cheerful, and kisses me. We make love for the first time in weeks.

There is an uneasy peace between us. Shahrukh seems relieved, as though going to India is a reprieve from inexpressible pressures. He calls his dad, arranges for his ticket. He is to fly out next Saturday. I hear him on the phone, making travel plans. School reopens on January 7th, but Shahrukh tells me that just in case he can't stand being with his family until then, he has left his return ticket open.

On Friday, I stay home from school and help him pack. I dig up his summer clothes, shorts and t-shirts, and fold them into his suitcase. He watches me silently, then catches both my hands in his own and says, "Come with me."

I free my hands as gently as I can, and shake my head.

On Saturday morning I call a taxi to take him to the airport.

Chapter 26

Patrick was jubilant when I told him Shahrukh had left for India. He cancelled his plans to fly back to Boston for Christmas, and asked me to go with him to California for the holidays, his voice drawing me towards him across the phone lines. We'd drive down the coastal highway, he said, spend a couple of days in San Francisco, then visit the Napa valley and come back up through the Cascades. "It's beautiful country," he said, and I found myself leaning forward in my chair.

It was hard to say no, but I did. "I need some time alone," I explained. "I'll call you in a week or so."

Then Sheila rang to invite me to spend Christmas with her and her family at their cottage in Carmel. When she described the cliffs of Big Sur, the spectacular California coastline, I was tempted. But in the end, I said no to her too.

Right now, being here by myself feels essential and right. I do yoga in the living room every day, then bundle up and go for long walks along the Willamette River. The sky and the river are subtle, shifting shades of grey; sometimes the pale winter sun glimmers through, rare as gold. I hold my face up to it, feeling its warmth penetrate my bones. Me, an Indian, savouring sun!

The past few days have been so peaceful. The pace of my

life has slowed to something close to my body's own rhythm. When Shahrukh was here, I'd get out of bed at five-thirty in the morning so I could have a couple of quiet hours to myself before he woke up and the noise of the TV drowned out my thoughts. Now, I stay in bed and read until seven-thirty or eight.

Last night it snowed. It's one of those rare mornings when the sky is a clear, limpid blue. Today, the whole world feels hushed, pristine. On the trees, ice crystals glitter like crushed diamonds.

Bombay, India
December 16, 1972
Dearest Shahnaz,

It's two in the morning; I'm wide awake and buzzing. The flight was long and boring without you. Santa Cruz airport was the usual nightmare of touts and tourists, and those head-wagging bureaucrats with paan-stained smiles who always seem to have their palms out for baksheesh. Mum and Zenobia picked me up in the old Caddy. We drove home via Rajan's. You should have been there. I had the best foot-long South Indian dosa, thin and crispy, stuffed with spicy potato filling and fresh coconut chutney.

Dad's in Madras and won't be back till tomorrow. The old lady's put on a ton of weight. She keeps beaming at me like a hungry crocodile; she pinches my cheeks and makes kissing noises as though I'm a tasty morsel she's checking out for dinner.

No TV here. Dad brought back a TV set from Japan, but this bloody country has only one channel. Agricultural shows from ten a.m. to nine p.m. How to plant maize and barley, how to paint your cows' udders with iodine, fascinating close-ups of diseased ears of corn. You'd love it.

Tomorrow my mother wants to take me shopping for wedding clothes. I told her I'm already married, but I think she has Plans. She liked the perfume and all the other stuff

321

you sent for her. I didn't tell her you were the one who'd bought it until after she said she loved it; I'm getting smart in my old age.

I met Cyrus, Zenobia's hubby-to-be, yesterday. Nice guy, but bit of a chumcha. Between my mum and my sister, the poor bugger doesn't stand a chance. He and I went out for a drink at the Taj last night. He's nervous as Hell about the wedding. I promised him I'd keep him stoked with scotch right through the ceremony so he won't feel a thing.

It must be three-thirty in the afternoon in Eugene. You're probably at school, or in your carrel at the library. My folks keep asking me why you aren't coming for the wedding. I told them you're busy with your research project. Somehow, I don't think that washes with them. Why aren't you here? I miss you.

I rang your mum as promised, and talked to her on the phone. Her speech was so slurred I couldn't understand most of what she said. If I didn't know better I'd say she was pissed to the gills, but I'm pretty sure it's the effects of the medications she's taking. Your dad's in Delhi. I haven't had time to ring him yet, but I'll try tomorrow.

My dad's office has a daily courier service to Los Angeles. I'll send my letters via him. That way, they'll get mailed in L.A. and should reach you in a couple of days. Otherwise, as you know, the mail from here takes forever and it's hardly worth writing. My letters wouldn't reach you until after I got back to Eugene.

I'm falling asleep so I'll stop now. I wish you were here. It's a crazy place, but it's home.

Love you.

Shahrukh.

I re-read Shahrukh's letter, trying to read between the lines, to imagine his parents' reaction to my absence.

I can hear his mother now: "Why for she is not coming to

Zenobia's wedding? What kind of besharam wife she is? I kept on telling you and telling you, don't marry this girl, she is spoiled like a peacock, but you! You do opposite only of what I say, just to eat my heart. You wait and see! You'll come crying to me when she runs off with some goraa."

And Shahrukh's laconic response: "Bugger off, Ma!"

Shahrukh's father is less predictable. Either he won't care, in which case he'll make no comment at all beyond telling his wife to shut up, or he'll say something oblique, like: "Shahrukh, your mother's giving me bloody Hell because you didn't bring Shahnaz with you. Talk to her before she drives me crazy." Then he'll get my mother-in-law to nag Shahrukh some more until she finds out why I really stayed behind in Oregon.

None of them would believe the real reason I've stayed here. This time alone is precious, the first I've had since Shahrukh and I got married. Each day, I feel myself shedding another layer of other people's thoughts and desires. Each day, I feel more like myself. I'm making friends with the landscape here: umber earth now sumptuously cloaked in white; thin branches of alder and willow arched under the weight of snow. I carry home fronds of balsam and cedar, blown by the wind onto the path that follows the Willamette river. The sharp scent of evergreens lingers on my palms, a clean, pungent freshness that fills my apartment with the smell of rainforest. There is a stillness here that calms my heart. I feel at home in my body for the first time since my mother returned to India and turned my world upside down.

Did she find peace in this winter world? Did she give it up to come home to us? Maybe what she found here was her own self; maybe she returned to India transformed, only to discover that nothing had changed. Did she feel suffocated by her family, the way I feel when I'm with Shahrukh? It takes solitude and silence to hear my own voice, to choose rather than be chosen. Did my mother know this? Then why did she return; why didn't she stay here and save herself? I wish I could talk to her, find out what she felt, why she came back. Does she regret the choice she made? She was always remote as a star, but she disappeared entirely from my horizon when she returned home from America. What remained was the empty husk of her body, animated only by a rage that seemed less hers than an impersonal force of nature, like lightning, or an earthquake.

The loss of her is a crevasse inside me.

Shahrukh will go and see her.

My mother, blind and trapped in that ill-fated house.

Bombay, India
January 1, 1973
Dear Shahnu,

It's nine a.m. and I haven't been to bed yet. Went to a New Year's Eve bash at the club last night and ran into a bunch of guys I used to hang out with at college. Sunil was there with his wife — sexy-looking broad named Apeksha. She says she knows you from Queen Anne's. Sunil's a big shot at Citibank now, something to do with international investments. Lucky bugger gets to fly first class to New York, Singapore, Hong Kong — all expenses paid.

A bunch of us ended up at his place for drinks after the club. He and Apeksha have one of those huge company flats on Breach Candy road, complete with ocean view and the edifying sight of thousands of bare brown arses defecating by the dawn's early light. We drank scotch all night and swapped "remember-when" stories while their cook kept the hot pakoras coming and the ice-bucket filled. My head feels like it's been run over by a B.E.S.T. bus.

A couple of days ago I went to visit your mum. She's in rough shape. She couldn't actually see me; she says she can only see blurry shapes, outlines. She wasn't swinging-from-the-chandeliers manic — the lithium seems to be working — but she was very agitated and couldn't sit still. I tried to make conversation, but it was tough because she kept pacing up and down the sitting room, muttering about how she was locked in the house and not allowed out by herself. She's very angry. I was glad to get out of there. It was like having tea in a cage with a sick tiger.

At home, my mother is driving everyone nuts over Zenobia's wedding. Since she couldn't bully you and me into getting married in a three-ring circus, she's going all out to create what she calls a "full-scale" wedding. Sounds like a war, no? She's got a real tamasha going: swing band, ten-course sit-down dinner for two thousand guests, complete with Pulav Dal, kebabs, catchumber and three kinds of lagan-nu-custard. She's booked the Mahalaxmi racecourse and has plans to convert it into a Hindi-movie fantasy of coloured fountains and twinkling fairy lights. She and Zenobia spend hours every day at the sari shops, and at the jewellers. They come home loaded down with loot, and change their minds at least twice a day about which sari Zenobia should wear for the wedding, which one for the reception. They have screaming fights about caterers and florists. These invariably end with my mother collapsing on her bed, hand to her brow, exclaiming: "Do what you want; what does it matter? I am an old woman. You are my one and only daughter. Why for you should care what I think?"

I keep telling Zenobia and Cyrus they should stage a pre-emptive elopement — just take off for Kody or Goa or someplace and come back after the show's over. They laugh; they think I'm joking.

I got the letter you sent via Roshan's Air France friend. I don't know when I'll be back. I haven't booked my return flight yet. I'm having a terrific time; nothing to do but eat, drink, sleep and party. My dad's offered me a job as marketing manager for his company. I have to tell you, Shahnaz, I'm tempted. The money's great, the perks are generous; we could have a good life here. Think about it, will you?

Love, Shahrukh

This letter reaches me on January 6th. School starts tomorrow, and Shahrukh has made no plans to return to Eugene.

I cannot go back. Shahrukh knows that. So what is he really saying to me?

Feeling uneasy and confused, I go for a long walk down by the river. I climb up a steep rise, feel the muscles in my thighs flex and stretch with every step. Snow crunches under my boots. My nose and ears tingle in the cold air, which smells of pine and juniper, woodsmoke, and decaying leaves. A robin struts along the path in front of me, his feet leaving tiny scratch marks in the snow. I stumble over a hidden rock and startle the bird. His wings blur as he flutters off and settles in a spray of snow on the berry-laden branch of a rowan tree. He remains dignified, even in his alarm. Cocking his head to look at me through one bright eye, he scolds me. I tell him I'm sorry I disturbed him. He scolds some more, then turns his back on me and begins pecking at a cluster of vivid red berries. He's a brave little bird, to take on a human fifty times his size!

As I walk up the steps to our apartment, I hear the phone ringing. It might be Shahrukh! My fingers are cold and I fumble with the key. By the time I've opened the door the ringing has stopped. I take off my coat and stare at the phone, willing it to ring again. When it does, I'm startled. It takes me a moment to pick up the receiver. Patrick's voice fills my ear. Our conversation is awkward, full of hesitancies, like that of people who once were close but have been apart too long. He asks me how I'm feeling. I say I'm fine. He tells me he spent Christmas in San Francisco, and has only just returned. I want to ask him if he went by himself, if he invited someone else — someone less recalcitrant than me.

I cannot ask. Instead, I invite him to dinner. He says he'll bring wine; he has a couple of cases of Napa Valley's finest. "Great," I say. "Seven o'clock?"

The doorbell rings just as I'm cutting up tomatoes to put in the salad. I wipe my hands on the kitchen towel and open the door. Patrick. He smiles at me with such warmth that I can only stand there, basking in his presence as though the sun has suddenly risen in my living room. He cocks an eyebrow and says, "Are you going to let me in?"

"Yes, of course, come in!" I blink, and step aside to let him through, and trip on my own feet. He extends an arm to steady me, then wraps both arms around me and gently kisses me on the lips. I close my eyes and mould my body to his.

We kiss for a long time, pulling back, finally, to catch our breath, and search each other's faces. "I've missed you," Patrick says, at the same moment as I murmur, "I feel as though it's been forever." We laugh, and start over. I take Patrick's parka from him — it seems inordinately heavy — and hang it on a hook by the front door.

"Careful with that parka," Patrick says, bending over to take off his snow-covered boots. "There's a bottle of Merlot in one pocket and a Chardonnay in the other." He stands up and wiggles his toes in his thick red wool socks, then pads over to his parka, retrieves the bottles of wine and places them on the kitchen counter. "Which one do you want me to open first?" he asks.

"Oh, the Merlot, please."

Patrick sighs. "You know what I've missed most about you?"

"What?"

"Your voice. That's what I fell in love with first. Don't ever change that accent!"

I look at him, alarmed. When he says things like this, I feel as though, to Patrick, I'm a collection of exotic parts: colonial English voice, brown Asian skin, black Asian hair; the demeanour, he claims, of an Indian princess. If I change or am different in any way from the image he's constructed in his head, he'll fall out of love with me as easily as he fell in love in the first place. Its absurd, and shaming. I'm not an exotic doll, to be cherished for the way I look and sound.

Patrick smiles at me quizzically. "Did I say something wrong?"

I shake my head. "You can't fall in love with a voice."

"Sure I can. I already have."

"That's not love. My accent — which you don't want me to change — is already changing. When I no longer talk the way I do now, will you stop loving me?"

The corners of Patrick's eyes crinkle as his smile deepens. "No, but I can't help the way I feel. You are exotic. A gorgeous mystery." He ruffles my hair playfully, strokes my cheek with the back of his hand.

I am angry, and close to tears. I pull away from Patrick and sit down on the couch in the living room. He follows me, sits beside me and wraps his arm around my shoulders. "Shahnaz, what's wrong?"

"You don't even know me." I turn my face away from him and struggle not to cry.

"Shahnaz, look at me."

I feel Patrick's breath tickle the top of my head. I focus on the back of his right hand, which rests on my right knee. It has veined ridges and a down of light brown hair.

"I'm in love with you," Patrick says. "I've no idea where this is going, but I'm willing to find out. Are you?"

A tide of grief surges through my body. I'm losing everything I know, and my future is shadowy and fills me with dread. I feel as lonely as I did when I was a child alone at home with my mother.

Patrick strokes my back, kisses my face, smooths my hair. He settles my head against his chest. His heartbeat in my ear is a steady, solid thump.

"What's really going on, Shahnaz?" Patrick asks.

"Shahrukh wants to stay in Bombay. He wants me to go back there to live."

Patrick's arm tightens around me. "Do you want to go?"

"No. But he's my husband. He knows me, Patrick. He doesn't

think I'm some exotic bird from the mysterious East. I'm his wife."

"Isn't 'wife' just another straitjacket? It doesn't define who you are."

"I feel as though I've disappeared, in my marriage. I can't be myself with Shahrukh. He acts as though I'm his mother and he's the rebellious teenager. Or else he has these notions of what a wife should be, and I can't be that either. These past few weeks, since he's been away, I've felt myself slowly coming back to life."

"Good. I'm glad."

"I feel your expectations of me too, Patrick. Exotic, mysterious. You think that's who I am, and I'm not!"

"I'm sorry. It's just that . . . Okay, truce. I'll never call you 'exotic' again, if you promise not to be mad at me any more."

I smile through my tears. Patrick wipes my wet cheeks with the sleeve of his sweater, and says gently: "You have a right to your own life, Shahnaz. Have you asked yourself what you want in all of this?"

"I want to be myself. Is that selfish of me? Since Shahrukh's been away, I've been happy."

"Good for you."

"Then why do I feel so guilty, as though I'm doing the wrong thing?"

"Because you're choosing your own life. That's a radical step."

"But Shahrukh agreed to come here. He wanted this freedom too."

"Lots of people think they want freedom. That's what the sixties was all about. But when it comes right down to it, most people don't want to pay the price."

"What d'you mean?"

"They don't want change. It's tough, giving up what's familiar, moving into unknown territory. Shahrukh's used to being top dog. He'd have to give up a certain amount of power and privilege, to stay here."

There's the crux of it. Shahrukh says he wants freedom, but he's not willing to start over in a country where his father's wealth can't serve up life on a silver platter. I say this to Patrick. He shakes his head.

"It's more than that, Shahnaz. You're changing and he's not. I can see the changes in you, even in the short time I've known you. You're unfolding your wings and beginning to fly. Shahrukh's stayed pretty much the same, since I first met him. If I were his therapist, I'd say he's comfortable with where he's at. If you stay with him, he'll clip your wings."

I close my eyes and take this in. Though I resent his know-it-all tone, Patrick is right. Shahrukh doesn't want to change. Nor does he want me to change. It scares him to be nobody special, to improvise his own place in the world.

He may decide not to return.

I will not leave here.

Chapter 27

Shahrukh is coming home. His flight arrives this afternoon, and Sheila has offered to drive me to the airport to pick him up. She'll be here in a couple of hours.

When the spring semester started, almost three weeks ago, and Shahrukh showed no signs of returning, I was angry. We began this adventure together; how could he abandon me to carry on alone?

But he called last week to tell me he's coming back, and to give me his flight arrival time. He has chosen me, after all; chosen to share in the adventure of our life here. I'm jubilant. And anxious. I've grown accustomed to being on my own.

The flowers I bought this morning — lilies and night-scented stock, pink waxflowers and shaggy white crysanthemums — are too tall for the Lalique vase we brought with us from India; their stems droop with the weight of the blossoms. I search the kitchen cupboards for something larger, and settle on a glass jug which we use as a container for orange juice. It is inelegant but wide enough and tall enough so the flowers stand upright. The lilies' creamy petals and dark yellow stamens exude a fragrance that blends with the clove scent of stocks, the delicate sweetness of crysanthemums; the entire apartment is filled with their perfume. I put the vase on the coffee table in the living room, rearrange a stack of papers, look at my watch. Another hour and a half to go. I'm too restless to concentrate on anything, so I go for a run around the track behind our house, come back, shower, dry my hair.

By the time I finish dressing, Sheila arrives, driving Bob's new Mercedes. "In Shahrukh's honour," she says, laughing. She teases me about being all dressed up. I blush, feeling like a school girl.

By the time we get to the airport, the United Air Lines flight from Los Angeles has already landed and the first passengers are emerging into the arrivals lounge. There is a small crowd of people waiting beside the barrier that separates the baggage area from the lounge. I make my way to the front, murmuring apologies as I brush by a woman holding a wet umbrella, a man dressed in a U of O track suit.

More passengers fill the arrivals area and stand waiting for their luggage as the first bags slide down the baggage chute onto the carousel. No sign of Shahrukh. Maybe his flight into Los Angeles was late. Maybe he missed the connection to Eugene. I'm trying to decide how I feel about this when I hear Shahrukh call my name.

He is standing a few feet away, smiling at me with such pleasure that my heart lifts. He looks fit and brown and very handsome in a new dark blue suit, with a cashmere overcoat slung over his shoulders. He strides over, puts down his carry-on bag and leans across the barrier to kiss me. His mouth on mine is insistent, proprietary; his hand on my neck is heavy and warm. I feel myself submerged, as if under water, fighting to breathe. A flash of anger tightens my belly and I pull back.

"Looks like your bag is coming down the chute," I say.

"Here, hang on to these, I'll be right back." Shahrukh hands me his coat and carry-on bag across the barrier, and grabs an empty cart, which he wheels over to the baggage carousel. He lifts his suitcase off the carousel and puts it in the cart. I expect him to turn around and head towards the gate, but he waits until another, larger suitcase comes sliding down the chute. He picks it up, grimaces as he wrestles it onto the cart. Then he turns the cart around and wheels it through the gate.

"Hey, you're the one with all the baggage this time," I say, laughing, remembering our arrival at this airport less than six months ago.

Shahrukh grapples with the suitcases, which wobble precariously and look as though they'll slide off the cart at any moment. He grins and shakes his head in mock bewilderment.

"Must be an Indian thing. I go to Bombay with one suitcase, and by the time I come back, it's multiplied, like everything else in India."

"What have you got in there?"

"Your dad insisted on sending a bunch of things for you, even though I told him . . ." He stops abruptly, looks at me, then lowers his eyes and shrugs. "It's just stuff. You can unpack it when we get home. My mum sent pickles and chutneys and wet and dry masalas. Oh, and a cook book. She thinks you're not feeding me properly." He looks at me slyly, and grins.

"Did you tell her my plan is to starve you to death and travel the world on the insurance money?"

"Sure, but she said, Why for you are making jokes? Send that girl to me and I will teach her how to be making proper Parsi food. You are becoming so-so thin, soon you will disappear completely. "

The eerie accuracy with which he mimics his mother's voice makes me shudder, and giggle. "Oh yeah," I say. "My one ambition in life is to have her teach me how to make dhansak!"

Shahrukh hugs me then, in the middle of the crowd. I hug him back, happy to be in his arms, glad he's returned in a good mood. I tell him, "Sheila's waiting for us out in the car."

Sheila drops us off at our apartment and turns down our invitation to come in for a cup of coffee. "I'll leave you two alone," she says, laughing. "I'm sure you've got more on your minds than coffee, right now." She waves as she drives off. I pick up the smaller of the two suitcases and head up the stairs to our front door.

"One thing about being in Bombay," says Shahrukh, as he follows behind me with the other suitcase, "there's always some poor bastard willing to carry your bags for a few rupees. About the only thing I had to do for myself was eat, sleep, shit and dress. And my mother would have had the servants do that for me if I'd only let her."

I jiggle the key in the lock until it clicks and turns. "God, don't remind me. I'm so glad not to be tiptoeing around servants all day."

"Hey, it has its advantages. Remember the first dinner party we threw in this apartment? We got up the morning after, and there was this bloody great mess waiting for us to clean up."

I bite back the retort that springs to my mouth. We hadn't done any cleaning up. I'd cleaned up all by myself, while Sharukh watched TV. This is a new beginning, I tell myself.

I open the door and carry the suitcase through to the bedroom. When I come back out, Shahrukh is standing in the living room, suitcase at his feet, looking stunned.
"Shahrukh? What's wrong?"

He shakes his head and looks slowly around the room. All at once, I see it through his eyes. The paper-thin walls pockmarked with thumbtack holes and lined with posters, the tacky gold carpet and sagging sofa, the cracked kitchen linoleum, the ceiling so low a midget could touch it by standing on tiptoe. The flowers in the juice jug.

"I can't believe we actually live here," Shahrukh says, disgust roughening his voice.

"It's a small price to pay," I say. "And it's only temporary. We'll be out of here as soon as we graduate and get real jobs."

Shahrukh sits down on the sofa, and pats the spot beside him. "Come here," he says.

I walk over and sit next to him. He turns to face me, strokes my hair back from my forehead, searches my eyes. I feel as though I should say something — he expects me to say something — but I don't know what it is.

Finally, he says: "Wherever you are is home for me, Shahnaz." He smiles and adds: "You should see what my parents have done. My dad's company has leased the flat next to theirs, for visiting dignitaries. They even brought in Neelum Advani to redecorate it. We could have it, to live in."

"What d'you mean?" His casual assumption alarms me. "We live in Eugene," I remind him.

"I know, but it's there for us whenever we want to go on holiday. And if we decide to return to Bombay at some point — say if I take the job my dad's offered me — we could live there."

I open my mouth to protest, but Shahrukh rushes on. "You should see the place. It's four thousand square feet, views out across the bay from every window, four bedrooms, four baths — same as mum and dad's, only on the opposite side of the building. And Neelum's done an incredible job. There are silk Tabriz carpets on the floors, some sort of pouffy raw-silk drapery thing around the windows — I don't know what you call it — Mughal miniatures on the walls. Completely furnished, down to towels and sheets even."

Dismayed, I look at Shahrukh; his eyes are shining with excitement; his voice is eager as a boy's.

"But I don't want to live in Bombay," I say. "And even if I did, I definitely wouldn't want to live next door to your parents!"

"We don't have to. We could move into another building. We could live wherever we want to," Shahrukh says.

"We live here," I reply.

"Of course," says Shahrukh, his voice restrained. "It's just a bit of a shocker, that's all. Coming from Bombay to here, I mean. I'll get over it, don't worry."

He puts his arms on my shoulders and kneads them. "Here, turn around," he says. "You're all wound up."

I do as he asks, and shuffle around on the couch. Shahrukh massages my neck, which feels ropy and hot under his hands. He works his way methodically down my back, pressing his thumbs into the muscles, carefully kneading around each vertebra. When did he learn to do this?

At first, my body braces against his touch. Then slowly my muscles relax.

"Lie face down," he says.

Obediently, I lie on the couch, my feet dangling, my head turned to one side. Shahrukh takes off his jacket and tosses it on the floor, loosens his tie, unbuttons his shirt sleeves and rolls them up to his elbows.

I close my eyes.

Shahrukh gets up and lifts my feet onto the couch. I hear him walk away, into the bathroom. When he returns, he kneels on the floor beside me and pulls up my blouse. He squirts something — lotion — onto his hands, then rubs it on my back in slow circles and continues his careful massage.

By the time he gets to my waist I've drifted into a state of dreamy well-being. He reaches under my hips to undo my belt, but can't quite get at it. I roll over and sit up.

"That was wonderful," I say. He looks up at me and smiles.

I slide my hands under his shirt. The skin on his back is smooth as silk. He touches my face with his fingertips, which smell of lotion. Then he kisses me.

We fumble with each other's clothes; he runs his hands down my spine, cradles my buttocks, draws me to him. Our bodies settle into an easy rhythm. He is tender, generous in a way he never has been before. Something has changed between us.

Afterwards, he carries me into the bedroom, lays me down on the bed. "You ready for presents?" he asks.

"You mean there's more?"

He laughs, and goes back out into the living room, returning with the big suitcase, which he plops on the bed and clicks open. He pulls out gifts with the air of a magician conjuring rabbits out of a hat: a red silk kimono, boxes of home-made sutherfeni and malido double-wrapped in thick brown paper, jars of pickles, the infamous cookbook, tapes of Ravi Shankar and Bismillah Khan. The bed is strewn with treasures. He digs deeper into the suitcase and unearths a blue velvet jewellery case.

"This is for you from your dad," he says, handing me the large square case. I open it, and gasp. Inside is a necklace of braided seed pearls, with a pendant of diamonds and emeralds set in gold. There are matching earrings, a bracelet, a ring.

"One thing I have to say for your dad, he has excellent taste. Put it on," urges Sharukh.

He lifts the necklace out of the box. I sit up, naked, my skin prickling in the cold. Shahrukh places the necklace around my neck, breathing through his mouth as he struggles to do up the clasp. "There," he says, smoothing the necklace flat against my collar bones. "You look like a princess."

"A princess with goosebumps," I say.

"Here. Put this on." Shahrukh holds up the kimono for me. When I slide my arms into the sleeves, the silk feels soft as clouds. It smells faintly of sandalwood.

"Where did you get this? It's beautiful!"

"Tokyo," he replies. "I had an overnight layover on my way to Bombay, remember? I saw it in the window of a boutique at the hotel. It reminded me of you."

"Thank you. It's absolutely gorgeous." I stifle my astonishment. Sharukh is not a gift-giver.

"Nothing's too good for my wife," he replies, grinning slyly at me.

He closes the suitcase and props it against the wall in the corner of the room. Then he climbs into bed beside me, and puts his arm around my shoulders. He says, "It's good to be here with you."

"I'm glad you're home," I reply. "I thought you weren't coming back."

"I couldn't leave you here by yourself. Too many good-looking men on campus," Shahrukh says with a laugh.

"Tell me about your trip. How was the wedding? What did you do? Who'd you see? You never wrote, after those two letters you sent me right at the start."

"I had so much going on, Shahnu. I tried to ring you a couple of times, but you weren't home."

"Never mind. You're here now. Tell me."

"It took me a while to get used to Bombay again. I'd forgotten how bloody crowded and noisy and frantic the place is. But my folks were great. They had this place all fixed up for me — for us — so I slept there most nights, but of course I had my meals and so on with them. The first few days my mum wouldn't let me out of her sight. After that, I hooked up with my friends and we went out together just about every evening."

"Who did you see? You mentioned Sunil and Apeksha. I didn't even know they knew each other. I only know of Sunil from the stories you used to tell me about your wild and woolly college days. And I haven't seen Apeksha since high school!"

"Oh, it's a hell of a romantic story. They met at a cricket meet at the Bombay Gymkhana. Sunil was playing for the Citibank team. Apeksha was sitting at one of those little tables on the verandah, having lunch with her friends and watching the game. Apparently she was halfway through her prawn vindaloo when she got stung on the belly by a bee. She screamed, and jumped up from her seat, spilling vindaloo down the front of her sari. Of course her friends began screaming too. The waiter came running over with a jug of water. Apeksha was flapping her arms, trying to get the bee out of the folds of her sari, and she knocked the jug right out of the waiter's hand. She was completely drenched. Sunil, who was just stepping up to bat, took one look at her and fell in love. Or so he says. He dropped his bat, ran over to help her, and they got married six months later."

"Wow. So how are they doing?"

"It's pretty funny, actually. He's having an affair with Binky Chatterjee — everyone knows about it, though no one says anything when Apeksha's around. On the surface, their marriage is very pukka. They entertain in great style. They're always out on the town together, and they're very lovey-dovey with each other — you know, sweetheart this and darling that."

"Shahrukh! Why'd you have to go and spoil such a splendid love story with such a sordid ending?"

Shahrukh shrugs his shoulders. "It's the way it is. Anyway, they were really good to me. They threw a big party for me so I could meet all their friends; fifty or sixty people, up on the roof-top terrace of their building. They have a swimming pool up there, and a garden, believe it or not. Lots of scotch and champagne, great food, nice people. Most of the guys work with Sunil; some of the women were Apeksha's friends from college. Several people knew you and asked why you hadn't come with me."

"Don't start that again . . . "

"Do you know a woman named Tehmi Irani?"

"Yes of course! She was in school with me. Did you meet her?"

"She was down from Cambridge for a holiday. She's doing an M.A. in linguisitics. She said to give you her love, and she sent a letter for you."

"Great. I haven't seen her since I can't remember when. Who else did you see?"

"My friends Cyrus and Nilufer. Remember I told you about that time Cyrus and I went up to Darjeeling together on our October holidays?"

"Vaguely."

"Well, he's almost chief engineer for Tata's now — his dad owns a chunk of the company. Nilufer stays at home with their little boy, Rustum. He's two years old, big black eyes, looks exactly like Cyrus. They have a huge apartment in Bandra, a chauffeur-driven company car, company servants, the works. Her grandparents built them a bungalow in Deolali when the kid was born — beautiful spread, surrounded by gardens. Her family has a flower farm up there, you know. Cyrus and Nilufer go there most weekends. I went with them a few times. We had a blast."

"Were you sorry to leave, Shahrukh? Was it hard to come home?"

"Nah, it's okay. Cyrus lined up a bunch of lunch meetings for me at his club. He introduced me to a couple of big-shots at Tata's. They'll set me up with a job, if I want one. If we decide to go back to Bombay to live."

I take a deep breath and bite my tongue.

Shahrukh keeps talking. "One night we drove all the way to Poona, to this little hole-in-the-wall biryani place, for dinner. We took along a couple of bottles of Glenfiddich, and a bottle of cognac. I got so drunk, I threw up on the way back — you know all those windy roads through the Ghats. It was bloody awful. The driver had to stop three times so I could get out and puke."

"Good thing you weren't driving," I say. "Are your friends still speaking to you after you threw up in their car?"

"Hell, they were all too bloody hammered to care. They cheered me on, and teased me all the way home about how I'd climbed up on the table at the restaurant and made a brilliant speech about friendship and the Nehru dynasty and the Indian economy. I vaguely remember looking down on all these people who were laughing and thumping and clapping. Then the room was whirling around, and I couldn't tell which was the ceiling and which was the floor because there were no overhead lights, only kerosene lamps. I must have blacked out after that, because the next thing I remember is being in the car and hanging my head out the window. I had the worst hangover in history the next day, but hey, I had fun!"

I don't know what to say, but Shahrukh doesn't notice. I want to get dressed and get back to work. I have a paper to present in class tomorrow. The world Shahrukh's describing seems very far away.

Over the next few days, we slip into a routine. I continue to wake up early and go out for a morning walk. By the time I get back, Shahrukh is up and has a pot of coffee brewing. I shower and make us both breakfast. Much to my surprise, Shahrukh helps me clean up. I leave for campus before he does, and don't see him again until the evening.

By the time I return, Shahrukh is home. I make dinner, he helps chop vegetables. After dinner I wash the dishes and he dries them. He still falls asleep on the couch, watching TV.

Much to my relief, he hasn't said anything more about returning to Bombay.

His friends phone him almost every night. He takes these calls in the bedroom, and talks for a long time. Afterwards, he's somber, subdued.

One night, he comes into the spare bedroom, which is now my study, and sits on the bed while I work. He doesn't say anything, just watches me for a while.

I put down the book I'm reading, and look at him. "Are you okay?" I ask.

"Yeah, I guess."

"You sound unsure."

"Shahnaz, how long are we going to go on this way?"

"What do you mean?"

"You know, living in this . . . hovel. We go to school every day like a pair of kids. We come home, we watch TV, we eat, study, go to bed. Then we do it all over again the next day. I'm sick of it."

"You're right, love, we should get out more. Why don't we go see a movie tomorrow? I can finish up early; we could have dinner together on campus and then take in an early show."

"I'm not talking about a night out!" Shahrukh sounds angry, frustrated. He stands up abruptly, paces the brief length of the room, turns around and says: "Look at this place. You call this a room? It's smaller than my mother's closet."

I smile and say, "Your mother has a lot of clothes."

"It's not funny, Shahnaz. We should go home. We don't belong here."

"This is our home. It's only going to be like this for a little while, Shahrukh."

"No. I've had it with living this way. You know what we got in the mail this morning? Our resident alien cards. We have to re-register with the INS at the beginning of each year. That's what they call us — resident bloody aliens!"

"Hello," I say, putting on a moronic smile and a robot voice. "I'm Shahnaz, from Mars. What planet are you from?"

Shahrukh slams his hand down on the desk, startling me so that I jump up from my seat and knock my chair over.

"Bloody Hell," he says, as I scramble to right my chair. "Why can't you take this seriously? I'm telling you, I've had it. I don't want to play student any more. I want to go home."

"Then go."

"What do you mean, go. If I go, we both go."

I shake my head. "You'll have to go without me. I'm not leaving here until I finish my degree."

"Why is that so damn important to you? Didn't you learn anything from watching your mother?"

"Gee, thanks, Shahrukh."

"I'm sorry, but I don't see why you want to stay here. We could have a terrific life back home."

"You keep saying back home as though Bombay were home. But it's not. We left there because we wanted a different life than our parents. Now suddenly you want to go back. Well, I can't go back there. I don't want to. You go if you have to, but I'm staying here."

"Fine. Then stay. But don't say I didn't warn you." Shahrukh storms out of the room and slams the door behind him.

I take a deep breath and realize I'm shaking. I pull on the

extra sweater I'd taken off earlier, and try to warm my hands by rubbing them together. I can hear Shahrukh banging about in the adjoining bedroom.

By the time I'm ready for bed Shahrukh is asleep on the couch. The blue light from the TV flickers across his face. I turn off the TV and cover Shahrukh with a blanket before going to bed myself.

The next morning, when I get back from my walk, there is no coffee, and no sign of Shahrukh.

Chapter 28

February 14, 1973

Valentine's Day. All my friends are going out to parties, or for dinner and a show, to celebrate. For the past month, the University Bookstore has had tall racks filled with Valentine's cards — red hearts, cupids, sexy jokes — on display. I wanted to take Shahrukh out to a play at the university theatre, and dancing after. If we could just get back to the camaraderie we shared when he first returned from Bombay . . . But he is very angry with me, and won't forgive me for refusing to return to India.

So when Patrick asks me if I'm doing anything Valentine's evening, I tell him I plan to work in the library until it closes.

He laughs. "Sounds godawful. Come spend the day with me. I promise it'll be more fun than the library."

I agonise over it for a couple of days. I want to celebrate this new holiday with Shahrukh. We spend so little time together, both of us busy with school and our own separate activities. I feel guilty, too, because he hasn't made any friends, seems to spend all his spare time, once again, in front of the boob tube. It would be good for us to go out and do something fun together. I try again.

"Shahrukh, remember when we used to go out dancing at

Firpo's? You loved to dance. Let's go out Valentine's evening, just for a little while. We'll have fun."

"Nah, I don't feel like it. Besides I have a show I want to watch."

"You can give up the telly for once. It'll be fun, I promise."

Shahrukh's face congeals and darkens, his lower lip prominent, his jaw set. "We're not going. It's a phony American holiday. Another excuse to sell more stuff to people like you. Valentine's bloody Day. Who gives a shit?"

"I do. It's not about the holiday, I just thought it would be good to do something together."

"I am doing something. I'm watching TV. You interrupted me." Shahrukh reaches over and turns up the volume.

"Well, if you don't want to go out with me, I'll make other plans."

"Fine, do whatever the Hell you want."

"Patrick's invited me to spend the day with him."

"Good for him."

"So you don't mind if I go out with him?"

"No. Go out with your useless friends, what do I care? Just stop bothering me."

I turn and leave the room.

I ring Patrick. "Is that invitation for Valentine's day still open?"

"You bet."

"Well, then . . . "

"You'll come? Far out! "

"Where're we going?"

"It's a secret." He won't say any more on the subject.

I'm in my carrel at the library. I should be working on my research project, but all I can think about is Patrick. It's funny how he finds everything about me fascinating. I tell him my life is ordinary, but I can see he doesn't believe me. He burrows after the most mundane details of my existence with all the zeal of Perin aunty's prize dachshund burrowing after moles. This

345

worries me. I wonder if his obvious attraction towards me is simply because I'm so foreign to him. Would he like me as much if I were blonde with blotchy pink-and-white skin, and a sprawling American accent?

His directness used to startle me. He'd ask me intensely personal questions, not seeming to realize how utterly inappropriate they sounded, to me. Then he'd listen to my answers with such rapturous interest that I didn't know whether to be offended or flattered. But now that I've known him for several months, I realize this is simply his way: an endearingly American notion that all mysteries can be dispelled by breaking and entering.

I realize, with a start, that I've been daydreaming about Patrick. I'm here in the library. I should be working, not mooning like an adolescent. The shelves on the wooden partitions of my carrel are sagging with books waiting to be read. I look at my watch. Eleven o'clock.

Cold hands cover my eyes. "Guess who?"

"Patrick! I was just thinking about you. D'you want to go get something to eat? I'm starving."

"Here, this'll hold you until we get to where we're going," he says, pulling a Mars bar out of the pocket of his parka and handing it to me. "C'mon, get your coat."

"Where're we going?"

He smiles his gap-toothed smile, those seagreen eyes crinkling. "Can't tell you, it'll spoil the surprise."

"Ah, come on, Patrick. A hint?"

"You'll need your coat," is all he'll say.

I get my coat. We walk down to the faculty parking lot and climb into his new car. After agonizing about it for weeks, Patrick has finally traded in his frigid little VW Bug for a much roomier hunter-green Volvo with heat. At first, he was filled with guilt about joining the ranks of the bourgeosie, but I managed to convince him the masses would be better served if he drove a car whose windshield he could actually see through. Besides, I want to be able to ride in his car without developing frost-bite.

"Here you are, ma'am. Heat!"

"Mmmm." I unbutton my coat and lean back. The seat is covered in a velvety corduroy fabric and is wonderfully comfortable. "Where did you say we were going?"

"Nice try, Shahnaz. You're just gonna have to wait." Patrick grins, looking very pleased with himself. "I've got a new tape I want you to hear," he adds, rummaging around in the glovebox and pulling out an eight-track cassette. He plugs in the tape and the car fills with John Denver's cool waterfall voice, singing "Rocky Mountain High."

Patrick drives out of the parking lot and onto the street. I watch as his long, slender fingers change gears. His hands are always chapped-looking, red around the knuckles, the rest of his skin white and flaky, like flour. So unlike mine, it fascinates me. Since that first time we kissed, I've become acutely aware of his physical being, the sheer dissimilitude of his body, which is big-boned and rangy, like an Irish setter; his smell, musty, meaty; his chameleon eyes the colour of the sea; his front teeth, which have a tiny gap between them, giving him the look of an impish child when he smiles; his deep dimples; his curly hair the colour of beach sand. He is as unfamiliar to me as the tall evergreen trees outside the window, trees whose names I am learning from him — pine, spruce, fir, balsam, cedar. Cool, green, temperate names, tangy with sap.

Patrick steers us expertly through the city. I love the self-assurance with which he drives. I haven't learned to drive yet, am not sure I want to learn. I like being chauffeured around. He turns onto Highway 126, heading west. "Patrick, where are we going?"

"You'll see. Hey, you ready to smoke a joint yet?"

I've never smoked marijuana, although its sweet, leafy smell is as ubiquitous as the rain on campus. Patrick smokes it occasionally, and gets very talkative and funny when he's high. He's offered it to me before. I've always refused, afraid to venture into murky territory. But today is Valentine's Day — whatever that mean — and I'm off on an adventure with Patrick, and . . . why the Hell not? "Sure," I say, gaily.

"Really? Far out! Open the glove compartment. It's in an old envelope under all my junk."

I do as he asks. His glove box is as untidy as the rest of him, crowded with odds and sods: a screwdriver; an electric torch; a couple of maps which haven't been refolded properly and which balloon out like paper fans; several receipts for gasoline; an old light bulb; a single leather glove, its fingers stuck together with chewing gum. How on earth am I supposed to find anything in this mess?

"Patrick, how did you manage to get this car so messy when you've only had it for a week?" I complain.

"I work at it," he says, his voice brimming with laughter. I laugh too. I switch on the torch, thinking it might help to shed some light on the chaos in the glove box. Finally, buried under a grease-stained copy of B.F. Skinner's Beyond Freedom and Dignity, I discover a battered manila envelope.

"That's it," says Patrick. I take it out of the glove compartment, stuff everything else back in, resisting the urge to tidy it up. Patrick steers with one hand, reaches into the envelope with the other. He takes out a joint, lights it with the car's cigarette lighter, inhaling in that peculiar pop-eyed way that makes me laugh.

"You look like a demented squirrel when you do that," I chuckle.

"Mmmhmmm," Patrick nods, holding the smoke behind compressed lips before letting it out in a slow stream. "Here, try it." He hands me the joint, which fizzes and pops like mustard seeds in Sunder ayah's frying pan. I hold it gingerly between my fingers, looking dubiously at the soggy end I'm supposed to stick into my mouth. "Go on, it won't bite," teases Patrick.

I lift it to my lips, sucking in the harsh smoke as I've seen

Patrick do. It burns my throat, floods my nasal passages. I burst out coughing, the smoke scalding and acrid in my nostrils. "Hey, not like that, you're wasting all the good stuff," says Patrick, laughing and thumping me on the back as I choke and splutter. He takes the joint from my fingers and relights it. "Watch. You take it in nice and easy, like so." He demonstrates, inhaling deeply, holding the smoke in his lungs till his face turns red, blowing a thin stream of smoke through puckered lips gently towards me.

After a few more tries I get the gist of it, and can hold the smoke in my mouth, let it cautiously into my lungs, without coughing. It tastes awful. I keep waiting for something to happen, but feel no different than before. Patrick's eyes shine like stars, his smile so wide his cheeks all but disappear into those deep dimples.

The rest of the ride is a blur; I remember only the feeling of freedom and laughter. There are sudden glints of gold as the sun emerges briefly through a break in the clouds and flashes off the bonnet of the car. The trees along the roadside shimmer, seem less intimidating in their tall viridian ranks. I roll down the window an inch or two, to let some of the smoke out of the car. The air that blows in is chilly and smells of the sea, a smell that takes me back, momentarily, to Bombay. I breathe it in, close my eyes. Hear the hoarse cries of seagulls.

"This reminds me of Bombay. The salt air. Only this is cleaner, less pungent."

"Yeah? Take me to Bombay."

"My parents' house is on the beach in Juhu. A white house, with white plaster walls and lots of windows. Our compound backs onto sand and sea. The sand is white too, and soft as powder. I'd wake up in the morning to the screaming of seagulls, and the smell of Bombay Ducks drying in the sun. That's a kind of fish. The fisherwomen spread them out on palm mats on the beach, to dry. They smell bloody awful. I never thought I'd miss that smell!" I laugh.

"Sounds like magic. I can't figure out why you're here, you know. Eugene seems so — drab, compared to some of the things you've told me about Bombay."

"I don't know. I love it here. It's beautiful, peaceful. I don't miss the heat, the filth, the rotting garbage piled in heaps on the street. And India breaks my heart. I hated the way we lived — we had so much of everything. Yet all the while, right outside our compound there were whole families — tiny babies with runny noses, big-bellied toddlers, nursing mothers — living in shacks made of cardboard and rags and flattened tin cans. For years, I would see them every time we drove in or out of our compound. They'd be washing their pots and pans in the water that ran through the gutter at the side of the road, or eating the leftovers from our kitchen, which the servants would give them each day, or playing dice games on the sidewalk. The children would play on the rubbish heaps, their parents would scour those same heaps for food, scraps of metal, paper which they could sell in the bazaar for a few annas. I felt so ashamed."

"That's the India I've always heard about. No one tells us about your India, with servants and beach-houses and chauffeur-driven cars."

"It's there, cheek by jowl with the beggars and the starving children." I sigh, and Patrick puts his free arm around the back of my neck. "I miss my family. And the food. And something in me yearns for a particular quality of light, more golden than anything I've seen here — maybe all the dust in the air accounts for this almost liquid radiance at certain times of day, early morning, late evening."

"How d'you mean?"

"You know how the more dust particles there are in the air, the more brilliantly coloured the sky is at sunrise and sunset?"

"Yeah."

"Well, the countryside around Bombay is really dry and dusty, except during the monsoons. In the evening, the sun's rays slant at such an angle you can actually see them shimmering to the ground. All that dust in the air makes those rays look like liquid gold, slanting through the sky and pouring right down to touch the earth at your feet."

"Wow! Have you got photos?"

"I've got snapshots of my family, but it never occurred to me to take any of the landscape. I don't think I realized I wouldn't see it any more, or that I would miss it. I'll ask my sister to send me some, the next time I ring her. You would love India, Patrick. It's a feast for the senses. Everything is out in the open, there, since so many people live and work on the streets. I miss that, the diversity, the richness of it all. But mostly I miss . . . small things . . . crows cawing in the early morning, masses of brilliant red chillies spread out on a sidewalk to dry in the sun; dew softening the sharp spears of leaves on the mango tree in our garden. And the smell of the sea . . . "

I look out through the window at a sky as pure and blue as any I've ever seen. "This is so lovely," I say, embracing the passing blur of trees and sky with a sweep of my hand. "But there are no people in this landscape. They're all in their own houses, with their doors locked. At home, there isn't such a separation between inside and outside. The doors and windows are always open, the breezes blow through. And people drop by to visit in the evenings, once the heat of the day is past."

"You miss that, having lots of folks around?"

"I'm so busy, I barely have time to see the friends I've made here. But I miss the ease with which people flowed in and out of our house, the lack of ceremony. We'd have ten or fifteen people sitting down to dinner with us every night."

"Every night? Wouldn't that get kinda hard on you? Cooking for all those people . . . "

"I'd never cooked a meal until I got here. Our cook, Hari, did it all. He'd come in and check with me around 9 o'clock, to see how many were staying for dinner. We'd eat around 10:30

351

or 11:00. He always made extra food, in case more people stopped by."

"Just like that, huh? What about Hari? If you didn't eat till eleven, he must have gone to bed at what . . . midnight, one in the morning?"

"I don't know. Isn't that awful, Patrick? I never thought about it. When we woke up in the morning the house was always immaculate. Poor Hari must have worked on long after we went to bed, cleaning up and getting things ready for the next day."

"I can't imagine your life back there. In my country, only very rich people have servants. I can't figure you out, Shahnaz. Why'd you leave, when you had so much there?"

"Not out of any burning desire to be a poor student, I assure you." I laugh. "I don't know if I can explain it. Everything is . . . set in stone, there. Your life is mapped out for you from the day you're born until the day you die, and you can't change much of anything. Only live out your life within these very narrow parameters."

I pause, thinking it through, then turn to Patrick, wondering if he can understand — he who has grown up with a kind of freedom I have never known. "I couldn't stand it. It was all laid out for me, Patrick, who I must be, what I must do, how I must live. There weren't many choices. I watched it happen to other women I know. Intelligent, vital women with much to contribute to the world. It's a . . . slow congealing of self into a simulacrum: the Indian Wife-and-Mother as depicted on stage, screen, myth and in the deepest recesses of the national psyche. All-giving, all-nurturing. Also pliant, graceful, drenched in the sickly stench of self-sacrifice. Sets my teeth on edge."

Patrick grins. "Hey, if it's any consolation, they did a piss-poor job of moulding you into Earth Mother."

"I don't know about that. I get so angry with Shahrukh when he tries to put me in my place. Its a mystery to me why he's suddenly begun to think my place is at home, taking care of

352

him. But I hate having to fight him for the right to be myself, to do what I choose. I want him to want that for me, just because he loves me. Is that hopelessly naive of me?"

"No. It's what we all want, isn't it? For someone to love us enough to let us be ourselves."

"It's not that simple. I say I want him to be free to live his own life. But I get furious when he chooses to watch TV instead of doing his share of the housework."

"How did the two of you end up together anyway? You're so different from each other. Did your parents arrange your marriage?"

"God, no! My parents aren't the old-fashioned sort. I met Shahrukh when I was in college. His younger sister, Zenobia, was in my class, we acted in a play together. Shahrukh used to come and watch us rehearse."

"Love at first sight?"

"Something like that. The first time we went out together, he told me — didn't ask, mind you, just announced — he was going to marry me."

"Far out!"

"I told him he was crazy. I was never getting married."

"That bad?"

"Oh, Patrick. I saw what marriage did to my parents. My mother went crazy, as you know. She should never have married, or had children. She doesn't like people. She'd have been happy living by herself, being an Oxford don and doing whatever it is mathematicians do. But she's an Indian woman. She was supposed to marry, so she did. And she made us all pay for her unhappiness."

"It can't have been any picnic for her either. What was your parents' relationship like?"

"I don't know. It's hard for anyone on the outside to know what really goes on in a marriage. The family story — my aunt's version of it, anyway — is that my father adored my mother, pursued her for years. She refused to marry him. He wrote her poetry, bought her jewels, had brocade saris made especially for her, that sort of thing. His family is rich, hers is poor."

"Far out! Cinderella and Prince Charming."

"My mum's no Cinderella. When she's manic she insists she only married my father for his money. I don't know if I believe that. I think she felt he could protect her from society, make a safe haven for her so she could be a mathematician and not have to care what anyone thought of her. Because he supported her totally in whatever she wanted to do."

"And of course he couldn't protect her."

"No. There were always these expectations, you know? If not from him, then from his parents and other people in our society. That she would be like other wives, even though she had her own career. That she'd entertain his friends and relatives, have children and love them, put her family before her work. She never did. She's a mathematician first and foremost; that's all she's ever cared about. But I think she swallowed all those expectations with her mother's milk. They became part of her. In the end, she couldn't do it — couldn't love my father and us kids as she was supposed to love us, or play the part she had to play. It ripped her mind apart. At least, that's my theory."

"And that scares you. You think you might end up like her?"

"Deep inside, yes. I'm always afraid. There's a genetic component to manic depression, and . . . "

"There's no causative link established, you know, only correlations. I've seen the data."

"I don't think logic has anything to do with it, Patrick. I'm just afraid. Sometimes I lie in bed after Shahrukh and I have had a particularly ugly fight and I think to myself, if I don't get out of here I'm going to end up hating him. Because to him I'm not a person, I'm his Indian wife. And he has five thousand years of history on his side, while all I have on mine is my crazy mother. That's when I get really scared. All I've known of my mother, these past ten years, is her hatred, her corrosive rage. It's as though all the love and tenderness in her vanished underground, buried so deep she can't reach them. That's not what I want for myself. I don't want to lose my heart or my head."

"You couldn't, not in a million years." Patrick strokes the back of my neck, his fingers warm against my skin. His voice is very low. "I'm crazy about you, you know. I feel like I've stumbled on a treasure right here in the wilds of Eugene, Oregon. I'm a lucky guy."

For some reason, this makes me want to cry. I turn my head away to hide my tears. It's been so long since Shahrukh spoke to me with gentleness, with such love in his voice, in his eyes. And yet, only a year ago we were sitting in his parents' car, driving from Calcutta to the tea-gardens of Assam. Shahrukh had rested his hand on the back of my head like this, stroked my neck with his thumb like this.

Patrick moves his hand onto the gear shift between our seats. "We're almost there," he says. I look outside my window as he slows down, turns off the highway. The green exit sign says "Florence."

Chapter 29

"Just call him and tell him you'll be back tomorrow." Patrick is trying to sound reasonable, patient, but his voice is edged with exasperation. "Are you happy right now?" he asks.

"Yes. This has been one of the best days of my life."

"Then how come you'd rather go home to Shahrukh than stay the night with me?"

"I don't want to go! But I can't just ring him up and tell him I'm staying with you. It would hurt him. He'd flip out."

"So let him. He's been acting like a jerk. You don't have to go back there if you don't want to."

"I do. I do have to. Shahrukh is my husband."

"Do you love him?"

"I did once. I married him."

"You've been trying to work things out with him for months now. The guy's not interested. You've got to let go and get on with your own life." There's enough truth in this to make me want to bury my head in Patrick's chest, lose myself in his smell, in the thudding of his heartbeat. I straighten my back, rub my neck, which is beginning to ache. Shahrukh isn't about to change. To stay in my marriage, I would have to resurrect an earlier self, hungry for love, eager to please, afraid of being alone. Careless of the costs of such a marriage.

This timid self hovers behind my eyes. She tugs at at the back of my neck with the anxious temerity of the weak. Let's go home, she whines. This love business is all American nonsense, what do they know? I shrug impatiently to throw off her presence, which clings like cobwebs against my skin. Look what happened to your mother, she whispers, viciously. Think about that, the madness, the loneliness. Is that what you want?

I turn to Patrick. "I can't stay with you tonight. I have to talk to Shahrukh first. Not over the phone, that wouldn't be fair."

Patrick's face changes; his eyes seem to disappear, dark pools in the moonlight. His face is as remote as a monk's.

My bones shudder in protest.

"Okay. Let's go." Patrick stands up. He looks away at the moon's shattered reflection trembling in the water. He shakes the sand from his parka, slides his arms into its sleeves. He does not look at me. The sound of the parka's zipper has a finality.

I scramble to my feet, bereft. "Patrick . . . Are we okay?"

"I don't know." He begins walking very fast along the beach. I have to run to keep up with his long stride.

"I don't want to lose our friendship over this."

Patrick stops so abruptly, I almost slam into him. "Is that what we are, Shahnaz? Friends? Who kiss occasionally?"

"I don't know. You're only the second man I've ever kissed."

"I forget sometimes what a different world you come from." Patrick's eyes return from the far horizon, look at me soberly. "I love you. I want to be with you," he says. "I'll be patient for now, Shahnaz, but you'll have to decide pretty soon what you want." He grins then, mischief creasing his face: "Race you to the car!"

Patrick takes off at a sprint, his shoes kicking up clumps of sand, his hair streaming in the wind. I watch him run. My own arms lift like wings into the wind, and I race after him across the beach.

A seagull soars overhead, filling the sky with its raucous cry.

Chapter 30

It is past midnight by the time Patrick drops me off at my apartment. I unlock the front door, step into the hallway, close the door quietly behind me. The apartment is dark. I let go of the breath I was holding, grateful that I don't have to face Shahrukh right now. I want time to think through the events of today, to make up my mind about what to do next. I slip off my shoes and tiptoe towards the living room.

"Do you know what time it is?" Shahrukh's voice is sepulchral in the darkness. Startled, I drop my keys, which jingle and clatter on the linoleum. I bend down to pick them up. "You scared me, Shahrukh! I thought you were in bed."

"Yeah, I'll bet you did."

"I beg your pardon?"

"Where the Hell were you!"

"I went with Patrick to the coast. I told you I was going."

"You didn't tell me you were going to stay out half the night. What were you doing out so late?"

"We had a late dinner and went for a long walk along the beach. After that, we just sat on the beach and talked. I lost track of the time."

"You lost track of the time."

"Yes. Look, I'm tired. Can we talk about this in the morning? I'm going to bed."

"No you're not. Sit down!"

I laugh uneasily at his peremptory tone. "Hey, you sound like the bad guy in a B-movie," I say.

"Not funny, Shahnaz. You're not to see that man ever again."

"That's ridiculous. He's my advisor. I work with him every day."

"Then you can bloody well get a different advisor. Or drop out of school. I'm warning you, Shahnaz, I won't stand for this."

"What are you going to do," I ask, genuinely curious.

"I'll file a complaint with the Psychology department. They have rules against this sort of thing, you know. They'll fire the bastard."

"Are you out of your mind? We haven't done anything wrong! You have no right to do this."

"I have every right. I'm your husband."

"Listen to yourself. You sound like some Victorian patriarch!"

I realize, shockingly, that Shahrukh means what he says. "Shahrukh, look, I know we have our problems. I've tried for months to get you to talk about them; you haven't wanted to. But it's past midnight. I've had a long day. I'm tired. Let's save this till tomorrow."

"Shit, no! If you're tired, it's your own bloody fault." Shahrukh's voice turns ugly, insinuating. "I want to know what you were up to, tonight."

I rub my eyes with the back of my hand and feel the scrape of sand against my skin. I can just make out the shape of Shahrukh's body, looming against the darker mass of the couch. I grope my way to an armchair and sit down.

"What do you want to know?"

"Are you in love with this man?"

"I don't know." I feel like a little girl. Forlorn.

"That's no answer."

"It's the best I can give you right now."

359

"Try. You try to do better than that." There is something rough, newly aggressive, in his voice. It makes me shiver. I pull my coat closer around my neck.

I say: "I love you; you're my husband." What does he want me to say? I'm sick of apologizing. "But since we left India and moved here, you've changed. You've ignored me and bullied me and told me I was worthless so often that I began to believe you." He has. He has done these things. "You don't want me, Shahrukh. You don't talk to me, or sleep with me or make love to me. You left me a long time ago, even before you went back to India."

"That's bullshit. Don't try to wriggle out of this by blaming me."

"I'm not blaming you, I'm just stating the obvious. You haven't slept with me in months, except for that one night when you came back from Bombay — you fall asleep in front of the TV night after night. You switch it on as soon as you wake up in the morning. When I try to talk to you, you turn up the volume. You make me feel invisible, as though I no longer exist for you."

"Did you have sex with him?"

"What?"

"Patrick. Did you and he . . . ?"

"No!"

"Then what were you doing out so late?"

"I told you, we were talking."

"Yeah, right!"

"Look, he wanted me to spend the night with him. I said no."

"You said no." Shahrukh stands up abruptly, knocking over the coffee table. There is a crash of things falling, things breaking. "Shit!" His huge shadow bends over, humped against the living room wall. "Bloody Hell! Look what you made me do!" His voice is shrill, the rasp of an overexcited, angry boy.

Shahrukh clumps towards me, stepping over the fallen coffee-table. Something —glass? — crunches under his heavy tread. Then I feel his breath on my face, hot, sharp, like burnt toast. He looms over me. I clutch the arms of the chair. My fingers are numb.

Shahrukh's arm snakes out, his fingertips jab my chest, bony, hard. He is breathing heavily, his breath rasping in that strangely childish, overexcited way. "What?" he says, "What!" He jabs me again and again; each time he says "what?"

I can't answer him, the breath gone from my body with the surprise of it. Blood roars in my ears. Shahrukh bends down, brings his face right up against mine, so close I feel the spray of his saliva when he hisses: "You're going to keep seeing this guy?" Jab. "This advisor. What advice does he give you, huh?" Jab. "Huh?" His voice descends from shrill to gutteral, thick as sludge. "Answer me!"

I cannot answer. I am seven years old again, and the face above me in the straining dark is my mother. Answer me! she shrieks. And my heart is as empty as the sky which frames Shahrukh's head through the living room window.

This is why I didn't want to go home. But Shahrukh has brought India back with him, and all the menace I thought I'd escaped hovers over me again.

Shahrukh grabs the back of my hair and twists it in his fist. Tears sting my eyes as my neck jerks back, exposing my throat. My whole scalp burns. "You're hurting me."

"It's your fault. You went gallivanting off with this . . . this American!"

"Shahrukh, you're scaring me. Stop this!"

"Stop this" he echoes, mimicking my voice. He lets go of my hair and prods me again in the chest, so hard my head snaps back and the chair I'm sitting in tips, lands again with a jarring clunk. "You think you can go where you want, when you want? You're my wife; you do what I tell you."

My mouth is desert-dry. I lick my lips and say, "Shahrukh, please. Let's just leave this till tomorrow." I haven't enough breath to finish the last word, which drops between us like a stone.

Shahrukh grabs me by my left arm, just below the elbow. I wince against his grip. He hauls me out of the chair, a rough, violent gesture. He pulls me towards him, so close the heat from his body burns my face. I am trembling. I close my eyes, feel my body dwindle into something impossibly distant, small.

"Now get in there!" He wrenches me around by the arm, pushes me towards our bedroom. I feel something tear in my shoulder; I scream involuntarily.

I hear this: Shahrukh's noisy breathing, my own frightened scream. And my mind goes white with resolution. I turn to face him, see, in the layered dark, that he is only a man after all. Only a man.

I reach across him and switch on the table-lamp with my right hand; my left arm still hurts too much to move. Shadows shift and reshape themselves to accommodate the sudden light.

"What do you think you're doing?" Shahrukh's bullying voice slaps the walls.

"I'm leaving."

"The Hell you are."

I look him steadily in the eye. He glares at me, makes a threatening movement, tries to stare me down. I stand silent, trembling, but not accepting his challenge. His face is sullen and red, like a sulky boy's. He mutters, "We'll talk when you come to your senses!" Then he turns on his heel and stomps into the bedroom, slamming the door so hard the apartment's flimsy walls shudder with the impact.

I pick up my purse. I walk to the front door, open it, step out into the chilly night. It has begun to rain; a fine, sleety drizzle mists my face. As I close the door behind me, my knees buckle. I grab onto the railing, and wince as my shoulder burns.

I've done it; I've left him.

And I'm alone. At two in the morning, with nowhere to go. I walk down the apartment steps and head over to the nearest streetlamp. In its sulphurous glow I rummage through my purse, find my wallet, open it. I have four one-dollar bills and fifteen cents in change. Not enough to get a taxi or to go to a motel. Enough to make some phone calls.

But its two a.m.

Who can I call? What will I say? I feel deeply ashamed.

I begin walking to the pay phone at the end of our street.

Epilogue

June 30, 1973

Bombay in June is a steambath. The air is heavy, raucous with the din of traffic, seething with dank discord. The trees are limp, their leaves a dessicated brown, choked with dust. The city reeks of feces and rotting garbage. An occasional breeze stirs the turgid air, bringing with it the foul stench of a sea transformed daily into a public latrine.

I am sitting on my sister's verandah, looking out on the dusty palm trees that line the Oval Maidan like so many rustling brooms. Behind them, the Tudor towers of Bombay university are just visible. The sky is a hazy white. Crows perch on the power cables and rooftops, cawing raucously. A taxi guns its motor on the street below. My shorts and t-shirt are drenched in sweat. It is seven in the morning. I feel disoriented, jet-lagged, my eyes itchy with lack of sleep. Last night, my plane arrived at Bombay's airport just before midnight. My sister and I stayed up until three a.m., talking. Now my throat is raw.

We are waiting for Perin aunty to arrive. Her flight gets in from Perth early this afternoon. This evening, when visiting hours begin, we will go to see my father at Breach Candy Hospital, where he is recovering from a heart attack. Tomorrow, there will be a funeral at Dungerwadi — the Towers of Silence.

My mother, who raged against the silences imposed on her, is dead, immolated. What's left of her body lies at the Towers of Silence. Wrapped in a white muslin winding cloth, she awaits the vultures.

So much has happened. I have returned to a city, a country, I never thought I'd see again. In a couple of hours, my sister will drive me out to Juhu, to visit what remains of the house where I was born.

Shahrukh is somewhere in this city. We haven't talked since he left Eugene, but the Parsi community in Bombay is small; I'm sure he's heard the gossip. How my mother set fire to our house. How she died. I keep picturing her as the mali described her: standing at the window of her bedroom in her gold wedding sari, flames roaring all around her. "She was smiling," the mali said. His voice was hoarse with smoke and surprise. "She waved," he said, flailing one gnarled brown hand in the air to demonstrate. "And she was laughing. Such a happy laugh, like a young bride."

She was wearing white gloves.

The firefighters, with their ancient ladders and inadequate equipment, struggled to reach her. She was on the second floor. She could have jumped. She didn't. Only smiled and waved as the flames engulfed her.

Acknowledgements

All creations are collaborative, nurtured by many hands, minds and hearts.

This book exists because of the skillful, dedicated help of my friends and colleagues. I have been blessed by their encouragement, support, and shared wisdom. The shortcomings of this novel are mine alone.

My deepest thanks to the following:

Keith Harrison, brilliant editor, teacher and friend, for keeping the faith through three years of writing. When I got bogged down, Keith always had a splendid idea to share. His unwavering spirit inspires me.

Ron Smith, for miraculously weaving the separate strands of the manuscript into a seamless whole, and for believing in me. Wisest of editors, and most generous of friends, his support, honesty and vision brought this book into being.

Pat Smith for her warm hospitality through months of revison and editing at her dining room table.

Jay Connolly for reading the text with such care, and for nudging me, gently but persistently, to go deeper. Also for typesetting, and designing a stunningly elegant cover. Linda Martin for speedy and impeccable copy-editing. Ursula Vaira for web page and promotional materials. Oolichan Books for publishing beautiful books.

Kate Braid, friend, mentor and blazer of trails, for showing me what's possible. Kevin Roberts for valuable editorial help and advice. Carol Windley for getting me started. The Creative

Writing Department at Malaspina University-College, for its support. Colleagues in Keith's novel-writing workshops, and my writing buddies, Colin Whyte and Liza Potvin, for reading and editing the manuscript in its many incarnations. Margaret Horsfield for generously sharing her knowledge of marketing.

Ruth Campbell, for allowing me to use her beautiful painting on the cover. Robin Chakravarti, for sharing his insights and experiences about emigration, India, and Eugene in the '70's. Jacqueline Wareham, Beth Taylor-Harris, Judith Snider and Mary Kagan, whose loving care and support made it possible for me to finish this book.

My family, Gordon, Jesse and James, for putting up with me through months of writing, and for being there and loving me. My family in India: Shireen, Amy and Sunder, who helped me grow; Parvana and Nivi, who grew up with me; and my mum and dad, who started me on this journey.

The Beloved, who is the heart of this book.

About the Author

Heydemann Art of Photography

Hiro McIlwraith was born in Bombay in 1949. She was educated at a private British girls' school in Bombay, and later took a degree in psychology in the United States. She moved to the west coast of Canada in 1976 and now lives with her husband and sons in Nanaimo, BC. Her short story, "Sunder Ayah," was a finalist in the 2000 CBC Literary Awards competition. *Shahnaz* is her first novel.

SHAHNAZ